THE BLADE THAT BINDS US

ISBN:
E-book 978-1-915585-29-5
Paperback 978-1-915585-30-1
Hardback 978-1-915585-31-8

Cover Art by: Andrew Thomson
Additional Illustrations by: Carla Jones

Praise for The Blade that Binds Us

"A swoon-worthy romance—fueled by dangerous magic and set against an eerie and evocative landscape—makes this a wild and heart-pounding adventure you'll never forget."
- Caleb Roehrig, author of *Teach the Torches to Burn*

""A dark, bewitching tale of love, loss, and healing. Wallace and Thomas weave together rich folklore, skin-crawling horror, and tender moments in this beautiful tapestry of a book."
- Kelsea Yu, Shirley Jackson Award-nominated author of *Bound Feet* and *Demon Song*

"A perfect fantasy for the dark at heart and an achingly beautiful queer romance that cuts to the bone (quite literally). A must read!"
- Kit Vincent, author of *Love Immortal* and *Us Et Cetera*

"*The Blade that Binds Us* is a captivating and dark fantasy unlike anything I've ever read. Thomas and Wallace deftly wove a haunting story of blood and bone with a bittersweet romance that will linger in my memory for years to come."
- Audrey Coulthurst author of *Of Fire and Stars*

"...readers drawn to folklore-laced fantasy and hard-won romance with sharp banter will find much to savor here. A dark, haunting fantasy in which magic binds hearts as tightly as it binds fates."
-Kirkus Reviews

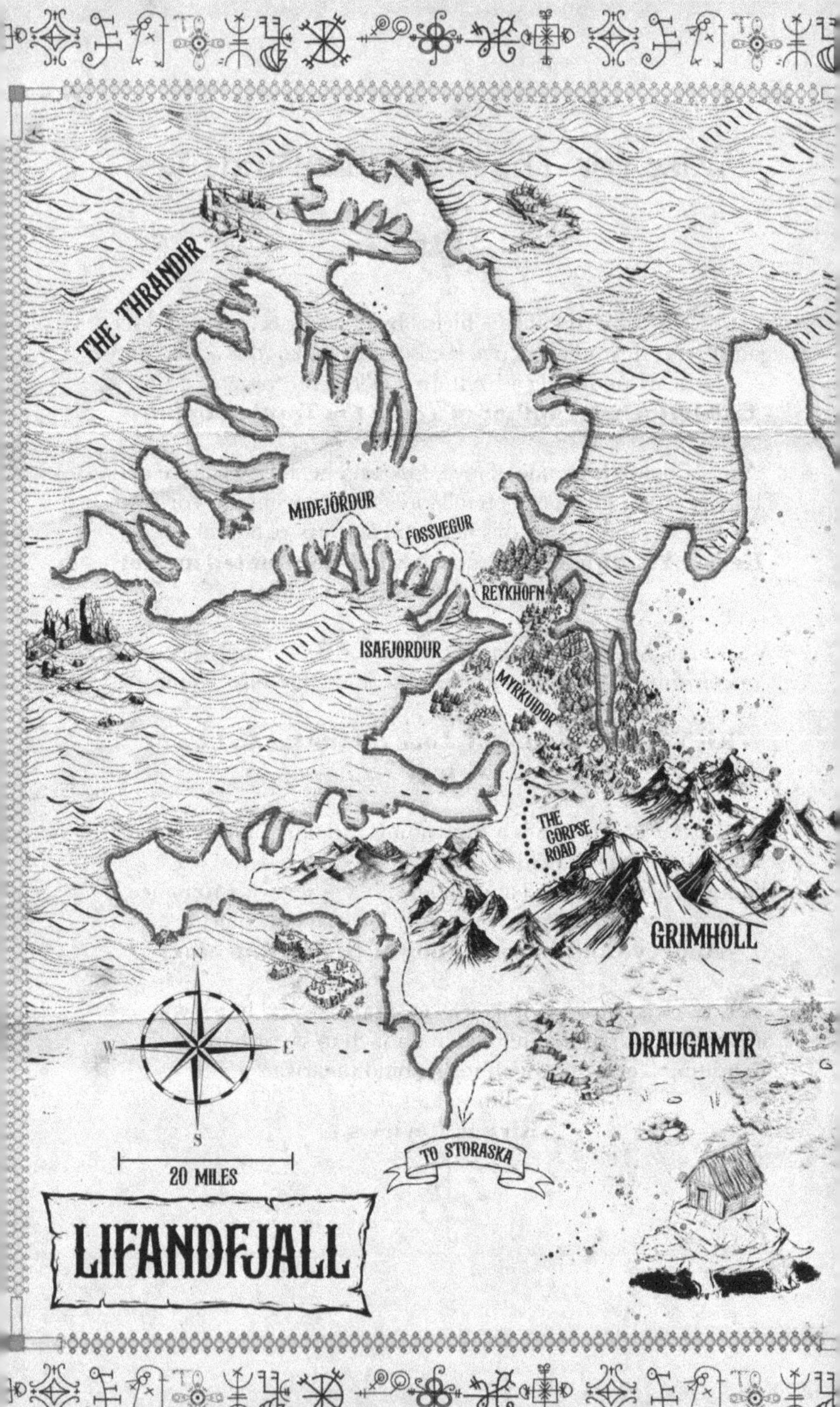

THE THRANDIR
MIDEJÖRDUR
FOSSVEGUR
REYKHOFN
ISAFJORDUR
MYRKVIIDOR
THE CORPSE ROAD
GRIMHOLL
DRAUGAMYR
N
W
E
S
20 MILES
TO STORASKA
LIFANDFJALL

*This one is for us
and for all the queer kids of any age,
and the witches, weirdos, and outcasts
trying to make a home in this world.*

THE BLADE THAT BINDS US

Leah Thomas & Kali Wallace

Tiny Ghost Press

*actual size

Chapter One
Work That Cannot Wait

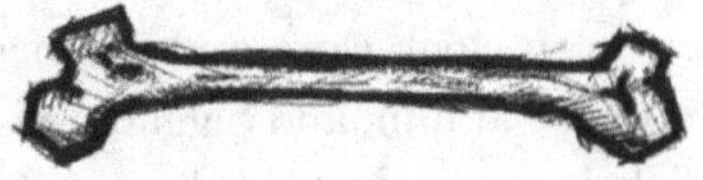

Siggi heard the creak of the wagon wheels even before the birds cried morning, not long after he had closed his eyes, and still he did not rise. Instead, he turned over on the sunken cot and burrowed deeper beneath his soot-caked sheepskin, reaching for his brother.

For a moment he knew Arnes would groan in protest and roll away. But then Siggi remembered Arnes was gone. This thought brought Siggi upright as Father opened the door. The wind off the sea blew into the turf house and snuffed out what warmth had been left in the charcoal.

More than this, the sag of his father's shoulders chilled him. Some part of Father, too, was always seeking Arnes. There was only Siggi now, and Siggi could never be enough.

"Boy. Fetch the bellows. There is work that must be done."

Siggi did as he was told, pulling the bellows from the hook and following Father outside. True darkness was a stranger to the Thrandir Coast during the summer months, when the sun refused to set and instead settled into a haze of mist that framed the world in curious silver. Siggi and his father needed no lanterns to guide them, but the icy quiet and the slumbering stillness of the sheep proved that however bright the world, this was not daytime. This was another White Night. The people of Midfjördur believed such nights were the domain of witches and worse.

Father's wagon waited beyond the door, and it was not empty. Siggi saw an amalgamation of pale limbs and tattered clothes stained black with cold blood.

"Who were they?" Siggi asked, voice cracking in the cold. "Warriors from the south? Or from the sea?"

"It doesn't matter who they were. Now they are work." Father ran one hand down the length of the old mare's neck before climbing aboard the wagon. "Quickly, boy."

Siggi pulled his woolen cloak close and climbed aboard beside him. Father would not look at him, and Siggi dared not look back at the rolling heads of their cargo. Instead, he faced forward, gazing down the narrow, muddied path that snaked away from their farm. The old mare began pulling, lifting her furred ankles with slow deliberation, and Siggi heard the corpses at his back bump and clank against each other. Beyond the village along the jagged coast, the whispering slate sea lapped the foundations of Thrandir's basalt cliffs, black against the White Night.

It was a short ride to the edge of Father's land, but the final path to Father's forge was never intended for people. Yet what part of the Thrandir ever had been? Unforgiving mountains ever-capped in viscous fog, serrated coastlines infested with screaming seabirds, volcanic terrain that resisted farming like wet fleece resisted combing.

It was sheep that had carved the winding way up to the sheltered cliffside cavern where Father had established his forge. The cave shielded the space from wind, and the bog beside its entrance provided iron. The steady dribble of a glacial stream down the mountainside fed into pools at its base, deep and cold enough for cooling Father's irons.

The mare stopped of her own accord at the fence that encased the bog, restlessly pulling her hooves from the sticking mud. The wagon jostled to a halt. Father pulled the sheep-stomach bellows from Siggi's grasp, hoisted his satchel of irons over his broad shoulders, and hopped down from his seat. He frowned at the cargo of dead men.

"Search every pouch and pocket, boy. Remember that wretched men often hide blades in their boots and all other places besides."

Siggi was afraid to look closely at the corpses. He had seen corpses before, had been woken on other nights to other work of this kind. He knew his mind was telling him lies. He knew there was no way he'd see Arnes's face among those of these new bodies. But still…

"Now, boy!" Father shoved him.

Siggi stumbled down from the bench and into the muck, catching himself with his hands, smelling damp sulfur and sheep dung and cold mud. He hurried to his feet. Father's eyes glinted in the white light. He opened his mouth as if to say something. Might it have been an apology?

But Father shook his head, voice gruff. "One corpse at a time. Lay their weapons at their feet. Do not pocket a single coin or treasure, lest you stir the wroth of a vengeful ghost. I'll go stoke the forge."

Siggi's eyes drifted to a single pale hand that dangled over the weathered wagon side. Its nails were chipped and filthy with blood, but around its wrist was a bangle of rare glass beads, a gift from afar. "But…where did they all come from? Not the Thrandir?"

"I did not ask. I only asked what the payment would be."

Siggi shifted his weight from foot to foot. "How long have they been dead?"

"Some days, by the look and smell of them."

Siggi swallowed. "But they were bad men, weren't they?"

"They were thieves."

Siggi frowned. "Not warriors?"

"Your brother asked fewer questions."

Father turned away and ascended the path, vanishing into the shade of the cavern. Siggi still had not moved when an orange glow blossomed in the dark pit. Father's silhouette was cast on the wall, much bigger than the man himself.

Siggi shivered. The dead men, unlike Father, seemed all too willing to look at him.

It was not the first burial ceremony Siggi had taken part in, but during the first Arnes had been beside him, and the world had seemed both smaller and safer.

When the fisherman Stong died of damp lung in his seaside hovel, the village priest, Brother Hamon, came to their door and demanded Father treat the old man's death as he would that of a fallen warrior. It was said in the Thrandir that dead warriors would rise as revenants if ever their weapons were not put to rest beside them, and to put a weapon to rest, the services of an ironsmith were necessary. The blade of a fallen warrior's weapon must be heated and twisted into a knot, lest he rise straight and sharp from the dead and wreak havoc on the living.

"But Stong was no warrior," Father said, in his soft growl.

Arnes and Siggi watched from where they lay on their stomachs beside the fire, playing Stones and Bones on a lattice Arnes had traced on the earthen floor.

Brother Hamon, clad in warm robes, a collar of fox fur, and shoes of real leather, pinched his pale lips. "By the end, he was no threat to anything but sharks and herring, that is true. But in his youth, Stong fought along the Ylffinn in the peninsula and took the heads of many rivals. Why chance a dead man rising?"

Siggi's mouth fell open, but when he looked to Arnes, the older boy was smirking, clutching Siggi's prince stone in his hand. "I win, Siggi."

Siggi scowled and reached for the piece, but Arnes laughed and held it just out of reach. With a cry of fury, Siggi leaped atop his brother, scrambling for the stone.

"Sons," Father warned, and immediately Arnes dropped the

piece. "Did Old Man Stong even own a sword?"

"He had several harpoons. They will knot just as well."

"There are some that believe such ceremonies are superstition," Father said carefully.

"Some do, but you know better, don't you, Arnes Thorsson." Brother Hamon grasped the carved visage of a saint at his throat and peered at the boys. "Two sons now, have you?"

Father stepped into the doorway, blocking the hovel from view. "I will be paid. One healthy ewe, or four fistfuls of ore."

The priest frowned but nodded. "Bring your children to the burial service. Both of them, not just the elder. Surely the younger would also benefit from taking part in prayer."

Once Brother Hamon was gone, Father at last unfolded his arms, murmuring curses.

Arnes stood, crossing his arms in his stead. "Father? Will Siggi go to the church with us?"

"Can I, Father?" Siggi had never been allowed to attend, had rarely been allowed to leave the hovel. His heart pounded at the prospect of going to Midfjördur, of meeting the village children Arnes often spoke of, of hearing firsthand the stories always withheld from him.

"Arnes will go." Father mussed Arnes's hair, then pointed a steady finger at Siggi. "Boy, you will not. Do not ask again."

Siggi stared at the ruined lattice on the floor, little fists curled into furious knots.

Siggi wondered what the payment for knotting so many swords would be.

There were six corpses in total. Six bodies that Siggi dragged, one after another, from the wagon and onto the mossy stones. The men were limp and soft as rotting fish but so much heavier. Siggi tried not to breathe in the stink, tried to ignore the damp that seeped from their flesh—blood or bile or some other thing that always left a body after death had found it.

The first man had two swords and one dagger. The dagger would be broken down to scrap, but the swords had to be knotted. He seemed a few summers older than Siggi, hardly a true man at all, freckles on his scarred cheeks. His empty blue eyes were open to the sky.

The second man had only one sword, but a shaving blade in his pocket along with a stone idol like Brother Hamon's. Siggi could not tell which of the church's storied Seven Saints it was meant to represent.

The third man was bearded, and his entire body was bruised. When Siggi pulled him from the wagon he realized the man had only one arm and his left eye was missing. He carried a sword and a hand ax with a name carved into its handle.

The fourth man was at least as large as Father. Siggi had to roll him, climbing into the wagon and gagging at the sludge that had congealed on the wooden floor. The man hit the mud with a heavy slap. By the time Siggi laid him beside the others, Siggi was gasping. This man had three swords, an ax on each hip, and, as Father suspected, a dagger in each boot. In the man's pocket was a bit of dried flesh with a witch's stave carved upon it, a ward against theft or a failed attempt to foil death.

The fifth man was different. The others were clad in the garb of warriors: woolen tunics and cloaks, sheaths and boots of hide. But this man wore a long robe of blue linen so fine it felt like water in Siggi's grip. His face was worn and strange, his cheeks tattooed with staves Siggi had never seen. He bore no weapon but carried several inscrutable bundles of parchment in a fish-leather bag at his belt.

The sixth corpse wasn't a man at all.

He was a boy, but unlike any boy Siggi had ever seen. Even now his skin was darker than anyone's in Midfjördur, his eyelashes long and shining, his hair as black as proper night. His frame was small, much smaller than Siggi's, his limbs as thin as broomsticks, and he wore iron manacles upon his wrists. His eyes were closed as though he were sleeping, and a small smile seemed to play on his cold lips. Like the man in blue, the boy had staves upon his cheeks—but his were pink scars, not tattoos, carved by another hand.

The boy was beautiful, and the boy was unexpected, and the boy was dead.

Siggi was crying again. Happiness, sadness, rage—any of these and more made Siggi cry, and always had, much to Father's fury. Though when Father told him word had reached the village that Arnes's ship had sunk, Siggi did not cry. Tears were so common and the loss of Arnes so uncommon, so impossible, tears would not come. Instead, Siggi laughed so hard he choked and lay down in the Erikson field and would not rise until Father hoisted him up hours later, just before the dew could freeze on his shaking limbs.

This dead boy was nothing like Arnes. Yet at the sight of him Siggi ached, and the tears that had never fallen for his brother fell thick and furious.

Sobbing, Siggi reached into the dead boy's pockets. In his trousers he found nothing. The boy was not wearing shoes, and his feet were scarred as well, as though he'd walked across a lava field for years. Siggi had never seen soles so filthy. Where had this boy been?

In the boy's sleeves Siggi found nothing, but his arms were likewise covered in curious staves and runes, some raw and red and some as old as the boy seemed to be, perhaps fifteen summers or so, like Siggi himself. Finally, Siggi reached into the boy's dirty tunic and felt the long, cold resistance of a blade.

He pulled it out into the light and his eyes widened. The knife—for it was too small to be a sword, only as long as Siggi's hand—was unlike any he'd ever seen. The central blade was black as the ash that spewed from the volcanoes when they spilled over, but it had four ivory tines along its length. These split away from the central blade, as though the knife had ribs of its own. It was as alien as it was beautiful, this little knife like a fern or fish skeleton, and before he could wonder what had come over him, Siggi tucked the blade beneath his cloak, pinching it between his arm and torso.

"What are you doing, boy?"

"F-father."

Siggi rubbed his eyes and looked up at his father, who had already gathered the weapons of the first two men in bundles beneath his arms. If Father had seen what Siggi had stolen, he did not say so.

"He's just a boy. Like Arnes."

Father froze, cold wind pulling the hair over his forehead. "Your brother is gone."

"I know, but why is a boy here?"

"Children can be bandits also. Does he have any weapons?"

"No," Siggi lied, as the spines of the black knife poked the flesh of his underarm. "There are marks. Staves. On his cheeks. All over him. What do they mean? And he's bound at the wrists. Why? He's just a boy, he shouldn't even be here—"

Father turned away from Siggi and the dead boy, moving instead to the next corpse "For once spare me your questions!"

"I know you won't look at me," Siggi breathed, voice trembling. In the wake of the tears, a deep rage stirred in his belly. "But Father, at least look at this boy!"

Father spun around, face twisted. His eyes widened, not at the sight of the dead boy, but rather the sight of the blue-robed dead man..

"What is this? What is he wearing?"

"You didn't see him when you loaded the wagon?"

"I didn't load the wagon. They had done it before I arrived. I did not see this man."

"*They* loaded the wagon? Who—?"

But Father was leaning over the corpse, eyes fixed on the man's tattooed cheeks. At last he looked at the dead boy, too. "Oh, by Storguð's hands, what have I gotten us into?"

"Father. Those staves. What do they mean?"

"And on a White Night," Father whispered. "We have to burn these bodies. All of them. Now."

"Burn them? Warriors should be buried, not burned."

"These last two aren't warriors," Father said. "This man. Your precious boy. These aren't people. These are witches."

"Witches," Siggi echoed, following Father up the hill to the forge. "But you always told us witches and wights are just superstitions, that only the seafarers and wild women believe such nonsense! You told us never to speak of witches!"

"I have said many things, true and untrue," Father said.

Siggi followed him into the choking air of the cavern. The charcoal in the belly of the forge glowed red and hot, and the air was clogged with the smell of burning wood and shark oil, used to spur on the flames.

Father pulled a pair of tongs from their hook on the wall and shoved them into the forge, sending sparks toward the ceiling. "Only fire will work. Witches must be burned before they can rise again. Before anything else, we must deal with those two."

The dagger beneath Siggi's arm felt warm against the pounding of his heart. "And…and what about a witch's weapons?"

"A witch's weapons? A witch's weapons are their hands and tongues and whispers," Father said. "A witch's weapons are their very flesh and blood." Suddenly, Father froze, turning slowly to stare into Siggi's eyes for the first time in months. "Boy, did you touch its flesh?"

"What?"

"Show me your hands," Father demanded.

"My hands?"

"Sigbert. Your hands."

Siggi proffered his hands, helpless at the sound of his proper name on his father's lips, at being called something other than "boy" or "not Arnes."

Father pulled the tongs from the fire and, in a single unflinching motion, laid the white-hot iron against Siggi's waiting palms.

Siggi screamed and fell to his knees, bright flashes marring his vision as flesh peeled away from his palms. Distantly, he was aware that Father had dragged him out into the cold and thrust Siggi's hands into the icy water from the little waterfall, that steam rose from the water as it met his bubbling flesh. Distantly, he felt Father slap him into wakefulness.

"My hands," he said. "Father, my hands."

"Rather burned than cursed." Father said, his voice hoarse. "You must never touch a witch, lest they bewitch you thereafter. Keep your hands in the cold water. I'll see to them."

"But witches aren't real," Siggi murmured, and vomited in the grass before falling into darkness devoid, for an instant, of pain.

How often Siggi had woken to the sight of Father's broad shoulders, on the mornings when he and Arnes lay huddled together. Father, his back to them as he tended to the fire, boiling broth or fish, muttering to himself. In those moments, Siggi would watch his father work without uttering a word, seeing the man in motion and unguarded as he prepared for the day ahead. Arnes's warm breath on his neck, Arnes's bothersome feet kicking his calf. Braced on both sides: Father's shoulders, Arnes's breath.

Never before had Siggi woken to see his father's shoulders backlit by a bonfire of this scale. Father must have poured shark oil on the blaze, the flames took shape so fiercely, and though Father stepped back, the flames threatened to snare him too. He lifted his arm to shield his face, heaving.

The fire burned, hungry in the White Night, and then, dazedly Siggi saw them: scarred little feet in the flames.

The dead boy. No, not Arnes. But a boy, a brother, a son, a boy, once alive.

Would no one wonder what had become of him?

"Father," Siggi groaned, "stop."

Siggi stumbled to his feet, pulling his hands from the icy bath with a gasp. Something sharp and insistent prodded his arm. Dazed and unthinking, stumbling thoughtlessly down the dung-streaked path toward the bright flames, Siggi reached for the boy's knife under his arm, forgetting the state of his hands.

And as he drew the spiny thing from beneath his cloak, the knife scraped his sodden skin, tasted his blood, and reached for him as well. Like the legs of a summer spider preparing to leap, the four sharp white tines of the witch-boy's knife curled inward, poking into the raw flesh of Siggi's seeping left hand, piercing the meat of his palm. Siggi screamed, watching the tines grow longer beneath his skin and extend to the tips of his fingers, watching the hilt and handle of the knife embed itself in his wrist. His very bones seemed to shift, making way for it.

In vain Siggi tried to drop the knife, but it was fused with his singed flesh, the center blade and handle sunk into his forearm like a shining tattoo.

At the sound of his scream, Father turned from the pyre and Siggi saw that tears were clearing a path through the dark soot on his grizzled cheeks. "Sigbert! No! Stay back!"

Siggi looked past those shoulders, into the flames. The knife—his hand—the knife—churned against his flesh like the whorls of waves at high tide, then the movement stopped as if the knife had settled somehow. The pain was gone.

But it was replaced by something more frightening. In the depths of his skull, Siggi heard or felt the echo of a second heartbeat that was not his own. Once, then twice, then again and again. The shock of it brought Siggi to his knees.

And the witch-boy sat up in the flames.

He stepped out of the fire even as his clothes turned to ash, his skin unburned but aglow with fire as he placed his feet on the cold, wet moss. The staves that marked his cheeks marked all the rest of him as well, his torso, legs, and arms a tapestry of scars and burns and runes. They burned bright like coals set alight, framing his shining black eyes in orange. There was no question he was alive.

The flames left his skin and the staves faded only after he inhaled the misty air, falling away like leaves in autumn. The witch walked right past Father, who fell back, weeping, on the stones. He stepped carefully up the little path to the place where Siggi had collapsed in the mud and knelt before him. He took Siggi's hands in his own, gazing both at the bewitched left and the fire-scorched right. At last he raised his black eyes, piercing Siggi straight through to his heart. "Sorry about all this," the witch-boy said, and then he smiled.

Chapter Two
When Stupid Men Die

Gudmundur Jarlsson was a stupid man who believed himself to be a smart man, and he was going to get them all killed.

Hrafn leaned against a jagged rock and closed his eyes. He had stopped listening to Gudmundur's scheming some time ago. The man had been talking, expansively and boastfully, for much too long, sharing the sound of his voice and the emptiness of his thoughts more readily than Randulfur One-Arm shared lice at every brothel they passed.

Not that they had passed any brothels in some days, or anything at all except black rock, heavy fog, and bird shit. The coast of the Thrandir was so far along the desolate ass-end of Lifandfjall that even the rock-clinging sheep had a wary, unfriendly look to them—a look that nevertheless suggested more interesting conversation than anything Gudmundur could offer, and probably cleverer plans.

Hrafn wondered what sheep would steal if they had a band of thieves and a couple of witches in their employ. Wheat, maybe, or rich green grass. The pelts of wolves to wear in mockery. Their own lambs on the verge of slaughter. Brandywine to forget when the slaughter happened anyway.

Probably not the body parts of dead saints. The men were arguing now about what body part the relic might be. A finger or an ear seemed to be the favorites, although Olafur was insistent that it would be a teat, which led the other men to laugh uproariously and ask if he was so eager because he had never seen one before.

The crunch of footsteps brought Hrafn out of his reverie.

Hrafn opened one eye to find Einar standing over him, the hem of his ridiculous blue robes stained with mud.

"Fuck off," Hrafn said

"You're needed," Einar replied.

The men fell silent and watched them warily. More than one hand twitched toward a knife hilt, as though they expected Hrafn to attack Einar like a wild animal. Perhaps he ought to have been listening more closely. Not that it mattered. Hrafn had chains on his wrists and ankles; he would manage about six stumbling paces if he tried to run.

"We need to know how many men are in the village," Gudmundur called to him. He had hefted himself to his feet but kept his distance. "The priest has gone to visit the church, but he's—"

"He's a fool, is what he is," Olafur said with a laugh.

A few of the others joined in. They had been mocking Ketill, the naive young priest from the Church of the Seven Saints, both to his face and behind his back ever since they left Storaska. Gudmundur wasn't happy about the priest's presence, but Ketill had insisted on joining them. He was the one paying them to steal the relic—*reclaim*, he insisted, to return it to its rightful place—so he got to make the rules, even if he was a fool. With his brown eyes always wide, his too-large mouth always on the verge of saying something idiotic, Ketill had absolutely no business coming along for thievery. He had even approached Hrafn to give him a bit of food the other day. The other men had stared in horror, as though they expected him to return missing a hand. Ketill had only smiled guilelessly, and the pang Hrafn felt in his gut at that moment had little to do with hunger.

The men stopped laughing when Gudmundur glared at them. "The priest is the one who will see us paid, and you won't forget it." He looked back at Hrafn. "You can count when you do your wicked trick with the birds, can't you?" A wary glance upward. "Birtingr said you retain your senses."

So it was going to be like that. Hrafn glanced at Einar and wondered what, exactly, Birtingr had told Gudmundur when he offered up two of his apprentices for a spot of lucrative theft. Birtingr hadn't bothered to explain anything to Hrafn before sending him along with the thieves, and Einar had no interest in sharing what he knew. Einar was a man of few words, mostly because he wanted everybody to mistake his long silences for ominous wisdom.

"Yes," Hrafn said. "I can count when I do my *wicked trick*."

Gudmundur scowled, as though searching for an insult in the words. "Do it, then."

"I need—"

Einar held up a short, dark feather. "We'll begin now."

"Don't do it here. Take him down there." Gudmundur's gesture was vague, but the meaning was clear enough. Down along the rocky barely-a-trail, away from the camp where the men were sharpening their blades and twisting greed into courage, where they would not have to watch their most useful tool being put to work.

Hrafn might have thought them squeamish about blood if they didn't regularly slit throats and split heads themselves. It was only witch blood that turned their stomachs.

The shackles and chains rattled as Hrafn stood and shuffled along behind Einar. The thieves' camp sat at the bottom of a sharp crack in the land, where the black rocks were slick with rain and covered by clinging lichens. Drifting fog rolled and curled into the ravine from every direction. The men grew louder as the mist thickened, perhaps hoping their boasts would drive away any spirits lurking in the gray.

Hrafn had walked into the heart of the haunted marsh beneath the great living mountain Grimholl when he was only a child. He was not afraid of ghosts. He would welcome them, even, if they saw fit to join the party.

What he loathed about that gray fog was the cold. Without shoes or a jacket or even proper clothes, Hrafn could not remember when he had last been warm.

"I know you weren't listening, so I'll tell you again." Einar always sounded bored when he scolded Hrafn. He sounded bored when he did almost everything, in fact, with very few exceptions, usually of the sort that ended with men weeping to the goddess Eldkona as their blood fed the ground beneath them. "Number of men in the village—"

"Only men, or shall I count particularly fierce women as well?"

"An estimate of how many boats are at sea, the location of the church, the look of its doors."

"All of which," Hrafn said, as he pulled his sleeve up to his elbow, "Good Brother Ketill can tell us, when he gets back. Or we could send One-Arm to scratch his balls and ask about forgiveness from the local priest. That's always enough of a show to bring the whole village out to watch."

"Sure, we could do that, and trust a pampered scholar with our lives," Einar said. "But we're doing it this way."

And trusting a cold, hungry, bored witch with their lives instead.

"Right," said Hrafn. He dropped to the ground and looked up at Einar. The sky was nothing but gray fog, on this quiet cusp of a White Night. "Give me my blade. I'll do it."

Einar hesitated. He had taken the knife away a few days ago, claiming it was to make the men less nervous, but they both knew it was because the colder and hungrier and more bored Hrafn got, the more likely he was to stab somebody's eyes out just to remind them he wasn't a well-trained dog.

After a second, Einar drew Hrafn's blood-forged knife from his belt and handed it over, along with the feather. It was from a kria. Hrafn scowled. He hated kria.

Hrafn rested his right elbow on his knee, palm up to expose the mind-theft stave carved into the skin of his forearm. It was an elaborate symbol, with four whorls around a three-ring center, crossed by five rune-marked lines and a single long meridian. Most of the lines were thin and faint, as they had been carved by Birtingr's steady hand and sharp blade two years ago. But the line that bisected the center of the stave was a fat pink line that stood out against his brown skin. The stave never fully healed, as it was sliced open often enough that it never had the chance to harden into a numb scar.

Hrafn pressed the sharp edge of his knife's center blade into that line.

The initial resistance. The first sting. The parting of his skin. The hot well of blood and the low, slow ache that would linger. These were sensations so familiar he knew them as well as hunger or thirst or cold. He set the knife down and picked up the feather. Einar watched without speaking. Einar couldn't do this. He couldn't do many useful things, which was why Birtingr often sent him along as Hrafn's minder rather than entrusting him with important work on his own.

Hrafn pulled the skin of his arm apart with his fingers and pressed the kria feather into the cut. Blood welled around it, surrounding the barbs and drowning the center shaft. He pushed the feather down firmly and pinched the skin closed over it.

He had just enough time to feel the blood dripping over his own skin, the pressure of his slick fingers, the odd sensation of enclosing something foreign into his flesh, before his vision blurred with a dizzying swoop. The black rocks smeared into Einar's blue robes, the gray fog smudged both away, and he was soaring.

He was soaring.

Had he still occupied his human body, Hrafn might have laughed. So it *did* get easier with practice. The mist flowed around him, over his wings and the unfamiliar shape of this borrowed bird's body, and below the rocky landscape raced past with all of its jagged features smudged together.

He turned, first to see if he could, then to aim in the correct direction: over the landscape until he found the ravine, then toward the sea. He spotted Ketill returning to the camp on the rough trail. The land dropped away, and there was the village, tucked into a fjord on this inhospitable coast.

It was the largest village for miles around, but that didn't mean much. He counted a dozen houses, with only two boats tied up in their sad little harbor and another three fishing at the mouth of the fjord. That made it easy to find the church, a wooden building at the edge of town, alone on a little rise that would surely bear the brunt of any squalls raging landward from the sea. Beside the church was a graveyard marked by the humps of turf graves. There were more graves than there were people living in the village.

Hrafn circled the village again, in part to make sure he hadn't missed anything, but also because it was very peaceful to be so high above the ground, to see so far and wonder what would become of him if he didn't go back, if he just kept flying away from the land, away from the men, away from his own body, to live a short, cold life diving for fish and resting on icebergs. It was appealing, in its way, but only until he remembered—

There was a lurch, like a gust of wind or an invisible kick, and as Hrafn tumbled and flapped he heard a scream that was not a scream, felt a fiery anger burst behind his eyes and a crush of pressure from both within and without, and the scream that was not a scream grew louder, and louder, and louder, and he fell with a nauseating swoop through cold and mist, back into his own body, where he rolled onto his side and vomited onto the ground.

It was always appealing, to stay as a bird, but only until he remembered that birds were *absolute raging assholes*. They never took kindly to having their minds stolen.

"Hrafn? Are you okay?"

With the words came the scuff of footsteps. It had to be Ketill. Nobody else in the group used his name. Or asked if he was okay. Hrafn grunted, and spat, and kept his eyes closed for a moment longer to let the dizziness subside.

"Here. Water."

Something nudged his shoulder. Only Ketill was foolish enough to risk touching a witch, even when all the great fierce men around him had warned that it would result in curses or boils or his cock rotting off.

Hrafn opened his eyes cautiously, found that he did not need to vomit again, and accepted the water. He rinsed his mouth and spat one more time.

"Are you okay?" Ketill asked again. He stood barely an ell away, close enough to kick, if Hrafn wanted.

"Men think they banished the world's unspeakable evils when they locked the hidden folk away," Hrafn said, with a tired sigh, "but that's only because they don't know how much wickedness birds carry in their tiny, wretched hearts."

He broke the scab on his arm to dig the bird feather out and dropped it to the ground, then dashed on a bit of water to scrub the blood away.

"Oh. Uh." Ketill smiled, then frowned, then smiled again, uneasily, as he took another step back. "Did you have—was it a premonition? What did you see?"

Hrafn sighed. Every day he hoped in vain to discover Ketill's sense of humor, and every day he was disappointed.

"Does your lonely god let you believe in premonitions?" he asked.

Ketill's smile grew calmer, as it always did when the conversation turned to the one topic in which he had confidence: his religion. "The nature of the Godhead is to allow us both wisdom and wonder, as well as the humility to recognize that we cannot ever know the fullness of creation."

"So where do the body parts of dead saints fit in? Are they wisdom or wonder?"

Ketill's eyes narrowed, just a bit, before his placid expression returned. "They are sacrifice," he said evenly. "The Seven Saints died so that the rest of us might know the forgiveness of the Godhead and one day live free of sin. In the church, there is no crime worse than stealing a relic that has not been entrusted to you."

Hrafn regretted asking. He looked away. Ketill's intensity needled at him, though it wasn't the man's fault. It was only that Hrafn couldn't imagine ever caring about something so much as Ketill cherished his faith.

"I need to tell Gudmundur what I saw," he said.

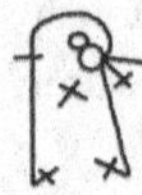

There was no true darkness to cover them on a White Night, but there was a muddled, murky twilight during which the people of the village would let down their guard, lose their sharpness, tumble into sleep. When that hour arrived, Gudmundur ordered the men down the trail, with himself in the lead and Hrafn rattling along in his chains at the back. They likely wouldn't need him until they reached the church. Ketill said he had not seen the stolen relic when he visited the church, which meant the local priest had hidden it away and likely used witchcraft to obscure it. For all their preaching about wickedness and fondness for witch-fueled bonfires, the priests of the Seven Saints had no qualms about using magic when it suited them.

Hrafn was good at finding things. He didn't know how well his finding magic would work inside a church, but that was a problem to solve when they got there.

He fell behind as they descended; the chain on his legs kept his steps short and awkward. The fog thickened as they neared the coast, wrapping around them like a shroud, obscuring the men ahead and the surrounding landscape from view. Hrafn followed Einar's blue robes as the noise of the seabirds grew louder and the smell of low tide grew stronger.

He thought it was another bird, at first, when the man screamed.

After the piercing scream came a shout, and that voice was Gudmundur's. There was another shout from up ahead, bellowing somewhere in the fog, and a sound very much like an ax chopping into wood.

Hrafn knew what the sound meant, in a land where there were no trees.

"Give me my knife!" he hissed. He did not want his voice to carry. "Einar, give me my knife!"

Einar took several steps forward, away from Hrafn, then turned back. Several men were shouting now, and the clash of metal on metal rang through the fog.

"Gods damn it, give it to me!" Hrafn said. "I can help them. You know I can."

After another second of indecision, Einar hurried back to Hrafn and drew the forked blade.

"It was a trap," Einar said.

Hrafn agreed. "Guess they cherish their saint's teat more than it seemed."

"What are you going to do?"

Hrafn looked at Einar. He looked, and he did not have to look for long, for he saw the precise moment when Einar understood that Hrafn intended to run. Guilt churned in his gut, but he ignored it. They would not risk themselves for him. Their screams were not his fault. He owed them nothing.

He only wished he had some fucking shoes.

"Don't be stupid!" Einar snapped. "You know Birtingr will hunt you down."

Hrafn grinned and spun the forked knife in his hand. "I don't care. Give me the key. Do you want to die in this sheep-shit hell?"

A man shouted, much closer than the others. Einar looked back again, wasting too much time in indecision, then finally reached into his pouch for the key. He tossed it to Hrafn, who caught it and crouched to unlock the cuffs about his ankles.

As he stood again, somebody staggered out of the fog. It was Randulfur One-Arm, with blood on his face and a wild look in his eyes. With his one hand he was grasping at his other shoulder, where the handle of a blade protruded. Another man leaped from the fog behind him, bellowing as he swung an ax; he struck Randulfur in the center of his back. Randulfur gasped, gurgled. He said a word—a woman's name, mother or wife or daughter, somebody who would miss him—and fell. The stranger yanked his ax free and raised it high.

A voice carried through the fog. "Kill the witch in blue, but capture the small one."

Hrafn's heart skipped. That was not the voice of a stranger. His hands shook; he couldn't get the key into the shackle on his wrist.

"We need him alive," the voice went on.

The stranger with the ax was listening; he turned his gaze on Einar.

"What," Hrafn said, his mind racing. "What are you—"

Einar was boring. Einar was untalented. Einar was good for nothing but babysitting. But in this one thing, he was cleverer than Hrafn.

Einar darted forward to yank the knife from Randulfur's shoulder; it came free with a slick, wet sound. Then Einar was in front of Hrafn again, blade raised as the man with the ax charged. Hrafn tried to run, he tried to dodge and flee, but he tripped over a stone. He would have fallen if Einar did not catch him by the upper arm. Hrafn twisted and thrashed to break free, but Einar held him tight.

"Sorry," Einar said, as blandly as he said anything. "I can't let them take you."

He thrust the knife upward in a quick, skilled underhand move, driving it directly into Hrafn's heart. He pulled it free, the blade bright with Hrafn's heart-blood, and drew it swiftly across his own neck. The stranger swung his ax. Einar's eyes widened and his mouth dropped open. Blood spilled from his neck and he toppled to the ground.

Hrafn was already on his knees. He did not recall falling. Somebody was gurgling painfully. It might have been Einar. The sounds of the battle had ceased. He was cold, and his heart could not beat, and every one of his staves burned like ice on raw new skin. Stepping out of the fog behind the man with the ax was Ketill.

Good Brother Ketill, with his hairless face and round eyes, had no tremble in his voice when he spoke Hrafn's name. Ketill, who had gone alone to visit the village. Ketill, who was smiling now with all the humor he had never shown before.

"Oh," he said, when he looked down at Hrafn. There was blood on his brown robes and his pale face. "This is going to complicate things. I was going to keep you for myself."

Darkness surrounded Hrafn, an impossible darkness on this White Night. All he could feel was the cold, and blood in his throat, and nothing. A moment passed, or an eternity.

And everything was fire.

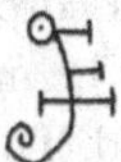

Hrafn knew quite a lot about pain. He knew the pain of hunger and thirst and exhaustion. Of a blade slicing through his skin. Red-hot brands and long needles and heavy fists. Skin chafed raw around ankles and wrists. He knew pain that felt like nausea, and pain that felt like fear, and pain that was indistinguishable from pleasure. He even knew pain that had no true cause, the pain of a child wanting something he ought not to want, of seeking something he did not deserve, of asking for something that could never be given.

This. This was different.

Every stave and scar on his body burned, glowing from within with a heat more furious than the heart of a volcano. They burned more fiercely than they had when they were first placed on his skin, more fiercely even than the earliest of his brands, the ones that he had endured only because four grown men had held down a skinny underfed child so that a fifth might carve his skin. It felt as though his skin was peeling away from his limbs, his flesh curling from his bones, his blood boiling through cracks and fissures that slashed across his body. He could not scream. The world was a thunderous roar. Every breath he drew seared his throat and lungs. Everything was agony.

Until, suddenly, it wasn't.

The pain vanished, but the fire did not. The relief was so sudden and surprising that Hrafn opened his eyes. Flames danced around him, tickling over his skin and eating at his clothing, but he felt them now as only the gentlest of spring breezes. His skin was neither blistered nor broken. The only pain that remained was a strange, dull ache in his arm and palm. He shook whispers of flame away but saw no wound.

When he rose to his feet, his bare toes nudged a knot of charred meat and scorched bone and, vanishing rapidly in the flames, blue cloth.

So. Somebody had decided to burn the witches.

Hrafn stepped over Einar's corpse and out of the flames. The ashes of his clothes fell away as he moved into open air, though the manacles on his wrists remained. The world outside the fire had the golden look of a White Night, but not like the one he had just left, leaden with fog and sapped of color. The clouds had broken overhead, and the breeze that whipped around the fire was cool, though it smelled slightly of manure. It felt so good on his naked skin that for a moment Hrafn did not care why he was alive when he should obviously be dead, why this should have happened when he had only ever heard whispers of such a thing before. It would matter later. Right now, he only wanted to kiss whoever had made the pain stop.

A man stood beside the fire, broad-shouldered and grim-mouthed. If he was speaking, Hrafn could not hear it, because he could not look at the man when his gaze was drawn to the boy behind him, a scuffed-up ash-dusted giant of a boy who was kneeling in the mud and staring at Hrafn with terrified, tear-filled eyes as deep and blue as the sea on a sunny day.

The boy's arms were extended awkwardly in front of him, as though some invisible force had tugged them forward. One of his hands was burned in furious, blistered stripes, untreated and badly seeping.

The other was veined with fierce black and white lines in a familiar pattern. A single central blade, four tines from the side, pressed into the boy's hand and forearm so deeply the knife had become part of him, deeper than any scar. Hrafn's heart skipped when he saw it, and in that skip he felt an echo, another heartbeat. The boy's eyes widened.

Hrafn walked past the man and knelt in the mud before the boy. He took the boy's hands in his own, the chains of his manacles clinking together. He could feel the same black lines that marked the boy's arm pulsing beneath his own skin, although outwardly it looked much the same as it always had.

There could be no mistake.

It was his own knife, forged of blood and magic and bone, now a part of the boy's arm.

Well. Fuck.

There were a number of things Hrafn suddenly wished he had taken more care to learn about when his elders tried to teach him.

Hrafn looked up to meet the boy's eyes.

"Sorry about all this," he said.

He tried a smile, because the boy looked like he was about to shatter into pieces. Beneath the ash and grime that made him look like a wary, overgrown puffling, the boy was actually quite fair. His hair was golden and tied back from his face somewhat messily, in a sweep of small braids and escaping strands. Perhaps no older than Hrafn, but taller and twice as broad, and well used to manual labor, if the corded muscles in his arms and shoulders were any indication.

"Did you, ah, did you do that on purpose?" Hrafn asked.

People did often try to bind a witch to themselves or meddle with the rules that separated life and death, and sometimes they even succeeded, but this boy looked so upset that Hrafn had to ask.

"I'm going to guess that the answer is *no*, because you look like a great skua has just snatched your mother into the air, when you were probably out here just hoping to have a nice peaceful witch-burning. But if you *did* do it on purpose—"

The boy made a startled sound, nothing like a word, and a tear slipped down his cheek.

"If you *did* do it on purpose," Hrafn pressed on, squeezing the boy's hands just a bit, just the tiniest bit, knowing that even that little bit of pressure would be agony for that freshly burned skin, "you should just tell me what you want and get it over with. I've been stabbed in the heart and set on fire. If you were hoping for a mindless puppet, I'm afraid you fucked something up. Tell me what you want. I'm not really in the mood to coddle a scared little puffling who's so surprised by his own success that he can't speak a single word."

"Witch," the boy said. "You're—you're—"

Hrafn rolled his eyes. "Yes, we can start there. You've dragged a witch back from the dead, so you must want something. What is it? Silver? Jewels? Treasure?" He looked around. There did not seem to be anything nearby except mud, manure, and rock. What did people who lived on manure-stinking cliffsides in the desolate westlands want, anyway? He really hoped this boy was not about to ask him for the teat of a dead saint. "Sheep? Fish? Good weather? Maybe a pretty girl? Or a pretty boy? One of each? Twice the trouble, but twice the reward, especially if they—"

"Witch."

The word came not from the boy that time, but the man, who Hrafn had, admittedly, completely forgotten about, because it was not the man whose flesh and skin had wrapped around a cold iron and bone piece of himself, whose blood now pulsed in time with his own. The man was tall and broad, as big as Gudmundur, and he lumbered toward them with his hands clenched at his sides.

"Step away from him," said the man.

Hrafn dropped the boy's hands and stood up, took a few squelching steps back onto blissfully mud-free moss. He wiped his feet as clean as he could and held his own hands up.

"I'm not going to hurt him. That would be stupid."

The man stared at him—not at his face, but at the staves carved into his palms—eyes wide with fear, as though he expected sulfurous worms to erupt and attack him where he stood.

"Get away," the man said again. "Sigbert! Come here!"

The boy staggered to his feet, swaying, and stumbled to the man's side.

"Father," he said. "Father, I don't know—"

He reached out, but the man recoiled in horror when he saw the blade embedded in the boy's arm. "What have you done, boy?"

Fresh tears spilled from the boy's eyes. "I don't know, Father, I don't know, I only—"

"That cannot be burned from the surface. The curse is too deep."

"Wait." Hrafn stepped forward. "Wait. He's not cursed. If

anybody's cursed it's *me*, but it won't—"

"Be silent, witch!" the man shouted. "The filth is beneath the skin. This cannot be cleansed from the surface."

"Cleansed?" Hrafn said, understanding dawning, and with it a roiling mix of anger and horror. *Don't touch a witch*, the common folk said, *or you'll be tainted*. "Is that why his hand is burnt? *You* did that?"

Neither father nor son answered. The boy was trembling so badly it shook his entire body. "What—Father, I didn't mean to, I didn't—"

"It's going to be okay," the man said. "This can be fixed. Come here, Sigbert."

He held out his arms, as though to embrace his son. The boy's expression lightened with something like hope, and his blue eyes shimmered. He stepped closer and leaned toward his father.

The man moved to the side swiftly and grabbed the boy by the back of his shirt. He jerked him off his feet and dragged him toward the fire.

"Father? Father! Stop! Father, what are you doing?" The boy flailed and kicked as he cried out, his voice rising higher and higher in panic. "Father, please!"

"You're bewitched," the man said. "There's no question now. This is the only way."

"He is not bewitched!" Hrafn shouted. "For fuck's sake, don't you know anything?"

"Do not speak, witch. Unnatural wickedness no longer has a place in this world."

"You fucking idiot, he's not cursed!"

"Father! Stop, please!" The boy was sobbing now, still kicking helplessly at the mud and moss. "I'm sorry! I'm so sorry!"

But the man heeded neither Hrafn's words nor his son's pleas. Hrafn ran a few steps after him, then stopped, looked around.

"There is no cure for a curse that flows in your blood," the man said.

"You really don't know anything," Hrafn snapped.

"Father," the boy cried, choking on the word. "Please."

"The witch's words are lies. A witch cannot speak the truth."

The boy found a well of strength as they reached the fire, and he managed to twist away from the licking flames for a few brief seconds. But he could not escape. His father was bigger and stronger and driven by terrible purpose. The man did not even have tears in his eyes.

Hrafn didn't know what the boy had done to get a blood-forged knife of iron and bone magicked into his arm, nor why that had brought a witch back from the dead. If anybody had ever tried to beat that particular bit of magical knowledge into him, he hadn't learned the lesson. He had never encountered such magic before. And he had no idea what it meant for him, or for the boy.

But he did know this: a father should not harm his son.

And a witch didn't need magic to kill a man twice his size.

All he needed was a big, sharp rock.

He hefted a chunk of black stone and charged. The boy's screams grew louder as the man drove him closer to the flames. It was one of the most terrible sounds Hrafn had ever heard. He felt the heat growing in his own left arm, a strange pain like brands pressing upward from the inside. His heart was racing and there was blood in his throat. He recognized it as fear, but it was not his own fear. He had none in this moment, only pure red rage. He threw himself onto the man's back and swung down hard, driving the sharp edge of the rock into the back of his skull.

The man spun around, trying to throw him off, but Hrafn struck him again, and again, and again, until the man's shouts of anger turned to wordless grunts, and he released the boy. The boy rolled away from the fire, and the father lurched toward it. Hrafn dropped to the ground, landing messily in the mud.

The boy was up on his feet almost immediately. "Father!"

He darted forward, reaching as the man toppled into the fire. Hrafn scrambled after the boy, grabbed him around the middle, and hauled him backward.

"Let go of me!" the boy cried. "He's going to—"

What the man was going to do was fall face-first into the flames without so much as a twitch or a sound. There was, for a moment, a gap where he had fallen, but the flames were hungry and soon closed over him.

The boy stopped struggling, but Hrafn did not release him until he had dragged him several feet back, far enough that the heat was gentle rather than painful. Then he let go and stepped away.

The boy sank to the ground, staring at the fire. There were still tears gathered in those big blue eyes, and streaks through the ash and dirt on his face, but no more fell. His breath hitched, softly, but he did not sob. He only sat in the mud and stared at the fire.

Hrafn had no idea what to do. The man had tried to burn his own child alive. Such a man did not deserve his son's grief. He crouched down, wrapped his arms around his bare legs and torso, and watched the boy watch his father burn.

It took a very long time. The night ended, and morning arrived, drawing the sun back from its skimming dip beneath the horizon. Seabirds woke and shrieked and whirled around the plume of smoke. By the time the fire began to die down, the corpses within were shriveled husks. There was no trace of Einar's blue robes left.

"Shark oil," the boy said.

Hrafn started. Neither of them had spoken in hours. "What?"

"That's why it burned so well." The boy's voice was low and hollow. "He must have used shark oil."

"Oh." Hrafn swallowed; his throat was dry. "That was wasteful. Einar had nothing but sawdust in his veins anyway."

Hrafn looked away from the fire to find that the boy was looking at him. But as soon as their eyes met, the boy looked down at his left arm. He traced the outline of the knife with the fingers of his right hand.

"You want to know what I want," he said.

Hrafn felt something crack inside of him, something cold and tired. What *he* wanted was a hammer to break his manacles, a warm blanket and a good night's sleep, and a hot meal of something besides moldy scraps.

And trousers. He could do with some trousers.

That's all he wanted.

But of course, the boy wanted something from him. Nobody captured a witch from the nether realm between life and death unless they wanted something.

"Sure," he said. "Tell me what you want. That's why I'm here, isn't it?"

The boy rose to his feet. When he stood upright, with his shoulders unbent, he was nearly as tall as his father had been. Hrafn hadn't noticed before.

"I want you to find somebody," the boy said.

Hrafn frowned thoughtfully. "I can do some tracking but—"

"Not track," the boy said. "Find. Whether he's dead or alive, in this world or another, you're going to find him. That's what I want." He turned to walk away from the fire. "They won't fit well, but I can give you some clothes, if you come this way."

Chapter Three
Of Hammers and Teeth

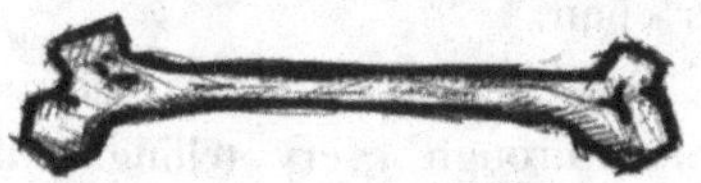

"A witch killed Mother, you know." Arnes kicked at the broken body of a langoustine, caught in a net of seaweed on the black sand, hollowed out by the beak of a seabird.

"Who says a witch killed Mother?" Siggi asked, trailing his elder brother along the shore, placing his feet in the indentations Arnes left behind. "Did Father say that?"

"Father never talks about Mother."

"Then who said so, Arnes?"

Arnes bent down suddenly, plucking the broken purple shards of a shell from the sand. "Everyone else. Everyone says a witch killed Mother to spite Father."

"But Mother died the same day I was born." Siggi did not say, *Because I was born.*

"That's what Father says. But Brynja Gottsdottir told me that her mother says otherwise." Arnes tossed the purple shard into the sea and turned his back on Siggi, facing the water. "Brynja Gottsdottir's mother says that Mother was strange, and she whispered to the hidden people in the rocks down here by the sea, inviting them back into our world to spread plague and madness. She says Mother visited an ancient trylla in a cave and brought him pieces of meat as offerings. She said that the day after Mother died, she came to this cove and found the heads of three devilfish in a gull's nest, and the fish had staves carved into their brows."

"Do fish have brows?"

"*Siggi.*" Arnes sighed. "The point is, that was witchcraft."

"How does she know that was witchcraft against Mother?"

"Brynja Gottsdottir told me that her mother says that Mother's golden hair was woven into the nest."

"Many people in Midfjördur have golden hair. How could she know it was Mother's hair?"

Arnes groaned. "Siggi, why not listen to a story for once? *Listen,* and not prod holes through every telling with your endless questions?"

Siggi tucked his cold hands beneath his arms. The water stretching before them was a cold shade of slate, impenetrable as the cliffs at their backs. Whenever the wind rose, ripples appeared atop the sucking waves, trails left by unseen fingers. "You say Mother was wonderful."

"She *was* wonderful," Arnes said sharply. "She was the most wonderful person in all the Thrandir. Never listen to a word otherwise."

"Then why would anyone want to harm her?"

Arnes laughed at the surf, a grating sound. "You think witches need a reason?"

"Maybe they do. So why?"

"Because Father is much less wonderful."

Siggi's eyes welled, and his face grew heated. "Father is respected."

It was only months from the day Arnes would set sail for the southern peninsula and vanish. Siggi was already as tall as his older brother, though four summers separated them. Even so, Arnes seemed to tower as he rounded on him, meeting Siggi's eyes with his own, just as blue. "Would a man worthy of respect blame an infant for a woman's death? Would anyone respect a man who refuses to love a boy as kind as you?"

Siggi asked many questions, but Arnes asked so few. Why was it so hard to answer him? "He loves me. He only loves you more."

"Siggi." Arnes placed one hand on Siggi's shoulder, the other on his side. Even through the thick woolen tunic, Siggi could feel the desperation in his grip. With one hand, Arnes pressed gently against his little brother's ribs and Siggi gasped for air, collapsing to his knees.

"Is this love? He never lays a hand on me, but you—Siggi. How can you still admire him?"

Siggi gasped and clutched at his bruised ribs. He longed to say Father had been right. He was right to thrust his boot into Siggi's chest, once and twice and again, because Siggi had broken a blade before it was tempered. Father was right to punish Siggi, because Siggi was so often clumsy and stupid and no matter what, he could not seem to stop crying.

Siggi tried once more to defend Father, but he could not breathe through the pain.

"Why not believe in witches, if the alternative is believing in a man like Father?"

Arnes's eyes were wide and scared and unfathomable, as though Siggi were seeing his own reflection and not his unshakable older brother. And for all the questions Siggi always asked, in that moment he failed to ask the right ones.

Then Arnes left Midfjördur and there was no one left to answer him anyway.

Father was a big man, but by the time the flames had finished with him, he was as empty as that langoustine husk. The air was cold and clogged with filthy smoke. Siggi found he could cry no longer.

Father's murderer sat beside Siggi, silent and unshivering despite the cold, naked but for those black manacles. Siggi waited for his fists to curl, for the same conviction that rose to his lips when he defended Father to Arnes to spur him into action. If witches were real, witches should be burned. There wasn't a child in the Thrandir who didn't know that much. And this witch, however small, had killed Siggi's sole remaining family member.

But if he hadn't, Father would have killed you.

Was it the bewitchment or his own voice in his head that uttered this truth to Siggi's heart? Father, wild-eyed and spitting, holding Siggi's mangled hands in his grip and dragging him mercilessly toward the pyre. Father, at last looking at him, but every ounce of his gaze oozing a vitriol Siggi could not fathom. How often had the eyes that gazed fondly upon Arnes gazed hatefully upon him?

And yet never did Siggi suspect Father would hate him enough to burn him alive.

Arnes must have suspected, and Arnes had left. Killing this witch would not bring him back.

Siggi remained unmoving as the fire died, as the White Night gradually shifted into chilly silver morning, as the fey blade in his wrist pulsed with a second heartbeat. He remained unmoving until the silence choked him more than the ash, and then he turned to face the witch-boy.

He really was a striking little thing. The intertwined staves that scarred his body were as unreadable to Siggi as the stars. The hollows of his cheeks, the blackness of his eyes. And now that he was alive—impossibly but undeniably resurrected—the self-assurance that imbued the witch's every movement captivated Siggi. It was as though the boy were a precisely aimed arrow that, however fragile, would always hit its mark. What must it feel like, to be so confident?

To lift a stone and bring it down on a man's skull as if it were easy?

Siggi understood that many frail-seeming things were not. The thinnest icicles were often the sharpest, capable of impaling those who stood beneath them. The most delicate of bearberry stalks survived the winter. A mere drop of shark oil could ignite a pyre.

"Shark oil," Siggi murmured.

The witch-boy jumped, shoulders tensed as though he were about to take flight. "What?"

"That's why it burned so well. He must have used shark oil."

"Oh." Though a wry note tinged the boy's voice, his expression belied some other emotion. "That was wasteful. Einar had nothing but sawdust in his veins anyway."

Siggi had to look away. As his face flushed, the knife in his arm drew his eye: ash black, bone white, and ice cold. He traced the blade's outline with the fingers of his right hand, recalling all the times Arnes had traced lattices on the earthen floor. Arnes, and all the memories he had left in his wake, like footprints on black sand.

"You want to know what I want," Siggi said.

The witch-boy's shoulders sank. "Sure. Tell me what you want. That's why I'm here, isn't it?"

In truth, Siggi could not fathom why this boy was here, but now that Father was dead there was no one else. No one but this slight stranger with long eyelashes and a thousand vicious scars and a stare as black as the deepest mountain caverns.

Could eyes like that see through the darkness? Could they find what had been lost?

Siggi stood. "I want you to find somebody."

"I can do some tracking but—"

"Not track. Find. Whether he's dead or alive, in this world or another, you're going to find him. That's what I want." Siggi turned away from the fire and Father and any semblance of the world he had known. "They won't fit well, but I can give you some clothes, if you come this way."

"Well, thank fuck for that in any case." The witch-boy drew himself up on unsteady legs.

Siggi quickly looked away.

"Oh." The boy's smirk was audible. "Do my staves scare you, Sigbert?"

"*Siggi*, not Sigbert," Siggi said, placing a hand over his eyes, wincing at the echo of Father's voice. "That's not…I didn't…you must be very cold."

The boy blinked in something like surprise, then chuckled. "Oh? So you're looking away to spare the witch the loss of his precious dignity? Don't bother. Haven't ever had any, *Sigbert*."

"Siggi."

"Fine."

Siggi bit his lip, fighting the impulse to look at him again. "And…what is your name?"

"If you know how to capture a witch, you must know better than to ask a witch his name."

Siggi frowned, because there it was again: this witch thought Siggi had *meant* to ensnare him, that Siggi had taken the knife to trap him. The witch believed Siggi had some understanding of witchcraft. Somehow, this boy did not assume, as most people did, that Siggi was an idiot.

Siggi knew nothing of witches that couldn't be heard in garbled children's stories, gleaned from Arnes's whispers while they dozed beside the fire. Siggi had taken the knife on impulse and wished now that he hadn't, that he hadn't been swayed by the scarred feet and empty face of a pretty dead boy that looked truly nothing like his brother.

But he could say none of this if he wished to enlist the witch's help. For once, Siggi bit his tongue as he led the witch, barefoot and bound, up the narrow track to Father's forge.

The mare had been so quiet that Siggi thought she must have fled the chaos. But she stood stock-still as they passed by the wagon, eyeing the witch-boy.

"She's afraid of you," Siggi observed, patting her as he passed.

"She's got more sense than you have, then. Storguð's cock, how do you tolerate all this muck?"

Siggi recalled the witch-boy's bare and broken feet. "Sh-should I carry you?"

"Fuck off. Just find me some damned trousers."

Siggi stopped and felt the witch-boy stumble at his back. "If you will tell me your name."

"Never had one, never needed one," muttered the witch-boy, but Siggi felt a curious twinge in his arm and a flutter in his chest. The boy was lying.

"Everyone needs a name." Even Siggi had been given that much.

"You know what I need? *Trousers*."

Father kept the last remnants of Arnes's belongings hidden in a driftwood chest in the forge, but he hadn't always done so.

The day news reached Midfjördur that the *Hvalfinder* had vanished and all aboard were lost, Siggi had retrieved the old clothes Arnes had left behind, clothes Siggi too had overgrown, from the little chest beneath their bed. He had pressed the worn cloth against his nose and willed himself to weep, willed himself to believe his brother was alive.

Father had torn the clothes from his grip. Wordlessly he hit Siggi upside the head with the flat of his hand, gathered all Arnes's things inside the chest, and set off into the night. But one day, while Father was outside harvesting bog iron and Siggi was sweeping ash from the cavern, Siggi spotted the chest tucked behind a woven basket of rags against the far wall.

Now, with the witch-boy at his back, tapping on the ironworking implements and muttering to himself, Siggi tried to pull the chest from its hiding place, but his wounded palm twinged sharply. Siggi whimpered and recoiled.

"Fuck!" Behind him, the witch-boy fell against the wall, his manacles clanking against the stone. Siggi looked at him. He was panting from exertion, muck staining his scarred shins, eyes streaming just as Siggi's were. "*Fuck*, but I felt that. What kind of Father…never mind. I met him."

"When I'm hurt…you're hurt as well?" Siggi said.

The boy rolled his eyes, shuffling toward him. "Wasn't that the whole point of binding me to you, puffling?"

Siggi looked down at his mismatched hands. The burned one was hideous, and already several blisters had popped and cracked. But more disturbing was the spined knife, fused with his other hand. The central blade had grown right into his forefinger, and those thin ivory branches reached the tips of his others. Siggi could see no seams, no clear place where the cursed knife ended and his skin began.

"Give me your hands."

Siggi was startled. Despite the manacles, the witch had moved as quietly as a fox after dark. He knelt before Siggi as though he'd always been there.

"Your hands." The witch-boy took firm hold of Siggi's wrists. "I'm not your Father. I can't kill you even if I want to."

The witch-boy peeled open Siggi's burned, seeping fingers. "Right to the bone. That'll need the stronger stave." The witch stared at his own forearms, scanning his chest and abdomen, letting his eyes drift across every rune that marked his naked flesh.

Siggi no longer tried to look away. "What are you doing?"

"Witchcraft, obviously." The witch-boy scowled, running his fingers over an ornate stave on the bottom-left side of his rib cage. "Fucking Randulfur One-Arm wanted me to fix his eponymous situation, but this stave's no good on old wounds, and what the hell would anyone even call him if he'd gotten that sorted? He's such a stupid—well. It doesn't matter now."

The witch-boy used two sharp, overgrown fingernails to peel the scab from the surface of the stave. He acted as though he were only combing his hair, and yet Siggi felt a needling flash of pain scrape his own stomach. He twisted in discomfort.

The witch-boy pulled Siggi's hand to his torso, pressing it against the blood beading there, inhaling through his teeth. His blood met Siggi's burns and a curious blend of sensations overcame him. Siggi felt the pain of the boy's reopened stave, like a phantom in his own belly, and a curious tingle of warmth in his bloodstream, and an almost tickling chill as his palm cooled and knitted back together. The exhaustion abandoned Siggi's bones.

The witch pulled Siggi's palm from his skinny abdomen, sweat on his brow. "There."

"You healed me." Siggi stared in wonder at his hand, devoid of burns and blisters.

"I didn't do it for you. Your burns were bothering me."

Siggi felt that twinge again, the one that felt like a lie.

The witch said gruffly, "Now get me some goddamn trousers or I really will curse you."

Siggi stared at his hands. Not for years had his skin looked so smooth, given Father's frequent switchings and the toll hard work took on a farmer's palms. Father's hands were mangled too, forever misshapen by years' accumulation of splinters, burns, and calluses. Siggi had felt the roughness of his palms every time he laid a hand on Siggi, had felt the weight of hard work when it bore down on him.

Father is dead. Once again, the thought stole Siggi's breath. *He'll never pull the switch out from above the door again. He'll never hit me again.*

Suddenly the witch-boy's hands were on Siggi's cheeks. "Gods, enough with your heartbeat! I can't heal that bit, so calm the fuck down!"

Siggi breathed through his nostrils, eyes streaming. "If you can heal my wounds, can't you heal your own?"

The witch-boy recoiled as though Siggi had struck him. "What?"

"All your scars. They must hurt you. Can't you heal them, too?"

The witch-boy dropped his hands, scowling. "What, heal all my staves? What use would I be to anyone then?"

Siggi looked into his strange eyes and then nodded, reaching under the workbench with renewed strength. He pulled Arnes's driftwood chest free, set it on the floor between them, and lifted the lid.

A spare tunic, too small and careworn. The shoes from Arnes's infancy, the woolen shawl that ensconced him in his youth. The Stones and Bones playing pieces, a single bead he'd traded two pelts for at the harbor. Yet Siggi couldn't smell Arnes at all, or if he could, he couldn't remember Arnes's smell enough to know it. He thrust the box toward the witch-boy's grasping fingers and turned away. "You'll find clothes in there."

When he looked back, there the boy stood, holding Arnes's trousers, twice as wide as he was, belted at the waist with a length of twine.

"There's a shirt in there as well."

The witch-boy rolled his eyes, holding up his manacled wrists. "Easier said than done."

"Oh." Siggi turned to the tools that lined the walls of the forge. Father's best hammer, scarred with countless years of ironworking, hung in its rightful place. Even on a night devoted to burning bandits, Arnes Thorsson was meticulous about his workshop. Siggi pulled the hammer from the wall, gripping its wooden handle with both hands.

"You know how to use this forge, then? Magic's nice, but there are a few heads I'd prefer to lop off the old-fashioned way."

Siggi shook his head. "Father only taught Arnes. I looked after the sheep. Here. Place your hands on either side of the anvil."

"You're going to what?" The witch's eyebrows shot upward. "Break a cursed chain with *that* lump of metal?"

"I don't know anything about that. But a hammer is a hammer, and a chain is a chain."

"Well, aren't you clever." But even as the witch-boy mocked Siggi, he shuffled closer and placed his hands on either side of the stone anvil, stretching the chain taut across its surface. "Don't say I didn't warn you."

Siggi was not Arnes. He was neither as coordinated nor as clever as Father had wished him to be, and perhaps he had killed his mother as an infant. But Siggi had strong arms, and could wield this hammer, and Father wasn't here to hit him for doing it wrong.

Never again.

Siggi swung with all his strength. The hammerhead collided with the chain and all but bounced away. Siggi gritted his teeth, arm shaking, and tried again, and again, until the noise was a steady racket and the witch-boy was cursing at him.

"Useless lout, *enough*, Einar magicked them! They're iron fused with huldu bone, likely unbreakable, I told you it was no good—"

Siggi swung the hammer again. With a clanging crunch, a link of the chain cracked and then broke. The witch-boy's eyes widened as he fell forward over the anvil, hands separated at last.

The two of them looked at each other by the dying light of the coals.

"A lout," the witch-boy breathed, staring at his hands, "but perhaps not *entirely* useless."

"Put on that shirt," Siggi breathed, wiping the sweat from his brow. "And then tell me how we're going to find my brother."

The forge was fading, and the cold was beginning to seep in from the mist outside.

"So last year your older brother stole away on a fishing boat." The witch-boy, fully clad at last, was perched on Father's workbench with his legs crossed and his eyes closed. "And soon after your village received word that the boat was lost at sea. Is that it?"

Siggi nodded, hugging his knees, back against the cavern wall. That was as much as he had shared. The reasons why Arnes had left, what he had hoped to achieve, his promise to return for Siggi as soon as he could—the witch-boy didn't need to know those parts.

"Well, that's simple enough. I can certainly tell you where your brother is."

Siggi drew himself up. "You can?"

The witch-boy shrugged. "Dead at the bottom of the sea."

Siggi stood. "You can't know that. You haven't looked for him!"

The witch-boy didn't bother opening his eyes. "And if you discover that he is drowned and gone? If I do all my scrying magic and discover your brother really is a fish-eaten corpse, will you release me from this bond?"

Siggi trembled, shaking his head. "Even—even if you learn that Arnes is dead...can't you bring him back to life? Like you were brought back?"

"You tell me." The witch's eyes snapped open. Slowly, he slid from the table, unctuous and threatening as a cooling river of lava. "*I* have never brought anything back from the dead. All my life I've been a witch, and I wouldn't know where to begin with reviving a corpse. But you did it so easily, didn't you?"

Siggi dared not answer.

"Don't tell me it really was an accident." The witch's expression soured. He peered up at Siggi's face, eyes prodding like knives, and then sank back on his heels. "Oh, bloated bloody trylla balls. Of *course* it was an accident. You didn't even mean to catch a witch, did you?"

Siggi did not lower his shoulders. "Does it matter, if you're already caught?"

"It may. It may matter a great deal, if it means you don't know how to break this bond you've created between us."

"I know how to undo it," Siggi lied, swallowing hard.

The witch-boy weighed him with narrowed eyes. "I don't think I believe you."

"Just tell me. If Arnes is dead, could he be brought back? Like you were?"

"Well, let's see, *Sigbert*. If *you're* not a real necromancer, and my breathing again has *nothing* to do with you, it must have something more to do with me. Did your beloved brother happen to be branded with a hundred staves of witchcraft, imbued with ungodly powers in his infancy against his will, and armed with a ritual blade of bone and blood?"

Siggi shook his head, eyes burning. "No."

"I thought not. If your brother is dead, he'll stay dead. And even if that's the case—if I find out he's dead for good—swear to me you'll still break the bond that binds us."

Siggi had no idea how the bond had formed in the first place. But he nodded, because this was no choice. "I swear it."

The witch watched him with his animal eyes, then he sighed. "Scrying is easier with fresh blood or flesh from the person being sought, but we'll have to make do with something older."

"You're wearing his clothes." Siggi drew himself up. "Isn't that enough?"

"No." He sneered at the tunic. "These stinking clothes are more closely related to the sheep who grew the wool than to your brother. It needs to be something *more* personal, more specific to who he was.

A vial of his blood, a leathered piece of his skin, a collection of his fingernails."

Siggi gaped at him. "Why would I have any of those things?"

"I don't know what sort of tokens people keep of their loved ones." The witch-boy threw up his hands, all but drowning in fabric. "A…a thick lock of his hair? I suppose you won't have any of his bones on hand, either?"

Siggi shook his head, helpless.

"You truly know nothing about anything. It's almost impressive." He paused, one pointed tooth buried in his bottom lip.

Siggi blinked. "Would…would one of my brother's teeth be enough?"

The witch-boy raised his eyebrows, cocking his head to one side. "Yes. Yes, you idiot, a tooth would work just fine." He held out an open palm, broken chain rattling.

"I don't have any here. But…at the church."

"The *church*? Why the hell would your brother's teeth be at the church?"

"The church collects all teeth lost by children. Father never took me to service, but he took Arnes, and Arnes had to pay the tithe like everyone else. Brother Hamon gave no choice."

"Well, isn't that horrid." The witch-boy frowned. "It's the church in the village, right?"

Siggi nodded. "There are no other churches in Midfjördur."

The witch-boy sighed, hands presumably on his hips—it was hard to tell, given the clothes that swamped him. "That fucking church really seems to want me dead."

"You've died already," Siggi pointed out. "What's there to be afraid of?"

"You aren't as simple as you look."

"Do I look simple?"

The boy scoffed. "Does piss look yellow?"

Siggi wondered whether the boy knew that each and every time he said something sour, his mouth twisted into a smirk but his shoulders tensed like a cat's before she fled. Did the witch-boy know he seemed ever on the cusp of running? Did he know that for all his power, he seemed so incredibly close to snapping in two?

"Fine. Let's go to church." The little witch knitted his fingers together and cracked his knuckles all at once. "I've got other business there to look into anyhow. And if you can find me a pair of shoes, maybe I'll let you burn it down once we're finished. As a special treat."

Chapter Four
Better Left Sleeping

Siggi was not, it turned out, terribly excited by the possibility of burning the village church to the ground, because he did not seem to understand that there was anything strange about it.

"You've never questioned it at all?" Hrafn asked, skeptical. "You do know that it's not normal for priests to collect children's teeth, right?"

Siggi shrugged. "I've never met a priest besides Brother Hamon."

"And when the Brotherhood collects tithes, it asks for iron, wool, barley, even gold. Not teeth."

Siggi remained unimpressed. "We don't join the rituals. I don't know what's normal for them."

"What's normal," Hrafn said, "is the good brothers chant a lot and douse themselves with spelled water and talk about how their Seven Saints let themselves be tortured to death to save our rotten souls. They definitely do not collect children's teeth."

"This one does," Siggi said.

"And that's suspicious," Hrafn insisted.

"If you say so," Siggi said agreeably.

They were following a rocky trail down from the forge, heading toward a small turf house tucked away in the lee of a hillside as protection against the wind. Siggi had only been able to break the chains from the manacles, not remove the cuffs, although he had only stopped trying when Hrafn started to worry that a misplaced blow of the hammer would shatter his wrists. He would really rather have something to eat than a pair of broken wrists, he had said, if it wasn't too much trouble. Hrafn had almost expected Siggi to swing the hammer at his head when he said that, because what kind of monster asked for a meal when he still had the blood of the boy's father on his hands? But Siggi had only muttered something about needing a better chisel to try again later before stepping out of the cave.

Hrafn did not trust his calm. It was the calm of a breathless seaside morning while storms gathered just over the horizon. The calm of a mountain that lay dormant for years before erupting. There had to be anger somewhere inside that strong body, buried beneath the hunched shoulders and sad eyes.

The turf house was small and humble and dark, but well sealed against the wind and warm enough to chase away the morning chill. Hrafn looked around shamelessly, but there was little to see. It was a thoroughly bleak excuse for a home. Not because of how humble it was, as he had seen houses smaller and dirtier, but because it revealed so little of who lived there. There were furs, wooden benches, tools, and clothing. A bucket of clean water. A charcoal fire.

There was only a single stool beside the fire, as though the father had built himself a place to sit but had not bothered to do the same for his son.

The only sign of personality was a tiny stone shelf wedged into a corner, on which somebody had collected a few pathetic treasures: pretty shells, a stone with a hole worn through the center, a small figurine carved from a nub of driftwood. The little carving had once been a whale, elegant and smooth, but it was broken in half.

Something twisted angrily in Hrafn's chest. It was all him, no spillover from Siggi. He grabbed the bucket of water without asking and went back outside, breathing through his nose so he didn't end up saying something stupid like, *How the fuck did you not bash your father's head in years ago if he made you live like this?*

He crouched beside the bucket to scrub his hands clean. The dead man's blood, his own blood, mingled together with mud and ash.

Everybody lied to witches. They lied when they caught them, lied when they asked favors of them, lied when they interrogated them, lied when they killed them. Men seeking curses lied about the unfaithfulness of their wives while leering at the stepdaughters they coveted. Women seeking children lied about the strength of their yearning while twitching under the weight of a family's or village's judgment. Everybody lied about how many sheep they had and who they had seen in the paddock at midnight and how often they met their lover for a tumble and whether they shat in the morning or evening. They lied about what they wanted, why they wanted it, what they were willing to do to get it.

The boy was lying about releasing Hrafn when his task was done. Of that Hrafn had no doubt.

What he didn't know was whether Siggi was lying because he had no intention of releasing his new pet witch until he'd used him up and drained him dry, or because he genuinely had no idea how to do it.

It was a problem for another day. Hrafn figured, if it came to it, he could try chopping the boy's arm off. If that didn't work, Hrafn would be as dead as he had been before the idiot stole his knife. And if it did, well, Siggi could go on tending sheep with one arm, and Hrafn could leave. He could go where nobody knew him. Across the sea, maybe, to the green island where the druids and mad hermits came from. Or somewhere even farther, to the hot distant lands where his parents had probably come from, whoever they had been. There were taverns in Storaska frequented by sailors whose skin was dark like his, who spoke languages unknown throughout Lifandfjall, who might be willing to trade passage to somewhere distant and warm in exchange for a scrawny witch's labor. He might, in this unexpected second life, finally find the courage to go somewhere nobody would recognize him or carry back word that he was alive. Where he would never have to be Birtingr's apprentice ever again.

Hrafn carried the bucket away from the house, toward the spot where the muddy wagon track descended toward the fjord. The village was hidden by the lonely rise of a mossy hill. Hrafn found a flat stone and scraped it clean of sand and moss. He wetted his hands again, taking care this time to cup the filth that washed from his skin rather than shake it away.

He dipped his forefinger into the ruddy-brown water and began to draw on the flat stone. He started with a single long line, gently curved like a feather. Added some of the dried blood from his side to add the shorter lines and curls.

"What are you doing?"

Hrafn jumped to his feet and whirled around. Siggi stood just outside the turf house, looking at him with a puzzled expression. His eyes went from Hrafn's hands to the bucket to the flat stone at his feet.

"Are you doing magic?" he asked.

"What does it look like? Of course I'm doing magic."

"What for?"

Hrafn gestured down the path. "How do you think the people of that charming, fish-stinking village down there will react if they learn you've brought a witch back from the dead and bound yourself to him? I'm doing this to keep your neighbors from stopping by and deciding they want a bonfire of their own."

"Nobody comes up here," Siggi said. There was no bitterness in his voice, only acceptance. He came toward Hrafn and peered down at the stone; one of his small braids slipped free from the knot in his hair. "How does it work? Are you warning them away?"

"That's one way of putting it."

"What's the other way of putting it?" Siggi asked, his innocent expression belying the sharpness of the question. "Will it hurt them?"

For fuck's sake, the boy didn't stop. "It won't hurt them. All it will do is make them think twice about coming up this way." But the stave was incomplete. Hrafn dug his thumbnail into a cut on the inside of his right elbow.

Siggi hissed at the sudden, shared sting of pain. "Do you have to do that?"

Hrafn looked up at him as the blood welled. "Well, puffling, normally I don't have to resort to such barbaric methods, but *somebody* took my knife."

Siggi closed his left hand into a fist. "No, I mean…do you have to hurt yourself every time?"

"It doesn't hurt," Hrafn said. The sting of the reopened cut was barely worth mentioning.

"Yes, it does. I can feel it."

"And who's fault is that?" Hrafn had blood enough on his fingers now. He traced the minor stave of protection on the black stone, adding four smooth circles of different sizes, connecting them with straight lines. "If you don't like it, give me another blade. A good, sharp one. It will make drawing blood easier."

"That's not what I…"

Siggi stopped, whatever he was about to say caught behind his frown. Hrafn wondered if the boy ever stopped frowning.

Then he wondered if stupidity was contagious, because here he was wondering about the lightness of Siggi's mood after he had just murdered the boy's father. Annoyed with himself, Hrafn finished the stave and placed his hand over it.

The response was no more than a faint tickle, like feathers brushing over his skin, but that's all it was supposed to be.

"That feels weird," Siggi said. "Does it always feel like that?"

Hrafn almost laughed. "No. It doesn't always feel like that."

"There's food inside. I have to go see to the animals and the…" Siggi gestured vaguely, then turned away, his broad shoulders hunched. "I'll be back."

It took Hrafn until the boy had already walked away to realize what belonged in that empty space between his words. The bodies. What remained after the fire. Siggi was going to tend the sheep and bury his father's charred corpse. He wondered if he should offer to help. He said nothing. Siggi climbed the trail back toward the forge.

Hrafn was left alone outside that grim little house, with fresh blood on his arm. He washed his hands again before he went inside.

When Siggi returned, quite a long time later, he stepped through the doorway of the house and said, "I have no shoes that will fit you, but these will work for now."

Hrafn stared from where he sat upon the floor. Siggi was holding two curious bundles of knotted cloth strips woven through pieces of animal hide.

He dropped them beside Hrafn and said, "And this."

He set a short, sharp knife down more carefully.

"There's rain coming. That will provide some cover when we go to the church."

Hrafn didn't answer. He picked up one of the bundles and turned it over in his hands. The sheepskin was old and heavily greased, the cloth frayed and slightly dirty, but the cuts attaching the cloth to the hide were fresh, as were the knots.

"You…made me shoes," he said.

Siggi sat on the bench and reached for his own food. "The paths are rocky."

"You made me shoes."

"Will they not work?"

Hrafn didn't know what to say. The idiot boy had gone off to tend to his father's sheep, bury his father's corpse, and make shoes for his father's murderer. He couldn't look at the ridiculous shoes a moment longer. He set them aside to examine the knife instead. It was nothing fancy, a blade useful for shearing sheep or gutting fish, but it had been freshly sharpened and the handle was firm.

Outside the hovel, the wind was picking up as rain clouds blew closer. Hrafn told himself that was what he was feeling in his chest, the force of that coming storm. The storm was the reason he wanted to take that knife and tear into those shoes, tear into the cloth and sheepskin, tear into the gormless boy who had made them, right into his chest where his heart beat an echo to Hrafn's own.

He settled for testing the blade on the inside of his arm. Siggi did not gasp that time, only jerked his arm a little in surprise.

"Get used to it," Hrafn spat out, annoyed. "Are you so stupid that you expect witchcraft to feel like nothing? As long as we're tethered, you're going to feel it. This will grow tiresome very quickly if you twitch and shudder at every little thing I do."

He moved the blade to the hollow beneath his ribs on his right side, to draw fresh blood from his stave for diverting attention. If he was going to walk into the middle of the village that had already killed him once, he wasn't going to trust in half-healed scars.

"How far to the village?" he asked.

There was a pause before Siggi answered. "Not far," he said quietly.

He looked like he wanted to ask something else, but for once he kept his questions to himself.

The village was far enough, it turned out, that sheets of lashing gray rain arrived before they crossed the headland and descended into the fjord. It would indeed serve as good cover, as only idiots and madmen would willingly stroll about in a bursting summer squall. The overly large clothing provided only so much protection. Hrafn was soon soaked through, and every motion made the hanging fabric around him slap and sway. His new shoes grew heavy with mud. Siggi was every bit as wet, but he bore it stoically.

Perhaps he was used to it. His father had not seemed the type to consider chattering teeth and sodden clothes a reason to let a boy put his chores aside for an afternoon.

When the village came into sight, they crouched in the protection of some jagged rocks to survey the scene. Seabirds shrieked and wheeled overhead, heedless of the storm. Hrafn glared at them for a moment and hoped the one whose mind he'd borrowed before was having a very bad day fighting against the wind.

"There are people by the docks, unloading and securing the boats, but nobody's near the church," Siggi said.

Hrafn peered through the rain. "Why are there no guards?"

"Why would there be guards at the church?" Siggi asked.

"Didn't the villagers who brought you a cartload of corpses tell you why there were thieves in this forsaken place?" Hrafn asked.

Siggi frowned thoughtfully. "I didn't speak to Brother Hamon or anybody else, and if they told"—a slight hitch of his breath—"Father did not tell me much."

Hrafn considered the wisdom of revealing more to Siggi, and decided there was no harm in it. Gudmundur and his thieves were dead, Einar as well, and Siggi was certainly not a devoutly religious person.

"We were hired to steal a relic from the church," Hrafn said. "But the one who hired us betrayed us and told the villagers we were approaching."

"Why would he do that, if he wanted you to steal for him?" Siggi asked.

It was a good question, and one to which Hrafn had no certain answer. Ketill had implied, right before Einar drove the knife into Hrafn's heart, that he still wanted Hrafn to find the relic for him. Perhaps he wanted it for himself, not for whatever priestly sect he represented—but he didn't need to betray the thieves to do that.

"Something must have gone wrong, when he went into the village," Hrafn said, considering. "Perhaps this Brother Hamon of yours was suspicious. Or we were spotted from afar, and our traitor spun a story so nobody would suspect him. It would be just like a priest to betray others to save his own skin." Hrafn shook his head. It didn't matter anymore what Ketill had been thinking. He had another task now. "There's nobody about. We should go."

They ducked their heads and ran for the church, lashed by the wind and rain. The waves were high, the spray cold, but already the worst of the squall had passed.

The church door was not locked. They stepped inside, and Siggi shut the door behind them, muffling the noise of the wind and waves.

52

The interior was cold and dark and quiet, the hush interrupted only by the drip of their clothes on the floor.

"Right," Hrafn said. "Where are the teeth?"

Siggi looked around. "I, uh, I don't know? I've never been in here before."

"Of course not. That would be too easy." Hrafn walked toward the center of the church, his makeshift shoes squelching on the floor. Wooden walls, wooden roof, wooden floor, whereas the rest of the village was stone and turf. And wasn't that just like a priest, to force village builders to carry logs from miles inland to erect a creaking, moldy temple for worship. "Children's teeth are used for protection. Probably for protecting something valuable."

The church was plainer than those Hrafn had seen in Storaska and villages to the south. On the wooden altar there were five fat tallow candles—one for each of the aspects of the Godhead—and behind it was an elaborate tapestry showing the deaths of the Seven Saints. The tapestry was faded and moth-eaten, which made the saints' horrible deaths look even more gruesome: this one beheaded, this one set afire, this one torn limb from limb. The saints had been hard to kill, claimed the church, because they were so very holy and beloved. The tapestry was obviously old, probably carried across the sea some decades ago. But the rest of the room was free of ornamentation. There were a few simple wooden benches at the front; most who joined a service would have to stand.

There was nothing else. No relic, no locked chest or box, no cabinet in which anything valuable might be. No sign of a collection of children's teeth. Hrafn supposed it had been rather too much to expect that the teeth would be displayed on the altar in a conveniently ostentatious chalice.

"How many children has the priest taken teeth from?" Hrafn asked.

"Perhaps about twenty. My brother Arnes was the first, when he was four, right after I was born." Siggi frowned—always with the frowns—and looked down at his blackened left arm. He made a soft, annoyed sound and scratched at it swiftly. "What is that? That feeling?"

Hrafn hadn't even noticed until he mentioned it, because the feeling was Siggi's, not his. He felt the strange itching only faintly; it was easy enough to ignore.

"It probably doesn't like our bond." Hrafn slanted a glance at Siggi and lifted an eyebrow. "You know, the priests are notoriously stodgy and disapproving, so maybe it's more than that."

"How so?" Siggi asked.

"Is that the hand you use to touch yourself? I don't *mind*, not really, but if it is we really should talk about how to handle it with a certain respectful awareness—"

"*What?*" Siggi yelped. "No!"

The puffling, Hrafn was delighted to learn, turned as red as a strawberry when he blushed.

Siggi stomped around the altar at the head of the church, his footsteps echoing loudly as he did so. "Where do these churches usually keep their relics?"

Hrafn was willing to put aside his teasing until later. "Usually they're on display for all to see, but we were told this one is hidden. By magic," he clarified.

"I thought priests hated witchcraft." Siggi walked slowly around the church, peering at the pews and walls and ceiling, looking into corners.

"Everybody hates witchcraft until it's useful to them," Hrafn said. "Then they hate the witch instead, while reaping the benefits of their craft. If the priest who hired us was telling the truth, this church is hiding a stolen relic from one of their saints." He gestured at the gruesome tapestry over the altar. "Some rotting bit of one of those sorry fools. That's the kind of thing that your local priest would use witchcraft and children's teeth to hide."

Hrafn drew his knife and extended his right arm. It was no easy thing to find something that was deliberately hidden by protective magic. It didn't help that he didn't know exactly what he was looking for—how big it was, how it might be preserved—but knowing that it was a body part of a saint was a place to start. He had already prepared for this search, when he had thought he would be searching to earn pay from Ketill, not to help a sad farm boy on a doomed quest.

He pressed the tip of the knife into the unhealed cut on the inside of his forearm. He dabbed his forefinger into the blood and walked a slow circuit around the church, smearing a tiny mark onto every wall and into every corner to trace an invisible perimeter. Siggi didn't ask Hrafn what he was doing, but he did watch carefully, the look in his blue eyes more curious than wary. After Hrafn completed his circle around the room, he walked to the center and raised the knife again. He tugged down the neck of his too-large shirt and flipped the knife in his hand to point the blade at his own chest.

"What are you doing?" Siggi demanded. He moved to Hrafn's side with a speed that belied all that muscle and height. "Are you— do you have to do that?"

Hrafn let out a sigh and looked at him. "Do you think it's easy to find things that are hidden by magic?"

"Well, no, but…"

Siggi was staring at the knife in Hrafn's hand—or maybe it was the stave on the center of Hrafn's chest that had his attention. Hrafn knew it was a particularly ugly one, long and knotty and uneven. His own fault, really, because he had squirmed too much when it was carved, at least until he had passed out. There was a reason so few witches could do the magic required to find anything, at any time, regardless of its nature or concealment. It required a stave etched partially in bone, as well as in skin, and that required—well, Hrafn was glad he had passed out halfway through the carving, and most of the time he was glad he had also woken up again. It barely even hurt anymore when he used it, at least not to any degree worth mentioning.

But Siggi just kept staring.

"What?" Hrafn asked, growing impatient. "Do you want me to find your brother's teeth or not?"

"In all the stories, witches are always hurting other people," Siggi said, his voice echoing strangely through the church. "Not themselves."

"What sort of idiotic stories have you been listening to?"

Hrafn pressed the tip of the knife into his chest, right above his sternum. It never bled much—the scar was too thick, the bone too shallow—but it was enough to remind the stave of its shape beneath all the scar tissue. It was an inversion of the stave that protected against thieves, combined with elements of those that protected against witchcraft. He pressed his hand to the wound to get some of the fresh blood, then pricked his arm again to draw even more. It didn't take that much, certainly not enough to justify the squeamish look on Siggi's face. Only so much that it remained liquid in the palm of Hrafn's hand rather than immediately turning sticky and dry.

He extended his hand, drops of blood cupped in the palm, and began to turn in a slow circle. He felt the blood warming almost immediately, a soft tingling sensation that tickled his hand and made his fingers itch.

"Do you have to, you know, say anything?" Siggi asked. He absently rubbed his own palm on his trousers.

"Like what?"

"Don't some witches recite verse? Or something?"

Hrafn glanced at him. "Is that in your stories too?"

"Some of them."

"Same for the witches. Some of them use verse, or song. I don't."

"Why not?"

"Because I don't need them."

The blood in Hrafn's hand was beginning to move, creeping up the creases in his skin and along the seams between his fingers. He turned again, again, watching carefully, until he determined that the response was strongest in the direction of the church's altar.

He took a few steps to be sure. There was no mistake, but the altar was just as empty as it had been before. It was nothing more than a simple wooden stand. Hrafn knelt down to look at its underside, then moved the candles to check underneath them. He even peered into the tallow, wondering if there might be teeth in the candles themselves, but there was nothing.

After a moment Siggi joined him to look around. "It's here?"

"Somewhere around here," Hrafn said. He felt it as a faint tug in the center of his chest, almost like being out of breath although he was barely moving. "But I don't see——"

"Huh." Siggi dropped to the floor suddenly and crouched beside one corner of the altar.

"Look."

There was a scrape in the floor, smaller than the width of a finger, just enough to show that the altar had been moved.

"Good eye," Hrafn said, meaning it. "Something's under there."

Siggi stood up and, with a strength and ease that Hrafn envied, lifted the altar to move it out of the way. There was nothing immediately apparent underneath, but Hrafn could still feel it, that insistent tug. He dipped his fingers into his cupped hand and flicked a bit of his own blood onto the floor, right over the small scrape.

Rather than sinking into the wood, the blood beaded, then rolled swiftly over the surface before spreading out into a thin line——a seam that had not been visible before, and would have remained invisible if not for Hrafn's spelled blood. He flicked another few droplets of blood to trace out a square, no bigger than a single pace across.

It was a trapdoor. There was no handle or strap, so Hrafn used the short blade of the knife to pry it upward and swing it open.

"Ah." Hrafn sat back on his heels. He absently rubbed at his chest; the tugging sensation was even stronger now. "Okay, to be honest, I've never been beneath a church before, but I don't think it normally involves quite this many runes and staves."

The entire underside of the door was carefully carved, and the carvings darkened by either ash or blood——or both——to press deep, dark lines into the wood. Hrafn recognized a few of the staves: there was one for hiding a secret, another for creating a barrier. The largest, in the center, was familiar in a way he couldn't quite place. He traced over it with his fingers, trying to memorize the lines, trying to recall where he had seen it before.

"Is this a lullaby?" Siggi asked. "These runes?"

"No, don't be stupid, these are..." Hrafn turned his attention from the staves to the written words. "Oh, come on."

"I can read, you know," Siggi said, bristling. "It's about going to sleep and staying asleep. It says—right there—better to stay asleep."

Hrafn realized he had been assuming Siggi couldn't read, but only because a lot of people couldn't. He wanted to ask who had taught Siggi the runes, because it sure as fuck hadn't been his father, but rather more pressing was the matter of what they said.

Because Siggi was right, in a way. The runes did form a lullaby, but it was also a spell, as many lullabies were. He remembered now where he had seen that center stave before. It was an old one, rarely used these days, carved only into waystones and fence posts by superstitious elders at the frozen edges of Bjornjokull, on the slopes of Bryreldfjöll, in the valleys of Thingvellir, in the mists of Draugamyr—all places where the boundaries between worlds were thin, where people still worried the huldufolk might return to the human realm.

The staves on the underside of the door had been carved by somebody who knew what they were doing.

A lullaby, a secret, a barrier.

It was a spell to keep something asleep and trapped beneath the church.

"Shit." Hrafn's heart began to pound. "Fuck fuck *fuck*. This is bad. This is really fucking bad."

"The teeth must be down there," Siggi said. "I can go down to—"

"No. We're going to leave them where they are."

"You said we need something of Arnes's." Siggi looked at Hrafn stubbornly. "This is where we can find it."

Hrafn let out a frustrated growl. "For fuck's sake, scrying to find out your dead brother is still dead is not worth fucking around with what's down there!"

Siggi just kept looking at him, those big blue eyes wide and serious. "What's down there?"

"I'll tell you after we leave. And get very fucking far away from here. We can't—"

Siggi grabbed his arm. Hrafn was so unused to being grabbed—so unused to being touched at all—that for a second he couldn't breathe, couldn't think, couldn't focus on anything except the pressure of Siggi's hand on his upper arm. His hand was big and warm and strong, and after the shock passed a wild stab of panic took its place.

"Let me go," he snapped. "Don't fucking touch—"

"Quiet!" Siggi's voice dropped to a whisper. "Listen."

The church had grown quieter since they'd entered, as the rain had stopped and the wind had slackened, leaving only the restless grumble of the sea. It was quiet enough that Hrafn could hear Siggi's breath right beside his ear. And a heartbeat, which might have been his, might have been Siggi's, might have been both tethered together.

And voices outside.

"That's the priest," Siggi whispered. "You have to hide."

"Hide? There's no place to—"

Hrafn swallowed. There was one place.

"I'll get rid of Brother Hamon, I promise," Siggi said. "It's just for a bit. Go!"

There was nowhere else to go. Hrafn swallowed his revulsion, dropped to the floor, and slipped through the trapdoor. He was small enough to fit, and the ground was only a few feet below. He wriggled down to lie flat on the rocky ground underneath.

Siggi shut the door. Hrafn heard the scrape of the altar moving back into place and Siggi's footsteps walking away, just moments before the church door opened.

"…I'm sure it's nothing to—oh!" A man's voice called out in surprise. "There is somebody here! Hello, Sigbert."

"Hello, Brother Hamon," Siggi said.

"This is one of the local boys," the priest said. "He's harmless. He and his father helped us with the…you know. But this is the first time you've come to visit us, isn't it, Sigbert?"

"Yes," Siggi said. "Father never wanted me to come before."

"I see," said another man.

Beneath the floor, Hrafn scowled. That was Ketill. He told

himself he wasn't surprised, but there was still a little ache, right below his heart, where Einar had stabbed him. *I wanted to keep you for myself*, Ketill had said. Hrafn would have bitten his fingers every time he came close if he had known the man would get them all killed.

"Have you decided to become a godly boy, Sigbert?" Ketill asked.

"I, um"—Siggi's voice shook—"I don't know?"

Fuck. He was going to give them away. The priest and Ketill would see right through whatever story he came up with, and he would blubber out the whole truth to them, and they would haul Hrafn from beneath the church for a fresh set of chains. Hrafn was still holding the little knife in his hand. It felt small and useless now. Sharp as it was, he would need to be quick.

As he shifted into a better position, his elbow nudged something that was not quite solid, but not quite soft either. He recoiled in alarm.

"My father doesn't know I'm here," Siggi was saying. "He wouldn't approve. But I thought…maybe it would be okay."

Slowly, Hrafn extended his hand to touch the object. It was round and bulky; it felt like rough cloth wrapped with thin twine that had beads knotted along its length.

Not beads. Hrafn's fingertips felt around gingerly. Teeth.

"All are welcome in the family of the Godhead, Sigbert," the priest said. "I can understand how you would wish to pray after the work of the past days."

It seemed a strange thing to say to a boy who tended sheep, until Siggi said, "I saw the witches among the men."

Hrafn felt a sudden, outlandish surge of hurt. He had expected to get caught because Siggi couldn't lie well enough. Not because Siggi would open his big mouth and tell the priest everything.

"I was glad to burn them," Siggi said, "because I know it's important. But it was still…a little frightening. Father doesn't believe there is reason to worry, but I thought…"

Siggi's voice trailed off.

"Your father will come around in his own time," the priest said.

"Solitary prayer is of course very important, but it isn't quite the same as attending a ritual. The saints themselves joined together to pray before their deaths, and it was their shared devotion that made their sacrifices so powerful. You will join us next time, won't you?"

"If Father allows it," Siggi said. Hrafn could only imagine what he looked like, but his voice sounded smaller, shakier than it had been when he had been weeping.

"Very good. You see? There is nothing to be worried about here. A boy finding his way into faith is cause for celebration, not alarm."

"Of course," Ketill said dryly. "You were the one who burned the witches, were you?"

"Um, yes?"

"It's okay, Sigbert. This is Brother Ketill, a fellow priest from the south."

"And they were both dead?" Ketill asked. "You know that witches have ways of deceiving us."

"They were both very dead," Siggi said. "There was, uh, they had been for some time."

"Don't bother the boy anymore," the priest chided. "He's of a…slightly delicate sort of mind. He has been since childhood. It's best we leave him to his prayers."

The two men took their leave. Siggi's footsteps followed them to the door after they were gone and lingered there awhile before he returned. The altar scraped on the floor again, and the door opened, letting weak gray light into the space beneath the church.

"They're gone," Siggi said. "It was the priest and a stranger."

"A stranger I'm going to skin alive inch by inch. He's the one that got me killed." Hrafn pulled himself out from beneath the floor, then leaned back down to grab the object his fingers had brushed against. "That was a good performance. Have you ever considered joining a troupe of traveling players?"

Siggi rubbed the back of his neck. "When everybody thinks you're simple, they don't even wonder if you can lie."

"I promise never to call you stupid again," Hrafn said. He hoisted the wrapped object up from underneath the floor. "Now this—"

Siggi made a face. "What is that?"

Hrafn set the object between them. It was about two hand lengths across and almost spherical in shape. Twine wrapped around the sacking so many times there was no risk of it ever coming unraveled. There were knots all along the twine, a few fingers' width between them, and at every knot was a child's tooth with a small hole bored through the middle.

In the spots not covered by teeth or string, the sack was stitched with fat black threads in the shape of staves and runes, many of which were marred with the unmistakable reddish-brown stain of blood. In some places, the black threads were twisted together with yellow hair that had been drawn through the sack from the inside.

It was, on the whole, a thoroughly unsettling object. Yet Hrafn knew the weight of it all too well. He knew what a spell woven from teeth and blood and hair implied. He told himself it wasn't fear that made his shoulders tense and his heart race.

"You've lived in this village all your life, right?" Hrafn asked.

"Yes," Siggi said, a bit faintly. He could not look away from the thing. "But what—"

"And it's a normal village. Full of normal people. People who fish and tend sheep and get scolded by the priest into praying for this god or another. You didn't even think witches were real before I showed up."

Siggi nodded. His throat bobbed as he swallowed.

"And all those nice normal people are human?"

"What? What else would they—"

"Humans who die when you chop their heads off? Like most people do?"

"What is it?" Siggi asked, his voice wavering.

"So tell me, Siggi, why the *fuck* does your nice little village full of nice normal people have some poor bastard's severed head bound by sleeping magic and children's teeth beneath its church?" Hrafn lifted his gaze to look at Siggi. "Do you have any fucking idea what kind of person *doesn't* die when you chop their head off?"

62

Chapter Five
The Hidden People

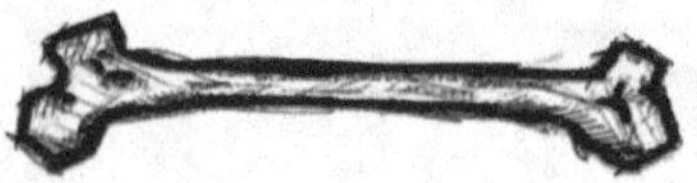

Siggi looked at the bloody object and then at the witch-boy. He couldn't tell if the boy was bemused or disgusted, holding the hideous object at arm's length.

"How…are you certain it's a severed head? It's all bundled up, maybe it's something else—"

The witch-boy shook his head. "Oh, I think I've severed enough heads to know the weight of one. Now, *whose* head it is and why the fuck it's here, that's another matter." Carefully, he set the bundle on the floor as though fearing it would bite him. For all Siggi knew, it might. "One we won't be getting into."

"Why would anyone's head be buried beneath the church?"

"I understand there are bound to be echoes in a church, but didn't I just say we wouldn't be getting into it?"

"But you said it's asleep, not dead? How can that be?"

"Haven't you heard?" The witch laughed without warmth. "Churches perform miracles."

Siggi had heard, but seeing the church from the inside at long last, he could not see how. The depiction of saints was captivating but far from grand, and Siggi found the wooden, windowless walls altogether smothering. Aside from the ragged tapestry, the church was hardly nicer than his own hovel. From the instant Siggi had stepped inside he'd felt queasy.

Arnes had always told Siggi that the church was nowhere he should long to be, worthwhile only for the whispering that went on among the villagers after prayer, and never for the prayer itself.

"And what the hell does Ketill want with something like this? And where the fuck is the rest of it?" The witch eyed the bloodstained lump. "Gods, but I'm a *little* curious."

"Brother Ketill." Siggi recalled the stranger who'd entered the church beside Brother Hamon, whey-faced and curiously young. "The frog-mouthed man?"

"Frog-mouthed? I thought he was rather…fuck. It doesn't matter what I thought. He was not what he pretended to be."

All of this meant little to Siggi, but a thought made his insides churn. "This frog-mouthed man is the one who killed you."

"He didn't kill me himself, it's just his fault I got knifed in the fight. Ketill said he wanted to keep me, which is even stranger than wanting to kill me. I mean, who doesn't want to kill a witch?"

Siggi noted the utter lack of sarcasm in the boy's voice. Had he never had a brother like Arnes, someone to tell him he deserved to live?

The witch-boy was pacing now, the remnants of his chains clinking as he threw up his hands. "I thought he only wanted to steal a normal relic. Not—not *this*. What would he want with this? And want it badly enough to hire a band of thieves and a couple of witches?" The witch stopped and shook his head. "And now I've gone and found it, exactly like he wanted. *Fuck*."

Siggi wanted to tell the boy to sit down and start making sense. But he doubted that would work, so he only shrugged. "It doesn't matter right now. We just need to get the teeth and go. Right?"

The witch gawked at him, stopping in his tracks. "No. I told you. We aren't going to disturb this thing. We want nothing to do with it. We shouldn't have even touched it! And we'd do well to get the fuck out of this horrible little village as soon as possible."

"Not without Arnes's teeth." Siggi reached for the bundle, but immediately the witch-boy placed himself in front of it, frail arms open wide, eyes big and black.

"I told you *no*."

Siggi frowned. "Is there any other way to find my brother? Some way you have not told me?"

He saw the answer in the witch-boy's eyes, and that was enough to make up Siggi's mind. The witch-boy let out a squawk as Siggi hefted him off the floor and threw him over his right shoulder, gripping him tight by the waist as though he were a bale of straw.

The boy really was skin and bones, hardly as heavy as a newborn calf, and though he kicked and cursed in protest, small sheep-hide-shod feet were nothing compared to Father's fists.

"You—don't—I fucking told you not to—put me down! *Never* touch a witch!"

"Or you'll curse me?" Siggi mused, turning the filthy bundle over on the floor, peering at each of the tiny teeth. "I think we're past that, little witch."

"*Little*—?" The boy kicked again, but Siggi paid him no mind.

There were a few dozen teeth of different sizes, indistinguishable from one another as the shell shards that peppered the black beaches. And yet, though they all looked the same, Siggi felt drawn to a single tooth among them. It seemed to gleam brighter than the rest.

The cursed blade in his arm twinged sharply, as though in confirmation.

"This one," he said. "That one's Arnes's tooth."

Abruptly the witch stopped kicking, limp as a kitten. Siggi rather liked the warmth of him there. "What? You're saying you can tell which tooth is your brother's?"

Siggi cocked an ear toward his voice, just over his shoulder. "Is that strange?"

"Fucking yes, it's strange. A tooth is a tooth is a tooth."

"But this is *Arnes's* tooth." Siggi looked down at his cursed forearm. "I know it."

"Even if you're right, puffling," the boy said, "cutting a single thread of that twine would be a mistake. I don't expect you to understand what you're dealing with, but please understand that this is as nefarious as anything can be. It's just not fucking worth it."

"Arnes is worth it," Siggi said simply, and gently he set the witch-boy on the floor so that they were kneeling across from each other. "Arnes is worth everything to me."

For once the witch was silent, his restless volcanic eyes confused. He didn't protest again as Siggi tugged on Arnes's tooth. The twine pulled away from the fabric. Siggi pulled his whittling knife from his satchel and the blade sliced easily through the bloodstained hemp.

Even as Siggi squeezed the tiny tooth in his healed palm, the ropes around the bundle began to unwrap of their own accord, twisting like maggots in a summer corpse, the tiny teeth clicking against the floor as they fell away. From within the fabric something moved, a jaw opening and closing, and there came a gasp as though the thing inside had woken from a nightmare.

"You've done it now," the witch-boy breathed. "We need to go."

But Siggi held in his hand the smallest piece of his brother and found himself frozen solid. How could it be that so little of Arnes remained in Midfjördur, and yet his presence still permeated every aspect of Siggi's existence, gave *meaning* to his existence?

"Come on!" The witch-boy's long fingers gripped Siggi's arms, trying and failing to lift Siggi from the floor. "Why the fuck are you so heavy? Have you been eating stones?"

Siggi climbed to his feet, feeling the prod of the tooth against his skin, and as he found his footing he felt a stinging pain in his healed hand. The witch-boy was slicing himself open again with the sheepshearing knife, blood bubbling from a many-pointed stave just below his wrist, gritting his teeth against the pain he pretended didn't exist. Both their heartbeats quickened.

The thing on the floor began to scream. Its piercing cry cut through the fabric and rattled the wooden rafters.

"Enough of that!" The witch-boy pulled his hand away from his fresh wound and slammed it down on the unrolling relic—

Nothing happened.

"Fuck! The wards are strong, it won't light!" The witch-boy stared down at his bloodstained hand. He lifted it and slammed it down again, pressing it again to his burbling wrist, but nothing happened. The thing kept screaming and rolling, gradually freeing itself from the tangle.

The witch-boy rounded on Siggi. "Why are you still standing there, you fool? Go!"

"It sounds like a woman," Siggi said hollowly, watching the fabric pull away as the object rotated on the floor, unwinding like a spool. "She's alive. Who is she, and why is she—"

The witch-boy shoved him in the chest, leaving behind a bloody handprint. "She's only half alive, and she was never human to begin with, and she's going to kill the both of us if *you* don't flee for the fucking hills and I don't use my magic to do away with her!"

"But..."

"Enough. Move." Suddenly the blood on the witch-boy's palm caught fire. A torch of otherworldly lavender flames ensconced his entire hand. He grimaced and pressed his fiery palm to the unraveled edge of hemp and held it there, setting the unwinding bundle afire at last.

The relic rolled itself free of its final binds and there she was, cradled in the nest of hemp.

The severed head of a beautiful, ageless, yellow-haired woman, not mummified in the least but seemingly alive, apart from two vacant sockets where her eyes should have been.

Her empty gaze seemed somehow to fix on Siggi even as the ethereal flames caught the tips of her tangled hair. She stopped screaming, and the fire went out.

Siggi's breath caught in his throat.

"Fuck, why?" the witch-boy cried, voice breaking, igniting his palm once more.

The woman began to smile, her sightless stare boring holes through Siggi's heart.

"Please! I think we should stop! Please!"

But the witch-boy coaxed his flames back to roaring life, bright and hot enough that Siggi threw up his arms to shield his eyes. Even then he could feel the witch-boy's heartbeat in his bones, could feel the sting of his boiling magic as he fueled the blaze to towering.

The woman did not scream again as flames licked her hair and traced the strands to their roots. She didn't seem to suffer as the fire crowned her forehead, as Siggi watched skin peel away from bone for the second time in mere hours.

The witch-boy took Siggi's hand and yanked him away from her pyre as she ignited in a vivid burst of scorching amethyst, and as they reached the doors the floor began to splinter and shake, giving way underfoot as the woman at last stopped smiling.

The turf on the cemetery mounds fell in clumps as the earth shook beneath their feet, and even as they tore across the churchyard the gate collapsed before them. Behind them the wooden walls creaked and groaned like a ship coming to wreck, unable to withstand the blaze.

Siggi gasped, falling against the shaking moss of a grave, captivated by the sight. This fire was no hearth or forge blaze. The flames shone golden and lavender, as strange as the remains of the woman being devoured by them. Like a fearsome aurora, the witch-fire lit the sky, a beacon that would certainly draw the eyes of every soul in Midfjördur.

"Normal churches," the witch-boy spat, dragging Siggi to his feet and through the crumbling gate as the flames intensified, "don't keep the heads of huldu women beneath the floorboards."

Huldu. It was an old word, one rarely used. Most people called them *the hidden folk*, when they spoke of them. It hardly seemed to matter. Human or inhuman, the woman had seemed so alive.

"This isn't right."

"Of course it isn't right. It's foul, and fouler still that Ketill wanted to steal such a thing."

"That's not what I mean!" Siggi cried, furious again, pulling his arm from the witch-boy's grip so abruptly that the pair of them tripped and fell into the dirt road.

Beyond the churchyard, the ground wasn't shaking. It was only ground, still and stony and cold. But the groan of the collapsing walls pierced the morning air like a wailing wind.

"I don't know who she was, or why she was there, but no one deserves such a terrible death!"

"I said I wouldn't call you stupid, but how *simpleminded* are you? That thing wasn't a woman. It was a monster. Of another kind than your bastard father, but a monster all the same. Why cry for either of them?"

Siggi leaned back against the gate, gasping, tears flowing freely. He knew the stories well. The hidden people were powerful, and that power could turn to cruelty. Sometimes they were generous; more often they were capricious. They toyed with humans as children toyed with dolls. But she had smiled so beautifully and screamed so terribly.

"I don't know."

The witch-boy threw up his hands, black eyes reflecting fey firelight. Fury rendered his skin pale, his scars stark. "Do you think they'd have cried for you, Sigbert?"

"Are you…are you worried about me?"

"No, for fuck's sake! I'm worried about myself! If you die, I die *again*, so for the love of shit, stop throwing yourself in front of awful men and howling beasts!"

Siggi stared at the boy's furious glowing eyes, the drawn expression on his small, wounded face. Something in his heart loosened.

"Okay," Siggi said. His tears were slowing.

The boy stepped back. "Okay?"

Siggi nodded, and the witch-boy's shoulders slumped.

"But…we could have asked her who she was," Siggi added, and like a branch snapping the witch-boy's fury returned and he opened his mouth to scream at Siggi again—

They were interrupted by the sound of rapid hoofbeats, and there he was: the frog-mouthed man with the eerie gaze, perched on his horse as though he were on nothing but a casual morning trot, frowning at the scene before him as though an otherworldly fire and collapsing churchyard were only a minor annoyance.

"Hrafn," he said to the witch-boy, his voice unctuous and soft. "My, but you do continue to draw attention to yourself."

"Fuck your face, Ketill," the witch-boy spat, on his feet again, bloody palms upraised.

Siggi blinked. His name was Hrafn, as in raven, as in a creature just as flighty and black-feathered and bold and unappreciated as he was.

"I can't say I'm entirely surprised to see you breathing," Ketill pondered, "although I am curious how you managed it. Oh, what I wouldn't give to thoroughly inspect every blasphemous stave on your body."

"And I'm curious about why you sold us all out for the sake of a severed huldu head in a church," the witch-boy spat.

Ketill's eyes flashed. "What have you done? That relic is more powerful than you can ever imagine."

The witch-boy's expression was incredulous. "That was no relic! That was a huldu! What the *fuck* is wrong with that ungodly mind of yours?"

The man inhaled shortly, and his face smoothed, hiding his anger as effectively as donning a mask.

"Such doting words, Hrafn. But I don't expect you to understand. You don't believe anything unless you can bleed on it, do you? And I see you've moved on rather quickly," he added, eyeing Siggi. "The village simpleton? I'm insulted. Unless there's more to him than meets the eye? He *was* very convincing when he lied to me."

Siggi had had enough of watching that frog mouth move, of watching his companion rankle at the man's biting words. He placed himself between Ketill and the witch-boy.

"Who was she?" he demanded. "The woman in the church."

"You woke her without knowing? Oh, but that really *was* foolish." Ketill raised his eyebrows. "She is from a world you have never conceived of. There is strength in her screams that could make this entire island of weak men cower."

"Not anymore," the witch said.

"Do you think she is so easily set aside?" Ketill asked, his voice trembling with anger. But even as it flared, he swallowed it down again. "But truly. Who are *you*, Sigbert, that you're not afraid of witches?"

"He's nobody," the witch-boy—Hrafn—spat. "Leave him be."

"Do you know what happens to those reckless enough to harm a holy creature? I brought my pet witch here to save her, not desecrate her."

"Huldu aren't holy," Hrafn said. "And they'd want nothing to do with a maggot like you."

Ketill peered at them with something like pity. "Oh, heathen children, you would never understand. But know this: you've broken the wards that hid her, and her kin will not be pleased. They will come for you."

"Her kin?" Siggi demanded, a pang in his heart, Arnes's face on his mind.

Ketill laughed, high and maddening. "Boy, don't people in this wretched village tell stories of the hidden people? Don't you know what happens when they are stirred to vengeance?"

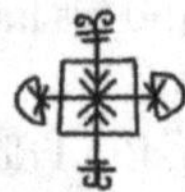

Of course the people of Midfjördur told stories of the hidden people, because when winters were long and even a blazing hearth couldn't keep them warm, at least a story could busy their thoughts.

The hidden people once lived in the mountains and caves, unseen unless they wanted to be seen. Alluring and elfin, tall and ageless, they were said to be descended from heavenly creatures who had come to Lifandfjall before the glaciers grew, long before men existed.

Holy they were not, but in some of the stories, the hidden people *were* beneficent. They appeared as children and helped farmers herd sheep, only to vanish forever thereafter. If a hidden person looked kindly upon one's family, their cows would produce milk as rich as cream. Those favored by the hidden people might find their pockets filled with perpetual gold and would never be lost at sea, no matter the tempest they sailed into.

But the hidden folk were fickle, as likely to be cruel as kind. Sometimes they forced mortals to bed them, only to give birth to cats with human faces and leave them on the unfortunate fathers' doorsteps. They hosted beautiful festivals in the meadows and danced until their unhidden guests dropped dead from exhaustion, and then they danced some more, the corpses of their human playthings no more than party decorations. The hidden folk were beautiful but did not cherish empathy. A hidden person might smash in a woman's head as easily as Siggi's father had crushed mice found in the grain.

Arnes told Siggi a story once upon a bitter winter's evening, while Father was at the forge. That night, the wind wailed so loudly Siggi feared their hovel would buckle. Tucked close beside Siggi beneath one blanket, Arnes spoke to keep their minds off their frozen fingers.

"Once, a woman was tending to her flock in the fields alongside her only son. He was just a little thing, but well behaved—"

"How little?" Siggi demanded.

"Six years. Exactly your age, to the very day," Arnes said, with a grin. "She turned her back to milk the goat and when she looked up from her work, her good son was behaving strangely. Thereafter, he was no longer good. When she left him with the goat, she returned to find the beast's eyes had been infected with worms, and it was covered with fleas. He drank all of their milk, ate all of their butter, and"—he paused, beckoning Siggi closer until Siggi cupped his ear by his brother's mouth—"he shat in the bathing pool!"

Siggi squealed in horror. "Why would he do that?"

Arnes laughed. "The woman's lovely son would no more do that than you or I would. And the woman knew this, and that's when she realized: this boy who caused so much trouble was not her son. He only *looked* like her son."

Siggi's eyes felt so wide he thought they might leave his head, land in the fire, and shrivel up like dried berries. "Who was he?"

"He was a changeling. You see, a woman should never turn her back on a child in the fields. While she was not looking, the hidden folk stole her son away to live with them in the boulders and left one of their naughtiest little monsters behind in his stead. Every one of the hidden people has a unique magic, and this changeling had the power to bring a scourge of insects onto their farm."

"But…if he was a changeling, why did he look like her little boy?"

Arnes let loose an exasperated sigh, bopping Siggi on the nose. "More magic. Obviously."

"Oh." Siggi nodded seriously. "Obviously."

"The woman realized the truth, but she needed to find a way to prove it, lest she never see her real son again. So she went to the village witch and asked him what she should do to escape the curse of the changeling. And the witch, do you know what he told her?"

"No, what did he tell her?"

"He told her that the only way to see her son would be to find herself a briarwood branch and use it to beat the changeling until he was within reach of death. He told her she had to beat the changeling boy so thoroughly that he cried out for his true mother instead!"

Siggi winced, feeling the marks on his arms and backside. Father didn't have a briarwood branch, but he did have a switch and large rugged hands. "So…what did she do?"

"Well, she did exactly as the witch told her to. She went into the woods of Myrkvidor and found a long and prickly briarwood branch. She took it home and she put the little monster over her knee and beat him bloody." Arnes looked at Siggi, clearly waiting for a reaction, but Siggi said nothing. "Just as promised, the changeling's mother appeared in the farmwife's doorway. She was tall and beautiful but her ears were pointed like a cat's, and she had a fox's tail at the back of her skirt. She was holding the woman's real son in her arms."

Silently, Siggi wiped tears from his cheeks.

"'I have spoiled your child and fattened him up with berries,' the hidden woman said, 'but you have beaten my son. I brought him here for a better life, but I will leave him with you no longer.' And so the hidden woman exchanged the children, and the mother held her son tight as the two hidden people vanished into the boulders, never to be seen again."

Arnes sighed and kicked at the ashes, clearly finished. At last, Siggi cleared his throat.

"But…what happened to the boy?"

Arnes shrugged. "Oh, I'm sure he grew up fine with his mother on her farm."

"No." Siggi shook his head. "What happened to the changeling boy?"

Arnes scowled. "Who knows. Does it matter? He was a monster."

Siggi's lip trembled, and he burst into gloopy tears, howling as though his heart had been pulled right out of his chest. Arnes gazed at him in shock.

"Siggi, what's wrong?"

"Am I a changeling, Arnes?"

"What? No. No, Siggi! Of course not."

"Then why does Father beat me?"

Arnes didn't answer, but pulled his little brother closer, resting his chin on his head.

"The hidden people," Siggi said, ears ringing. "But they're—aren't they all gone?"

Hrafn shook his head. "There are very few left in our realm, but those that remain are as bad as the stories say."

"Are they bad, or are they above such human qualifications? The huldu see all realms with wisdom we can never comprehend." Ketill looked down at the pair of them. "You know, Hrafn. My one regret is that I shan't be able to make a pelt of that wonderful hide of yours, once the huldu have exacted their vengeance."

"Go, Ketill," Hrafn said, through gritted teeth. "Or I'll set fire to you, too."

"Oh?" Ketill said, blatantly unafraid. Whatever this Ketill was, he wasn't an ordinary priest, nor an ordinary bandit. "I have no more business in this village. Farewell then, pretty little Hrafn."

He rode away from the burning church as though it were any other morning, as though the two boys were corpses already.

At last Siggi looked at Hrafn, noting how very pale he looked, swaying on his feet.

"Are you all right?"

"He wanted to keep me, all right," the witch-boy murmured, and then collapsed to his knees. "As a trophy."

Siggi hoisted him to his feet as voices echoed from the bottom of the hill. Clearly, the burning church had been noticed.

"Why should the hidden people harm us? If we only tell them what has happened, that we did not trap her there, then maybe—"

"Then what?" Hrafn's voice was bitter. "You think they'll understand? If you've heard tales of the huldu, you'll know that's not likely. At best we could beg for another day before they peel our skin from our bones."

"How do you know, if there are so few of them?"

"Tonguð's eyes! I can't be bothered to explain the entire history of witches and huldu at this very terrible moment! For now, we've got to go before your villagers show up with knives, wondering who torched their ugly little church."

"But things could be worse." Siggi looked into Hrafn's eyes. They were as guarded as ever. "We have the tooth. We aren't dead. You said you'd help me find my brother. Else what was the point of…of hurting her?"

Hrafn looked at him, searching his face for something. Siggi couldn't imagine what, so he simply met his gaze with as much conviction as he could.

"Fine. I'll need a still pool for scrying," the witch said, exhaling. "Water undisturbed by tides or fish."

Siggi nodded. "I know a place."

"And a wooden bowl. And a sheep. The oldest, meanest one you

76

know."

"Okay, Hrafn."

"Don't. I didn't choose that name. I didn't choose any part of this."

Siggi was thinking of the birds on the cliffs, feathers caught in the grass and collected by the villagers in springtime. "Ravens are beautiful birds."

"I hate birds," Hrafn muttered. It was impossible to be certain, given all the pink scarring, but Siggi thought the boy's cheeks had reddened.

The boys hobbled up the hillside, headed for the cliffs again as the church collapsed behind them, sending ashes toward the white sky.

Chapter Six
Shadows in Water

Hrafn was a child the first time he saw one of the hidden folk. He had been with Birtingr for a number of years at that point, so he might have been nine or ten. They had traveled to a small, dirty village at the edge of a glacier, where black ash from a recent eruption blanketed every surface and meltwater from under the ice threatened to overwhelm the banks of the river. Many of the villagers had moved elsewhere when the mountain changed its mood and floods became more common.

It was winter and darkness came early. Hrafn was aware of faces behind shutters, whispers behind walls, doors that snapped shut as they passed. He was tired from walking all day, and his stomach was a knot of hunger. He knew better than to complain, but what he refrained from saying out loud was not the same as what he kept inside, and inside he wished for one of those doors to open, for the warm yellow candlelight to draw him in, for a plump woman with a pink smile to coo and tut and offer him a hot meal and a pile of furs by the fire. He wanted Birtingr to leave him behind, forget about him, abandoned like a changeling, so he might become that kind woman's new son.

It was a stupid yearning. Nobody would ever want to keep him.

The only villagers out in the cold were two men standing guard outside a crumbling turf house, armed with pitchforks and knives and dressed in heavy furs. Hrafn stayed behind Birtingr as they approached. He stepped on something that crunched loudly. He recoiled in surprise: it was a dead gull, frozen into the mud.

Hrafn looked around, alarmed. The ground was littered with dead birds. Gulls, petrels, shearwaters, so many more. There were dozens of them, and most were smashed, bloodied, twisted in some unnatural way, with feathers and fine bones sticking out of the frozen muck. They formed a ring of carnage around the turf house.

One of the men grunted. "Took us awhile to make it stop calling them."

The captured huldu must have summoned the birds with magic. A cornered huldu would use every shred of their terrible magic to escape, regardless of who or what was harmed.

Birtingr glanced at the birds with disinterest. "He's inside?"

The man cleared his throat. "We thought the madwoman would come. This is her sort of work."

Birtingr's eyes narrowed. He hated to be compared to Ylfa Sifsdottir, the witch most people preferred to summon when there were hidden folk to deal with.

"Inside?" he said again.

The man must have heard the ice in his voice. "Aye, bound and stunned, at least for now."

"Show me."

The men exchanged wary glances. One of them opened the door with obvious reluctance before stepping aside. Birtingr always said common people were cowards, but their fear did not make Hrafn feel brave. It only made him want to turn and run away.

He couldn't run. He had to follow Birtingr into the house, where it was even darker than the night outside. Birtingr lit a tallow candle with a pass of his hand and held it up.

The huldu was slumped against a wooden post in the center of the house, bound with so many coils of rope half of his body was hidden. Aside from the rope he was naked. His face was mottled with bruises and cuts, as were his shoulders and legs and what remained visible of his pelvis and torso. The wounds on his head were especially severe: the white bones of his skull showed through dark, crusted blood and hair that was, when clean, probably as golden and fine as summer flax. The hay on the floor around him was also matted with blood. His throat had been cut with a deep gash, but still he breathed, a hoarse and gurgling sound that filled the small, cold house.

The villagers had beaten him to subdue him. It had probably taken ten of them or more, armed with every tool they had on hand. Had he been human, he would have been long dead. Only a huldu could survive such damage.

He was still the most beautiful person Hrafn had ever seen.

He was the opposite of Hrafn in every way: pale as milk, long limbed, well muscled. Hrafn inched closer. It was said that the beauty of the hidden folk could beguile a man with a single glance. He wanted more than a glance. He wanted to wash the blood away, to tend the wounds, to see what this man might look like standing tall and strong in the sunlight.

Birtingr mistook his movement. "Don't be fooled by his current state. The hidden people are devious, and those living in exile are mad with rage. Do only what I say." He set the candle down and drew his knife from its sheath. "We'll take what we can before we kill it. You collect the hair. As much as you can shear. A single strand is worth more than your skin, so don't be careless."

Hrafn was never careless, although Birtingr did not always believe him when things went wrong. He removed his gloves and knelt beside the captive. The huldu's hair was soft to the touch; Hrafn wanted to stroke it rather than cut it, but if he tarried Birtingr would notice. He took care as commanded not to lose a single thread, while Birtingr set about his own tasks: removing the fingernails and toenails, peeling away patches of unmarred skin, pulling teeth one by one. Taking all the parts that were useful for witchcraft. The soft, slick squelch of his knife and sickening cracks of teeth separating from jaw made Hrafn's stomach churn. A few times he heard the flutter of wings outside, followed by the thump of feathered bodies striking the building and falling onto the snow. The huldu was weak, but his magic still called the birds to their deaths.

As Birtingr finished with the teeth, Hrafn cut through the last strand of hair. He tied the bundle of it neatly with a string.

"Here," said Birtingr. "I need your small hands."

Small hands to reach into the man's chest, which Birtingr split with a blade and magic, to take the huldu's heart. Hrafn gagged at the horrible cracking noise. He swallowed back acid and bile when Birtingr directed him to cut through the arteries and veins one by one. The quiver of the heart, still beating until it was severed, made his entire body tremble.

He glanced at the man's face.

The huldu was looking at him.

Hrafn rocked back on his heels. The man's eyes were the soft-green color of moss, vibrant even rimmed with red. There was no confusion in his expression, no anger or fear. Tears slipped down his cheeks, sliding through the grime to mingle with the blood trickling from the corners of his mouth. Hrafn wanted to wipe that blood away, but instead he curled his hand into a fist at his side. Even bloodied and dying, the huldu was too beautiful to be smudged by a dirty little thing like Hrafn.

"Wrap it and put it away," Birtingr said.

"Okay." Hrafn scrambled to his feet. The heart had stopped beating with the last cut of the veins. He wrapped it in oiled leather and placed it in one of Birtingr's bags.

Birtingr stood over the huldu, his face impassive. "Come here. Take off your coat and tunic."

Hrafn hesitated. "But it's…"

"Now."

"But it's cold," Hrafn said, his voice small.

It was not all he wanted to say. It was cold, and his skin still hurt from the staves Birtingr had given him days before. The pain was only now starting to fade to the point where every movement, every rasp of his rough clothes, did not make him shudder and wince.

"Do you disobey me?" Birtingr said, his voice low and calm.

Hrafn couldn't answer. It would hurt if he did as Birtingr said. It would hurt if he tried to refuse. His stomach was tied into knots and he was shivering so badly his knees felt weak. He knew what finishing their task meant. Cutting out the man's heart was not enough. There was only one way to kill a huldu for certain.

"There's oil," he said to Birtingr, his voice shaking. "We have oil and there's probably fuel in the village, in the empty houses, we can make a pyre—"

Birtingr spun around, grabbed Hrafn by the hair, and dragged him forward. His grip was so tight Hrafn saw stars.

"Oil and charcoal are valuable," Birtingr said. "I won't waste them."

With trembling hands, Hrafn removed his coat and waited. The cold air bit at his skin, raising bumps all over. He was not going to cry. The huldu was still looking at him with those green, green eyes. His mouth moved, forming words that had no sound. Hrafn could not tell what the man was saying. It might have been a curse. It might have been a plea.

Birtingr grabbed Hrafn's right arm and drew his knife, the knife he used only for carving staves, the one with a handle wrapped in nykur hair and a blade etched with runes. The knife Hrafn hated more than anything. He pierced the tip into Hrafn's wrist. Hrafn caught a pained whimper behind his lips, buried it down in his throat. It was not a simple mark. Birtingr carved carefully, making several distinct cuts. By the time he was finished, Hrafn's arm was a hot, bloody mess of pain.

But it wasn't that bad. Others had been worse.

"Your other hand," Birtingr said.

He didn't wait for Hrafn to react; he grabbed his left wrist and carved a stave into the heel of his hand. Hrafn felt dizzy and dazed; he only noticed Birtingr was done when he pried Hrafn's fingers open. He pressed Hrafn's open left palm against the stave on his right wrist, his own much larger hand holding Hrafn's in place. Heat spread from Hrafn's wrists and hands through the rest of his body, a heat so powerful he thought he might burn up from it. He was certain he would smell his own skin and hair burning any moment.

Then Birtingr pulled Hrafn's palm away from the stave and shoved him forward, slamming both of Hrafn's palms onto the huldu's bare skin just below his neck.

Shimmering purple fire erupted around Hrafn's hands, exploding across the huldu's skin. It seared the ropes to ash in an instant and spread with fast, licking flames along every smear and line of blood. Blue and green joined the purple, flames surging out from the huldu's wounds, from the gash in his neck, the crack in his skull, the strips where Birtingr had taken his skin, and finally from his mouth, his nose. His lips moved even as flame engulfed him. He made no sound that could be heard over the roar of the fire, but outside the stone and turf walls birds began to scream. Whatever the man meant to say, with his cracking and twisting lips, with his green eyes obscured by smoke, it was lost as the witch-fire devoured him.

Birtingr pulled Hrafn back. There was a horrible, sticky tear as his skin separated from the dead man's. Pain exploded on Hrafn's palms; the skin blistered and tore.

"With more practice, you'll learn not to burn yourself as well," Birtingr said. "Stop weeping like a child and get up."

There was only one way to kill a huldu for certain, and that was with a witch's fire, cast so that it consumed every part from the inside out. The huldu man burned for some time, his pale skin blackened and crumbling, his elegant form ruined.

They watched him burn until he was gone and the birds fell silent once again, then waited until the bones were cool enough to collect. The villagers paid them well before they departed.

As he and Siggi climbed the steep hills away from the village, Hrafn found himself wishing Einar were still alive, because Hrafn had questions. Who is that piece of shit Ketill, really, and what does he want? Did he need a witch only to find the relic, or did he have something else in mind? Did you know the relic was the severed head of a huldu? Are all of the church's dead saints huldu? What did Birtingr tell you about this job that he didn't tell me?

And: How will the huldu retaliate, when they learn what I've done?

And: *What the fuck is going on?*

But Einar was dead, and Hrafn had no answers. This little village on the Thrandir Coast had been keeping the severed head of a huldu in undying torment beneath the floor of its church for several years. Whoever she was, however she had come to be there, Hrafn was certain that every magical and monstrous thing within a hundred miles had felt her final, unnatural screams.

What they would do about it remained to be seen—but Hrafn had no doubt as to what the villagers would do. They would do what they always did when a witch disturbed their dull little lives. Hrafn didn't think he would come back from a second pyre.

"We don't need much," Hrafn said. "Only—"

"A wooden bowl, a sheep, a calm pool. I was listening." Siggi walked a few steps before adding, "Will the sheep's meat still be usable after you're done? I know you probably think it's a stupid thing to worry about, but if we must waste it—"

"I'm not going to kill it," Hrafn snapped, suddenly annoyed. Is that what Siggi thought of him? That he went around killing things even when there was no need? "I only need some of its wool and blood. Not enough to harm it."

"Oh." Siggi sounded relieved. "Why does it have to be old?"

"Old and mean and full of spite, preferably, because that makes it more…" Hrafn gestured vaguely, although Siggi's back was to him. He wasn't quite sure how to explain it. "It needs to be a part of the world. More than something young and…new. It needs to be more like the world."

"The world is old and mean and full of spite?" Siggi said.

Hrafn kicked at a rock and scowled at the boy's back. "It is in every place I've been."

"Stay here and warm up for a bit," Siggi said. "And—"

"What? No! We don't have time—"

"*And*," Siggi went on, looking right at Hrafn with his obnoxiously blue eyes, "pack up some things that we need. I'll go fetch the sheep. And a chisel. I've thought about it, and I know I can get those chains off."

Hrafn felt the sudden urge to hide the shackles on his wrists. He hadn't been thinking about them at all; his face warmed to know Siggi had been. "I told you, all I need is the sheep and a bowl."

"I mean for after that. We're going to have to leave, right? The flames and the priest will lead people here, and we'll have to go to wherever Arnes is. There's no reason for you to be jingling all the while."

Hrafn stared at him. "I'm not taking you to the netherworld."

"There's food over there, and a bag for carrying there," Siggi said. "I'll be back."

He left Hrafn alone in the sad little house.

Hrafn hoped the calm was only for show, that somewhere beneath his very broad shoulders and very bright eyes Siggi was as much a roiling mess of confusion as he was. Because if he wasn't, and things like undead witches and murdered fathers and screaming severed heads didn't have him panicking internally behind his plentiful tears, then the moment when Hrafn performed the scrying and revealed that Siggi's beloved brother was actually dead and gone forever—that was going to be bad. It was going to be so very bad.

Maybe, Hrafn thought, maybe the brother wasn't—

He couldn't hope for that, even if only to spare Siggi the hurt.

He stoked the fire a bit warmer and began to search the little house. Siggi was right; they would need supplies wherever they went next. Hrafn found two bags and divided the food and waterskins and flints between them. Siggi would go his own way as soon as their bond was severed. A blanket for each as well. He hesitated, then swept the little trinkets from the shelf above the bench into the bottom of one bag, along with some of the tools Siggi had brought down from the forge earlier. He placed the wooden bowl in his own bag.

Thrice he went outside to look toward the fjord and the village.

It might take a few days for the huldu to arrive. He only wished he knew what to expect. When the huldu had lived in the human realm, witches knew they could sense the amethyst flames of witchcraft from any distance. But nearly all of the huldu had been trapped in their own world for a hundred years, and they interacted with the human realm so rarely the extent of their powers was less clear. They could still work some of their strange, wild magic across the boundary, they could communicate in limited ways, and they could banish their own kind through gates that were otherwise sealed against crossing. Beyond that, Hrafn didn't know what they could do.

Siggi hadn't yet asked what would happen to the village. Maybe he wasn't thinking about it yet. Hrafn didn't know what to tell him. Every story he knew of the vengeance of the huldu was horrific: entire villages wiped out by glacial floods or storm surges, plagues that turned livestock into living carcasses, fishing boats crushed to splinters by sea creatures. The village of Tindurgos on the eastern shore had protected a man who killed a huldu child, and as a result the entire village had been cursed so that every infant born for ten years emerged from its mother shriveled and wizened, with wispy white hair and cloudy eyes, aged to the brink of death before drawing its first breath.

The woman in the church must have been an exile, or she had been trapped in the human realm when the last gate closed at Draugamyr. But the huldu lived for centuries, and their memories were just as long.

He could not get the woman's screams out of his head.

Eldkona's ashes, to behead and trap her as the church had done—that was an absolutely wretched thing to do to a person, no matter what she had been. Hrafn should have set the priest on fire too. Maybe he would still get a chance, if the man led an angry mob of villagers to find them.

It wasn't long before Siggi returned, and with him an evil-eyed ram with large, curved horns and lingering winter wool shaggy enough to hide a few scrawny children. The animal looked at Hrafn like it wanted to butt him right off the edge of the world, but it lumbered behind Siggi like a faithful dog.

Hrafn couldn't really blame it. Between the two of them, that's the choice he would make too.

Siggi also had both a hammer and a chisel. To Hrafn they looked no different than the ones he had used before, but Siggi told him exactly how to position his hands, at this angle in this spot on the table, and finally broke the shackles with a few swift, strong blows.

"There," he said. "I knew that would work. It's about getting into the weak spots, you see. Every piece of forged iron has a weak spot."

Hrafn rubbed at his newly naked wrists. "Thanks."

They closed up the house and left. Siggi looked back twice as they walked away. The first time Hrafn wondered if he was having second thoughts. The second time he knew that he wasn't. He felt no nervous patter across their shared heartbeat, no shudder of doubt. Siggi didn't think he would be coming back anytime soon.

Hrafn could already feel the ache of Siggi's inevitable heartbreak when he learned his brother was well and truly dead. He could feel it, not through their bond but inside his own chest. This was a fool's errand. He knew what the scrying would show. He had killed Siggi's father, turned his village against him before dooming it to vengeful catastrophe, and now he was about to break the last delicate thread of hope the boy was clinging to.

"It's not going to be what you expect," Hrafn said.

They had been walking in silence for some time, climbing farther and farther away from the farm and forge. Siggi had turned off from the rock-hewn trail and strode across the unmarked landscape with the confidence of someone who had been traversing these hills his entire life. The ram ambled along with them, stopping to eat mouthfuls of grass here and there. Thin fog whirled as they climbed, making the air cold and damp. When Hrafn looked back he could see the broad, black sweep of the coast and the sharp turn where the land bent into the fjord.

"I know that Arnes might be dead," Siggi said.

"That's not what I mean. Listen. If he is, what you see when we scry for him isn't going to be what you expect."

"Am I going to see something too?" Siggi asked, surprised.

"If you look." Hrafn scraped his fingernails over his own left arm and saw Siggi's fingers twitch in response. "Most people can see a little anyway, even if they haven't stolen a witch's blade directly from a funeral pyre."

"Next time I'll ask you first what I should steal from a witch's funeral pyre," Siggi said. "Since you have such strong feelings on the matter."

It took Hrafn a second to realize he was making a joke, and when he did he was too stunned to laugh. He looked away before Siggi could look at him.

"Coins and boots," Hrafn said. "All good things to steal. Everything else is too likely to be cursed and should be knotted or destroyed, but money changes hands too often for any magic to cling to it."

"And the boots?"

"If you're stealing from funeral pyres, you probably need a new pair of boots."

"I see," said Siggi. "I'll remember that. What did you mean, it won't be what I expect? I don't even know what scrying *is*, not really. Only that it means looking for something, like they do in old stories."

"Maybe you aren't making offerings to the old gods and weren't praying down at that church, but you've surely got some idea what it is you expect to happen after you die. But whatever it is, it's not what you see when you scry somebody who's dead. There are no women with large axes ferrying anybody into a feasting hall full of victorious warriors."

Siggi walked along quietly for a few moments. "What did you see?"

"It's different every time, is the thing, and you never know—"

"No, I mean, when you were dead. What did you see?"

Hrafn stopped. He didn't know why the question surprised him. They were talking about the netherworld, the lands beyond death. Of course Siggi, a farm boy with a thousand and one questions, would want to know.

"Nothing," he said. He was as surprised by his own honesty as he was by Siggi's question. He didn't feel like he had been dead. He felt like he had closed his eyes with a knife in his heart and awoken in a fire after a dreamless sleep. "I didn't see anything. It was like no time passed at all."

Maybe witches didn't have netherworlds. Maybe they were so despised even after death there was no heaven or hell or feasting hall that would accept them.

"And that's not what you see when you scry somebody who's dead?"

"No," Hrafn said slowly.

"What do you see if they're not dead?"

"If it works—and it doesn't always work—you see what they see."

"Like you've taken their place?"

"No," Hrafn said quickly. "That's different. This is as though you're looking from their eyes, but you can't do anything while you're there. Sometimes you can't even be sure what you're looking at."

"Huh."

They fell into another silence.

Siggi led Hrafn and the ugly old sheep into a broad valley high above the coast, following a rough livestock trail that wound its way up alongside a tumbling creek. The sides of the valley were green with moss, the peaks of the hills hidden in the clouds. The entire valley was hushed and still, as though the clouds and the long climb cut it off so effectively the rest of the world had forgotten about it. Even the call of the seabirds was distant up here. There was a falling-down rock wall across the mouth of the valley and an abandoned turf house, even smaller than Siggi's, tucked into the base of a short cliff. Aside from that, there was little sign anybody except sheep ever visited this place.

"This isn't anybody's land anymore," Siggi explained. "Not since Erik Erikson went south to Storaska after his mother died last year. Father wants—" A catch in his breath. "My father wanted to claim it, mostly so nobody else would be going up and down past his forge all the time, but it's difficult to get to and doesn't have very good grazing. I come up here sometimes to…to be alone."

Hrafn wanted to ask why somebody whose life was so utterly lonely as Siggi's would ever want to be alone. But it wasn't hard to understand. The loneliness of a high, empty valley with no company but the sky was very different from the loneliness of living with a father who hated you so much he didn't even build you a stool to sit on by the fire on cold nights.

They followed the creek to where it tumbled down the hillside in a burbling, clear cascade, and there they climbed a bit more, up the steep slope, to a level area at the head of the valley. There Siggi presented his pool.

"Will this work?" he asked, looking at Hrafn expectantly, even a bit nervously.

The pool was small, about two paces across, and almost perfectly round, but so deep that its bottom was swallowed in darkness. Foul-smelling steam rose from the surface as hot water from below mingled with the cool trickles that seeped in from the sides. The surface was still and smooth. Hrafn walked around it and looked back down the valley.

The abandoned house looked like a broken box, the crumbling wall a hastily sketched line, and beyond that the world dropped away, hidden by clouds. He could easily imagine Siggi coming up here to sit, to keep his own company away from the world that was so unkind to him.

"It's perfect," Hrafn said softly.

Siggi looked away, suddenly very interested in the ram. "What do you need to do?"

He directed Siggi to hold the crotchety old ram while Hrafn cut a tuft of its matted wool, then dug in deeper to prick its skin and spill a bit of blood into the bowl. The ram responded with what were no doubt some very rude words in the language of sheep, but Siggi was strong—Hrafn nearly cut his own finger off at the sight of Siggi's arm muscles straining as the creature fought—and Hrafn got what he needed. When Siggi let the ram go, it bounded off to glare at them murderously from several feet away.

Hrafn carried the bowl over to the pool, crouched down, and rolled up his sleeve.

"Do you have to do that?" Siggi asked.

"Do you see another witch nearby willing to do it?"

"The ram's blood isn't enough?"

Hrafn snorted. "Not unless you want the ram to be the one doing the scrying. You can *try* asking him what he sees, but he looks like a dishonest fucker. He'll probably lie."

Siggi started to roll his own sleeve. The left one, to reveal the black-tainted pattern of the knife. "Then what about using my blood?"

Hrafn gave him an incredulous look. "What good would that do? You don't know how to scry. Just grit your teeth and deal with it. It'll be barely a scratch."

"That's not what…" Siggi trailed off as Hrafn opened a cut on his arm and held the wound out to drip blood in the bowl. "Okay. But would it work, if you used my blood?"

"Only if you also learned to draw staves on still water," Hrafn said. "Why does it matter? Give me the tooth." When Siggi passed it over, he said, "I really hope you're right about this one being your brother's."

"I am."

There was absolutely no doubt in Siggi's voice, and it bothered Hrafn as much now as it had in the church. He could only assume that Siggi was feeling some effect of the spell Hrafn had used to find the relic. Perhaps their blood relation meant that the magic affected Siggi differently, or the priest had done something to the teeth when he collected them. Hrafn had no blood family; he had no idea what effect that would have.

He hated not knowing what his own magic was doing.

He grabbed some moss from beside the pool and used the knife to mix it in with the blood and wool, then he scraped up a bit of the sparse black soil and did the same. Finally, he cupped a bit of water from the spring, warm to the touch and faintly sulfurous. Pieces of the world, parts of a whole, all stirred together.

He mixed the elements slowly, waiting for the pool to still again. When he had a loose reddish slurry, he dragged his forefinger through it to draw the stave for an all-seeing eye on the back of his right hand, then did the same with the left. When the lines of the second eye connected, Hrafn felt a cool breath skating over his skin, raising his hairs and pricking playfully at his scars.

"Oh, that feels strange," Siggi said softly.

"Sorry, but it's about to get even stranger," Hrafn said.

The easiest way to make use of the target material was to put it inside his body. And there was one straightforward way to do that.

He popped it in his mouth.

"Hrafn!" Siggi burst out. "Did you just swallow it?"

"What? No! It's under my tongue, for fuck's sake. I'm not going to eat a tooth. And we might need it again if this doesn't work." Hrafn spread the blood mixture over the palms of his hands and set the bowl aside. "It might not be pretty. You might hate what you see."

"I know."

"Then come closer if you want. But don't disturb the water and fuck everything up."

Siggi moved closer, and it turned out his idea of close was actually *really close*, so that Hrafn could feel the heat of him all along his side. He thought about telling him to move away but didn't say anything. He had learned to focus under more distracting conditions. He scooted forward on his knees and leaned over the water to begin drawing the scrying stave.

It took a few tries, because water was a finicky medium. The trick was to trace his blood-touched fingers just over the surface, close enough that the water pulled up to meet his fingertips, but not so close that he sent ripples through the pool. He had to get the lines and curves of the stave exactly right, even though he couldn't see them while drawing—until he *could* see them, when they began to linger on the surface of the water as a faint red glow where no light should be.

"Oh!" Siggi's heart skipped across their bond. His breath was a puff of warmth in Hrafn's ear.

Hrafn smirked. A scrying stave was pretty damn impressive when it worked. The elaborate pattern sat atop the water for several seconds, lines and curves and circles shifting together with the smallest adjustments. Hrafn flattened his hands just above the surface of the pool and waited for the stave to fade.

As it did so, a deep, empty darkness took its place. No longer did the pool reflect the gray sky or their faint outlines. It was black, darker than black, a hollow void.

Hrafn thought, *oh,* and it tasted bitter, the disappointment, to learn that poor beloved Arnes was dead after all. He hadn't realized how much he wanted to learn otherwise.

But even as he was hoping that Siggi saw what he saw, that he understood what it meant, Hrafn saw that the darkness wasn't empty after all. There was a faint flicker of patchy, broken light to one side. The image did not have the sickly, nauseating unreliability of a view into an afterlife, but he couldn't make sense of it. The tiny patches of light brightened, forming a grid-like pattern that was familiar in a way Hrafn couldn't quite name. Then they moved suddenly—all of them, together—and golden light flared.

It was a candle. Blurry at first, then clear, backlit by light of a pale, murky gray. It was a fucking candle, and there was daylight behind it, framed by an arched opening. It looked like a cave or a grotto, every surface jagged and unhewn.

Siggi's bloody brother was *alive.*

Siggi let out a strangled sound. Hrafn ignored him. He couldn't be distracted now.

The man holding the candle was a looming shape. He was using a long, long bone as a walking stick, and in that hand, flapping against the bone, was a dark sack of some material. That's when Hrafn realized why the grid of lights had looked familiar: there had been a hood or bag over Arnes's head.

As his eyes—as Arnes's eyes—adjusted to the light, he could better see the man before him, even with the gray daylight at his back. His skin was loose and shriveled and browned, as though it had been leathered while he still lived. His hair hung in filthy, matted hanks around his face, which was covered with a beard. He wore no clothes except strings of bones carved with runes and staves around his neck and waist. His limbs were lashed with wounds that had not yet healed, although they had been stitched closed with rough threads.

No sound carried through the scrying, but Hrafn saw when Arnes kicked at the man's legs, saw the way the man danced easily out of reach, as though acting out steps he had performed dozens of times before. The man lifted his head slowly and pushed curtains of hair back from his face. As he did so, the skin on his arm and hand shifted, slid over his body, and Hrafn stopped breathing.

That was not his skin.

Those were not his wounds.

He was wearing a cloak of skin over his own, one stitched together from a dozen pieces or more. His face was covered with a mask of the same, showing nothing of his true self except his unruly beard, his grinning mouth, his dark eyes. As he spoke he wagged a finger reproachfully. Whatever warning he gave, it did not stop Arnes from trying to kick him one more time. *Good for you,* Hrafn thought. *Keep fighting.* There was a thick knot of rope around Arnes's bare ankles.

The shrouded man stepped closer and set the candle on a narrow ledge of rock. As he leaned down, Arnes went still. The man laughed silently, perhaps in response to something Arnes said, and his grin was so wide it became all that Hrafn could see, that wet red mouth in the candlelight. The shrouded man moved closer, closer, and Hrafn felt like he was slipping toward him, like his control was water falling through his fingertips, and he knew he was looking now through his own eyes. His own eyes, staring right into those of the man stitched into his hide of stolen skin.

The man reached out of the pool with his free hand, the one not holding the bone-stick, and Hrafn was reaching as well, without even meaning to. He was aware of a noise behind him, like a voice coming from a great distance, but he could not make out any words.

The man grasped his wrist. It felt like fire and ice at the same time. He gasped as the man pulled, and Hrafn plunged face-first into the pool.

Darkness surrounded him, and so did laughter. A raucous, bellowing laughter, so loud it filled his ears and his mind, chasing away every other thought. Somewhere distantly, beneath the laughter, he heard another voice, one angry and demanding and scared, asking questions that received no answers, but the laughter and the rush of water soon drowned it out. Water flowed into his mouth and throat, and the hand on his wrist kept pulling him down, down, the cold from the man's slimy, wrinkled grip becoming the cold of his own skin. There was no golden candlelight anymore, no daylight just beyond reach, no light at all. The man was still laughing. His laughter was the only thing in the world.

Then there was a tug, soft at first, then stronger, and finally so powerful that Hrafn felt it in his hip and shoulder. He struggled to break the man's grip on his wrist, felt it when the bony fingers fell away, and he was being pulled upward swiftly, and in seconds he was out of the water.

Siggi was shouting as he hauled him onto the moss.

"What the fuck was that? What was that? How did it grab you?"

He shook Hrafn's shoulders and shouted, then quickly rolled him onto his side as Hrafn began to cough up bitter spring water.

"Are you okay?" Siggi asked, still shaking Hrafn's shoulders. "Hrafn? Say something, for fuck's sake, are you okay? What happened? How did—something *grabbed* you! I thought we were just looking! How did it grab you?"

Hrafn wanted to answer him, he really did, but he had to stop coughing first, and then he had to struggle to sit up. Siggi helped him, and Hrafn couldn't even be bothered to brush away his warm, solid touch this time. He couldn't tell if the drumming in his chest was his own heartbeat or Siggi's.

"Hrafn, say something," Siggi pleaded. "What happened? What was that?"

Hrafn coughed a few more times, his throat raw, and spat out Arnes's tooth onto the ground. He gasped for breath for several long seconds. Siggi's hand was resting on his back and he didn't want to move away, but as he regained his breath, he started to laugh. It was a wild, mad sound, but he couldn't stop it.

"Hrafn! What was that?" Siggi's voice was tight with fear. "Are you okay? What happened?"

Hrafn gasped for breath. "Your brother—your brother—"

"Was that Arnes? I don't understand."

"Your brother is alive," Hrafn said. He sucked in another breath, trying to steady himself. There was nothing worth laughing about, but he felt it burbling back to the surface all the same. "Does it run in the family, do you think? Do you have a family tradition of having really truly terrible luck with witches? Do you do it on purpose?"

"I don't understand," Siggi said again, more quietly. "What are you saying? Was that person we saw—was that—"

"A witch. Yes." Hrafn raised his wrist. The empty skin-hand was still clinging there, torn at the wrist where the stitching had pulled away. He shook his hand to fling it aside. It landed on the mossy rocks with a wet slap. "You know, puffling, there aren't many witches left in Lifandfjall who use skin magic. It's gone a bit out of fashion lately. But you want to know what they all have in common?"

Siggi tore his gaze away from the ragged piece of skin to meet Hrafn's eyes. "What?"

Hrafn grinned. "Every last one of them is a complete fucking madman."

Chapter Seven
Monstrous Heather

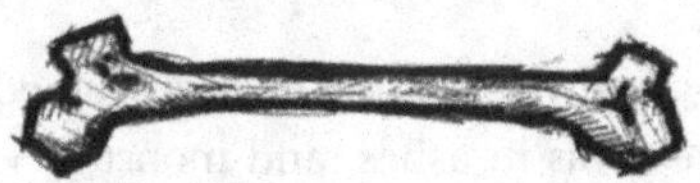

Arnes had been the first to tell Siggi that one day he would die.

He hadn't said it to make him cry, but of course Siggi had cried nonetheless, sobbing into his brother's lap. Siggi had seen stillborn lambs and knew his mother had met her end; he had seen old ewes rotting in the fields and fish floating on the surface of a stream. And yet it had never occurred to him that death would find him too, and worse: death would find Arnes.

Even after watching the dead rise and seeing his father burn and scrying alongside a black-haired witch, Siggi still couldn't fathom this one inevitability. Wherever Arnes was, whatever had befallen him, Siggi's heart said only: *Arnes cannot die, not ever.*

So Siggi didn't know what he was saying as he pulled Hrafn limp-limbed from the pool and laid him on the grass, didn't know what he was shouting as Hrafn coughed and spluttered and finally confirmed the cry of his heart.

"Arnes is *alive*," Siggi repeated, and some terrible tangled knot unwound in his chest. He couldn't stop his hands from trembling, all of him from trembling. *"Arnes is alive."*

"Don't you start crying again," Hrafn warned, looking uneasy and spent, but Siggi pressed his fists into his eyes and breathed deep. "He's alive, but he's in foul company."

Siggi pulled his hands away and laughed. "*He's alive*! Hrafn, my brother is alive!"

"Enough," Hrafn said, flinching, but Siggi wrapped him in his arms and squeezed him tight, smiling into his collarbone.

"Thank you," he whispered. "Hrafn, thank you."

"Stop that," Hrafn said, sounding panicked. "Don't thank me."

But Hrafn did not tell Siggi not to touch him, and for a moment, the pair of them knelt in the muck with their hearts pressed and pounding together.

Magic was grisly, and violent, and gory, it seemed to Siggi. Father was dead, the church was in ashes, and monsters were all too real, and magic fueled all these terrible truths. Yet painful as it was to watch Hrafn slice open his skin so often, as though harming himself were no more meaningful than plucking shallow-rooted plants from the stones, Hrafn's magic had given Siggi a priceless gift.

Arnes is alive.

Siggi felt keenly the shape of Hrafn's ribs against his own, the unsteadiness of Hrafn's shallow breaths against his neck. Something shifted in Siggi's navel. Abruptly he let Hrafn go, face warm.

"If he's alive, we can find him." Siggi cleared his throat, climbing to his feet.

Hrafn's gaze was fixed on his knees, his ears tinged pink. "Maybe we can, or maybe we can't, but either way we can't stay here. That fire will draw all kinds of trouble this way."

"Won't they have doused it by now?" Siggi asked.

Hrafn still did not look at him. "That's fey-fed fire. Buckets of water won't be enough."

Though they were too high above the village to hear any commotion, the morning fog had already lifted. Had Brother Hamon told them that the village idiot Siggi Arnesson had been seen there before the flames erupted? How far had the fire spread beyond the churchyard?

"What will become of the people of Midfjördur?"

"The huldu don't take kindly to those who've slighted them, and binding a huldu in teeth in a dark pit is no small slight."

"I didn't know about the woman in the church," Siggi said. "I doubt many of the villagers knew about her, either."

"Tell me, puffling. When the head of a fish rots, do you eat the rest of it?"

"Well…"

"*Ew. No.* You throw the whole thing out." He found his feet and stood behind Siggi, staring down into the fjord. "That's how huldu view humans. A rot to be cut away."

"These are people," Siggi said, "not fish."

"Makes little difference to the huldu. Have you ever heard of what happened to the village of Tindurgos, far to the east? Or the farms at Mulbotn?" When Siggi shook his head, Hrafn let out a frustrated huff. "Well, neither of them exists anymore, because they made the mistake of offending the huldu. Tell me you've at least heard of the Ghost Marsh? The haunted battlefield at Draugamyr? A huldu's curse begins the moment they die. You saw those flames. They'll burn until there's nothing more to burn. All the villagers can do is run."

"Can't *you* put it out?" Siggi asked.

Hrafn's eyebrows shot up. "Even if I could, why would I?"

Siggi gaped at Hrafn, stunned by the ice in his voice.

"Siggi. Listen." He sighed. "I can't put it out. I can't do *anything* about a huldu death curse. The rain and this rocky shore will keep the fire in the fjord, probably, and any soul foolish enough to stay will find themselves facing every vicious witch or vengeful huldu who shows up to nose around. That's why you and me? We're fucking leaving. Now."

"But if the villagers flee, they can survive?"

Hrafn looked at him, long and hard. "I can lie to you. Will that make you feel better?"

"We could warn them," Siggi said.

"Certainly, if you want to walk right into their pitchforks. Much good you'd do your brother then." Hrafn seemed to consider, then he sighed. "I don't know, okay? I don't know how far the huldu will reach or how thorough they'll be. The fire might be the extent of it.

If there are huldu in this realm, they would have the power to starve the villages by killing every fish on the Thrandir Coast. Or turn all the fishermen into fish themselves. Or raise the dead from the churchyard to form a mob. Nothing they do is ever simple or straightforward, and nobody even knows what they can do from their own realm. *I don't know.* That's why we're getting the fuck out of here."

Siggi steeled himself, turning his back on the horizon, the last glimpse of the houses in the fjord. Everything Hrafn described sounded like the stuff of stories, the sort of tales Arnes had told him on long winter nights to make the both of them shiver and laugh. Too big to be real, too big for someone like Siggi to change.

"What happens will happen," he said.

"And here I thought you were soft." A hint of sadness colored Hrafn's voice.

"Did you think that?" Siggi asked, and Hrafn unfolded his scarred arms.

"No. No I didn't, in fact."

Siggi hefted both their packs from the ground. "The easiest way out of Midfjördur is through the mountain pass at the Fossvegur."

"Oh, yeah?" Hrafn didn't offer to take the bag from Siggi's shoulder but followed him up the trail like a specter. "And once we're away, what then? I told you. I don't know where the hell your brother is."

Siggi looked back at him over his shoulder. "But you're clever, and you have magic, and you found him once already, and you don't want to die again. So you'll find him, I know it."

Hrafn's face soured and he spat into the mud. "You don't know me."

But in his chest, Siggi felt something flutter, something that was Hrafn's. Siggi had felt it a few fleeting times in his life, in those beautiful moments when Arnes told him he wasn't worthless.

Arnes. The thought of his brother's face, the wry smile and thoughtful eyes, sapped the exhaustion from his aching bones. Siggi thought he could walk forever, until he walked into an unknown darkened cavern and into his brother's embrace.

The pair left the Erikson farm behind, walking into the mist of morning.

Siggi had never left Midfjördur, but he knew the way. In the dying days of autumn, he and Arnes had often snuck over the driftwood fence in the dark evening hours, laughing as they darted from shadow to shadow. Avoiding the main road that rose from the heart of the village, the brothers instead took a narrow, unseen path that traced the cliff just above land belonging to Snorri Arnarson, the wealthiest man in Midfjördur. Snorri had four ships to his name in spite of hating the sea and its fish and its squalls.

Arnes and Siggi hadn't cared about Snorri's wealth. They cared only about the bathing springs on his land. Snorri charged travelers on the Fossvegur for their use, but Arnes and Siggi had found a way around his wretched toll. From the crumbling cliff, they would hop down only when the overgrown heather met the rock face. Shielded from view, they crept like bandits toward the steady cloud of steam rising from the springs.

It was this overgrown path that Siggi led Hrafn down now. The morning dew left the stones slippery, and omnipresent sheep shit made the path downright treacherous. Even so, there was no better way to leave Midfjördur.

"How you keep your footing here, I've no fucking idea," Hrafn mumbled, stumbling in Siggi's wake.

"Shall I carry you?"

"Stop asking that."

By the time the pair approached the end of the cliff, the sky had cleared to reveal a bright, unexpected noonday sun. Siggi stopped as Snorri's land unfolded before them, fields of overgrown heather only just beginning to sprout purple buds. Though Snorri's fences were high, his land was vastly untouched. In the distance, his impressive lodge guarded the Fossvegur's opening, from this side of the field no more than a jagged black cut dividing the cliffs.

"That's a lot of heather," Hrafn observed. "Where are all the sheep?"

"Snorri doesn't keep any sheep," Siggi said.

"Then who's been shitting on this trail?"

Siggi almost laughed, but the sight of that grand but silent home instilled in him an uneasy quiet. The field of heather seemed impossibly wide.

"No one's here," Hrafn said. "Not a *great* sign."

"He's probably gone down to the village," Siggi said. "They would have sent word."

"They should be running away from the village, not toward it."

There was yellow smoke rising from the fjord, tinting the sky a sickly hue. Siggi could only guess what such a sight portended for Midfjördur. And yet Siggi felt curiously empty at the thought, as though he himself had only ever been a relic in that place, the smith's idiot son hidden on the hill. The village had hardly been welcoming to Siggi, its people all but strangers. Siggi wondered whether that might be why he couldn't bring himself to grieve their fate.

"Come on," he said quietly, turning his back on the sight.

They climbed down the stones and dropped feet first into the brambles.

Without sheep's teeth or a farmer's scythe to tame it, the heather proved a formidable foe. Mature and wiry, the brambles stretched as high as Siggi's hips and scraped against Hrafn's waist. Carefully, Siggi picked the way forward through the zigzagging fissures in the cover.

"Should really just burn through it all," Hrafn said.

"No!" Siggi said, more sharply than he intended. "Is starting fires all you know?"

He waited for Hrafn's biting retort, but it didn't come. He turned and saw that the witch had stopped in his tracks. Suddenly his posture was entirely different, as though he really were on the verge of flight. And the way he was looking at Siggi—

Siggi had seen it before, fleeting instances when he felt the witch-boy weighing him with apprehension. "Hrafn. What is it?"

"I'm awaiting the eruption," Hrafn said, almost to himself.

"The what?"

"Forget it." Hrafn shook his head, but there remained something fragile about his posture.

"Hrafn. I will never hurt you," Siggi said, relaxing his shoulders. "I swear I won't."

"Why are you saying that?" Hrafn demanded, face twisting. "Did I fucking ask?"

"No. You just looked…frightened." Siggi frowned. "And…felt frightened, too."

"Frightened?" Hrafn's eyes shot up. "You think I'm frightened of you, puffling?"

Siggi didn't answer. He couldn't guess what was going through Hrafn's mind, but he knew that Hrafn hadn't put all those staves and scars on himself. Siggi had felt the blows from fists and boots a thousand times, but rarely the slice of a blade. Each and every time Hrafn cut himself, Siggi felt it, and he felt something much worse than the momentary sting: a certain familiarity and indifference to the pain.

"I just wanted to say it. I won't hurt you."

Hrafn's face had worked itself into a real tangle.

"You may want to reconsider that. I've killed before. I killed your father. I set fire to a huldu. And if it weren't for the knife that binds us, I might kill you too. Don't forget that."

Ears ringing, Siggi turned away. "I haven't forgotten."

"And that's what scares me," Hrafn whispered, and Siggi turned to face him again, to ask him what he meant by that and how he could possibly make Hrafn believe that maybe one day he'd have killed Father himself, if only he'd been less of a coward—

"Gods' eyes, but that was quick. Not even half a day since the fire." Hrafn gazed past Siggi's shoulder.

Siggi turned to look as well, casting his eyes across the field.

For a moment he saw nothing, heard nothing. Just the wind in the heather, the distant whisper of the sea. The cries of coastal birds and wind singing through the cliffs.

"What is it?"

And then Siggi saw it: a rustling in the heather, a susurration accompanied by a roiling that passed through the field as though a wind were rising beneath the surface of the buds. Inexplicably, the heather rose into a mound, elevated from the earth around it. And then, like some sea monster breaching the ocean's surface, the hill of heather as big as the village church moved toward them, its ovular silhouette growing clearer as, bobbing up and down, it accelerated across the field.

"A—a quake?" The Thrandir was rattled by earthquakes less often than the southern parts of Lifandfjall, but tremors were not unheard of. "Or is it the huldu?"

"Afraid not," Hrafn replied. "But at least as devastating as either, when she's in a mood."

"Should…should we run?" Siggi asked, disturbed by Hrafn's smirking calm.

The mound of heather came all too close, tearing through the stationary brambles like a knife through milk. The thing was as big as a turf house—in fact, it looked a *lot* like a turf house. Siggi could even spy the wooden outline of a door, tucked among the bristles.

"Hrafn!" He reached for Hrafn's hand, but Hrafn tucked his palms beneath his arms.

"There's really no point," Hrafn said. "No one avoids Ylfa."

"You know what that thing is?"

"I know *who* it is," Hrafn said, and then the thing was upon them—

Siggi tackled Hrafn, shoving the swearing witch-boy into the brambles as the barreling mound came to an immediate halt barely an ell's length from Siggi's face.

Jutting from the underside of the heather leviathan, Siggi saw a pair of massive, clawed feet, seemingly grown from twisted roots. Carved into talons, they flattened the mud beneath them. They looked like wood but moved like something livelier.

Siggi's grip on Hrafn loosened as his eyes traveled upward. The house of heather was being carried upon the back of a monstrous behemoth: it looked something like a whale, with a large, rounded snout pocked with fungal bumps, but also nothing like a whale, given it was land-bound and coated in green moss. Its slitted silver eyes, peering out from the forest of brambles, were each as large as Siggi's head. The heather bushes sprouted from the creature's fertile flesh, spilling from its crown and thickening as they spread across the span of its massive, curvaceous back. Like a turtle carrying its shell, so did the leviathan carry its bramble patch.

"A beast," Siggi breathed. "What is it?"

"It's a lyngbakr," Hrafn said, from just beneath him, and Siggi saw that his black eyes were shining. The smallest smile marked his lips, altering his face entirely. For a moment Siggi forgot the looming beast entirely. "It's Ylfa's lyngbakr."

There came the sound of a door creaking open and shut and a wracking cough, and then a voice called down to them from the crest of the lyngbakr's back.

"What in Storguð's ugly name have you gotten yourself into, Hrafn the Feckless?"

Hrafn got to his feet, pulling Siggi up with him. "Ylfa. Hello."

The lyngbakr bent its driftwood knees and lowered itself to the ground, and only then could Siggi see the woman who stood upon its back, akimbo before that door—it really was a door—in the mound of heather.

Ylfa was unlike anyone Siggi had ever seen. And though Siggi had seen relatively few people over the years, he thought that she was probably so unlike other people that *no one* had seen anyone like her.

She was short in stature but broad in the shoulders, her skin weathered with age and toil. She wore a tattered shawl of wool and a leather patchwork vest, as well as a many-colored skirt, tied in a knot at the middle so that she almost appeared to be wearing pants. Ylfa's silver hair was a tangle that mirrored the brambles, although she'd fastened bunches of it away from her wrinkled face with knots of twine.

Around her neck, Ylfa wore a curious oblong talisman—Siggi couldn't quite make out what was carved upon it, but he recognized that it was a stave. On her shoulder was perched yet another creature Siggi had never seen, like a specter from a ghost fable. The creature looked like a bird, a small raven, with feathers black and gleaming. But in place of a bird's head, the naked skull of a human infant bobbed on its shoulders.

"The minute I heard some witch was fool enough to set fire to a huldu in the Thrandir, you know what I said? I said I know exactly the unthinking little witch who might have just such a death wish. It pains me to be right at times, Hrafn."

"Sorry," Hrafn said, though he didn't sound sorry. He sounded pleased.

Siggi squinted at the woman who could make Hrafn something close to happy, and she looked at him too, eyes narrowing. She coughed again, and the bird-thing on her shoulder fluttered its feathers.

Suddenly Ylfa's round face split into a toothy smile. "Come on up, you fools."

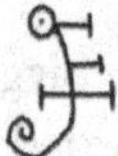

A brief clamber up the mound of heather, aided by a rope ladder Ylfa dropped from above, and the pair of them found themselves sitting on a bench beside a bright long fire, safe inside Ylfa's inexplicable home aboard the lyngbakr.

Hrafn sat across the fire from the strange old woman, telling her of all that had occurred across the long day past. Siggi remained standing, gawking at the walls, cultivated to form a wide, insulated dome.

The heather had been tamed, by magic or some other means, into tangled but sturdy walls that allowed light in between their branches. Tiny staves had been carved into the surface of those branches. Siggi could only guess, but perhaps the staves could explain how Ylfa's home felt much larger on the inside, or how the floor remained steady even as the lyngbakr traversed the field and climbed into Fossvegur, carrying them away from Snorri's farm.

The long fire burned merrily but never seemed to escape the confines of its circle, no threat to the heather or the beast below them. Siggi spied a cot covered in woolen blankets, upon which a small orange cat lay sleeping. Beyond the cot, there was a small shelf overflowing with more books than Siggi had ever seen, seven at least, and beside that was a wooden perch, perhaps where the bird-thing on Ylfa's shoulder spent its nights.

Siggi craned his neck. A stone slab and shelves of bowls and curious plants were displayed in cluttered piles along the walls. A bowl of beads clinked when the lyngbakr's strides were widest, but otherwise, the house did not shake. Pacing the floor, Siggi peered through the heather. He saw the dark gleam of the canyon walls and knew that it was raining.

"Why doesn't everything get wet?" Siggi said, turning to the pair of them.

Hrafn paused midsentence, and Ylfa raised her white eyebrows. "What's that, boy?"

"It's raining outside, and there's fog too. But it's dry here, even though there are gaps in the heather. Is that a kind of magic?"

"Of course it is," Ylfa said.

"It's wonderful," Siggi said, thinking of the cold wet winters in Midfjördur.

"Strange creature, isn't he?" Ylfa said to Hrafn.

Hrafn's lip twitched. "An understatement."

"It isn't a bad thing, being strange," she added, smiling knowingly at Siggi.

He felt his face flush and turned away as their conversation recommenced.

Siggi wandered closer to the cot, peering at the books. Arnes had taught him runes, but none of these were familiar. He reached a hand down to stroke the sleeping cat. The cat stretched himself out, long and carrot-furred and unusually fat, pushing his warm head into

Siggi's palm.

"…and when the huldu's head unraveled in the church, it began to scream," Hrafn said, and Ylfa tutted.

"You say they kept it there as a relic? How the church has fallen, and they were already crawling on the ground to begin with. Foolish as they are cruel."

"I thought so too."

"And yet you also thought it'd be wise to ignite the huldu's head?"

Siggi froze, and Hrafn hesitated before answering.

"I had to. She was screaming and she was cursed and…Birtingr always said a living huldu is a deadly huldu."

"Birtingr would kill anything if he thought doing so might line his pockets. He never has a care to who he angers or what dangers he brings down on your head." Ylfa shook her head, frown-lines deepening. "All those summers you spent with me, and you never learned a thing."

"*You* try dying and see how thoughtful you'd be in the hours after." Absently, Hrafn rubbed one of the staves on his shoulder.

"You say that as though I never have," Ylfa hummed. "Tonguð's teats, but you really were a terrible student."

Hrafn fell silent, snuffed out. Siggi felt the need to speak. "He was trying to help me, when she started screaming. He was trying to help me save my brother."

"Was he now?" Ylfa said, raising her eyebrows. "Well, that certainly doesn't sound like you, Hrafn."

Hrafn shifted in his seat. "I told you. The boy and I are bound by that blade. I have to do what he asks, or he'll never break our bond."

"Oh, yes. The witch-blade. Boy. Let me see that arm of yours."

"My name's Siggi," Siggi said, frowning. "Please don't call me *boy*."

Hrafn shook his head in warning, and Ylfa narrowed her eyes. She snapped her fingers and Siggi found himself in her grasp, his forearm caught in her bony fingers.

"Well, *Siggi*," she said, as he tried to regain his balance. "This is quite a bind indeed. Where did a hulking farm boy from the remote

Thrandir learn such advanced necromancy? Was it your father? Your mother?"

Siggi felt Hrafn's eyes on him, wondering the same. And for an instant he wanted to continue the ruse, to pretend that he'd known precisely what he was doing when he stole the knife and bound his life to Hrafn's. But he looked into the woman's piercing eyes—bright green, like grass after rain—and found himself speaking the truth:

"I don't know any magic. I don't know how or why any of this happened."

"I fucking knew it," Hrafn said, standing up. "I knew it!"

"Hrafn," Ylfa warned.

"But if he doesn't know how he bound me, he won't know how to unbind me, either!" Siggi cringed at the fury in Hrafn's face.

"Sit. Down." Ylfa snapped her fingers again, and Hrafn's legs buckled. "In any case, you're better off than you were, cold on a pyre. Should be glad this farm boy didn't try to burn you again. All I taught you, and you still ended up dying and on the wrong side of priests and huldu to boot!"

"Oh, yes," Hrafn hissed. "You taught me a great deal, and then you sent me straight back to Birtingr!"

"Whatever I did needed to be done," Ylfa retorted, though there was a note of pain in her voice. "You refused to learn. You refused to change. You refused to take care of yourself. And I couldn't bear to see you bleed any longer."

Siggi saw darkness sprouting in her verdant eyes, and a new tension in Hrafn's birdlike shoulders. In the space between them he felt the weight of unspoken pain.

"I didn't mean to bring Hrafn back to life, or bind him to me," Siggi said, and Ylfa raised her eyes. "But I'm glad it happened. I'm glad he's not dead."

Hrafn stilled, staring straight through the softly breathing floor.

Ylfa eyed Siggi with the strangest of expressions. "Hrafn said you recognized your brother's tooth at a glance."

"Yes," Siggi said. "I did."

"Hmmph." Finally she let go of Siggi's arm. "That blade binds you together, that much is true. Your souls are intertwined. And if there's a way to undo that binding, you won't easily find it in this world."

"How can you be sure?" Hrafn demanded.

"Come now, Hrafn. Haven't you guessed? That which binds you, it isn't black magic or skin magic or blood magic or stave magic. It's *huldu* magic."

Hrafn seemed startled. "Just because—the knife handle was huldu bone, but that doesn't mean I can use huldu magic. That's ridiculous."

"Yet it happened. I'd wager that only the hidden folk will know how to break such a bond without killing the both of you. Unfortunately, I can't imagine any huldu will be keen to help, given what you did to one of their own. Mark my words, the instant that fire spread, so did word of it, farther than my sympathetic ears. I've heard a few whispers across the realms."

Siggi gawked at her. "You speak to people in the hidden realm? What are they like?"

Her mouth twisted. "That's a question with as many answers as there are huldu. Proud. Arrogant. Clever. When I was young, they were like animals rattling in a cage, trapped as they are in Hulduheimer. They had expected to defeat the humans the same as they'd defeated the trylla, ages ago, but they failed, and they were vanished. What they're doing now in their hidden realm, I have no idea. But if I had to describe them as a whole, I'd say…vindictive. Had this huldu woman any allies in this realm, or any powerful enough to work magic across the boundary, they will come for you. The village is only a tantrum. You will be the target."

"Isn't there anything we can do?"

Ylfa cooed softly to the raven-child on her shoulder, which nestled into her neck with an eerie squeak. "You say your brother is missing, is that right, Siggi?"

"Yes."

"And what would you do if someone roasted his skull on a whim?"

110

Siggi didn't answer and could not bring himself to look at Hrafn. He had asked Hrafn not to do it, but he hadn't stopped him, hadn't prevented the screaming woman from catching fire.

"Magic leaves a mark, a signature. For a huldu or druid, tracing magic to its source is an easy task. Every witch can be identified by the residue his workings leave behind." Her voice dropped. "Hrafn, you really have been foolish this time."

"I won't let them hurt Hrafn," Siggi blurted. "I won't."

Ylfa looked up, expression unreadable. "This one's a real idiot, isn't he?"

Hrafn opened his mouth and closed it again. "He isn't. Not entirely."

"And not bad to look at, either, is he?" She smirked as Hrafn squirmed. "Boy. No, *Siggi*. I've never known a huldu to forget a slight or fall easily in a duel. Your best hope is there are none in this realm who cared overly much for that woman. And if there are…run far, and run fast, and never stop running."

"That's impossible," Hrafn muttered.

"Tell that to my lyngbakr," Ylfa said wryly. "He knows well never to stop moving."

"If you say that they'll catch us eventually, then in the meantime…there's no reason not to look for my brother."

Ylfa laughed, loud and long, and Hrafn just shook his head. The rain hit the heather rooftop in a quiet patter, and the smell of damp moss drifted in through the branches. Suddenly, sleep invaded Siggi's very pores.

"Well," Ylfa said at last, clearing her throat, "foolish he may be, but a coward he is not."

"We're very tired," Siggi said at last. "May we sleep here?"

Hrafn looked at him then, and Ylfa nodded. "You won't find anywhere so warded as this. Have a kip in my cot, the pair of you. And I'll try to think up some way to keep the huldu from skinning you alive too quickly."

"Thank you," Siggi said.

Ylfa smiled. "You're welcome."

Lying beneath the heather brambles, Siggi caught glimpses of gray sky. On the opposite side of the room, Ylfa busied herself over the bowls and herbs on her wall, humming a quiet tune to the raven-child on her shoulder.

Siggi rolled over to find Hrafn was watching him, eyes like nightfall in the half-light. The orange cat lay purring and outstretched between them, a furry barrier.

"Ylfa cares for you."

"Ylfa is a stubborn old witch," Hrafn replied.

"Who cares for you."

Hrafn hesitated. He seemed so small, like a newborn lamb, and Siggi felt the peculiar urge to wrap him up in his arms. Instead, he watched and waited for Hrafn to speak.

"She could have killed me a thousand times over, and never has."

"Yes. Because she cares for you."

Hrafn closed his eyes, a crease in his forehead, and exhaled. "More fool her."

"I don't think so," Siggi said, and soon after drifted into the deep sleep of the truly exhausted, lulled by the subtle footsteps of the monster that carried them away from Midfjördur.

Chapter Eight
A Witch's Skin

Hrafn was exhausted. Apparently being dead for a couple of days did not count as rest. But his thoughts would not settle.

He kept slipping his hand underneath the too-large shirt to feel his newest scar, the slightly raised line where Einar's knife had pierced through to his heart. He didn't like the feel of it, unfamiliar and useless. He tried to remember if it had hurt when the blade went in. It seemed like a thing he should remember.

Finally he gave up on sleep. He sat up and carefully crawled over Siggi, took a few steps before turning back to tug a coarse wool blanket up over the boy's shoulders. The orange cat had curled up in the bend of Siggi's legs. It gave Hrafn a narrow, baleful glance before going back to sleep. Ylfa was tinkering with something at the far side of the room, muttering to herself and paying him no attention.

The skin of his wrist was itchy and hot where the skin-hand had gripped him from the scrying pool. Hrafn stepped closer to the fire for better light. He scratched his wrist roughly, although it brought no relief. The itching blossomed into pain along his arm, and the purple shadows of a bruise appeared.

The bruise was shaped like a hand, with the four fingers and thumb encircling his wrist.

"Ylfa," Hrafn said quietly. He cleared his throat. "Ylfa? There's something…"

She was at his side instantly; he hadn't heard her approach. She hissed sharply and grabbed his arm. "Why did you not mention this? Did you not think it important?"

"Oh, you know me, I'm so stupid I forget things like magical bruises that appear from nowhere."

Ylfa was unimpressed. "Embarrassed to let that farm boy see? Is there pain?"

"Itching," Hrafn said. "And I'm not *embarrassed*. It's where the skin-witch grabbed me."

Ylfa prodded at the bruise, which in truth did not resemble much of a bruise anymore. It was peeling and cracking around the edges. "You burnt the skin he left behind?"

"Uh. No. I just…flung it away." Hrafn didn't want to admit that he had been so distracted by being hugged by Siggi that he hadn't even thought about it.

Ylfa jagged her finger at the bruise. "Fool! Whyever not? You know how easy it is for another witch to leave a mark!"

Hrafn scowled. "First you yell at me for burning something, then you yell at me for *not* burning something. I can't keep all these complicated rules right in my mind."

"Don't pretend to be stupid, child," Ylfa said. "I know you're not."

The bruise hurt more and more as Ylfa poked and prodded at it, but he didn't let himself flinch. "I'm not pretending right now. I really don't know how he did this." He took a breath, let it out. "But I know who it was. And so do you."

"Aye," Ylfa said softly. "We do."

She prodded at the bruise again. Picked at the edges with her fingertips. Hrafn hissed as it tugged away from his skin, and Ylfa leaned closer, so close her nose was only a finger-length from his arm. She sniffed, tried to peel the strange black mark back a bit more.

Hrafn's heart skipped anxiously. "Stop fussing, old woman, and tell me what you know. How can Haraldar Swift-Eye reach through a scrying and leave a part of himself behind? I've never heard of a witch who could do that."

"I guess you've heard of one now," Ylfa said distractedly. She scratched her fingernails beneath the black skin. "Does it hurt when I do this?"

It wasn't anything Hrafn couldn't handle. "Just take it off."

"I asked you a question, Hrafn. Does it hurt?"

"It's fine, just—"

Ylfa looked up at him. Her mouth quirked, but it wasn't quite a smile. "Answer as though you're speaking for that fair-haired farm boy over there, or some ordinary person with a sensible understanding of pain. Does it hurt?"

There was something in her eyes that he was not used to seeing, something that put a chill through him in spite of the warmth from the fire.

Ylfa was *worried*.

Hrafn swallowed. "Yes."

"Ah. That's too bad."

Before she had even finished speaking, Ylfa grabbed the crackling dried edge of the mark and tore it away from Hrafn's skin.

The pain was like a punch in the chest, sudden and overpowering. Hrafn let out a shout and tried to pull away, jerking Ylfa's arms so strongly the utburdur flapped off her shoulder in alarm.

"Sit still, boy. You've gone and startled Anna."

Hrafn glared at the utburdur. "Anna is undead. She doesn't scare easily."

"Same could be said of you, these days," Ylfa said. "This will hurt even more."

Her grip was too strong to break. She peeled the mark off swiftly, without mercy. Through the thundering roar in his ears, he realized that he wasn't feeling the pain only in his arm. He felt it all over, like the mark had planted a thousand barbs into every part of his skin.

Then, as quickly as it had flared, it was gone. Ylfa dropped the leathery black mark into the fire. It crackled and spat and curled as it burned.

"*What are you doing to him?*"

Siggi stumbled from the cot and crossed the room. He grabbed Hrafn by the shoulders and shoved him back, placing himself between Hrafn and Ylfa. Hrafn was so surprised he didn't even think to struggle.

"What did you do?" Siggi demanded. His right hand was clenched into a fist at his side. "What was that?"

Ylfa laughed her snorting, mocking laugh. "My, that bond really is sensitive. A little tickle can bring you out of a dead sleep, can it?"

"That was *more* than a little—"

"Siggi. It's okay."

Hrafn opened and closed his hand. There was still a bruise there, purple and ugly, but the leathery black mark was gone. There was no lingering pain aside from a faint soreness.

Anna flew back down and landed on Ylfa's shoulder. Ylfa ran a soothing finger along one of her wings and murmured, "There, there. Don't mind the loud lad. His fuss won't hurt you."

The utburdur ruffled her feathers in annoyance. She tilted her skull toward Siggi, and though she had no eyes in those dark sockets, it still looked very much like she was giving him a disapproving glare.

Ylfa picked up a stick and jabbed at the shriveling remnants in the fire, now little more than a twisted strip of leathery black.

"Doubt that fool meant to send a piece of his shroud with you," she said thoughtfully. "Most likely he didn't expect there to be somebody strong enough to pull you back."

Siggi looked at Hrafn with a question in his eyes, and whatever he saw in Hrafn's face seemed to be answer enough. He sat beside Hrafn and reached down absently to scratch the orange cat, who had followed him out of the bed. "That's, uh, that is…that man in the scrying, you know who it was? Why didn't you say before?"

"Because this foolish child didn't want to frighten you. It was Haraldar Swift-Eye or one of his followers," Ylfa said, with a nod at Hrafn. "It was always too much to hope they would all kill each other and finish the job Thekla Igullsdottir started."

"I don't know who that is. Are they witches?" Siggi asked.

"Are they witches, he wants to know," Ylfa said with a laugh. "Don't you hear any of the best stories out there in the Thrandir?"

"He doesn't. I've already learned that. Yes, they're witches," he said to Siggi. "Witches who use skin magic."

"And that means…wearing cloaks made of skin?"

"Among other things," Hrafn said. "Haraldar used to have a powerful coven, but he got greedy and began pissing off too many people. Thekla Igullsdottir is his sister. She's the one who gathered a group of witches to drive him away."

"Where did he go?" Siggi asked.

"To lick their wounds somewhere here in the north. Last I heard they were lurking at the edges of the Myrkvidor," Ylfa said. "Nobody's bothered to go after them since they've kept to themselves well enough, but I do wonder what they're getting up to." She nodded at Siggi. "And why they'd want this one's brother. What sort of business was your brother involved in? Anything to do with that huldu head in your village church?"

"I really don't know," Siggi said. "Arnes had nothing to do with the church if he could help it. We've never known any witches before. I don't know how Arnes ended up with that man. I don't know *anything*. When Arnes left, he said he was going to find our mother's family, but we never knew them." Siggi's eyes widened suddenly. "Father never spoke of it, but there was—there was a rumor in Midfjördur that a witch killed our mother. I've always thought it was just another child's story but could they—could my mother's family have some sort of quarrel with witches? Could they *be* witches?"

Ylfa looked at Siggi for a long moment. Hrafn wished he knew what she was thinking. She knew everybody in the witching world; if Arnes had set out looking for somebody, Ylfa would know who they were.

"That's all you know about your family?" Ylfa said finally.

Hrafn didn't like her thoughtful expression. It was the same one she wore when she was turning something over in her tangled skein of a mind, following threads of ideas that drew on knowledge he couldn't even begin to imagine.

"What was your mother's name? *Her* mother's name?"

"I—I don't know her mother's name," Siggi said, as though he had only just realized it. "My mother was called Salka."

"And you know nothing else about her people."

"I never knew her. She died when I was born."

"But if your brother went looking—"

"He said he doesn't know," Hrafn snapped. He didn't like the way Siggi's shoulders were hunching down, like every word of Ylfa's questions was a weight he struggled to bear. "Does it matter? We know Haraldar Swift-Eye has his brother, so that's who we need to find."

Ylfa raised an eyebrow. "Is that the whole of your plan, child?"

It was, and they both knew it, but Hrafn didn't see the point in talking about it anymore.

"How did you find out about the fey fire so quickly? You never said. And don't try to tell me you were already in the area."

Ylfa laughed. "People talk to each other, Hrafn, when you don't alienate them with your foul temper. And people talk to me, especially when something strange happens in a place where nothing strange should be."

"Did we put you in danger by coming with you?" Siggi asked. The cat nudged at his hand; he started scratching its ears again.

"Farm boy, the day I'm in any danger from huldu or gossips is the day I lie down and let the worms turn me into soil." She huffed and stood up. "I'm growing bored of all this talking. You'll need more rest if you're going to run about and do something reckless in the morning."

"But we—"

She tugged Hrafn's hair before he could finish. "Rest. We'll get you as close as I can, but that won't be as close as you like."

"Close to what?" Siggi asked.

Ylfa snorted. "The woods of Myrkvidor. *You* might be able to walk right up to them—well, you could have before you stole this boy's knife—"

"I didn't *steal*—"

"But I can't. The people who live there aren't fond of trespassers, and they consider every witch a trespasser."

"Especially you," Hrafn said.

"You won't fare much better, with your sharp tongue," Ylfa said cheerily. She patted the tangled heather wall of the hut. "But we'll get you there."

They parted ways with Ylfa early the next morning. She sent them off with an admonishment to be wary near the Myrkvidor, even going so far as to grab Hrafn's arm to tell him again what danger awaited witches who wandered into the forest uninvited.

For a moment Hrafn was afraid she might do something insane like *hug* him, but in the end she only gave him a good shake and said, "Don't do anything stupid."

Hrafn and Siggi set out on foot, heading south along the Fossvegur. There were few travelers, and news of what had happened in Siggi's village did not yet seem to have spread. Hrafn covered his arms and ducked his head every time somebody approached, because nobody liked to encounter a witch on the road.

He noticed, after a while, that Siggi began placing himself between Hrafn and the strangers as they passed. Siggi didn't say anything about it, and Hrafn didn't ask. Siggi was just trying to avoid trouble. That's all it was.

By late afternoon the day's clouds had cleared, revealing a clear blue summer sky. A gentle breeze whispered through the heather. They passed a fork in the road: west to a fishing village tucked into the fjord, east to the dark, dense forest of Myrkvidor. The road through the Myrkvidor was shorter and faster, but Hrafn steered them toward the fjord instead.

"That's the way Ylfa warned us about?" Siggi asked, looking toward the smudge of dark trees filling the valley in the distance.

"That's the way she warned *me* about," Hrafn corrected him.

"You would probably be safe."

"I've heard people talk about the Myrkvidor, but mostly they just say not to wander off the road or you'll get lost. Why is it especially dangerous for witches?"

"It started about two hundred years ago," Hrafn began, "when the first Lifandfjall settlers were growing old and their children were having children of their own. Some king across the ocean to the east came to dislike the idea of people raising sheep and catching fish in their little stone and turf houses without any of it benefiting him. So he sent warships to claim Lifandfjall for himself."

"Oh, I know all of this," Siggi said. "I know you think all I know about is sheep, but I have heard that story before."

"I don't think that about you," Hrafn said. Maybe he had at first, but he knew better now. "Do you know what happened next?"

"What I learned is the king's people tried to convince the powerful men in Storaska and the Brothers of the Church of the Seven Saints to collect taxes for him," Siggi said. "When they all declined, he sent a force of berserker warriors to take what was not offered freely. The king's witches used magic to drive the berserkers mad with rage and make them more fearsome—is that part true?"

"The king did use magic to make them stronger, yes," Hrafn said. "They were marked with staves and runes. But I don't know if that's why they were mad with rage."

"Maybe somebody should have asked them," Siggi said thoughtfully. "In all the stories, the people of Lifandfjall led the berserkers north, into a trap in the Myrkvidor, where the hidden people were waiting in the woods. The hidden people called down storms from the skies and made the ground tremble, and they transformed the trees into darkwolves as black as the night, with fur as coarse and sharp as needles. The wolves tore the berserkers to pieces. When they were finished, the hidden people woke trylla from caves to drag all the corpses away. And eat them, I suppose." Siggi paused, as though expecting Hrafn to interrupt. "Is all of that another silly child's story?"

"Not a child's story at all," Hrafn said. "It's partly true, but not entirely."

Siggi slanted a glance at Hrafn, amused. "You mean darkwolves aren't born from trees?"

"You've spent your life on a farm and you don't know where puppies come from?" Hrafn asked. "Do you need me to explain it to you? I can draw a picture, if you like, let me just—"

He made a show of drawing his knife and crouching to sketch in the dirt, but Siggi rolled his eyes and pulled him to his feet. "I don't need a *picture*. I thought we were talking about magical beasts coming from trees."

Hrafn tucked his knife away and told himself he was not disappointed when Siggi released his arm. "The picture was going to involve trees. It would have been very detailed and *very* shocking."

"We can pretend I am very shocked," Siggi said dryly, but his cheeks were pink in a way that made Hrafn stare.

He tore his gaze away and cleared his throat. "That part of the tale is true, actually. The darkwolves did spring from the trees of the Myrkvidor. But it wasn't the huldu who called them. The huldu didn't do shit to help. They probably watched from a distance and placed wagers on how many villagers the berserkers would kill."

"What about the trylla?" Siggi asked. "I've heard stories about them. Big monsters, live underground, hides as hard as iron, eat people—are they even real?"

"They're real, but they're all dead now," Hrafn said. "The huldu killed them off long before any of this happened. And even if they hadn't, the huldu never had power over them."

"So who raised the darkwolves and stopped the berserkers? Was it witches?" Siggi guessed.

Hrafn shook his head. "It was the druids."

Siggi made a thoughtful noise. "Huh. I don't know much about druids. All I've heard is that they're secretive women who live a very long time, but I don't know anything else."

"That's all most people know," Hrafn said. "They like it that way. They came here with the first settlers, after the Church and its priests drove them out of their own lands. They've made their home in the

Myrkvidor. They'll let travelers pass through the woods, but if a witch gets close the darkwolves wake up again."

Siggi looked over the land toward the wooded valley. "The ones who came here centuries ago are still alive? But how could they…" He stopped, shook his head, and laughed. "You don't have to say it. I've already realized it's foolish to ask how they could still be alive when walking alongside somebody who has come back from the dead."

Hrafn hadn't even been going to say that, but mostly because he was so taken aback by the sight of Siggi laughing that all of his thoughts scattered. It had been this way ever since they had discovered that Siggi's brother was alive. Siggi still carried sadness and hurt like a burden he had long since grown accustomed to, but it was lighter, somehow, now that he had hope. He had wondered before how a son raised by a father such as Siggi's could have grown up so very kind, but the answer was clear every time Siggi mentioned his brother.

"I understand now why Ylfa warned us away from the woods," Siggi said. "But why would this Haraldar Swift-Eye be hiding nearby, if it's so dangerous for witches?"

"I don't know why Haraldar Swift-Eye ever does anything," Hrafn said. "But probably because he knows other witches will stay away, and he fears them more than he fears the druids and their wolves."

They walked a few steps in silence, then Siggi asked, "Does he really wear people's *skin*?"

"Oh, yes," Hrafn said. "Skin taken from his willing followers, all stitched together into fetching clothes and carved with staves too deadly or insane to ever be used on a living person. Are you sure you want to know? If the magic I do makes you squeamish—"

"It doesn't," Siggi said quickly. "It's not—you're not—" He glanced at Hrafn, squinting in the sunlight, then looked away again. "I want to know."

"I've never met the man," Hrafn said after a moment, "and I have no great desire to do so. But I'll tell you what I can."

And he did, as the road carried them west. He told Siggi of how Haraldar Swift-Eye and his coven used magic that nearly all other witches of Lifandfjall scorned, and how his own sister, Thekla Igullsdottir, had finally confronted him, fought him, killed many his followers, and driven the survivors into hiding. None of it explained what Haraldar would want with Arnes, and Hrafn kept his speculations to himself. Siggi did not need to imagine what torments his brother might be suffering, not yet, not before they knew.

The land dipped toward the fjord, where a small fishing village was tucked against the steep slopes. The wind now carried the scent of the ocean. Birds wheeled and screamed from their cliffside nests along the shore. The road was muddy but broad, and the hillside was dotted with white and blue summer flowers.

Ylfa had hissed countless warnings into Hrafn's ear before leaving them. He had heard them all, but he didn't know what else he could do. He was magically bound to Siggi and did not yet know what that meant or how to break free. Haraldar Swift-Eye knew they were coming. The hidden people were likely looking for him. Soon Birtingr would be looking for him as well. Every witch with a rusty knife and a greedy disposition would be looking for him when word spread that he had come back from the dead and killed a huldu, because both of those things meant he was probably a lot more valuable as a magical object to be gutted and skinned than as a witch himself.

There was danger on every side, waiting for them as surely as the sun would set tonight and rise again tomorrow.

Yet it was a fine day, and not a bad way to spend it, walking with Siggi and answering his hundred questions about witches and druids and warriors of old.

It was late in the day by the time they reached the village on the north side of the fjord, but there were still people out and about, taking advantage of the good weather. A few villagers stared, a few muttered, but nobody spat on Hrafn as they made their way to the docks, so it was better than many towns he had walked into.

Or so he thought, until they started making inquiries among the fishermen at the harbor.

He had hoped to hire somebody to take them across the fjord, so they could more easily approach the Myrkvidor from the south to search for signs of Haraldar's coven. Siggi made the inquiries, because Siggi was very tall and very polite and didn't terrify people with his visage, while Hrafn lingered in the background, trying not to look so frighteningly witchy that the villagers chose to run them out. But he was obviously unsuccessful, because no matter how politely Siggi spoke, the boatmen glowered at Hrafn before flatly stating that they would never take a witch aboard.

The last boatman listened to Siggi's question before rising up from where he crouched curling rope on the dock. He was as tall as Siggi, and even broader, and with one hand on the knife at his belt, he said, "We'll keep our skin to ourselves, boy, and you'd be wise to do the same."

"Oh," said Siggi, surprised, as though he was only just understanding their glares and their refusal. "He's not one of them. We only want—"

"Leave it," Hrafn said. He felt a tiny bit gratified when the big man started at the sound of his voice. "To them, all witches are the same."

The man snorted. "Never yet met one that didn't mean harm to decent folk."

Hrafn was deciding between an insult for the man's entire heritage and suggesting they give up for the night when a voice called out, "Can you row?"

Siggi's head whipped around. "Yes?"

"I need another pair of hands. You look strong enough."

The person asking was not a glowering and suspicious man, but a glowering and suspicious girl, no older than sixteen or seventeen, seated in the sixth and last boat at the village's small dock. Her fair hair was messily braided with string and beads, and she wore a tunic and trousers that had seen better days—probably a very long time ago, if the number of patches and stitches meant anything. She stood in a small boat about four ells long, along except for a mess of nets and crates. She had a smudged face and she smelled of fish. Everything smelled of fish.

"My cousin was supposed to help me with this," the girl said, scowling, "but he's probably got himself drunk and forgot. I can take you over if you help me row and unload."

"I can do that," Siggi said. "But it has to be both of us." He nodded toward Hrafn.

The girl looked at Hrafn for a long moment, so long that he was certain she would refuse.

"Can you carve a bounty stave?" the girl asked.

Hrafn was so surprised to be addressed directly that he stumbled over his answer. "I, uh, yes. You mean for a bounty of fish? Of course you mean for fish. Yes. I can do that."

"Good." The girl pointed at him, then at Siggi. "Stave from you, rowing from you. Hurry up. My uncle will beat me for being late."

Siggi looked at Hrafn again, eyebrow lifted in an obvious question. They didn't have any other choice, not if they wanted to cross the fjord.

Hrafn sighed. "Fine. Let's go."

There was a wind blowing from the west, making the water choppy, but the girl did not raise her square sail. She sat at the other end of the boat and let Siggi do most of the rowing, even though he clearly had little practice with it.

"Where do you want the stave?" Hrafn asked.

"There," said the girl, nodding toward the prow.

That was all she said. Hrafn shrugged, drew his knife, and set to work. A fisherman's bounty stave carved into wood would be more effective traced with blood, but the girl was only taking them across the fjord, and Siggi would be upset if Hrafn cut himself again. So he traced it with seawater instead, dipping the knife into the sea to carve every line just a little bit deeper. He could feel that it would work, although perhaps not very strongly. The magic seemed reluctant to cling to the wood.

"What are you doing?" Siggi said suddenly.

Hrafn looked around, but Siggi wasn't talking to him. He was talking to the girl, who had stopped rowing entirely and now sat with one hand resting on an oar, the other at her belt. Siggi stopped as well.

The sun was low in the sky now, painting the high clouds in vivid shades of red and orange, giving Siggi's golden hair a fiery look. The wind had died down, and with it the roughness of the water. Hrafn's heart skipped with sudden fear, and he felt the echo of Siggi's doing the same. There was no sound except the cry of the birds wheeling around the cliffs and the lap of water against the boat. They were in the middle of the fjord. The Myrkvidor stained the land deep green to the east, swallowing the entire valley from the end of the fjord to the tops of the hills and beyond.

"Who are you?" Siggi said to the girl. He moved one hand slightly, as though to reach for his bag, but stopped.

The girl didn't move at all. Her eyes were golden, like her hair. He supposed she might be pretty enough, if she cleaned up. Her unkempt appearance was no glamour, but her messy hair had shifted away from her face, revealing her ears.

Hrafn adjusted his grip on the knife.

Only the hidden people had ears like that, pointed at the tips.

Hrafn had been expecting them to come boldly, like an earthquake or a landslide, or sneakily under the cover of night. He had not been expecting a girl who smelled like fish.

"What do you want?" he asked.

"You're going to take me to your foul master, raven-hearted witch," said the girl. There was a tight anger in her voice, iron that had not been there when she was weaving her lies on the dock. "And after you have brought me to him, I'm going to kill him."

Hrafn's breath caught, and a wild thought stormed into his mind: they'd come for him, their vengeance would reach Birtingr as well, he'd fallen into their trap. His freedom had been so, so brief.

But the huldu had no reason to hunt Birtingr. And the girl had not yet mentioned the woman in the church.

"Oh, is that all?" Hrafn asked, raising his knife. He struggled to keep his voice calm. "And who is this master of mine that you so want to murder? What has he done?"

"Haraldar Swift-Eye. You're going to help me kill Haraldar Swift-Eye."

Chapter Nine
The Hidden Girl

Other people had been, for the most part, as removed from Siggi's existence as the opposite shore of the great gray ocean, as unexplored as the wider world beyond the weathered little houses that huddled together in the basin of the fjord. Yet unwelcoming as the people of Midfjördur had been, this fisher-girl unsettled Siggi more than they ever had.

It was the way her fey golden eyes fixed on Hrafn, tracing the lines of his staves. It was that the other fishermen had been avoiding her as much as they'd been avoiding Hrafn. Siggi knew fear when he saw it, and the people of Reykhofn feared this girl.

Pushing the oars through the icy water of the Isafjordur, haunted by the dark shadow of the Myrkvidor to their right, Siggi's unease spawned from a single thought:

This boat they'd boarded was entirely *wrong*.

Siggi was no fisherman, but Midfjördur was rife with them, and he'd come to know a fishing faerig when he saw one. Sometimes Father had been summoned to the shore to collect pieces of clinker-built boats that needed welding.

This wooden rowboat was no more fit for fishing than Siggi was. All told, the boat was only three ells long; she might have easily rowed it across the fjord by herself. There were several nets and crates aboard, but the crates were not only empty, but clean, as though they'd never once been used. The stink of fish did not emanate from the ship, but from the girl herself.

Superstition was a fisherman's lifeblood. Though they sometimes enlisted a witch's help, they never took one aboard with them. Yet Hrafn had seemed so determined, and whatever else, Siggi felt certain this girl, however fearsome, could not best the pair of them in a struggle.

When she turned on them and made her demand in a voice as cold as glacial pool, Siggi was not surprised.

"But we don't even know Haraldar Swift-Eye," Siggi said, tightening his right hand around an oar. "We're looking for him too!"

"Liar." With a bitter growl, the girl turned to look at him. "Only witches who serve Swift-Eye would come to Isafjordur."

Her eyes glowed like the sun, and beneath the grime, her skin was as smooth as milk and devoid of freckles or lines. She looked to him like the carved figurehead of a ship, like the clay doll he'd once seen displayed at a trader's booth, like—

"The woman at the church," Siggi said, recalling the huldu relic's final cry. "Are you…are you one of the hidden people?"

"Do I look as though I'm hiding?" the girl demanded, rising to her feet.

Siggi registered for the first time that she was inordinately tall, possibly as tall as he was.

"I don't know," Siggi answered, scanning her face. "But that's what you are, right?"

"Keep asking questions and I'll throw you overboard."

"But you promised us passage!" Siggi argued, gripping the oar tightly. "Hrafn did what you asked, and you promised!"

The girl laughed, sharp as a knife. "I owe no honesty to witches."

Siggi felt the burn of a blade as Hrafn sliced open his palm and held it over the wooden prow. "Siggi. A huldu would sooner kill you than keep a promise."

"So says a filthy witch," the girl hissed, pulling a long, curved ivory blade from her belt.

Hrafn's fist hovered above the bounty stave. "Put that away."

"And let you bewitch me?"

"Rather late for that, pisslocks," Hrafn said simply, and Siggi watched his fingers unpeel, watched him slam his bloody hand down atop the stave he'd placed on the prow.

The golden-eyed girl snarled and bounded forward with uncanny speed, and Siggi was on his feet as well, pulling the oar from the water.

The boat rocked suddenly from side to side.

Siggi felt the jolt in his heart, the strain in his muscles and blood, and some other force that ran through him that he'd only felt when Hrafn used his magic. Whatever was coming, Siggi knew to brace himself. He wrapped one arm around the mast, oar held fast in the other, staring at the blade in the girl's fingers.

"What have you done?" the girl demanded, brandishing her blade.

"Siggi's right," Hrafn trilled, blood seeping from his palm and into the wood grain. "I did as I promised. I carved a stave."

Suddenly, a flash of silver shot out from the water on the aft side of the ship and landed with a heavy plop at Hrafn's feet. It writhed against the deck, slapping its tail along the wood.

"A cod," Siggi said, and it was.

"You asked for a bounty," Hrafn said, clenching his bloody fist closed. He smiled.

And the barrage began.

From the water came a flurry of silver movement and splashing, and then fish were falling thick and fast onto the deck of the little boat. Cod as long as Siggi's forearm, haddock at least half as long, overfed saithe, and countless other fishes leaped from the inlet and aboard the boat, smacking themselves against Hrafn's glowing and bloodied bounty stave, flopping helplessly against the deck.

Siggi covered his head as fish smacked against his skin. They were no paltry minnows. These were full-grown arctic behemoths, enough to feed a family through a winter week. One struck his shoulder with a wet sting. Siggi felt mighty bruises in the making.

Almost immediately the floor was squirming and Hrafn darted forward, knife in hand, aiming for the hidden girl's throat as she hollered in the bizarre downpour—

Siggi knew that Hrafn would kill her without hesitation, that he would cut her head off and leave her just like the woman in the church, he could feel it in Hrafn's heartbeat and see it in the sudden cruel twist of his scarred face, and maybe that's why Siggi, almost unthinking, shouted a warning:

"Look out!"

The hidden girl spun around, slipping on the writhing floor, and Hrafn fell forward with a yelp, knife kissing the air as she stepped aside.

The girl cried out and kicked Hrafn twice in the stomach, and Siggi roared, furious at himself, because why in Storguð's Heaven had he tried to spare a girl who would dare kick Hrafn in the stomach?

He stumbled forward, but slipped on the mass of muscle and scales, seeing spots of white as another large fish struck the side of his head.

If they were big enough to leave him dizzy, Siggi could only guess what they'd do to Hrafn. Hrafn had curled himself in two on the deck, half-buried in the falling fish, covering the back of his head with his hands. The girl had cast her sights on the bounty stave, burying her blade in Hrafn's handiwork once and twice and again and again, making mince of the wood. For some reason Siggi could not fathom, no fish seemed to hit her; they even seemed to avoid her as they fell.

"Hrafn!" Siggi stumbled forward over the first rowing bench and plucked him from the pile of fish as the barrage of falling creatures finally subsided, leaving the three of them shin-deep in flopping wet bodies.

"Don't touch me!" Hrafn spat, and though it was far from the first time, this time the words felt like knives, piercing and defined. Siggi let him go, face hot with shame. Hrafn's glare was almost feral with fury, and for an instant Siggi thought he might turn his knife on him.

"Hrafn, I—"

"Enough!" The girl turned away from the stave, face flushed, rounding on the pair of them, eyes white with rage as she raised her blade.

Siggi shoved Hrafn onto the bench behind him and pulled his oar upward with both hands as the girl met him, catching her blade along its length. The handle splintered but held as Siggi strained against the blow. The force she put behind it was stunning. This girl was unfathomably strong, much stronger than her stature warranted. Siggi took one step back, pressing his calf against the rowing bench to stop himself from falling as fish tails scraped his ankle. Her blade slid as he stumbled, passing close to his knuckles, the tip of it mere inches from his eye.

And just as he'd known Arnes's tooth when he saw it, he knew instinctively that her blade was bone, the rib of a whale or some other deep-dwelling sea monster.

With all his strength he pushed against the oar, forcing the huldu's arms back. Siggi felt as though he were trying to press a tree into the earth, to break a boulder in two as the ship rocked beneath them, threatening to overturn.

The girl shouted as the oar snapped at last, and her bone-blade slid through the air where it had been with the sudden vim, slicing downward along the length of Siggi's tunic, cutting him from collarbone to hip. The girl raised the blade again as fire shot up Siggi's side, blood escaping the shallow but lengthy wound, and Siggi could only hold his hands out to stop her—

Hrafn's flames rose at the girl's back as he ignited his fire stave once again, and she darted back from the both of them, balancing on the side of the ship, panting.

"Fucking fuck, Siggi," Hrafn whispered at his back, and Siggi wanted nothing more than to look at his face, to apologize, to see how he was feeling or what he was thinking, to ask if he could please touch him or even hold him, please—but he dare not turn his back on this girl again.

The girl's golden eyes narrowed as she straightened up. She pointed at Siggi. "What the living fuck are you?"

"I'm Siggi, a blacksmith's son," he huffed, pressing a hand to his stinging, bleeding side.

"No blacksmith's son is strong enough to parry a huldu!" A fish slapped against her shin. Moving quicker than a whipcrack, she slammed the heel of her boot down on its skull, stopping it cold. "What are you, and why are you here?"

"He told you," Hrafn grumbled, on his feet at last. "We're looking for Haraldar, not serving him."

"Why should I believe that?" she demanded.

"Haraldar is holding my brother captive!" Siggi cried, and Hrafn groaned.

For a long moment, the huldu stared at him, and there was no sound but Hrafn's breath at his back, the slowing smack of the fish dying at their feet. "Your brother."

"Yes," Siggi said. "We're trying to save him. Please, you promised to help us cross."

Slowly she sheathed her weapon.

The huldu girl leaned back against the prow, stomping another fish flat beneath her heel. "Oh? You think I should join forces with a witch and his black-handed pet, then?"

Siggi nodded. "Why not?"

"*Why not?* He's just tried to slit my throat!" She laughed suddenly, sharp as a plummeting icicle. She directed her next comment toward Hrafn, glaring at her from beneath Siggi's arm. "Raven-hearted witch, if it weren't for your hulking idiot, I'd have gutted you already."

"He's not an idiot," Hrafn said, eyes flashing.

"No, you wouldn't have," Siggi argued. "You need someone to help you get to Haraldar, right?" The bloody tear in Siggi's side seemed to pound in time with his heart, and he could hear his own breath in his ears.

"Not just any witch will do. It has to be one of Haraldar's." The girl tossed another fish overboard, nonchalant, as though adjusting her shirt. "Even the druids can't find Haraldar. He's shielded by pitch-dark magic."

Hrafn ducked under Siggi's arm and stood before her, sharp shoulders squared. "I've never met a magical barrier I couldn't break."

She eyed him. "With skin so mangled, it would be a crime if you couldn't do as much. I've never seen a witch as pitiful as you."

"And I've never met a huldu that smells like fish and looks like a pisspot turned over," Hrafn growled, "so I suppose today's a day of firsts for all of us."

The girl scowled. Siggi leaned back against the mast, pressing down against the wound at his side, hot blood seeping between his fingers. He wondered whether he should mention it, or if such a wound would mean little to Hrafn, given his own scars.

"Why do you want to kill Haraldar?" Siggi asked, and she raised her eyes to him. "Did he take someone of yours?"

"Not someone, but somewhere," the huldu girl said. "My people have long since lived in the Myrkvidor, cultivating the magic and retaining the sanctity of the ley lines that vein these fjords. But Haraldar and his cult have grown greedy and invaded our lands as if they are their own, spreading the sickness of their black magic. Even the Myrkvidor is suffering its effects, shriveling and dying."

"You're a *druid*?" Hrafn asked. "Didn't know they were taking stray huldu home."

The elf girl scanned him from head to toe, expression unreadable. "As if a monster would know what it is to have a home. Tell me, raven-hearted witch, how many men have cut you and told you it was love?"

Hrafn flinched at that, and Siggi felt a deep pang that was far removed from the long wound igniting his torso. "Please stop fighting. Couldn't you just…ask Haraldar to leave? To take his…um, cult…somewhere else?"

Hrafn snorted. "His own sister drove him away. You think he's here because he wants to be?"

"Easier to kill a witch than reason with one," the girl said, and it struck Siggi then how similar she was to Hrafn, how her words might have been his. "And he'd only plague some other settlement."

"Huldu have their own magic," Hrafn said. "I know that much. Each and every one of you has magic. What's stopping you from finding him?"

"I have magic," the huldu said, her voice tense. "But I was not raised by huldu, and my magic is…it is not what I need to find the skin-witch."

"What sort of magic is it?"

For some reason her cheeks flushed, and she didn't answer.

"Oh, so you're useless, then."

"Unlike you, witch, I need not be useful to have value!"

"Stop bickering," Siggi groaned.

They turned to him as one, and Siggi wondered if they knew how alike they looked, or if they looked nothing alike and the blood loss was starting to confuse him.

"The witch is the one bickering."

Siggi saw that even if her words remained sharp, her posture had eased. Her pale face, her golden circular eyes, the sharp petals of her ears, the tough strength of her frame. The boat was gently adrift, but the water was calm enough. None of the fish had life enough left to wriggle any longer.

"I'm Siggi, and this is Hrafn. What's your name?"

She flinched. "What? Why should I tell you?"

Hrafn snorted, sharing a commiserating glance with the girl. "He's just…*like* this."

Siggi tried to draw himself upright, but the wound on his side felt curiously heavy, an anchor strapped to his torso. "If we're going to help you, I need to call you something."

"What, you don't care for Pisslocks?"

"Fine," she said, ignoring Hrafn. "Holta."

"What's that?" Siggi asked.

"It's a flower that grows even on the sides of cliffs, even in the driest places. Even without soil. They're yellow and white."

"They're also used in medicine," Hrafn supplied, "although I doubt they'd fix what's wrong with this one."

"Fucking—maybe I'll kill you after all, witchling."

Hrafn smirked and the girl glared at him. The wind rose and rocked the boat from side to side, the normal tides returning at last. Siggi felt a swooping in his stomach, in his head, and…

"Oh," he said, and suddenly he couldn't stand anymore. When he lifted his hand away from his tunic, it was drenched in blood.

"Fuck's sake, why didn't you say something?" Hrafn demanded, rushing to his side as Siggi slid down the mast, knees on the slippery deck.

"Didn't you feel it too?" Dazedly, Siggi looked into Hrafn's eyes, into that beautiful true darkness that persisted even now, during the longest of white summers. Hrafn's long eyelashes were so incredibly near as he leaned over Siggi, cursing and pulling his ragged shirt open.

"I didn't feel it," Hrafn said, voice hollow. "Or I did, but didn't…I didn't notice. Fuck."

Because you're far too used to pain, Siggi thought.

Hrafn ran his fingers over the scars that marred the entirety of his own sunken torso. Siggi's ears were ringing, his mind hazy, but he wondered why Hrafn seemed so scared.

"Move aside," the girl—Holta—commanded.

Hrafn tried to fight her, but she pushed him aside as easily as Siggi might have, and knelt before him. Her long, sharp-nailed fingers plucked the cloth away from his wound.

"It's deeper than I intended."

Hrafn put his knife to her throat, but she barely blinked. "Don't touch him."

"How are you going to heal such a big wound, little witch? With that paltry stave on your sorry excuse for a stomach? Please." Holta pushed his knife away. "Find me the largest fish aboard, little witch."

"What?"

She held out her hand and waited, saying nothing more. And Hrafn, for once, did what he was told. He lifted the largest remaining fish from the deck and shoved it into her open palm. To Siggi, woozy and cold, it seemed he was watching another of Arnes's stories unfold.

"It'll have to do," she said simply, and then she pressed the body of the pollock onto Siggi's open wound, drew her bone-made blade, and sliced the head clean off its body so that its blood met Siggi's brokenskin.

The salt water seeped into his wound and he cried out, and even Hrafn staggered. But almost as soon as it started, the pain lessened, and the cold chill of the fish's flesh seemed to ameliorate the burning fire of the salt. As Holta pressed the fish's body into his skin, he saw her golden eyes were glowing, and so were her fingertips, and he felt a rush of bittersweet strangeness—was it her magic?—flow through him.

When Siggi looked down at the wound that had split him from shoulder to stomach, there was no scar, and there was no skin. Instead, where the wound had been there gleamed a long line of silver and gray scales. Siggi pressed a wondering hand against them and felt the coolness of fish flesh on his fingertips. The scales were a part of him now, just as the witch-blade was.

Holta tossed aside the fish's naked skeleton, the offal still trapped inside it. With a heavy, exhausted sigh, she fell back on her haunches, sweat streaking lines down her dirty face. And Hrafn was there, inspecting Siggi's new skin with eyes even wider than usual, big as the sky, stopping just shy of touching him.

"You didn't use a stave," he said, voice imbued with fresh wonder. "I'd heard that about huldu magic, but…I never saw…"

"Staves are for mortal wretches," Holta said, catching her breath. "True magic requires no such monstrosities."

Siggi waited for Hrafn to snap back at her, but a deep, strange hurt registered in the depths of his eyes instead. Quietly, he said: "This is far from useless, Holta."

Siggi felt he knew exactly what Hrafn was thinking: that his magic was ugly, and he and his scars were as well, when Siggi knew it could never be true, but there was no way to say so now and here and with someone watching.

"Holta," Siggi said. "Thank you for saving me."

"Don't thank me," she said, but her beautiful, filthy face seemed to shift. "Once we find Haraldar, you're likely to die all the same."

"Even if you didn't use a stave…" Hrafn said, running his eyes down the silvery scales on Siggi's torso.

Siggi tried not to react, but gods, despite the circumstances he felt blood rushing to the wrong parts of him under the weight of those grazing eyes. Perhaps it was an aftereffect of the magic, but he wanted Hrafn to touch him.

"I thought huldu magic was all about altering nature, manipulating matter or changing the weather and the tides and other extravagant bullshit. You just bonded a dead thing to a living thing, didn't you? What kind of huldu uses flesh-binding magic?"

"One that was raised far from home," she said wryly. "An outcast."

Without warning, the deck began to shake beneath their feet, rollicked by a sudden tremor on the water.

"Fucking hell, what now?" Hrafn said.

The fish that remained rolled as something massive parted the water before them, nearly overturning them as it breached the water's rippled surface. Hrafn and Siggi clung to the side of the boat, but Holta drew herself up and stood on the bow without losing her balance, eyes fixed on the thing that rose from the water, salt and seaweed slipping down its sides.

Even as it surfaced, the stench of decay surfaced along with it. Siggi gagged in his throat, eyes streaming, and watched in abject horror as a great rotting whale carcass rose from the water like a new-formed island.

Water slid down its back, but no air was expunged from its blowhole, for this thing did not breathe. The dead whale was thrice the size of Holta's little vessel. It rose from the water until its belly rested on the surface, heedless of the laws of water and wind. Seabirds screamed and swarmed above it like a hysterical crowd. The air grew colder as mist rose from the water's surface.

The undead whale, gleaming and coated in barnacles and bumps of flesh, slowly opened its stinking maw as Holta's boat struggled on the rolling waves.

Standing on the whale's desiccated tongue, as water drained from the bowl of its mouth, was a man.

He did not lose his balance as the whale rose from the water. He stared holes into the three outcasts on the wooden boat and, when the mouth of the beast was level with the prow of their boat, stepped from the tongue and onto Holta's boat as easily as other men strolled along a beach.

He stood tall, lean as a sapling but taut as a bowstring. He wore a translucent garment made of silk or some other fluid material, belted at the waist, and his arms were as white as snow. His hair was silver, but it can't have been with age, for his face was as timeless and unmarred as Holta's, his ears as pointed as hers, too. He had the same sharp cheekbones and high brow as the woman in the church, but the bottom half of his face was a mass of winding blue scars, as though icicles had formed beneath the surface of his flesh.

"I am the third son of the Godi of Hulduheimer, the seventeenth lord of the hidden realm," he said curtly. "I have come to avenge my most wayward sister, and shall kill you where you stand."

The huldu raised a silver weapon and aimed it at the heart of the little wooden ship. Siggi took each of his companions by the arm and yanked them both to the floor even as the mast splintered above them. Where the harpoon struck, the wood became ice, cracking and dividing, spreading like a blight down the mast.

Siggi glanced from Holta to Hrafn, lost for words.

Hrafn's expression was almost indistinguishable from those of the gape-mouthed fish on the deck, but Holta was *grinning*, her teeth as sharp and silver as fishes' spines.

Chapter Ten
Blood, Ice, and Bone

Hrafn steadied himself with one hand on Siggi's shoulder. Holta stood as well—she didn't need a strapping farm boy for balance—her smile sharp and hungry. The ice spread through the boat with an ominous crackling sound, and the huldu stood at the prow, watching and unmoving, that wretched behemoth of a carcass at his back. It was as if every bad smell Hrafn had ever encountered had joined together to animate that unfortunate whale.

"You will not go unpunished, witch," said Godi the Shit-Stain, or whoever he was. "Have you forgotten how easily your kind grovels before mine, fearful and weak? Your memories are so feeble, so fleeting. I shall remind you."

His voice creaked strangely, as though it were emanating from inside the spreading ice, not from that frozen, dead-eyed face. Sunlight shone on the frost that rimmed every surface of his body. His skin was not just pale but translucent, clear enough to reveal the outline of a skull beneath.

"Oh, fuck him," Hrafn said, with a spark of realization. "He's not really here."

"What?" Siggi yelped, swaying as the boat rocked. "He's right there!"

"The witch is right," Holta said. "It's a sending. There is something dead beneath that glamour, and he's controlling it from the other realm."

Hrafn slashed his knife across his fire staves, first on his wrist, then on his palm. Blood spilled freely as he clasped his hands together. "Try not to let him sink the boat, fish-girl."

Holta was already moving forward, still grinning. Around the boat, the water churned and sloshed with silver scales flickering beneath the surface.

Siggi looked at Hrafn with wide eyes. "Wait, wait, what are you going to—"

"Stay down," Hrafn said shortly.

Hrafn didn't know much about huldu magic beyond what every witch knew. The huldu was animating both the whale and the man from the other realm, using a captured horde of ghosts to send his own image and possess the leviathan's corpse. But the real danger was in his elemental magic: the unnatural ice cloaking the skeleton and spreading so voraciously over their little boat.

The best way to fight ice was with fire.

And Hrafn was very, very good at setting things on fire.

As flames licked along his hands and arms, he jumped onto an empty crate, then launched himself toward the silver harpoon stuck in the mast. As he suspected, it wasn't silver at all but a shaft of ice so solid and dense it felt like metal when he gripped it. The mast groaned under his weight, and cold seared his skin. Nothing he couldn't ignore, however, as he swung his leg up over the harpoon and reached for the mast with both hands. The ice cracked and hissed as soon as he touched it; steam surrounded him in a blinding burst. He smeared his own blood over the veneer of ice, willing fire into every crevice until he heard a series of sharp snaps. He dropped from the harpoon, grasping clumsily at the mast to keep from crashing into the boat.

The mast broke just below the harpoon, and the top half fell into the sea, taking the harpoon with it. Hrafn hoped that would slow the spread of the ice, but it wasn't going to stop the huldu. The only way to stop him was to break his control.

Hrafn dropped back down to the deck. The boat rocked violently and he stumbled, would have fallen, but suddenly Siggi was behind him and catching him with his incredibly unfair amount of solid muscle. The boat jolted again, because the whale carcass was surging forward, driving against the side with relentless force. A horrible grinding sound filled the air as its massive jaw pressed into the wood. Rotting baleen swung like curtains as the boat tilted and lurched.

And all the while the huldu stood, impassive, with ice spreading around him.

Holta was balanced precariously on a bench with her bone-knife in one hand. "Don't stop now, witch! Make yourself fucking useful!"

Siggi said, "What do we do?"

Holta's grin returned, briefly, as she swept her free hand outward over the edge of the boat. The water churned and foamed, a storm caught between the boat and the whale's mouth. Silver flashes of scales appeared in the foam, only a few at first, but gathering and growing in number. Fish began to fling themselves out of the water and toward the whale, flipping themselves higher and higher, like flies swarming carrion.

The fish nipped swiftly at the carcass. It seemed to have no effect at first, but there were a great many fish, and the smell attracted a great many birds too, all converging now to feast upon this unexpected bounty.

The huldu was unimpressed. In that terrible, cracking voice he said, "Your human tricks are charming, but to me your world has only ever been an arena for play."

He held his hand out over the side of the boat. A fountain of water erupted to meet it, forming into another sleek harpoon. The man's eyes, empty beneath the sheen of ice, fixed on Hrafn. He took a graceful step forward.

There was a clatter of wood as Siggi hefted one of the oars like a club. He looked uncertain, as though he didn't think it would do much good as a weapon, but Hrafn couldn't let him hesitate now.

"Just crack the ice!" he shouted. "I'll do the rest!"

Siggi charged toward the man, oar raised. The man shifted both his attention and his harpoon to meet him. Hrafn took the

142

opportunity to dart forward, scrambling over toppled crates and tangled ropes to climb onto a bench. He ducked as Siggi swung at the huldu's shoulder. Hrafn's hands were already slick with his own blood; he needed barely any effort to bring forth new flames. In his right hand he held the little sheepshearing knife, tight so it didn't slip from his grip, and he focused the flames on the blade, heating the well-honed metal until it glowed.

Siggi swung the oar at the huldu, aiming for where his neck met his shoulder. Hrafn felt the energetic beating of Siggi's heart through their bond, felt the vibration of the oar rattling through his own hands and arms, felt the burn in the muscles of those impressive shoulders. There was a loud crack as both the ice and the wood broke. The huldu stumbled under the blow—were all farm boys from the Thrandir so *strong?*—and lashed out with his harpoon, catching the oar with a matching blow that knocked Siggi to the side.

Hrafn saw a ripple across the huldu's visage, the barest blur beneath the frosty surface.

The glamour had slipped. The spell was wavering.

Hrafn jammed the blade, red-hot, into a crack in the ice at the man's neck. It went in as smoothly as it would into soft flesh. Steam hissed around the metal, searing Hrafn's skin, but the pain wasn't worth noticing. He scrabbled at the man's shoulders, struggling to hold on. The ice was too smooth, the man too strong when he grasped at the shirt on Hrafn's back. The mouth of the whale yawned above him, putrid and dark and impossibly huge, even as Holta's fish gnawed away at its flesh, tearing its lower jaw free from the rest of it.

He heard Siggi shout something, heard the sound of ice cracking, and felt a rain of shards around him. He hoped that was the second harpoon shattering. He couldn't waste a glance. With his free hand he drew a fire stave in his own blood, larger than he ever had before, vivid and angry right in the center of the man's chest.

The glamour was almost completely gone now. The skeleton within was a filthy and weathered thing with bits of flesh still clinging. The huldu, cowering in the other realm, was losing control of his spell.

But he was not defeated yet.

"I will cut you down, blackhearted witch," said the huldu. He grabbed Hrafn's hair and yanked his head back. His voice was no longer deep and powerful; it no longer sounded like the voice of one man at all. Instead it echoed like a thousand distant screams woven together, the voices of the captured ghosts he was using to reach this realm. "I will freeze your land into a winter that never ends. For my sister whom I loved, I will have revenge."

Hrafn didn't let go, couldn't let go, not yet. The pain in his scalp was nothing.

"The sister you left rotting beneath a church for a decade?" he spat. "The sister you loved so much it took you ten years to notice the priests had cut her head off?"

Something swung over his head to strike the man's arm. The ice cracked cleanly, right at the elbow, and crumbled away, letting the skeleton's old bones fall.

Hrafn dug his fingers into the cracks at the man's neck, dug them in so far he felt the skin of his fingertips split open. A high, faint wailing surrounded him as the captured ghosts grew angry enough to fight the huldu's spell. Water could not burn, nor could ice, but air could, and that was what Hrafn was counting on as he coaxed the flames into the cracks. The ice was so cold it felt like fire itself, but soon there were flames licking around his fingertips again.

Steam billowed from the boat, hissing and spitting. Meltwater boiled away from the huldu's head, revealing a weathered skull with crab-eaten chunks of gray flesh clinging to it. The melt roiled downward, revealing the bones piece by piece. The skeleton collapsed in its wake.

Then something slammed into the iceman from the side—not something but someone, Siggi, barreling into the man and grabbing for Hrafn at the same time. He pulled Hrafn away and tossed him back as easily as he would a bolt of wool, then he grabbed the skeleton's spine. Hrafn felt a jolt as he did so, as though the act of grabbing the spine had sent a shock through Siggi's entire arm. Siggi's blood was racing, his muscles tensing, his skin tingling, his very bones humming, and for a moment Hrafn could feel all of it.

There was a sharp cracking sound—not the ice, but the bones themselves, as they shattered into a shower of splinters. Hrafn flinched and ducked his head; the bone shards pricked like needles where they glanced over his skin.

When he looked again, Siggi was lifting the rest of the shattered skeleton, still held together by tendons and seaweed and frozen flesh. With a smooth, strong motion, he hefted it over the side of the boat and into the mouth of the dead whale.

"What the fuck," Hrafn said. He struggled to catch his breath. "What the *fuck* did you just do?"

Siggi looked back at him, his eyes wide. "I didn't—I just wanted, I wanted him to stop, I don't…"

He trailed off, staring down at his hand, which the bone shards had sliced open in half a dozen places. Hrafn felt each of those tiny cuts as well; his own fingers twitched as Siggi closed his hand.

"How did you do that?" Hrafn demanded.

"I don't know!" Siggi answered, his voice rising to a frightened shout.

"You broke a fucking huldu spell!"

"I didn't! You did that!"

"Both of you, shut up!" Holta threw one of the oars at Siggi. "The whale will take us down when it sinks. Row, you idiot."

Both Siggi and Holta were rowing, but Hrafn was pretty sure the fish beneath the boat were doing most of the work to push them away from the foundering whale. As soon as the huldu's grip on the human skeleton had been broken—as soon as Siggi had *shattered the bones* with his *bare hands*—so too had the man's control of the whale. All that was left was the carcass, sinking to the seafloor again.

"The villagers will have noticed that," Hrafn said, staring at the birds wheeling angrily overhead, diving down to grab what bits of whale or fish they could.

He splashed water onto his hands. The salt water stung every one of his cuts and small burns, but he needed to scrub some of the blood away. He felt shaky and a bit weak; he had bled more than he intended keeping the fire going. His ears still rang with the howls of the captured ghosts. They hadn't sounded like the ghosts of Draugamyr, where he had first learned to hear the dead years ago. They had sounded older, wilder, as though they had long ago forgotten how to cry with human or huldu voices.

"You killed a huldu," Holta said. "That's why he came for you."

"Yes," Hrafn said. "She was mostly dead already, but I finished her."

"What do you mean?" she demanded.

Hrafn lifted his head to look at her. "Her head was bound in a spell and buried beneath a church."

Holta made a face and spat. "Priests."

"Every last one of them is a bastard," Hrafn agreed.

"How did he find us?" Siggi asked.

Hrafn twisted around to look at them, then turned back to Holta. "How *did* he find us? Did he track us? Did you lead him here?"

Holta narrowed her eyes. "You said yourself, witch, I am an outcast. I have nothing to do with him."

Hrafn flipped his knife around in his hand. He couldn't tell if she was lying, and it bothered him. But that wasn't the most immediate problem. The huldu had found him once; they would find him again. He had to locate Siggi's brother before they came back.

He said, "What do you know about where Haraldar and his men are hiding?"

She glowered at him. "If I could find him, I wouldn't need the likes of you. They make their home in this fjord, in a hidden cove or cave. That is all I know."

There were fish entrails in her hair. Hrafn decided not to tell her.

"Right. Well, you know that they're here because other witches stay away, right? But even if they're hiding themselves with magic that druids can't see, there will be traces." He took a breath. He was

146

so tired. The last thing he wanted to do was slice another stave open, not when his skin was smarting with cuts and burns.

But they couldn't just drift around until he felt better, not with the village fishermen no doubt coming soon to investigate the commotion. Or Haraldar Swift-Eye, for that matter. Hrafn pressed the blade to the finding stave in the center of his chest. Behind him, Siggi made a quiet sound, neither a gasp nor a word, and Hrafn expected him to protest, to ask again if he had to do that—but Siggi said nothing. Of course he said nothing. They were going to find his brother. What was another splash of Hrafn's blood compared to that?

Hrafn closed his eyes to concentrate, focusing on the feel of the fresh blood in the palm of his hand, the way it teased and shifted. The sound of the oars was rhythmic, almost soothing. It would have been as effective as a lullaby--if it weren't for the shrieks of the stupid seabirds screaming over dead fish and chunks of whale.

It was much harder than it had been in the church. Haraldar Swift-Eye was a skilled witch; he had hidden his coven well.

The tug, when he felt it, was faint. So faint he thought at first he was imagining it. It didn't feel like anything big enough or strong enough to be a powerful concealment spell. It felt, instead, like the barest memory of a trail, a flickering whisper of something magical.

"That way," Hrafn said, pointing. He didn't open his eyes to see what he was pointing at. It was easier to feel the tug without letting his vision confuse him. "It's that way."

Siggi and Holta rowed for a little while, adjusting their direction as Hrafn pointed, until finally the sound of the oars slowed, then stopped.

Siggi said, hesitantly, "But there's nothing but—oh! Look at the water."

Hrafn opened his eyes. They had rowed the boat right up to the southern side of the fjord, where a cliff of crumbling black basalt met the water. It looked like there was nowhere to go—but at the base the water rippled smoothly rather than lapping against the stone.

It was the illusion of a cliff face, but even a very good illusion had its flaws. Holta reached over the side of the boat and, with a flick of her wrist, directed a large fish to swim toward the cliff face, just beneath the surface of the water. There was no hesitation as it passed, no shimmer or falter, and a moment later the fish returned, unharmed.

They passed through without incident. Beyond the illusion was a dark inlet, surrounded on both sides by high rock walls that blocked the evening sun. Holta and Siggi slowed their strokes and let the boat drift along. There was no beach, only a bit of gravel among jagged black rocks, with a small, rickety dock. From the dock, a narrow trail twisted deeper into the inlet, out of sight. There were no people to be seen, no buildings, no hints of light. Only that lonely dock and the trails and the silence.

It was utterly quiet. The seabirds in the fjord sounded as distant as dreams, and the lap of the water against the boat was no more than a whisper. When the boat tapped against the dock, that small thud felt so loud Hrafn started.

Holta jumped out to tie up the boat, then looked around warily.

"Is there anybody here?" Siggi asked softly. He helped Hrafn out of the boat before following himself. His expression was hard to read in the dim light. "Do you smell that?"

The air smelled of salt and fish and low tide. A hint of blood, but Hrafn knew that was coming from himself. Wet stone. Something earthy and green.

Faint smoke, barely lingering.

And rot. Not the rot of the dead whale they carried with them, but the septic, sickly-sweet stink of meat rotting in the open air.

They moved up the path quietly, bunched together as a small group. Hrafn felt absolutely no shame about letting Holta go first; she was the strongest of them, even if she wasn't currently commanding her own berserker army of fish. But he made sure to shoulder himself in front of Siggi. He still had blood left to shed, if he needed to.

The path wound through the narrow ravine of rocks before opening to reveal a small cluster of buildings. There was a stonewalled longhouse in the center; its wooden roof had been burnt away, recently enough that the black wood still smelled of char. A woven mat hung over the doorway. There was blood splashed across the mat, the doorframe, the flat stones of the threshold.

There were a few small huts around the longhouse. A broad stain of blood darkened the ground outside one of them. Near another, a group of birds picked greedily at a dark clump. The birds squawked and scattered as they approached, but returned to their scraps quickly.

Just beyond that pathetic little village, the ravine ended at a steep rock cliff, and at the base of the cliff was a cave. Siggi pushed past Hrafn and ran to the mouth of the cave. It wasn't very deep; they could see the back from where they stood, even in the shadows of the ravine. The entrance was arched, the stone black and weathered. Hrafn took a couple of steps inside to look around. It was the same cave they had seen in the scrying. There was nobody inside.

"Arnes," Siggi whispered.

He looked around helplessly. It was all Hrafn could do not to reach out with a reassuring touch. It was never going to be as easy as walking into a camp of skin-witches and finding Arnes right there for the taking, but Hrafn realized that at some point he had started to think that maybe—maybe they might find Siggi's brother. Maybe they could save him, as Siggi wanted.

Maybe.

There was a ratty blanket in a heap, a cracked wooden bowl on the ground with days' old food spilling from it, and scuff marks in the dirt. Beside the blanket was a polished wooden ring driven into the stone. There had obviously been some sort of struggle—it was so easy to imagine Arnes flinging the bowl at Haraldar in impotent rage— but nothing remained of whatever shackle or rope they had used to bind Arnes.

On the stone wall near the entrance was another smear of blood, much like those they had seen outside. It was roughly the size and shape of a man, as though somebody had been slammed against the wall repeatedly, until his body broke open.

"What happened here?" Siggi asked. "Where is everybody? Where did they go?"

"Most of them are still here," Holta said.

They turned to find her standing at the mouth of the cave.

"In the longhouse," she said. "Dead and burned."

"No." Siggi was still for a moment, so terrifyingly still it was as though he had been frozen. His voice was small, strangled. His face drained of blood. *"No."*

He turned quickly, boots scraping on the dirt, and stumbled as he ran out of the cave.

Hrafn had been doing fairly well, not thinking about how he had been dead and burned only a couple of days ago. He didn't remember any of it except the surprise of Einar knifing him in the heart and the pain of waking. He had no scar but for the small line left by Einar's blade. He didn't want to remember it. He had seen witches burned before. He had seen their fear beforehand, heard their screams while they died, turned away from their twisted remains after. It wasn't as though he could ever forget. He didn't need to think about it.

But it wasn't the stink of the dead or the buzz of swarming flies that made his stomach churn and his gorge rise when he stepped into the longhouse. It was knowing that this could have been him—that it *had* been him, and he would have stayed that way had Siggi not picked up his blood-forged knife.

There were seven corpses in the longhouse, laid out in two rows. The fire had died out before it consumed them entirely. There was enough left of each to see that their skin had been torn—not flayed, not peeled away, but ripped apart, seemingly from the inside. There was no pattern to the wounds; one man's entire chest was shredded, whereas another's face had scarcely any skin left. Hrafn could not imagine what weapon or magic could cause such wounds.

Flies swarmed over every body, lifting into dense clouds as Siggi stepped from corpse to corpse, peering at every face. Some of the faces were burned, others were skinned. Siggi shook his head at each one before moving to the next.

"Arnes isn't here," Siggi said. His voice was tight, still scared, but there was a tremble of hope in his words. "He's not here. None of these men—they're witches. They're all witches, aren't they? They aren't—he's not here. He's not here."

Hrafn looked over the corpses. "Neither is Haraldar Swift-Eye."

Chapter Eleven
The Women of the Wood

Briefly Siggi imagined that every corpse in the longhouse bore Arnes's face. Not until he had stared at each of them in turn, noting the staves tattooed on each, did he convince himself otherwise. He exhaled, relief flooding his veins, but suddenly the stench of ash and death was overwhelming, the buzzing of the flies loud as roaring tides.

Hrafn did not enter the longhouse, but waited in the entrance, tilting his face away from the mausoleum. Like Siggi, Hrafn had seen too many ashes of late.

Was Siggi another fire burning, then? Ever since Siggi had shattered the skeleton's spine in the fjord, Hrafn had not met his eyes. Siggi felt the absence of his gaze like another wound, one he couldn't see the edges of.

Why was it then—in that terrifying instant when Siggi watched the melting ice-huldu vie against Hrafn and his breathtaking flames, as the huldu gripped Hrafn by the hair and Siggi felt the searing burn on his own scalp, as Siggi roared and leaped toward them both— that Siggi felt a sense of belonging?

Siggi hadn't thought. He had simply shoved Hrafn away from that monster, gripped its sopping spine in his cursed hand and willed the bones to shatter, to disassemble, to *cease being*. Like scratching an itch or pulling a splinter from a sheep's hoof, Siggi had identified the problem and dealt with it.

And as the spine splintered into a hundred pieces, Siggi had felt, for the first time in his existence, that he had done something entirely *right*. Like there was nowhere else in the world he should possibly be other than between Hrafn and those things that might harm him.

But now Hrafn would not look at him, and Arnes was still lost.

"If Haraldar's not here, where's he gone?" Holta said, pushing past Hrafn and kicking at the coals of the fire. "Purging the colony's one thing, but Haraldar needs to die too."

Siggi allowed himself to hope. "But wherever he is, Arnes must be with him."

"Perhaps he is, but perhaps Swift-Eye's wearing him as a coat," Holta mused, crinkling her nose as she leaned down to inspect the nearest witch. "No telling, really."

Siggi flinched, but Hrafn snarled at her. "That's his fucking brother. Doesn't that mean anything to you, Pisslocks?"

"Haven't any brothers," Holta said, indifferent to the chastisement. "Hmph. Whoever killed this lot must have been a witch, or someone equally foul, to have found the place. Those strange wounds look like witchcraft to me."

"Perhaps," Hrafn said, "the attacker was Haraldar himself."

Siggi looked at Hrafn, whose eyes remained fixed on the corpses. "What? But—why? Why would he kill his own cult?"

"I'm not sure," Hrafn said, almost to himself.

"Oh, there could be a thousand reasons," Holta reasoned. "All witches are mad, and Haraldar the maddest among them. Frankly, I don't care what's killed them, only that they're dead and gone from here."

"You'll care if whoever or whatever's done this isn't gone and has no plans to leave your woods alone."

Holta's eyes narrowed. "Let them try. Our darkwolves are always hungry." She eyed the dying embers. "We need to report this mess to the yfirmaður."

"The yfirmaður? What's that?" Siggi asked.

"Not what, but who." Holta nearly smiled. "She'll want to know our wretched neighbors have come to a well-deserved end."

Siggi stared back at the lonely dock as they rowed back the way they'd come. When they reemerged in the fjord, they found the water patterned with choppy waves, the opposite shore lost in the gloom of a thick fog. The air was glacial enough to make Siggi shiver, and he knew Hrafn must be cold as well. None of them spoke of it.

Holta took the helm. "Just row. I'll get us there."

The oars creaked in their hands, and the waves smacked against the hull, and Siggi was all too aware of Hrafn's silence. The lingering smell of the corpses and the fire made Siggi's nose itch, and the rocking of the boat made him queasy.

Hrafn had sat behind Siggi so Siggi could not steal glances at him, but Siggi would not abide that. He stood and turned himself around, rocking the boat and bumping his knees against Hrafn's before taking up his oar again. Against the white fog and silver light, Hrafn was more striking than ever, black and red and delicate despite it all.

How was it that so cold a figure warmed Siggi so?

"You won't look at me," he said.

Hrafn pursed his lips and raised his eyes to Siggi's. "I'm looking at you now."

He was, and now the black glass of his unusual irises reflected the white of the world around them. Siggi wondered whether Hrafn had thought about his own family, whether he'd ever questioned where they came from, whether it was a land far away from Lifandfjall.

"Siggi," Hrafn said. "What haven't you told me?"

In the depths of the mist, a lone seabird called out to no one.

"About what?"

Hrafn stopped rowing. Holta perched on the prow of the ship, cloaked somewhat in the fog. If she was paying any attention to them, she didn't show it. "About *you*."

Siggi felt the strangest thrill tickle his chest at that, but before he could wonder at the feeling, Hrafn spoke again.

"I know you're no witch. But when you destroyed that sending today? That was magic. Magic of a kind I've never seen. No staves, no blood. And I can't stop thinking about the tooth."

"The tooth?"

"Never mind."

Hrafn began rowing again, but the moment he dropped his gaze, Siggi grabbed Hrafn's arm, holding him still. He felt the sting there, as he'd felt all the wounds Hrafn had given himself, felt the woozy loss of blood. But mostly he felt the weight of Hrafn's stare, the marked distrust in those round pools.

"Hrafn. Please? Tell me what you're thinking."

"Your brother's tooth," Hrafn said, staring at Siggi's cursed hand. "The huldu girl is wrong about many things, but it's true you're no ordinary farm boy. I've ignored it when I could, but…I can't anymore. Have you been keeping secrets from me?"

"I haven't! I wouldn't!" Siggi cried, wounded. "I don't know what's happening to me, or how I know things I know. I just…know them."

"I should have realized," Hrafn muttered. "Your kindness was always implausible."

"Is that what you think?" Siggi said, and he let Hrafn go. "You think I've been lying to you this whole time."

Hrafn looked at him. "My witch-blade. The soul-bond. That was no simple magic."

"I told you, I don't know why that happened, why any of this has happened—"

"And you know," Hrafn said, and Siggi felt Hrafn's pain infecting his heart, an ache in his sternum profound enough to make him gasp, "I *do* know better. The sight of a witch sends any *decent* person fleeing for the hills, but you? You were too kind to me. You…you *touched* me. I should have fucking seen the truth."

"Hrafn," Siggi choked, reaching for him again. "Hrafn, don't—"

But Hrafn got up and walked to the back of the little boat, arms folded against the cold. And though it was no great distance from one end of the ship to the other, the fog hung so heavy that Siggi could hardly see Hrafn at all.

The fog obscured Myrkvidor until the ship ran ashore and Holta led them forward. Siggi smelled wet earth and a sharp clean scent that must have come from the pines. He felt the wind die, caught in boughs on all sides. He could see glimpses of the blight Holta had mentioned: leaves and needles withered black, branches broken with dough-soft wounds inside, grasses withered to gray in the underbrush.

"This is what having Haraldar so close did to the forest?" Siggi asked.

Holta nodded grimly. "Witchcraft is greedy. It cares nothing for the harm it causes. The yfirmaður says it can heal. Maybe now it will."

"What Swift-Eye does is *not* normal witchcraft," Hrafn muttered. He was behind Siggi, out of sight and out of reach.

Siggi didn't want them to start arguing again. "Will you be able to find your way in this fog?" he asked.

"It's my home," Holta scoffed, stepping over a fallen tree, tracing a path Siggi couldn't see. "I could find my way without eyes."

"Ooh, then perhaps you're ready to give up an eye at last?" purred a voice from between the trees.

Siggi felt Hrafn tense and raised his arms to shield him.

"Fidelma," Holta growled. "What in Eldkona's name are you doing here?"

"A fine question to ask, and one you should answer as well," said another voice, this one older, deeper. "We sent you to the harbor to fetch supplies, not two ragged children."

"Show yourselves!" Hrafn called, and Siggi felt the flames flare up on Hrafn's hand, that stave reopened for the thousandth time. From all sides, Siggi sensed movement within the fog.

"Put that fire out," chided the deeper voice. "This is a forest."

From the mist, they emerged. Silhouettes that Siggi had mistaken for tree trunks stepped forward and revealed themselves to be something else entirely. A dozen women of every age in strange, patchwork garb braced them on either side, bows drawn and arrows notched. Though some of them looked like the pale women of Midfjördur, others had clearly come from elsewhere, skin nearly as dark as the volcanic black beaches, hair as black as ink bound in long braids, plaits heavier than Siggi had seen. One or two looked as though they could have been from the same far-off land as Hrafn, their dark, angled eyes shining and dark as his. These were women of the world, women who had seen and been places Siggi had scarcely dreamed of. Stone and glass beads adorned their matted hair, and they wore bones and stones and wooden talismans around their necks. They were clothed in thick, worn leather jerkins and pants.

Their faces bore curling tattoos, and every one of them, old and young, had a round red stone in place of where a right eye should have been. One of these astonishing women, her skin the brown of damp juniper driftwood, her hair voluminous as a blazing fire and matted like a bristle bush, held a bow unlike any Siggi had ever seen before. The bow was made not of iron or wood, but of curiously smooth stone.

"Kind of you to meet us so close to shore," Holta said to her, with a grin.

"Daughter, you made a racket profound enough to draw every creature from hiding," she said, revealing herself to be the second speaker. She placed a black-nailed hand on Holta's shoulder. "It's not like you to bring home guests. And magical ones, at that."

"Well, today has been an exceptional day."

"So we've seen." The woman raised her eyebrows. "I assume you'll tell me all about it?"

"I will." Holta's lips twisted. "Witch, Siggi—meet the yfirmaður, leader of the Women of the Woods."

The flames in Hrafn's hands grew brighter, and the bowstrings tauter, but the bristle-haired woman, the yfirmaður, laughed.

"Didn't I tell you not to cast a flame in this wood?"

"He's an idiot," Holta said. "They both are."

"I'd expect nothing else of any *friends* of yours." It was the first voice they'd heard, and it belonged to a girl, dark haired, brown skinned, and freckle faced.

"Shut it, Fidelma," Holta spat.

"An idiot I may be," Hrafn snarled, "but Siggi isn't one, and I'm not foolish enough to trust fucking *druids*."

Siggi threw an arm out in front of Hrafn, heart pounding. "Please, he means no harm."

"Oh, but he does," the bristle-haired woman said, gazing at Hrafn, her expression strangely sad. "And why wouldn't he? A creature carved from hate has never known how to be anything but hateful. To think the witches have stooped to maiming children. It disgusts me, boy, what they've done to you, and whatever else may pass between us, I'm sorry for it."

Hrafn seemed taken aback, but he didn't put out his flames even as she signaled for the women to lower their weapons.

"Thank you," Siggi said, and he looked at Hrafn. "Please."

With a sigh, Hrafn curled his fist shut, extinguishing his little fire.

"My name is Siggi, and this is Hrafn. What are your names?"

The yfirmaður laughed as her comrades shifted in discomfort, beads clinking.

"Oh, you are an odd thing." She held up a hand. "Of course, I am known for being polite." One of the other women snickered. "My people call me yfirmaður, but you may call me Gráinne of the Dark Wood. I am this child's mother, and the leader of this *humble* little band of priestesses."

"She's not my real mother," Holta said.

At that the freckled one—Fidelma—snorted. "Oh no shit, fish-elf."

Gráinne laughed. "Daughters, you are as charming as ever. Tell me, dearest guests: did you have anything to do with the sudden exodus of birds from the north side of the fjord, the fish washed ashore, and the rising reek of huldu magic on the water? Was it a sending, or something worse?"

"A sending," Holta confirmed. "A powerful one."

Siggi couldn't help himself. "You could smell the magic? From all the way over here?"

"Oh, yes. We could smell it, and see it, and very near taste it. It's a thick haze in the air, boy, thicker than this fog." Gráinne tapped her red-stone eye. "You may not be able to see the sheen of magic, but we certainly can. I hope our guests are willing to tell us why the huldu have attacked our fjord today?"

"Oh, that's the least of it," Holta said with a grimace. "We found Haraldar's camp."

At that, a susurrus rose among the witches.

Even the mocking one, Fidelma, seemed astounded. "What, just like that? Did you kill him, Celestina?"

"Enough!" With a single gesture, Gráinne silenced the druids. "Come. We'll talk over supper."

Siggi's stomach groaned. "That would be wonderful."

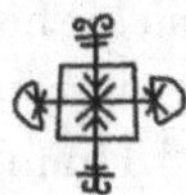

The druids did nothing to bind them as Gráinne led them into the woods. They did nothing, but surrounded them on all sides as the path led deeper into the dark forest. Even as the fog lifted and the path narrowed, the women branched away from it, walking alongside them over browning pine needles, through drooping ferns, under curtains of thick moss, making nary a sound. As the women moved, Siggi thought he could smell a strange perfume, like the peculiar spices Arnes had brought home from the harbor once, the scent of another world.

Siggi had never been in a true forest before. There was a small grove of trees near the Erikson farm, but nothing more than a copse of rowans. Here there were evergreens tall and looming, stretching the arms of their laden branches toward one another as though longing to embrace, closing the travelers off from the sky. The pungent scent of sap, the curious absence of birdsong, the distant trickle of an unseen stream, and the soft crush of needles underfoot. All of it was new, and all of it may have been wonderful, but Siggi could not seem to ground himself.

Hrafn had placed himself silently in front of Siggi once more. Hrafn's shoulders were slumped, and Siggi felt the pulse of his exhaustion. Bleeding himself took more than he'd ever admit. Siggi stared at the nape of Hrafn's neck and remembered the rows of corpses, the empty cavern where Arnes's shadow still seemed to linger. He felt the warm solidity of the skeleton he'd shattered at will, he recalled the mistrust in Hrafn's eyes, and then his mind cycled through it all again, until Siggi could barely feel himself walking.

He stumbled on a root.

Gráinne looked back at him, cocking an eyebrow. "Clumsy for a huldalf, aren't you."

"Sorry," Siggi said absently, blinking, regaining his footing.

"Keep moving," Holta said, but Hrafn had stopped, stock-still on the shadowy path. Siggi couldn't see his face, but the renewed tension in Hrafn's shoulders gave him pause.

"What did you call him?" Hrafn demanded, ice in his voice. "What did you say?"

"Your friend," Gráinne said, frowning at him, holding up a hand to stop the others. "I said he's clumsy for a half-huldu, a *huldalf*. Not that being huldu is any certain guarantee of grace, mind you. I mean, look at my errant daughter—"

"Gráinne," Holta said quietly, "he doesn't know. *They* don't know."

"What?" Siggi said, deeply confused, ears ringing. "We don't know what?"

The druid women, even one above who had been trailing them through the branches—all of them began to whisper again, a sound that rose like an uncanny breeze in the deep woods.

"Say it again," Hrafn demanded.

"What?" Gráinne's eyes went wide. "But he reeks of huldu magic, and there's huldu magic binding him to you, clear as water! Come now. It's beyond obvious, isn't it?"

"Obvious," Siggi echoed, ears ringing, breath suddenly broken. "What's obvious?"

Hrafn turned slowly to face him, and the look on his face was one Siggi couldn't begin to quantify, equal parts horrified and sad and scared.

"H-hrafn?"

"*Of course.* You're not human."

Siggi dropped his hands and fell to his knees as if he'd been kicked, and then everything went black as he forgot or remembered himself in the dark of the Myrkvidor.

On the day Arnes set sail from Midfjördur, Siggi found him digging through the chest beneath their bed. Arnes's woolen coat was laid out on the cot, and his sheepskin gloves, and a little knife he'd forged for himself. His rucksack was open.

Immediately, Siggi could not breathe.

"You're leaving?"

He waited for Arnes to deny it, but Arnes never lied to Siggi. "Siggi. I'm sorry. The ship is waiting."

"You weren't going to tell me?" Siggi couldn't stop the tears; he never could. "You weren't going to say goodbye? Arnes?"

"Siggi—"

"I'll tell Father," Siggi said, tears falling. "He'll stop you. He needs you in the forge."

"Needs me," Arnes muttered darkly. "Oh, I'm sure he thinks so."

"I'll run there now and tell him."

"You won't," Arnes said simply. "Siggi. Please. Come here."

Siggi sat beside him on the cot, staring at the seams of the coat, the weave of the blanket, anywhere but at his brother's face.

"Siggi, you're as tall as I am now," Arnes said softly. "Won't you look at me?"

"No." Siggi wiped his running nose.

Arnes sighed. "I know it's bad when you've no questions. Won't you even ask why?"

Siggi hadn't thought to ask that question, because he could think of ten thousand reasons to leave Midfjördur. To escape the bitter cold and bitter words of the villagers, to escape the pounding of Father's fists, to experience a world less prone to icing over.

"I've told you so many stories, haven't I, Siggi? About all kinds of things. But there are some stories I've never learned the endings of. And one especially, it's unbearable. I can't stand not knowing who she was."

Siggi knew *she* meant their mother.

"Brynja Gottsdottir says a witch killed her," Siggi remembered. He knew by then not to take the blame for her death, not in front of Arnes.

"Brynja Gottsdottir talks a load of shit," Arnes said with sudden spite. "And I'm tired of listening to whispers. Mother died, and Father will not say a word about her. But she came to Midfjördur from the North. We must have family out there somewhere, and I'm going to find them, Siggi. I *need* to find them."

"But…Arnes. Why now? Must you leave me alone with Father?"

Arnes hesitated. He looked uncertain as Siggi had rarely seen him, staring at his hands, where burns and calluses shone red and pink and glossy. "I just…I need to know who they are, and why she left them, and if she…who she was." He swallowed. "Who *we* are."

"You're my brother," Siggi said firmly. "That's all I need."

"Is it? Is it really?" Arnes took both of Siggi's hands and squeezed them tight. "Do you know, Siggi, that I have questions too? Not nearly so many as you, but…well. Some of mine I dare not ask aloud."

And Siggi realized that Arnes's hands were shaking, his voice tremulous.

"Arnes…are you afraid?"

"Sometimes I wonder," Arnes said, as if to himself, "what she was running from."

"Arnes?"

Arnes lowered his hands. "Siggi. I will come back for you, with answers and endings to share. But in the meantime, you must do your best to heed Father, to keep yourself to yourself, and avoid the villagers, Brother Hamon, and the church especially—"

"No. I'll go with you now." Siggi flipped open the lid of the chest, pulling out his own tattered woolen coat, Arnes's hand-me-down, far too small for either of them now.

"You *can't*, Siggi."

Siggi ignored him. He was old enough, strong enough now to pull Arnes's hand away. In silence, he gathered a few paltry things from the shelves, his sheepshearing knife, his scrying stone, a crumbling lump of soap, a patchwork pair of trousers drying beside the fire.

"Siggi, I said no. It's going to be dangerous."

"More dangerous than Father?" Siggi asked, pulling his winter boots and an iron spade out from beneath the bed. "Have you packed a cooking pot? Blankets?"

"Siggi," Arnes said. "I've booked passage only for one."

"No."

"*Siggi*," Arnes said, and suddenly his tone had changed.

Later, Siggi told himself it never happened that way, that he must have imagined it.

But in that instant, he felt cold metal tighten on his wrists, watched the fire poker stretch longer and wrap itself inexplicably around the sturdy wooden pillar at his back, strapping Siggi to the pole that upheld the ceiling. In an instant, Siggi was bound to the turf house like livestock to a post.

"Arnes? What? How did you—Arnes, no!"

"Siggi," Arnes said, lowering his hand, voice broken. "Stay."

"Arnes! *Arnes!*"

Siggi pulled against the inexplicable manacle with all his strength, until the beam threatened to give way. Arnes kissed him on the forehead, ignoring his cries and questions. Face set, he pulled on his pack, opened the door, and left Siggi alone in the groaning cabin, kicking his feet against the dirt, sobbing to no one.

Father found him that way some hours later. He hit Siggi and asked where Arnes was, and when Siggi only wept he hit him again and again until Siggi finally choked out an answer. Father cursed and left him bound there, hurrying down to the harbor, but the boat and Arnes were already gone.

Later, Father used smelting tools to free Siggi from the post, burning Siggi's wrist as he did so. Siggi wanted to look closely at the bent poker, wanted to know how Arnes had contorted cold iron without fire. Was such a thing even possible? But Father pulled the poker away and held it firmly in his hand.

"Say nothing of any of this," Father said. "Come to the forge. It's time you become a useful creature."

"Idiot. Incredibly heavy thing to carry, you are."

Siggi opened his eyes. He found himself gazing at a ceiling of woven wood through which stripes of sunlight permeated.

"Idiot," she—Holta—said again, as Siggi sat up.

He was lying in a heap of blankets in a little wooden hut. A fire burned in the center of the room. The wall was hung with handwoven tapestries, and the air was clogged with an odd, spicy-sweet incense that barely escaped through a hole in the roof. Holta sat beside the fire on a stone-carved stool, frowning at him.

"Where's Hrafn?" Siggi croaked, trying to stand. He put his hand on his chest and felt Hrafn's heartbeat there beneath his own, faintly, but knew somehow he was not nearby.

"I don't think he wants to see you at the moment, half-blood."

"Half-blood," Siggi said, slumping. "I'm not."

"You are."

"I didn't...I don't know. I didn't know!"

"I believe you, not that it matters. You aren't clever enough to hide something like that." Curiosity lurked beneath her scowl. "Was it your mother or your father?"

Siggi pressed his palms into his eyes. "What?"

"Which of them was a huldu?"

"I…I don't know." He lowered his hands. But Siggi did know, and wondered that he had ever failed to know: it wasn't Father, so it must have been Mother.

"Did you know all along"—he swallowed—"what I…that I was what you say I am."

"I knew when I saw your magic. The magic of the hidden people isn't the same as black, human magic. There are no staves, no mutilations. Huldu are born with the ability to control a single element or a single form of life. For me, it's fish, which is fairly fucking useless and caused all sorts of trouble for me, before my banishment. But for that bastard in the fjord, it was ice, and for you it's obviously—"

"Bone," Siggi breathed. "Bone."

"Yes. And magic like that—well. That's no small thing. Maybe you're descended from huldu royalty." She spat in the dirt. "Classist assholes, the huldu."

"Can…can the hidden people…can any of them bend iron?"

She shrugged. "It wouldn't surprise me. They can do all sorts."

Siggi recalled Arnes, the manacle he'd made from that poker, every time Father had said Arnes was made to be a blacksmith, the real heir to the forge. Siggi wondered how a man like Father had ever met a huldu, how she had ever loved him enough to bear two children with him. Or if she had endured it only because the place she was fleeing from was more terrible.

Sometimes I wonder what she was running from.

And how had she died, or did she die at all, or—

The eyeless woman in the church had smiled at Siggi.

Siggi pressed his palms into his temples and squeezed his eyes shut.

How much had Arnes guessed about their mother before leaving home? Did he remember Mother, did he know she was never human? All the stories he told, and never a word of that. Siggi stared down at his body, the fish scales in his torso, tracing a winding line from his lowest rib to his clavicle. He looked at the blade that had fused with the bones of his hand when he'd brought Hrafn back. Magic he'd done without meaning to. Hrafn was right, then. Siggi must have created the soul-bond that tied them together. So why should Hrafn ever believe he hadn't *meant* to? That Siggi had been so terrified of Father, of being dragged toward the pyre that he'd done it on instinct, as easy as screaming?

Siggi's breath caught. "I *need* to talk to Hrafn."

"No. You need to stay here until we figure out what to do with you, huldalf."

But Siggi stood up, casting the blankets aside. "Where's Hrafn?"

"Sit down, that little witch wants nothing to do with you or anyone else—"

But Siggi was already outside, half-clothed and gasping. He found himself looking upon a huddle of beautiful wooden huts that encircled a communal firepit. The women were convening there, sitting on stone benches. Several stood and drew their weapons as Siggi, shirtless and wild, burst outside.

Gráinne smiled at him. She pointed to the trees. "He followed the stream that way."

Siggi barreled through the woods with Holta hollering at his back, but he didn't hear what she said. He followed the path where it ran alongside an icy little brook, clambering over stones until the stream bent down into a waterfall, and Siggi looked down at the churning pool below and saw Hrafn there, sitting beside the rippling water with his knees up, his head buried in his folded arms.

Hrafn must have heard him, but he didn't look up as Siggi slipped down the stones and sat beside him, panting from the exertion. Siggi sat and Siggi waited.

"Can't have a witch sleeping in the druid camp," Hrafn said quietly, after many minutes passed. "That's an ill omen."

"Did they tell you that, or did you tell yourself that?" Siggi asked.

Hrafn didn't answer, and for a moment they sat there only breathing. Siggi watched the stream descend without cessation, the lapping of the water in the pool.

"I truly didn't know," Siggi said finally. "If I'd known, I'd have told you."

"Does it matter?" Hrafn nearly laughed. "You owe me nothing. And I owe you my worthless life."

"It's not worthless, Hrafn."

Hrafn finally pulled his face from his arms, gaze fixed on the falling water. His eyes were swollen and red, the staves on his cheeks stark. "There was always something wrong with you, Siggi. No normal boy watches his father die and then befriends his killer. No normal boy sees blood magic and embraces the one who weaved it. Fuck's sake."

Siggi frowned, searching Hrafn's face. "You're doing it again. You're trying to hurt me, but you're only hurting yourself."

Hrafn flinched. "What?"

Siggi wanted to take him by the shoulders and shake him, but instead he stood up on the stone and pulled at his own hair. "Hrafn. I'm not good with words! I don't know how to explain…how to convince you?"

"Convince me of what?"

"You call yourself a wretch, you call yourself ugly, a monster, a thing to be scorned. You cut yourself and say you deserve it, that you deserve to suffer. But you're wrong!"

"You barely know me."

Siggi shrugged, feeling Hrafn's flurrying emotions in his own veins. "I disagree."

"Really?" Hrafn stood as well, fingers forming clenched fists, eyes shining with fury. "You've just learned you're a *blessed* magical creature and you don't see anything wrong with a magical perversion like me?"

"The only thing wrong is the way you keep hurting yourself," Siggi said.

"Shut up!" Hrafn said, with an empty laugh. "I killed both your parents, most likely."

There it was, the thought Siggi did not want to think.

He shook his head. "We don't know that the huldu woman in the church was my mother. We don't know that."

"Come off it. How many fucking huldu do you think ever came to the nowhere place you called home?"

Hrafn stared shaking on the stone, on his feet but looking all too pale and scared.

"Hrafn. Do you hate me now?"

"What?"

"Now that I'm not…" Siggi swallowed, fought the sob behind the words. "Now you know I'm not human."

"No, Siggi." Hrafn's pulse quickened more, throbbing in Siggi's arm and chest. "No! I don't fucking hate you."

"Then why does it matter, what I am or what you are?" Siggi stepped closer to him, so that Hrafn's raised hands brushed against the skin of his chest, the skin and scales and the beating heart pounding beneath it all.

"Historically speaking, huldu and witches don't get along. There was a whole war about it and everything. Thousands died, and let me tell you, their ghosts are still angry about it. Witches are an aberration. We aren't pure, wonderful creatures like you. You saw what Holta thinks of me. And all the rest."

"They're wrong. What was done to you is ugly, but your magic is part of you now. And I think it's amazing. Because I think you're amazing, too."

"Stop that. You don't know."

Siggi took Hrafn's shaking hand in his and pressed it against his chest, above his beating heart. "It's amazing. It's beautiful. I know you well enough to know that. *You're beautiful.*"

Siggi tried to find the words, but they seemed both too big and too little for him, and so he took hold of Hrafn's perfect little shoulders and pulled him close and kissed him firmly on the lips. Hrafn stiffened but did not pull away, and Siggi felt the heat of one of his hands cupping the back of his neck, felt him stand on tiptoe to kiss him in turn, biting Siggi's lip, breathing into his mouth.

"Oh," Hrafn breathed, face red as blood as his heels at last hit the stone again.

Siggi searched Hrafn's face, combing strands of his shining black hair aside. "Please, Hrafn. What does it matter?"

Hrafn buried his head in Siggi's chest, shoulders relaxing at last. "Haven't I told you? You should never touch a witch."

"That ship has long since sailed," Siggi said, and wrapped his arms around him.

Chapter Twelve
To Free What Has Been Locked Away

He was going to die. He was going to *die*, because there was no way his heart, which had already been stabbed once, could survive with the way it was beating—so fast he was sure it would burst out of his chest. Siggi's heart was racing too, an echo that Hrafn could feel in his own, but his arms around Hrafn were solid, everything about him was solid, whereas Hrafn was shaking like a fragile leaf in winter's first storm.

He had to say something. Something clever, something true, something Siggi would *hear*. No words came to mind.

Hrafn wasn't sure how long they stood there, the two of them alone by the pool at the base of the waterfall, surrounded by forest and mist as though there was nobody else in the world. Time enough passed that his heart finally, finally began to calm, and the parts of him that weren't pressed against Siggi felt the beginnings of a chill.

Then Siggi laughed, a quiet little huff that was somehow both teasing and self-deprecating. Hrafn spared only a second to be surprised by how well he could decipher that sound. Perhaps they had only known each other for a few days, but their heartbeats were intertwined, their pain shared, and he had spent the last few days staring at Siggi quite intently.

He hadn't noticed that Siggi had been staring back at him.

A squirm of embarrassment pierced the calm that had enveloped them. Hrafn shoved at Siggi's chest—gods and monsters, why the fuck wasn't he wearing a *shirt*? How was that even remotely fair? He tried to step away, feebly, and muttered, "Shut up."

Siggi didn't let him go. He only laughed, and, oh, oh, the things Hrafn would do to hear that laugh again and again.

"Let me go," Hrafn said, without much force.

"No," Siggi replied.

Hrafn tilted his head to glare up at him. "Let me—"

Siggi kissed him again, chasing all protests from his mind. The kiss was soft, questioning, and Hrafn decided that whatever he'd thought so important to say could wait a little while longer. Siggi was still holding him like he didn't have any intention of letting go, and it was—it was too much. It was impossible. It could never last. For all that Hrafn rather liked the idea of spending the next day or season or year trading kisses in these quiet woods with Siggi, with this foolish, impossible boy, he would have to let go eventually. But for now, Siggi was touching Hrafn like he was more than a knot of anger and scars, he was brushing Hrafn's hair back from his brow so gently, he was kissing the staves on Hrafn's face and not shuddering in revulsion. It was too much. Hrafn's heart was racing again and it was—it was too much.

"You're ridiculous," Hrafn said, more sharply than he intended. He couldn't *think* when they were so close. He pushed at Siggi and tried to scowl. He was pretty sure he didn't quite manage it; Siggi certainly didn't look impressed. "Is that what you're going to do now, every time you want to shut me up?"

"I never want to shut you up," Siggi said, his blue eyes wide and innocent, but he ruined it almost instantly when his lips quirked. "Well, except for when you're insulting somebody who's trying to help us, or somebody who could hurt you, or yourself, then I sometimes do want to—"

"I can't believe I ever thought you were shy," Hrafn said. He pushed Siggi away more firmly, and laughed when Siggi stepped back and tripped over a rock beside the creek. "You really are clumsy for a huldu."

It was the wrong thing to say. Siggi's expression changed, his teasing half smile dropping away so quickly it might have been slapped from his face. The look of dismay that took over made Hrafn want to draw his knife.

"I didn't…" Siggi began, but he stopped, shook his head. He turned away from Hrafn to stare into the pool.

"I know you didn't know," Hrafn said.

But that wasn't quite the truth, because he *had* doubted, when Gráinne first spoke, and those careless words had reverberated around them like thunder. He'd thought about it since then, after he'd fled the druid village because the alternative was wailing over Siggi's unconscious form while all the women stood about and snickered.

He tried again, with more honesty: "I realize now that you didn't know. It was obvious, when I thought about it. You would never have…"

Put up with such a father, if he knew what power was available to him. Suffered the scorn and indifference of the villagers, if he knew there was another family, another home, elsewhere.

Befriended a witch.

"I think my brother knew," Siggi said, after a brief silence. He was still staring at the pool. His shoulders were hunched now, his voice low and strained. "Or he suspected. When he left…he said some things that didn't make sense at the time. But there's much more I have to ask him."

There were quite a lot of things Hrafn also wanted to ask Arnes Arnesson, starting with how the fuck he could have left his younger brother in the care of such a brutal father, regardless of his reasons.

"My father must have known," Siggi said. His voice was so quiet it was hard to hear over the sound of the waterfall. "It makes sense, how he could barely look at me. He had his reasons. He didn't see…a son."

"Horseshit." Hrafn was gratified when Siggi looked at him, startled, as though he hadn't realized he was speaking out loud. "Your father treated you as he did because your father was a cruel man. What he saw when he looked at you was due to his own weakness and spite, and nothing at all to do with you."

Siggi didn't respond, and Hrafn was afraid he had gone too far. As though it wasn't enough to murder the man in front of his son, now he was stomping over his memory. Maybe it wasn't much of a memory, maybe the man did not deserve a second of mourning or a single breath of fond recollection, but that was Siggi's choice to make, not Hrafn's.

After a moment, Siggi rubbed his hand over his face and sighed. "The woman in the church," he said.

Hrafn stepped back. It wasn't a conscious choice, his legs were moving without his permission, but at those words every inch of his body was seized with the need to tear himself farther from Siggi's warmth. He felt sick, although his stomach was empty and had been for too long. There were a thousand thoughts in his mind, screaming like seabirds above a cliff, and none of them were adequate.

He had believed the woman monstrous. He had not hesitated to destroy her.

He had been wrong.

He had been wrong, and he had killed her, and he knew now, with a certainty he rarely felt about anything, that he had burnt to ashes Siggi's only chance to know his mother.

He had reacted exactly as the villagers who captured and tortured witches reacted. He had given more thought to killing Siggi's father than he had to burning that woman, because she had not been, in that moment, a person. Only a thing. A relic to be sought and stolen. A tool for men like Ketill to covet and use for their own purposes. A weapon that frightened him, because he was so easily frightened, as senseless as a child.

"Do you really think…?" Siggi said, the question fading into quiet. The look on Siggi's face made Hrafn want to draw his knife and plunge it into his own stomach. He spun away from Siggi and took several rapid steps, clattering over the damp rocks beside the creek.

"Hrafn, wait," Siggi said.

Hrafn didn't stop. "You still smell like fish. You should wash. I have to…"

He didn't know how to continue. He didn't know what to do except get away from Siggi's sad blue eyes, from the still-warm sensation of his lips. He scrambled up the hillside beside the waterfall. Siggi called out for him again, but Hrafn strode into the woods and didn't stop until he was alone.

He bent double, hands on his knees. He wanted to vomit, or scream, or cry, but all he could manage was a few moments of strained, pathetic wheezing. He straightened up, feeling faintly ridiculous as he rubbed his hands over his face, and followed the creek back toward the druid village.

He hadn't realized how much time had passed as he was sitting alone by the water. It was early morning now, inasmuch as midsummer ever had any distinction between day and night, but the air was heavy with fog. Sound was curiously muffled in the Myrkvidor, with even the chirping of the morning birds very far away and the babble of the creek soft and shy.

Hrafn smelled the village before he saw it: somebody was cooking fish. His stomach grumbled; he had not eaten since midday yesterday. He had no idea what his welcome would be, so he hesitated at the edge of the woods. There were a few druids gathered around the firepit, the yfirmaður and Holta among them. They ranged from very young to very old, with more shades of hair and skin than he had seen anywhere outside of Storaska's harborside taverns and inns, where foreign sailors gathered.

It was Holta who first noticed him. Her expression changed from one kind of scowl to an entirely different kind of scowl. "What did you do with him?"

Like she was worried Hrafn would hurt Siggi. Like she thought he could. Like she had any *right* to pretend she knew the first fucking thing about anything.

"He's bathing," Hrafn snapped. "It's what people do when they don't want to smell like dead fish all the time. You should try it."

He turned around, ready to stomp into the woods again. He was stupid. He didn't want to be here. He didn't want to sit with all the druids staring at him, disgust and disapproval written clearly on their faces.

"So you've decided to flee like a coward again?" Holta said. "Or has he already figured out how to free himself from you? He can shatter a bone with a touch. No doubt he'll do the same to that twisted bond that ties you together."

Hrafn stopped. Looked down at his left hand. He thought, for a second, he could feel the cold rush of water over his dry skin, an echo of what Siggi was feeling as he bathed, but it passed quickly. He bent his fingers, tried to feel the blade that Siggi was always feeling. The blade that had until a few days ago been so familiar to Hrafn it was as another limb, but now wasn't even his anymore.

Unless Siggi wanted to give it back.

"Stop that," said Gráinne sharply.

Hrafn spun around to tell her she couldn't tell him what to do—then realized she wasn't talking to him.

"Daughter," she said, her voice stern and clear, "I know you have not forgotten that we treat guests kindly until they give us reason to do otherwise."

Holta snorted. "His existence is reason enough."

"Celestina," Gráinne said, the sternness turning icy, "it seems the lessons you have learned from living outside the forest have been the wrong ones. Go now and fetch food for our guest." She added, as Holta rose to her feet, "Do *not* spit in it."

The affronted look on Holta's face would have been hilarious, if Hrafn weren't so distracted by realizing two things in quick succession. The first was that Gráinne was defending his presence in their village, which meant that if he ran away again he would offend a centuries-old druid who was likely more powerful than every witch he'd ever met.

The second, rather less important but all the more intriguing, was that Holta's real name was apparently *Celestina*. The girl who was one part huldu, three parts fish, and all scorn was named for the beauty of the heavenly stars in the language of stuffy scholars and priests. It took every bit of Hrafn's self-control not to snicker and shout the name after her. He very much wanted Siggi to return so he could tell him.

"Come over here, child," Gráinne said. "Warm yourself. Talk with me."

Hrafn stepped forward cautiously. The other women had moved away from the fire, but they hadn't gone far. They lingered nearby, hands on their axes and bows, watching him. It was all well and good for Siggi to insist that Hrafn was being paranoid, but Hrafn had been chased out of plenty of pleasant-looking villages by people who offered food before they offered violence. He sat on a stone bench, not close to Gráinne, preferring instead to be able to look directly at her.

"I've sent some of my daughters back to the skin-witch village," she said. "Thank you for finding it for us. They will look for anything Haraldar might have left behind."

"He took everything he needed," Hrafn said. "The skin of his followers. And Siggi's brother."

"Is this brother half-huldu as well?" she asked.

"Yes. I think so. Ask Siggi."

"I will, when he returns. I take it he found you? He was very worried when he ran off."

Hrafn shrugged. He knew he was blushing, but he couldn't bring himself to care. He had questions, and while he didn't know if she had the answers, she seemed at least willing to let him ask.

"You said it was huldu magic tying us together," Hrafn said.

Gráinne tilted her head thoughtfully. "It is. Mostly. I admit I've never seen a binding quite like this one before. How did you come to be bound?"

Well, wasn't that the question. Hrafn held his hands out to the fire and tried to act far calmer than he felt. Gráinne was looking into the flames, not at him, but he still felt like she was *seeing* him, seeing the scars on his hands and face, the dried blood he could not scrub from beneath his fingernails, the lingering warm spots where Siggi had touched him.

After he had run into the woods—fled like a coward, Holta was right about that—he had tried to calm himself by remembering everything he could about the druids of the Myrkvidor. It wasn't much. They had come to Lifandfjall hundreds of years ago. They kept to themselves. They gave up a single eye in exchange for the ability to see magic. They killed witches who trespassed in their territory. They had no use for men or boys. That was all he knew. He was as ignorant as a child. As ignorant as Siggi had been a few days ago.

He felt bad as soon as the thought entered his mind. It wasn't Siggi's fault his entire life had been built on the shifting black sands of a lie. And Siggi was, admittedly, a great deal better at taking in every new thing he saw or learned than Hrafn would have expected. Better, even, than Hrafn himself.

"If you do not wish to answer…" Gráinne began.

"It's not that," Hrafn said quickly. "It's only—did you ask Siggi?"

Gráinne smiled. "He ran after you as soon as he woke."

"Well, he was the one who did it. I was dead at the time."

"You do not trust me," Gráinne said.

Hrafn just looked at her. "You don't believe me."

"I do not think you are lying, Hrafn. But your surprise—and your friend's—suggests that the two of you are rather more ignorant of your current circumstances than you want to be."

That was, Hrafn thought, putting it extremely mildly.

"I am not a witch," Gráinne said, "and I am not huldu, and I have no obligations to or debts from either. But I have been around for a very long time, and my people have always been collectors of knowledge. And I have," she added, smiling again, "spent a few too many of those years avoiding the ire of angry and self-righteous men. You may ask questions of me, if you like. The answers are offered freely, if I have them."

Hrafn took a breath. An ordinary person would not believe him. A fellow witch would think him an unlucky and accursed mistake—he was pretty sure that's what Ylfa thought, even if she hadn't said as much. To priests of any creed he would be an abomination.

But Gráinne had lived for centuries already. Little would surprise her.

"I spoke the truth. I was dead when he did it," Hrafn said. "Stabbed in the heart and left for days on a pile of corpses. Siggi was stripping the bodies of weapons to knot."

"The knotting of the blades is an old custom," Gráinne said thoughtfully. "People still do it, out of habit, but it has fallen somewhat out of fashion since the huldu have been banished, and there is rather less…concern about magic breaking the boundaries between life and death."

"Right, well. His father was a blacksmith who wed a huldu. Maybe he knew more about it than he said." For the very first time, Hrafn regretted killing the man so swiftly, if only because Siggi deserved answers that nobody else could provide. "Siggi found my knife and—I don't know if he did anything besides pick it up but, well, ask to look at his hand, when he gets back."

Gráinne looked thoughtful. "It was no ordinary blade."

"No. It was huldu bone and iron, and it was forged with blood."

Gráinne raised an eyebrow. "You are quite young to have a blood-forged blade. How much of it was your own blood?"

"All of it," he said shortly.

Birtingr had said it would be more powerful that way. Hrafn had been in no position to argue. It was not a story he cared to share.

"Other people have touched the blade before," Hrafn added. "Nothing happened to them."

"Were those other people huldu?"

"Probably not, but who can tell these days? They seem to be everywhere, for a people long exiled."

"And hunting you, my daughter tells me."

"I don't know if they're *all* hunting me," Hrafn said. He suspected he would be dead already if there were multiple angry huldu looking for him. "So far just the brother of the woman I burned. Killed."

"It is true that huldu don't get along with each other any better than humans do," Gráinne said, amusement making her tone wry. "Sometimes even less than that. Ah, Celestina has brought your food."

The girl stalked up to them, still glowering, and dropped a wooden bowl into Hrafn's lap. He caught it before it tipped, then looked up and gave her a sunny smile.

"Thank you, Celestina," he said.

Her eyes narrowed. "That name was not given for you to use."

She didn't wait for his answer before whirling around and stomping away again. Gráinne watched her with a soft expression, one that spoke of both fondness and sadness. Hrafn looked away in discomfort.

The bowl held chunks of cooked fish and barley porridge. She hadn't seen fit to offer a spoon, so he used his fingers to pluck at the food. He was very hungry, and the food was filling and warm, but after a few mouthfuls he lowered the bowl again to look at Gráinne.

"So you've never heard of something like me before?" he said, pushing the words out in a rush, before he could lose his courage. "A dead witch brought back to life by huldu magic? I've only ever heard of witches bound and turned to puppets. Made into unliving things with no will of their own. This isn't like that."

She was quiet for a moment before she answered. Her expression was serious but not marked by worry. She seemed to be perfectly relaxed, looking from the fire to the forest around them, enjoying the misty gray morning.

"I have seen a great many things in my life," she said, "both wondrous and terrible."

Hrafn snorted. "And we know which one I am."

Gráinne looked at him, her head tilted slightly. "I don't think we do. Yours is not a situation I have seen before, but from what you have told me, there was no ill intent behind Siggi's actions."

Hrafn ducked his head to scoop up another bite of food. He hadn't meant to imply that *Siggi* had done something terrible.

But Gráinne knew that, and she said, "I think, if you are searching for a reason for your revival, the explanation will be found in both your own blood magic and in Siggi's huldu magic. You know as well as I do that the confluence of the two types of magic is not an area many have explored. And certainly not recently."

Her words were something of an understatement. In fact there was only one example Hrafn had ever heard about in which a witch and a huldu combined their magics for common cause, and that had been the closing of the gates to the huldu realm a century ago. Which had been an impressive piece of magic, to be sure, but it had nothing to do with bringing the dead back to life.

"I am certain you've already considered this," Gráinne said, "but with such unusual magic, it might not be possible to know beforehand what the consequences would be if you should sever the bond. Siggi is huldalf and can survive a great deal. But you are, after all, still human, and one who has already passed into death. You might not survive the severing."

She was right: Hrafn had considered it already. And he considered it still, because every time it entered his mind, his thoughts were a storm of confusion. When he had first stepped out of the funeral fire, he had been furious to find himself bound by magic to a weeping farm boy who could now feel every beat of his heart. But he had also been relieved, because he had not wanted to die. He still did not want to die, nor did he now find the bond to be unpleasant.

But their bond went two ways. As much as Hrafn was bound to Siggi, and might suffer if the bond was broken, so too was Siggi bound to Hrafn—and he was already suffering because of it.

Footsteps crunched through the woods nearby, and Hrafn looked up to see Siggi stepping out of the forest. His hair was wet, his skin damp, and he looked really, truly, unfairly beautiful, especially when he spotted Hrafn and his face lit up with something almost like relief. Hrafn's pulse skipped, and he didn't know if it came from his own heart or Siggi's. He felt a pang of guilt; he hadn't meant for Siggi to worry that he was leaving him behind. And Siggi couldn't really have thought that, otherwise he would have charged into the woods after him. But it was still there, that doubt that broke away like clouds clearing from before the sun, and Hrafn was annoyed at himself for causing it, however lovely the expression was that took its place.

Siggi strode over to join them. He hesitated for just a second, barely worth noticing, before sitting on the stone bench right beside Hrafn—and not just beside, but close enough to touch, angled so that one of his shoulders was tucked behind Hrafn.

"Oh, food!" Siggi said.

"It's mine," Hrafn grumbled. "Get your own."

But he moved the bowl so that Siggi could reach it.

"There is plenty to share," Gráinne said, with a knowing smile. "And when you are done, we have a place where you can rest. If my daughters have found anything in the witches' village, you will be welcome to examine it." She stood up and nodded at Siggi. "Perhaps they left behind some hint about where they have taken your brother."

After she walked away, Siggi asked, "Do you think they did? Leave something to help us find Arnes?"

"I don't think Haraldar is careless," Hrafn said thoughtfully, "but something clearly happened in that village that he wasn't expecting."

Siggi was quiet for a moment, then he said, "If he didn't…could you…would it be too dangerous to use the tooth again?"

Hrafn glanced down at the fading bruise on his wrist. It would be a terrible risk to scry when Haraldar knew he was being hunted, but their options were limited. If there was nothing in Haraldar's village to point to why he was holding Arnes or what he wanted, Hrafn could think of only one other way to try to find them.

And that one was even more dangerous than scrying.

"We'll find another way," Siggi said quickly.

"Right." Hrafn leaned back against Siggi, hesitantly at first, then less so when Siggi shifted to curl around him, so warm and solid. "We'll find a way."

It began to rain around midday, and the druid women offered Hrafn and Siggi a hut for shelter. Siggi started a fire in the center hearth, while Hrafn pulled a wool blanket from a stack and wrapped it around himself like a cloak. It turned out that even getting kissed by Siggi could not dispel the chill from a night spent shivering miserably by a waterfall.

He had managed only a short nap when the door of the hut swung open and a druid girl marched in without waiting for an invitation. She was the smirking freckled one they had met in the woods, the one Holta had called Fidelma. She had been mocking Holta the night before, which made Hrafn inclined to like her, but he didn't like that Holta came in right after her.

"This is what we found," Fidelma said. She tossed a bundle onto the floor and sat cross-legged right beside it. "None of the skins. I wanted to bring some of the skin, but nobody else would allow it. So? What were those wretched witches doing?"

Hrafn eyed the bundle warily. It wasn't much, just a stack of wet bark, old leather, and tattered vellum tied up with a thin rope, all of it carrying a foul, smoky stench. "Are you sure you didn't bring any of the skin? It smells like you did."

"Are you squeamish?" Holta said, her face twisted in a sneer. She stood behind Fidelma with her arms crossed. "And here I thought the raven-hearted witch was supposed to be clever and fearsome."

"The raven-hearted witch is going to rip your tongue out and use it for fish bait," Hrafn said. He unknotted the rope and began to pick through the bundle. "Do you think that would confuse the fish, being lured in by the flesh of one of their own?"

The tattered and charred scraps did have staves and runes written on them, but most seemed to be notes rather than actual spellwork. Some of it was exactly what Hrafn would have expected from Haraldar's coven: methods for obtaining and preserving human skin, ideas for concealment, protective spells. There was very little to do with the huldu, and nothing that explained why Haraldar would keep a half-huldu captive.

Hrafn stopped to look over a thin strip of vellum, about as wide as his palm and as long as his arm. The strip was old, weathered, and cracked. It had staves on both sides, scraped into the vellum and painted with blood that had long since dried to a ruddy-brown color. He wondered what sort of skin it was, how likely it was to be human, then decided not to wonder about that anymore. He turned it twice, examining the staves and runes.

"What is it?" Siggi asked.

"Not sure," Hrafn said distractedly.

It didn't look like anything more than a list, the same sort that anybody might use to teach runes to a child. But it was clearly very old and had been kept in relatively good condition. At the top was the vegvísir, the wayfinding stave, with its eight lines splayed like rays from the sun. It was the most important stave in all of witchcraft for any sort of seeking, searching, finding one's way. It was the stave Hrafn had carved on his chest, deep enough that the blade nicked the bone.

Beneath the wayfinding stave was a column of other staves. Spells for the control of ice, wood, earth, iron… Bone, too. Not a stave he had seen all that often. Bone magic was extremely rare—maybe, Hrafn thought, with a tinge of amusement, because Siggi was hoarding all of it.

At the bottom of the vellum, last in the list, was another familiar stave: the complicated combination of lines, whirls, and runes for using blood magic with other elements.

Hrafn's pulse quickened.

"What do people normally want from the huldu?" he asked.

"Wishes. Good luck. Power." Fidelma rested her chin on her hand. "To own and control beauty, because men are idiots. Riches. The usual reasons they want magic."

Hrafn shook his head. "Then he would use witchcraft, because there are so few huldu left in this realm. What can't he get from witchcraft?"

"Magic that isn't tainted and foul," Holta said. She still had not sat down, nor had she stopped scowling.

Hrafn looked up at her incredulously. "You think that a man who wears other people's skins cares about what's tainted and foul? You're even stupider than you look."

Siggi wasn't saying anything. He touched the vellum strap gently, as though he was afraid it would crumble beneath his fingertips.

"You obviously have some thought in your mind, witch," Fidelma asked. "Let's skip over the part where you force us to admit you're cleverer than we are, and just tell us what you're thinking."

Hrafn pointed at the vellum. "This is the wayfinding stave, for finding things that cannot otherwise be found. And here"—he moved his finger down the list—"is a way to combine ice and blood. Earth and blood. Iron and blood. And bone and blood."

"Those are the elements combined in the gates to the huldu realm," Holta said.

"You think he's looking for the gates?" Fidelma asked.

"The gates aren't hard to find," Hrafn said. "I've seen a couple of them myself, and all I've got is this foul and tainted magic to guide me. No, I think Haraldar already knows where they are. What he wants is a way to open them."

Siggi was looking at Hrafn now, not at the vellum, staring like he was trying to read something in Hrafn's expression. "Isn't that supposed to be impossible?"

Fidelma shook her head. "It was supposed to be impossible to seal them, but a witch managed that a century ago. What can be done can also be undone."

Hrafn nodded distractedly. "People have been trying to reverse the seal ever since. Nobody has succeeded, because the witches didn't seal the gates alone. They had huldu help. They used both kinds of magic."

Fidelma climbed to her feet. "We should tell Gráinne about this. She always wants to know when witches are trying to do something stupid."

She left the hut, but Holta did not follow right away. She was staring at the vellum, her eyes wide, the scowl gone from her face.

"Is it possible?" she asked. "Can the gates be opened?"

Hrafn looked up at her. "How the fuck should I know? This isn't a list of instructions. There is nothing here about what Haraldar thinks he can do."

"Is all of your cleverness so useless?" Holta said, the scowl returning. "Do you know nothing about your own witchcraft?"

There was the slightest tremble in her voice, so brief that Hrafn could not be sure he hadn't imagined it. He lifted his gaze to meet her eyes, held until she looked away.

"This is not witchcraft anybody has tried before," he said. "But Haraldar has done a lot of things nobody else wants to attempt. It's probably best to assume he's onto something, don't you think?"

Chapter Thirteen
The Bone Bag

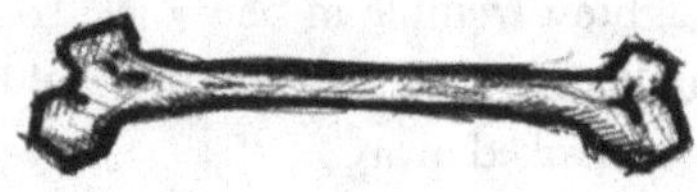

"To open a gate to the hidden realm," Siggi repeated, after Holta left them alone together. He leaned closer, peering at the debris on the floor. "Why?"

"Well, it won't be because they're bored. The hidden realm is filled with wild magic. Maybe they want to sneak into Hulduheimer to steal weapons or magic fruit or strands of huldu hair or—or whatever, it's always been a mad idea. But anything taken from that place would be powerful."

There was, as always, so much Hrafn wasn't saying, but more and more, Siggi recognized two things. The first was that Hrafn always told Siggi what was most important. Secondly, soul-bond aside, Hrafn's face was more telling than he ever intended. Hrafn couldn't keep his eyes and lips from relaying, if not his thoughts, at least his emotions.

Hrafn hadn't moved away from Siggi's fingers, still resting on his forearm.

"What other stories have *you* heard about the hidden realm, Siggi?" Hrafn asked. "I don't know what commonfolk know about these things."

Siggi raised his eyebrows. "Oh. Am I commonfolk?"

Hrafn's face flushed, and he muttered something under his

breath.

"What?"

"I said, 'rather the fucking opposite,' and I know you heard me."

Siggi watched him for an instant, strangely pleased by Hrafn's discomfort. Since they'd kissed, nearly all of Hrafn's expressions made Siggi want to do it again. If even pensive scowls made Siggi want to kiss Hrafn, they'd be in real trouble. Hrafn scowled rather an awful lot.

Siggi leaned away from Hrafn's neck, fighting his instincts. "I don't know much apart from fairy stories, like I told you. The hidden people live in another world, just out of sight, but they used to visit our world from time to time. And there were doorways between the two worlds in sort of…special places. Like, behind waterfalls and in tunnels and things like that. And in the stories, sometimes hidden people come through to steal sheep or spread a blight or cure a sickness. Sometimes just to cause mischief. Sometimes they're a blessing and sometimes they're a curse."

Siggi hesitated. Some uncomfortable thought he'd been quashing, buried in his belly, was climbing its way back up inside him.

Hrafn sighed; again, Siggi wanted to kiss him. "More or less— well less, but it doesn't matter—that used to be true. When early settlers came to Lifandfjall, the hidden folk had the run of both worlds, and always had. They passed between two realms on a whim for centuries. But I suspect they didn't even mind when the humans arrived. It probably entertained them, to turn the humans against each other with tricks and spells. To see them suffer, or to bed them. Huldu are capricious."

"Oh."

"But if they didn't mind the settlers, they certainly minded witchcraft." Hrafn didn't seem upset, only resigned to this fact of life. "I told you that huldu and witches don't get along. That was putting it mildly."

"But huldu are magic, right? And witches use magic too, so…shouldn't they have understood each other?"

Hrafn's lips twisted into the smallest of smiles. "It's very like you to think so, but no. Their magics and mindsets are far too different. What happens when oil meets fire? And in a land this unforgiving, it was all too easy for everything to burn. The huldu tried to chase the witches from Lifandfjall. The witches didn't want to go. I don't know all the details. Every witch tells it differently."

"They fought?"

"Yes. There was a great battle, and it culminated in separating the worlds. A witch and a huldu worked together to close all the passages between the hidden realm and this one. They trapped the hidden folk in their realm, against their wishes."

"When did this happen?" Siggi asked, frowning.

"A hundred years ago, or so."

"But my mother must have come to Midfjördur not that long ago," Siggi said, "and Holta's here in Lifandfjall, too. If the gates are all closed, how can that be? And how…"

How do I exist? Siggi didn't say it, but Hrafn's eyelids fluttered as though he knew. He placed his fingers on Siggi's hand. Siggi's stomach flipped over, and Hrafn felt it too, based on his expression.

"The huldu are also cunning. They can't properly open the remaining gates or restore the paths between the two worlds, but they've found a partial way through. The gates are sealed on *this* side, but from the other side they're like a waterfall—easy enough to tumble down it, but doing so causes great harm, and it's impossible to climb up it again. That's why the huldu can still send their fish-girls and other outcasts away if they don't care what happens to them. Most don't survive the journey."

"The huldu ghost we met on the water. The whale, too. What did you call it?"

"A sending. The summoner wasn't actually present." Absently Hrafn rubbed the bruises on his arm, left by the icy phantom's fingers. His eyes had that sudden busyness to them again, as if he were riffling through his mind like he'd riffled through the bag of skin and scrolls on the cabin floor. "A puppet, dead flesh possessed by spirits, using huldu magic. Think of it like…advanced scrying. The huldu was probably in the hidden realm. They can work magic across realms still, but it doesn't seem to be very easy for them. They would wreak a lot more havoc if it was. The question is how he heard the news so quickly. I'd have said it was unlikely, until…well."

"What?"

Hrafn bit his lip. "Well. Ylfa has a huldu friend, and she won't be the only one. But until recently, I've hardly ever met a living huldu."

"A living one," Siggi echoed. "But now you've met Holta." He swallowed. "And me."

If Hrafn frowned any deeper, Siggi thought his face might collapse. Siggi realized he couldn't really tell which emotions were Hrafn's and which were his own, they were so tangled up.

He said he doesn't hate you, Siggi told himself, but that needling feeling was growing more persistent, very near escaping his throat, even as he willed it not to, tried not to name it.

"There might be more of them than we realize. Making lives for themselves here." Hrafn's gaze flickered. "Having kids in Midfjördur."

The thought rose again, and Siggi bit it back, saying instead: "I told you. I don't blame you, for what happened in the church."

Hrafn almost laughed, disbelief etched in his face. "Who wouldn't resent the bastard who killed both his parents on a fucking *whim*?"

"It wasn't a whim," Siggi said, "and I don't resent you."

And that was the question, the thing clawing Siggi open. He couldn't bring himself to resent Hrafn, no matter how he knew he should. And he had to wonder why. Because Siggi had been given an answer to a question he'd never known to ask, an answer that gutted him.

"Haven't you just told me that…the huldu…that things like *me*…don't feel the same things other people feel?"

"What?" Hrafn's eyes widened. "What are you saying?"

But Siggi had to let it all out now. "You just said the huldu find human suffering entertaining, they think *commonfolk* are only good for bedding or robbing or cursing. And if that's what I am, too…maybe my feelings are all wrong. Maybe they aren't feelings at all. Shouldn't I be sobbing over Arnes still? Over Father? Over Mother? Over finding out I'm a…thing, over leaving home, over *everything*?"

"Stop that," Hrafn snapped, clutching his own chest as if to soothe Siggi's panic. "Siggi, there's nothing wrong with you!"

"But it's true." Siggi hadn't realized his voice was rising, hadn't realized he was clutching his knees close to his chest. "Father…the villagers. Even Arnes, maybe. They've all been right about me. There's always been something *off* about me, some good reason I didn't belong. Only now it has a name."

"Stop that! You've barely had time to think, let alone grieve!"

"And if I never grieve?" He locked eyes with Hrafn, seeing himself reflected in the shining black. "If I'm just…like this? An unfeeling…*thing*?"

Hrafn growled like an angry cat. Suddenly he hooked one hand around the back of Siggi's neck and pulled him close. Siggi rose from his haunches, shocked by the sudden strength in Hrafn's movement, catching himself on his hands as Hrafn pressed his mouth to Siggi's.

Before they pulled apart, Hrafn's tooth nicked his lip, deliberately, like a warning.

"What…" Siggi said, forgetting everything but Hrafn's heat, the breath they shared, their tandem skeletons. On the roof of the sheepskin tent, the patter of rain began.

"You kiss me when you want me to shut up. I can do the same." Hrafn's face was flushed and warm and fierce as he pushed his forehead against Siggi's, enveloping him in those thrice-damned cavernous eyes. "The boy who *sobbed* at the sight of my sorry corpse, devoid of empathy?"

"But—"

With a snarl, Hrafn silenced him with another fierce kiss. "The boy who befriends witches and cries at the sight of a pretty shoreline, devoid of feeling?"

"I just mean—"

Another kiss, this one longer, more soothing.

"Come the fuck off it, puffling. Of all your troubles, *unfeeling* isn't

190

among them. Gods."

Siggi wrapped his arms around Hrafn's shoulders, catching his breath. *Their* breath.

"But you look at me sometimes like you're waiting for me to hit you," Siggi whispered. "And other times, like you want to run from me. I don't know how to feel…or how you feel about me."

"Siggi. We literally share every feeling."

"That's not the same…I don't think it is."

Hrafn stiffened and closed his eyes, but remained pressed against Siggi, his heartbeat as fevered as Siggi's own. The rain grew louder, a heavy drum building to a steady roar that seemed to separate them from whatever monsters and ugly truths awaited them in the woods.

"Siggi," Hrafn said at last. His voice was a feathery tickle on Siggi's neck that straightened Siggi's posture and made his chest and trousers feel so much tighter. "Shall I lie to you? Shall I pretend I'm *not* afraid of you?"

"No," Siggi said. "Whatever else, don't do that. Don't lie to me."

"As if it's easy." Hrafn breathed, and his little chuckle, so much sweeter than usual, made every muscle in Siggi's back tense. "I'm a witch. I bleed. It's what I exist to do."

"*Hrafn.*" Siggi pressed his lips against the scars on Hrafn's neck.

"I'm not afraid you'll hit me. But you're—you're not like everybody else, with me. And that…that scares me. No matter what I've done, what I still do…you look at me with those feckless big eyes and I'm just entirely, helplessly fucked."

And Siggi didn't know how it had happened, but Hrafn was on him now, straddling him, his thin frame pressed against Siggi's torso. Perched in the nest of Siggi's lap. Siggi could feel every part of him, brittle and soft and otherwise.

"But soon enough, that's going to change, and you'll give me what I deserve," Hrafn whispered into Siggi's ear, looping one leg and then the other around Siggi's back. "And it's going to hurt so much more than any of these staves ever have."

"That last bit is bullshit," Siggi said. "But I'll give you what you deserve. Right now."

Hrafn's legs tightened around his back as Siggi laid him on the floor atop the scrolls and skins, as the rain played its thumping tattoo on the roof. Hrafn's raven hair was so incredibly soft, Siggi couldn't seem to keep one hand away from it even as he fumbled with the neck of Hrafn's tunic with his other. Hrafn finally took hold of his wrist and gasped, "Just leave it on."

"But—"

Hrafn's eyes flashed in the firelight, and he rose on his elbows, catching Siggi's lip with his teeth, speaking into his mouth. "I said leave it, puffling. Your attention is needed elsewhere."

And Siggi groaned as Hrafn's pelvis pressed up against his own, firm and unrelenting.

The flap to the cabin lifted open, allowing the barrage of rain to break the confines of the cabin, and then Holta made a noise like a strangled sheep. "Fuck's sake! Really?"

Hrafn was away from Siggi before Siggi could even register it was over, red-faced with humiliation, on his feet. Beyond the cabin wall, Siggi could hear Fidelma laughing in delight.

"The fuck do you want, *Celestina Pisslocks*?"

"It's not me," she said, shaking her head. "Gods, but I don't want anything to do with you. It's Haraldar's village. Gráinne's found something else."

"I thought you'd brought us all you found," Hrafn said to Holta as she led them into the woods again.

Hrafn's neck was still flushed, but Siggi doubted anyone else would notice. As for himself, the pressure in his groin was hard to bear. He was all too aware that Fidelma was whispering to Holta as they rushed through the light rain, finally arriving to meet with Gráinne not far from the falls where Siggi had bathed and he and Hrafn had…

Hrafn nudged him with his shoe. Even that almost set him off.

Hrafn coughed and looked away while Holta hurried them forward toward the center of a luminous green clearing, an exhale amid the heavy, looming trees.

What seemed like every member of the Myrkvidor druids had gathered in an aged stone circle. There where the grass had been shorn—by a scythe if Siggi had to guess—was a stone altar carved with marks like those tattooed on the women's faces. Though it was still raining lightly, not a drop landed in the stone bowl atop the altar. The air was cold, but Hrafn's heat, there at Siggi's side, seemed almost enough to leave them both steaming in the drizzle.

Gráinne watched the pair of them as they entered the circle, glancing at Holta with a question in her eyes. Holta shook her head.

"I see you found the lodging to your liking," Gráinne said, and Fidelma snickered.

"Thank you," Siggi said quickly. "Yes. Um. Very warm."

"And you made it warmer," Fidelma said, and this time Holta kicked *her* shin.

Once again, Siggi thought Hrafn and Holta were very similar. He would never, ever tell them.

"You found something worthy of a warded altar?" Hrafn said. "What is it?"

"Rain is often revealing," Gráinne said, and she nodded at a druid. "Show them, Dryade."

Siggi was taken aback by the youth of the girl who stepped forward. It was clear that the red stone that took the place of her right eye was newly implanted. The skin around it was puckered and pink, but her expression was set. Her hair wasn't braided like the rest but cropped short above her ears, and her complexion and features were not unlike Hrafn's. Rain had left her face striped with mud.

Dryade leaned a long, curious object against the stone altar and stepped away. All around them, the druids muttered. Hrafn leaned in closer, and Siggi placed himself at his back, shielding Hrafn from the rain.

Hrafn inhaled sharply and his emotions expanded, but Siggi couldn't make sense of what they were looking at. The object appeared to be a long spear of iron, atop which was affixed the feathered corpse of a raven. Its beak had been sewn shut with a blood-red string, and attached to its back, where its wings should have been, were a horrid replacement: skin from two degloved human hands, every inch of the dried flesh carved with staves.

A wave of nausea overcame Siggi, accompanied by a strange, sweet odor. He staggered, even as Hrafn put up a hand to catch him.

"Where was it?" Hrafn demanded.

Dryade looked to Gráinne, who answered for her. "Dryade does not speak. She came upon this totem beyond the mouth of the small cavern."

"Where Arnes was held?" Siggi demanded, but the women could not answer.

"Tell me," Hrafn said. "I know you one-eyed women see more than I can. What is it?"

"It reeks of huldu," Fidelma answered, stepping out from the circle. "Iron, too. And blood magic. Witchcraft, and something else. The fog of it all is so thick it's clogging the vision in my stone eye."

"It's emanating huldu magic," Holta repeated. She swallowed back what looked like gorge, hair dripping in the rain. "And the blood. Is that from the huldu captive?"

"Most likely," Gráinne replied, and Siggi knew that could only mean Arnes.

"But…what? What is it? What did they do with Arnes? Hrafn, what is this thing?" Even through the swirling in his stomach, Siggi saw how intently Hrafn's gaze was fixed on the dead raven.

Hrafn's frown deepened. "A totem like this could do many things, most known only to its enchanter. He left it behind for a reason."

Another wave of the putrid stink washed over him, and Siggi could no longer bear the emptiness of the raven's eye sockets. Dizzy, he fell to his knees, cursed arm burning, his eyes watering like another downpour. Hrafn knelt beside him, searching his face, but for once it was Siggi who could not look at Hrafn.

"Something's in its mouth," Siggi said, ears ringing. "The raven's beak."

Siggi felt a sudden pull, like another pulsing bloodstream, not so different from the pull that had planted Hrafn's blade in his hand. He found his feet, reaching for the totem even as someone grabbed hold of his hand.

"Don't, Siggi." Siggi blinked in the rain and turned. To his surprise, it was Holta, not Hrafn, who held him tightly now. She looked as ill as he felt, and a sudden fragility had overtaken her features. "It won't help you to see it. It won't."

"Let him go, Holta. There's no point lying to him." Hrafn spoke quietly, pulling her hand from Siggi's forearm.

Gone was the usual venom he spat at her. She must have seen something in his face as well, because she let go and turned away, covering her mouth. Gráinne placed one hand on her shoulder.

Siggi straightened up, fighting the urge to vomit. Hrafn passed him the sheepshearing knife. Siggi severed the red string from around the head of the desiccated raven. Its beak fell open with a curious cracking sound, the smallest smack of thunder as the rain faded to a dribble. From the beak fell a small cylindrical object, pale and cold.

Siggi caught it in his cursed hand, where it struck him like lightning, bringing him to his knees.

All around him, the druids stepped back as if they'd felt the strike too. There was no muttering now. There was no sound at all, not that Siggi could hear.

Hrafn held his shoulders, but Siggi barely felt him there. He could not feel the rain, or the mud beneath his knees, or the eyes that stared at him. He felt only the weight of the object, familiar as it was impossibly changed.

"It's Arnes's," he said. "It's Arnes's little finger."

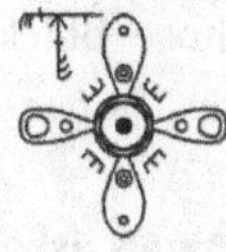

"Siggi," Arnes said, holding his hand out. "Come on. It's not far now."

Siggi always trusted Arnes. Even so, as they clambered over the mossy rocks that rose up the near-vertical ascent alongside Nebenfoss, another of the dozens of small waterfalls that accented the cliffs of Midfjördur, Siggi hesitated.

Siggi was not afraid of heights. But these rocks were damp, the path nonexistent, and Father did not know they had stolen away when the goat needed milking.

But Arnes's hand and smile had remained, and Siggi took the former, and Arnes pulled him up the last few slippery stones into a new world. Not a hidden realm, but a wondrous secret all the same. Kneeling on the floor of the cavern, Siggi gaped at the ceiling, the etchings carved into the smooth underside of the stone.

"What is this place?"

"The Cavern of Whispers," Arnes said, wiping his filthy hands on his trousers. "Brynja Gottsdottir told me a hermit lived here once. She said it was Thorfinn's uncle, but that was just to be unkind. Brynja doesn't care for Thorfinn ever since he put a slug in her hair." Taking hold of Siggi's hand again, Arnes helped his little brother find his footing. "But come on. There's something to see further in."

"Won't it be dark?" Siggi asked, wiping his nose.

"It will be, and then it won't be," Arnes said, and pulled Siggi into the depths of the cavern.

The pair of them stumbled through damp darkness, and the light from the cave mouth behind them was not nearly enough to illuminate the way, and they hadn't brought a torch, and—

Light graced their toes, and suddenly they stood on the cusp of a vision. Laid out before them was the sea to the right, and to the left extended fjords beyond fjords, the lands that stretched beyond the unclimbable walls of Midfjördur. There was no way down from this landing, no way to touch those black hills and green fields and unknown red and sable shores, but seeing them in itself was a gift Siggi had never been given.

"Are you crying again," Arnes asked, ruffling Siggi's hair. "Oh, Siggi. What will we do with you?"

Siggi didn't answer, and Arnes didn't expect him to.

"And look there!" Arnes pointed to a column of rock just to their left, home to hundreds of seabirds. One of them felt the Arnessons were far too close to her nest and screeched at them before swooping toward them. The boys ducked, and the tern carried on into the valley below, her cries piercing the distance.

"For all we've seen, imagine what *she* has," Arnes said, watching the tern until the wind caught her and carried her farther into the distance. "The world is vast, Siggi. Doesn't it make you want to see it?"

Arnes's finger was so very small in Siggi's palm. And perhaps it could have been anyone's finger, but it wasn't. It wasn't any finger but one of the ten that had guided him through his childhood, that had combed his hair when Father neglected to, that had held Siggi's hand in the skylit cavern.

What had Arnes suffered in that camp, captive among witches? Siggi found breathing almost impossible, his face hot as the sun. He held the finger tighter.

"Where was this found, precisely?" Hrafn asked. His hand remained on Siggi's shoulder. "We didn't see it, and you didn't even earlier today, before the rain. If it reeks so strongly of magic, how could it have been so well hidden?"

Gráinne looked to Dryade, who gesticulated with her hands, a language Siggi couldn't read. But he understood her frown and the sudden fear in her eyes.

"It wasn't hidden, she says," Gráinne said, and her posture stiffened. "It was displayed in plain sight."

"Waiting to be found," Holta muttered. "Planted after we left?"

"Then tell me one more thing, druids," Hrafn said, and Siggi felt the slice of the knife against Hrafn's burning stave, felt the fire start licking Hrafn's palms, as though from an ocean away. "With a totem this powerful here in your sight, fogging all you see—how well can you sense any other magic that might enter this circle?"

"Fuck's sake," Holta breathed, drawing her bone-blade. "We took the fucking bait!"

"Never expect a warm welcome from druids, they say," rasped a voice from the trees, as Haraldar Swift-Eye entered the sacred circle, boots squelching in the mud. "And Old Haraldar listens, but still, my dears, I hoped for a kinder greeting!"

Fidelma cursed in the old tongue, pulling a blade from beneath her cloak, and the other women reacted with similar alarm, drawing weapons and raising bows—apart from two.

Gráinne's expression was grim but unsurprised, as though she had expected nothing less. The gleam in her solitary eye looked, Siggi thought, even victorious. She signed a gesture to Dryade, who nodded and stepped behind Gráinne, obscured by the older woman's shadow as she set to work. Kneeling in the dirt, Dryade pulled a wedge of charcoal from her belt and began etching runes in the mud.

Who is baiting whom? Siggi wondered.

Whatever the case, Haraldar was a terror to behold.

Stories of Haraldar's fearsome stature proved more than warranted. Hulking as a boulder, his footsteps weighty as thunderclaps, he stepped into the white light, his filthy grin just visible through the mouth of his skin-suit mask, teeth browned with age. Haraldar approached the druids at a languid pace, as though the arrows pointed directly at him did not. He appeared to be unarmed, adorned in a hooded cloak of patchwork flesh that covered him to his elbows and kneesHe wore a strange leather glove on his left hand, which had empty fingers far longer than his own, dangling like vines at the end of his arm.

Siggi felt a surge of sudden fury, removed from all else: there wasn't a single scar on Haraldar's own exposed flesh, though he'd carved merrily away at the skins he wore as garments. He looked to Hrafn and knew he'd felt something as well, though his gaze remained fixed, his posture graceful and firm, his night-eyes reflecting his flames in the gray light.

"Haraldar Swift-Eye," Gráinne said. "You know you are not welcome here."

"Gráinne Redstone," he said, his drawl archaic and peculiar. "Neither were you welcome in my settlement, but visit you did all the same! Can you blame Old Haraldar for coming to seek what you've taken?"

"What they've taken," Siggi echoed, staring at the finger in his palm. "What about what you've taken? Where's Arnes?"

"Siggi!" Hrafn hissed. "Don't."

"Ah. So you'll be the other huldalf, then?" Slowly, so that the skin-cloak bent and creased with a gentle squeak around him, Haraldar turned to look at Siggi. His black, beady eyes glinted through the sockets of his mask. He pushed his long, tattooed tongue through the gash of the mask's mouth, wetting the dead leather lips. "Heard much about you, haven't I, though it took some time. Yet let it never be said that Old Haraldar can't make a body speak!"

"Where is Arnes?" Siggi asked again, nudging Hrafn and his fiery hands aside, stepping closer to the hulking figure. This close, Haraldar smelled of old rot and fresh blood.

"I'll tell you where, if you answer me a question first. Tell Old Haraldar, Siggi Arnesson, is it true you have bone-bending magic? Can those clever fingers of yours really break the very roots of living things? We have not seen the likes since the gates closed, and what a loss it is. What a loss!"

"Siggi, say nothing," Hrafn warned.

"Daughters, stay your hands," Gráinne warned the others. Behind her, Dryade drew furiously in the mud, a roving spiraling pattern taking on the shape of something larger, something Siggi couldn't yet discern.

Low, grating laughter shook Haraldar's shoulders. "Yes, yfirmaður, do ask them to wait. Wait while this huldalf pleads before Old Haraldar. Go on, then, lad. Beg for Arnes."

"Fuck off," Hrafn hissed, and the flames on his palms grew taller.

Haraldar's eyes lit upon Hrafn. "Is that Birtingr's pretty little carved boy? Smile a bit, lad. Show me all those lovely marks."

Siggi felt Hrafn's burgeoning rage ratcheting up alongside his own, felt it might be enough to tear his focus from Arnes's severed finger.

"Why are you trying to enter the hidden realm?" Hrafn demanded.

"Ah, such beauty is wasted on a fool, is it not? You who have traded a little huldu-bone knife for the living thing, and you still ask? The reasons for Old Haraldar's sneaking and stealing are mine own. It's not you I've come for, appealing as your lovely skin may be."

"Shut the fuck up," Hrafn spat.

"Yet I must offer you my thanks, Hrafn Ravenhearted, for showing me the way to this treasure most rare."

Haraldar raised his sagging hand to gesture at Siggi.

The flames on Hrafn's hands flickered. "I said *shut up*."

"My huldalf pet kept his secrets well, he did, until this foolish witch scried Old Haraldar. And then I thought, well, who's this tall lad, and why is my pet saying this name now? 'Oh Siggi, Siggi! How I miss thee!'"

Siggi moved but Holta held him back, and Fidelma too, each on one of his arms. Words wouldn't come to him, nothing but rage would, staring at Haraldar's gleeful smile, semiobscured by the skin of his victims.

"After all that, your brother proved a volatile disappointment, Siggi Arnesson. All I asked, yes, all Old Haraldar asked was a bit of help, but that lad hates his own magic too much to even try."

"His magic," Holta repeated. "Bending iron? You tried to use him to open the Gate of Iron and Blood?"

"Old Haraldar did ask most politely," Haraldar said, shaking his head. Again his long tongue snaked out to linger on the dried skin of false lips. "The huldalf would not be persuaded."

Siggi gave up all efforts to bottle his fury. He raised a hand and tried to extend his magic, tried to feel each and every bone of Haraldar, tried to shatter them all at once as he'd shattered the sending puppet. But Siggi didn't know his own magic, didn't know how to get past the warded coat of skins, didn't know anything but futile fury. He roared in frustration and sagged against Holta's grip.

"Oh, I feel that," Haraldar hissed, with a curious shudder. "*Oh,* but it is a proud attempt. *Oh*, but this magic, this is better than what your sorry brother has to share! If only your kin knew what wild power they let run about in this human realm while they malinger and molder in their own!"

"Where is he?" Siggi demanded, blood screaming in his ears. "Where is Arnes?"

"I'll take you to him if you like," Haraldar said, and beyond the hanging mask of his mouth, the gleam of his grin was visible. "Come along with Old Haraldar, boy."

"Touch him and I'll kill you." Hrafn's flames flared with his anger.

Siggi stared at Haraldar, and Haraldar stared back. The finger was cold in Siggi's fist.

He knew he should fight. But he felt numb from head to toe, apart from a pounding that was building in his cursed arm.

"My patience has worn thin, Haraldar," Gráinne said.

Behind her, Dryade had finished her illustration. Siggi could see past her to the completed drawing, made of intricate runes.

She'd drawn a large wolf, snarling and black-eyed.

"Gráinne." Haraldar came closer, moving with the agility of a much younger man. "I've longed to wear your skin, too. It would be a gift as lovely as a huldu queen's, and you've invited me right in."

"Silence, witch!" spat one of the druids, a brawny woman with black hair. She let loose an arrow, perfectly aimed at his heart. But as the arrow neared its mark, one of Haraldar's long empty glove fingers whipped it from the air like a kraken's arm might swat a fish away.

"Hold your arrows," Gráinne warned, as the women recoiled. "He is already defeated, daughters."

"Oh, you think so, do you?" Haraldar cooed, and he took two steps closer to Gráinne, but Siggi stepped directly into his path.

"Swear to me," Siggi choked at last. "If I come with you, you'll give Arnes back."

"Siggi, shut up now," Hrafn growled, but Siggi looked only at Hraldar's hooded eyes.

"Help me open the old gate to let me slip inside, quick as a shadow, and I'll happily, joyously, lovingly give you what remains of your brother."

"Siggi," Hrafn said. "*No.*"

Siggi clutched Arnes's finger close to his chest, willing the tears to come. He felt the cold inside him expanding instead. Once he'd cried for a dead witch, and now he couldn't cry for his brother's torment. He felt nothing but an icy pit of rage, so deep down that the water was only now beginning to stir.

Calm as a still pool, Gráinne stepped forward and clapped one hand over the sodden mouth of Haraldar's mask, muffling his voice.

"Enough," she said calmly. "There will be no more talk. Your words have poisoned the air long enough, as your magic has blighted the forest. Did you really think you could scurry away like the rat you are and settle elsewhere, to poison someplace new? Did you really think you could come here, to our sacrosanct home, *uninvited*?"

Haraldar began to laugh, pushing his tongue against her palm, but Gráinne did not flinch.

"Dryade," she said, and Dryade spun around, plucked her red-stone eye from its socket, and pressed it deep into the heart of her runic drawing.

A sound began to surround them, spreading through the trees on every side, like rain and whispers and the creak of branches in a wind. But there was no wind, and the rain had softened to a mist.

"Daughters," said Gráinne. "The wolves are waking."

Chapter Fourteen
The Wolves of the Wood

The Myrkvidor protected itself against witches.

Hrafn had shared the tale with Siggi only yesterday, so confident in his knowledge, so proud to be telling him things about the world of witchcraft and magic, but he had put it out of his mind. The druids had been welcoming, more or less. He had forgotten that they had survived for centuries by keeping people like Haraldar at bay.

He had forgotten the kind of power they could wield.

Something moved in the mist behind Haraldar, a gray shadow detaching itself from the dark silhouettes of the trees.

"No, wait! Just tell me!" Siggi's voice was shaking with anger. Hrafn wished that Siggi would, just this once, be less brave. "Where have you taken him? What are you doing to him?"

Haraldar laughed. He laughed that stupid, coarse laugh, the one that boomed like waves upon a rocky shore, the one he was said to have laughed when the witches of Lifandfjall came together to shatter his coven. His own sister had stood before him, promising death, and he had laughed.

"Are you going to keep bleating like a lamb," Haraldar said to Siggi, "or come with me?"

"Siggi," Hrafn said quietly. The mist was growing thicker, softening the edges of the pines around the clearing. "He's a liar. His words mean nothing." To Haraldar, he said, "He's not going anywhere with you. We're not that fucking stupid."

"Witch-boy," Holta murmured, right beside Hrafn's ear. "Follow me. Both of you."

Hrafn reached back without looking, grasping for Siggi's hand, and found his wrist instead. In the woods behind Haraldar, a single shadow split into two, slinking along the ground low and swift. Branches snapped. There was a tearing sound, like wood splitting along the grain, and the scrape of crumbling bark. A low growl.

Haraldar looked over his shoulder. "Ah, you think I'm afraid of those beasties, woman?"

"It doesn't matter whether you are or not," Gráinne said. "They'll end you all the same."

"Siggi, we have to go," Hrafn said.

Siggi tugged his wrist free of Hrafn's grip. "No. I'm not leaving until he tells me how to find Arnes."

"Don't be stupid," Holta snapped.

"We'll show you the way," Fidelma added. "You have to—"

"Not until I know where Arnes is." Siggi's jaw was set, his eyes narrow, his shoulders tense. "He's going to tell us."

"Wait any longer and your witch will be torn to pieces," Holta hissed.

Siggi looked at her in surprise. "What?"

"*Daughters*." Gráinne's voice was a warning. "The hunt begins."

With a look of exasperation, Holta gestured for Hrafn to follow as she darted toward the woods. Hrafn spared one more glance at Siggi, still stubbornly unmoving, before he ran after her. He ran without looking back. There was a snarl and a snap behind him. Haraldar was still laughing, Siggi was still shouting, and Hrafn didn't care anymore. Siggi could stay if he wanted. He wasn't the one in danger of having his throat ripped out.

It was all Hrafn could do to keep up with Holta. She moved swiftly through the forest, winding through the trees and leaping over logs with ease, until she reached a path and broke into a flat run.

The trees closed around the trail, dense and dark; the ground was muddy and slick where it was not tangled with stones and roots. It was an old trail they were racing along, worn deep into the forest floor. The voices of Haraldar and the druid women faded, and the eerie, hollow howls of the darkwolves echoed. They did not sound like natural creatures, nothing like dogs or foxes, but like the wails of spirits wrapped in the crackling of autumn leaves and the creak of old, old wood. It was impossible to know how far away they were. Every cry sent a fresh wave of fear through Hrafn.

He risked a quick look back. Siggi was nowhere to be seen.

If that was what Siggi wanted, so be it. Let him fall into Haraldar Swift-Eye's trap. Let him believe the lies and risk his own skin. Only days ago Siggi had known nothing of witches or their craft, but now that he had discovered his huldu blood he would disregard everything he learned.

A low growl came from the forest to Hrafn's left.

In the heavy fog, the darkwolf looked sleek and black all over. It was about fifty ells away, little more than a shadow between tree trunks and draping curtains of moss. The mist whirled, breaking apart just enough for Hrafn to see that it was covered with pine needles, not fur; its limbs had the uneven shapes of knotted wood. But there was nothing wrong with its teeth: long and white and sharp, glistening as the beast snarled.

It turned toward him. Its eyes were the color of bright forest moss, shining from its face like gems.

The sight was so startling that Hrafn stumbled. His foot caught on a root, and he fell, landing hard on one elbow and knocking his chin into a protruding rock. Stunned for a moment, he blinked the stars from his eyes and pushed himself up on his hands and knees.

The wolf growled again. Those eerie green eyes were much closer, and it was not alone. Points of green light appeared in the murky fog, surrounded by hulking dark shapes. A howl rose from somewhere in the forest, echoing through the trees until the other voices joined it.

Hrafn scrambled to his feet in a panic, but he slipped again.

"Fuck. Fuck!" A strap on one of his makeshift shoes, the ones Siggi had made for him, was broken. "Fuck!"

Hrafn had his knife, but there was no magic he could use to deter darkwolves. Anything he tried would only anger them more. He picked up his broken shoe to fling it at the nearest wolf, even though it would do no good.

As he swung his arm back to throw, a hand caught his wrist.

"Up, up!" Siggi shouted, tugging Hrafn to his feet hard enough to wrench his shoulder.

Siggi didn't let go of Hrafn's arm as he hauled him forward on the trail. The wolves howled again, a chorus of threats from all around. The nearest one lunged for Hrafn, swift and deadly as an arrow. Siggi jerked Hrafn to his other side, placing himself between Hrafn and the darkwolf. He swung at the creature, as though he intended to do something ridiculous like punch it.

Although his fist did not connect, the darkwolf snapped back suddenly and let out a pained yelp. At the same moment, Hrafn felt tension across the magical bond he shared with Siggi, like the strain of a caught breath, or the pressure of teeth clenched too tight, and through it all the drumbeat of their hearts—not, for once, matching, but wildly out of sync. The wolf toppled to the ground, pawing at its face with its forelimbs. As it writhed there, Hrafn saw blood flow from its snout—from where its teeth, the only bones in its unnatural body, had been split and shattered.

"What are you doing?" Fidelma was right behind Siggi, all of her beads and bags jangling as she caught up to them. "Run, you idiots!"

Hrafn looked at Siggi, but Siggi wasn't looking back at him. He was looking at the darkwolf with an expression that was part surprise, part disgust—and more than a small amount of satisfaction.

Siggi's magic kept the wolves wary until they reached the edge of the forest. The trees ended abruptly, as though they had been cleaved away with an ax, and the trail sank into a boggy marshland. They slowed their pace, mostly because Hrafn and Fidelma were gasping for breath, whereas Siggi and Holta weren't even winded.

The rain had stopped, but the mist lingered, thick and cold, making it impossible to see more than a few paces in any direction. Hrafn had not gone more than twenty strides before a misplaced step had him sinking to his knee in cold, murky water. He was still holding his stupid broken shoe in one hand. Siggi tried to help him up, but Hrafn shook off his grasp. Hrafn's heart was hammering. Siggi had to feel that. There was no way he couldn't. Hrafn was cold, he was damp, he was exhausted, and he really, really did not want to deal with Siggi acting concerned right now.

But neither could he keep his mouth shut. "What the fuck were you thinking?"

Siggi's eyes widened. He took a step back from Hrafn.

Guilt churned in Hrafn's gut, but he couldn't stop. "Did you think you were going to take on Haraldar Swift-Eye by yourself? Or just ask him nicely to tell you what you want to know? He was baiting you! And you fucking fell for it!"

"He has my brother!" Siggi answered, his voice rising.

"Yes! He does! He has your fucking brother!" Hrafn was shouting now as well. "He has him because he wants a huldu, and you were about to strap yourself down on the butcher block instead!"

"I know it's dangerous, but I have to—"

"You have no fucking idea how dangerous it is! That man has murdered more people than you've met in your entire miserable life." Hrafn let out a harsh, strangled laugh. "You were ready to go off with him like he wanted. You would have been dead or worse before you ever saw your brother."

"You don't know that," Siggi said, very quietly, as though shouting just once or twice had been more than he dared. "And even if it's true, I have to try something. I have to help Arnes. I can't leave him with a—that man."

"With a witch?" Hrafn said. "That's what you were going to say, right? You can't leave him with a witch."

"No, that's not what I—"

"And you'd be right. How many of your own fingers are you

willing to give up to do what Swift-Eye wants? All your fingers? All your toes? Do you know what it feels like to have your skin peeled off while you're still alive to watch?"

"I'll give him all of that, and more, if I can save Arnes," Siggi said.

Hrafn felt a stab of wild, irrational jealousy toward that idiot Arnes. He may have thought he was clever, going off to search for their huldu kin, but he had fallen prey to Haraldar Swift-Eye as soon as he dared leave that grim little hovel they'd called home.

Had Arnes known he was leaving behind something more precious than anything he would find with the huldu? He couldn't have known. He never would have left if he had. What must it feel like, Hrafn wondered, to have somebody love you so much, to be so rich in love's warmth and certain of its comfort, that you didn't even realize how breathtakingly lucky you were? That you could leave it behind without a look back and know that it would be waiting for you should you return?

He could no more imagine it than he could imagine what it would feel like to be a mountain spewing ash to bury a village, or a winter storm drowning a fleet of ships. It was too big, too wild, never meant for something like him.

"Haraldar will kill you as soon as he gets what he wants," he said. His chest hurt, and he thought that pain was all his, none of it Siggi's.

"I have to try anyway." Siggi's voice was rough but maddeningly even. Tears streaked down his cheeks, carving tracks through a splattering of dirt. "He's my brother. He's the only family I have—"

Hrafn turned abruptly and started walking.

"Wait, Hrafn, I didn't mean—"

"Yes, you did," Hrafn said. He knew he shouldn't say anything, but the words were like blades in his throat, slicing open wounds he could not control. "He's the only family you have left, because of me. We both know it. I'm bored of talking about it."

Hrafn almost slipped into the mud again but caught himself. Holta and Fidelma were a little ways away. He hadn't quite forgotten they were there, but he had forgotten, kind of, and he felt a fresh spark of anger at their presence.

"One of our sisters keeps a hut not far from here," Fidelma said. "She'll be at sea this time of year, but we can use her shelter for the night."

Neither Hrafn nor Siggi spoke as they followed the girls through the marshland and onto more solid ground. Through the midnight gloom and the patchy fog, the Myrkvidor was a sweeping black swath behind them. He could not hear the wolves anymore. He hadn't heard them since leaving the forest.

The druid's stone house was built into the side of a small hill. It was humble in appearance but protected by more than the usual number of staves and runes. Hrafn felt the shiver of warning over his skin as they drew close. He didn't let himself glance to see if Siggi felt it as well.

The hut was small but solid, and the inside was comfortably dry. Hrafn had brought forth a flame to light a couple of tallow candles, revealing a bed pushed up against the back wall, a pair of stools, some shelves and supplies, all of it clean and tidy. Holta knelt by the hearth to get a fire going, and Fidelma plucked a bucket from a hook by the door.

"The marsh water is foul, and the good spring is a bit of a walk," she said. "I'll go and fetch water."

"I'll help," Siggi said quickly.

He made to follow, then stopped and looked down. He was still holding his brother's finger, wrapped up in its ragged scrap of cloth. He stared at it for a long moment, his hand twitching as though he wanted to toss it away, before he awkwardly set it on the table. He grabbed a bucket and hurried outside.

Fidelma looked after him and shrugged. "I guess he's helping." As she followed Siggi, she shouted, "You're going the wrong way!"

The door closed with a click, and Hrafn jumped to his feet. He grabbed Arnes's finger and unwrapped it, dropping the soiled cloth to the floor.

"What are you doing?" Holta demanded.

"Not your fucking concern, fish-girl."

Hrafn held the finger up to the firelight. It was such a pathetic little thing. Too small to have come from the brother Siggi so revered. Men always looked small when they were reduced to pieces.

This would be better than the tooth. It was more recently alive and taken by force. The pain that had accompanied its taking would still linger in the blood.

Hrafn drew his knife and cut a sliver of pale skin from the finger's ragged end. Made sure to get a bit of dried blood and flesh. He didn't need the whole thing—better not to use it up. They might need it again if this didn't work.

Siggi might need it, to ask somebody else for help, if Hrafn didn't come back.

"What are you *doing*?" Holta asked again, her voice rising in alarm. "Is that—"

"Magic, stupid," Hrafn said. "Filthy, ugly, bloody magic, the kind you hate. You can turn away. Most people do."

He grinned and held up the sliver of skin and flesh; he was only a bit disappointed that she didn't flinch or gag. He felt wild and unsteady, as though he was held together by only the thinnest of threads. He always felt excitement more than fear when he tried a spell he had never done before.

It wasn't going to work. It was impossible. It had to work.

He pressed the tip of the knife against the stave on the inside of his right forearm. Blood welled and dripped onto the floor. The druid woman who called this hut home would hate that.

"None of them ever did, you know," Hrafn said.

He glanced up at Holta, but she didn't appear to have heard him. For all her sneering about his magic, all she was doing now was sitting there and staring, staring, staring like one of the fish she had the power to command.

He set the knife down to pick up the little scrap of Arnes's skin and flesh. He rolled it between his fingers. Holta's lack of reaction annoyed him.

"Not one," he said.

Holta blinked and glared at him. "Not one what? What are you talking about?"

"You asked me—what did you say? How many men cut me and called it love?" Hrafn pressed the stave on his arm open. His skin was slippery with blood. It was a deep cut. He really needed to hurry. "That was a stupid question. Why the fuck would they ever do something like that? Nobody needs to tell pretty lies to a witch."

He pushed the scrap of Arnes's skin into the stave and pinched his own skin closed around it. His vision began to blur around the edges, shadows creeping in to chase away the candlelight.

"Throw water on me if I don't come back," Hrafn said. "Usually works. But if that doesn't"—he nudged his knife toward her—"stick it somewhere it'll really hurt. Elbow or knee. Under a fingernail. I'll probably feel it."

Holta took the blade without hesitation. "I could stick you with it now, to stop you doing whatever stupid thing you're doing."

"But you won't." Hrafn tried to smile at her, all teeth, but he could already feel his control slipping away. His words slurred. "You want something, something you haven't told us about, or else you would have stopped us long before this. So you're going to let me—
"

And she was gone. The candles, the fire, the hut, all of it was gone in a shadowy whirl, like being plunged into a dark lake, and what closed over him was not cold, suffocating water but fire, overwhelming fire, searing through every inch of his body, and fuck, fuck, *fuck*, he'd made a mistake. There was a reason nobody did this kind of spell, and it wasn't because witches were overly concerned with right and wrong, it was because when it went wrong it went *so fucking wrong*—

The fire vanished in an instant, although the pain did not recede. It changed, instead, to something more familiar, something easier to handle. Physical pain, the ordinary kind. It wasn't Hrafn's pain, he didn't know these aches as intimately as he knew his own, but they weren't so different. He felt a lurching motion and panic seized him—and with that came a splutter of confusion, a burst of sleepy, muddled unease that was not his.

The confusion gave him an opening. Arnes didn't know what was happening, because he was only just rousing from sleep. Maybe, just maybe, he would believe this all a dream.

Hrafn opened his eyes. The world was moving around him, filled with scraping and plodding sounds. The sky was solid gray, the sun nowhere to be seen. He was in the back of a cart. There was a heavy fur draped over him, almost too warm, and points of pain radiating all over his body. His hand, throbbing, was the worst of it. The rest felt like the aftermath of a rowdy tavern fight. There was a strip of cloth tied across his mouth.

His hands were bound; both wrists chafed under the knotted ropes. He kicked his legs experimentally: they were bound as well. The slightest brush of his hand against the fur sent fresh waves of pain rolling through him. There was a bandage wrapped where his little finger had been, stained with dried blood.

But he did not, at least, seem to be missing any skin. Whatever it was Haraldar wanted with Arnes, it wasn't that.

He took a breath and struggled to sit up. He needed to see where he was.

A low laugh came from the front of the cart. "Finally waking up, are you?"

Familiar laugh. Familiar voice. He recognized the slope of his shoulders, the cut of his hair. The dull brown of a priest's humble traveling robes. When the man turned, Hrafn thought: Siggi had been right. He really did have a frog's mouth.

"Stay down," Ketill said. "You might have found it amusing to let the villagers catch a glimpse of you, but let's not keep making things difficult. I will knock you unconscious if I have to." He chuckled again and turned back to face the road. "Perhaps I should do that anyway. It's another two days to Draugamyr. You'll need your strength."

Draugamyr. The word echoed through his mind. The Ghost Marsh, a dead and isolated place beneath the shadow of the fiery old mountain Grimholl. Site of the battlefield where the huldufolk had fought the witches a century ago. It was said there were still corpses rotting slowly in the peat, so lifelike in appearance they might have lain down to die only days ago. It was the most haunted place in all of Lifandfjall.

It was also where the last of the huldu gates had been sealed: the Gate of Blood and Bone, locked shut with a terrible sacrifice, forever separating the two worlds.

Hrafn had been to Draugamyr. He never wanted to return.

As soon as that thought crossed his mind, he felt a spike of anger. A furious question, sharp as a jab, and immediately on its heels something even worse: recognition.

Witch.

The scorn was sudden and overwhelming. Hrafn felt it surge around him, with the force of storm-churned waves, an encompassing, rage-filled refusal to let him slip away.

Witch!

He was used to anger trying to push him out of a shared mind. Birds fought like they wished to tear him apart from the inside. Rats fought with single-minded fury. Sheep fought, dogs fought, cats fought, they all fought him, their little animal minds shrieking and bucking and twisting even though they had absolutely no concept of what was happening to them. But this was different. Arnes's rage was pulling him in, trying to drown him, and the shock of it had him thrashing against it, both in mind and in the borrowed body. The cart lurched to a stop and Ketill spoke sharply, but he couldn't hear the words over his own thoughts pleading to be let go, helplessly, *uselessly*, because words never worked, not when he was walking through other minds, but he could not stop himself.

Please please let me go let me go please please pleasepleaseplease…

And the answer he received, breaking through the clinging desperation, was something like a laugh.

Witch. Filth. Monster.

He felt, distantly, suddenly cold. Then came a sharp pain in his left hand. He did not make a noise, but a scream broke through the storm of fear and anger, loud enough to tear him away from Arnes's tumultuous thoughts.

He returned to his own body with a gasp and a whimper.

Chapter Fifteen
The Burning Barrow

"He said you'd have to hurt him to wake him!" Holta hollered, as Fidelma overturned a bucket of water across Hrafn's shaking form.

Siggi, arm pulsing with Hrafn's wound, tore the knife from Hrafn's pale hand. He pulled it once, twice, thrice across his witch-bladed palm, furious tears escaping his eyes.

When Siggi's slashes didn't work and Hrafn remained altogether too still, Siggi tried it again. And again, until the gouges felt deep enough to cut through to the other side of him, but Siggi knew they couldn't be so very deep, because he hadn't reached a solid thing yet, hadn't even found the place where Hrafn's knife had fused with his bones.

Hrafn's sudden gasp was like another piercing blade as his eyes shot open. Color didn't return to his cheeks, but—

"He's awake," Holta breathed, and her relief was apparent.

Siggi fell back on his knees, sick and dizzy, blood seeping from his palm with all the heat of a hot spring.

Fidelma wiped a strand of hair from her sweating brow. "I didn't think that would work."

Siggi leaned over Hrafn, resisting the urge to shake him, to kiss him, to scream. Hrafn's skin was frosty when Siggi placed a hand on his cheek, and Hrafn didn't seem to feel his touch. His lovely black eyes were dull, somehow, as though much of him was still far away. And Siggi knew, instinctively, that Hrafn *had* been far away. Siggi didn't understand much about magic, but he was beginning to understand Hrafn.

Unlike during that first scrying in Midfjördur, this time Siggi hadn't seen whatever Hrafn had. It was only that, when he and Fidelma were together filling buckets at that trickling little spring in the fog, he'd felt a sudden tightening in his chest, a sharp slice on his arm that had all the familiarity of Hrafn cutting himself yet again, and suddenly, an empty vacuum where half his heart had been.

Hrafn had lost himself on purpose, gone to a place Siggi couldn't feel or follow, and his sudden absence felt worse than any wound. Whether that was because they shared a soul or because Siggi had fallen in love with Hrafn, he didn't know, but—

Oh, Siggi thought, pulling his hand away from Hrafn's cheek. *Is that what's happened?*

Hrafn was the boy Siggi was, yes, in *love* with, claws and scars and all, and how *dare* he leave him alone like that, knowing how it felt?

"What the fuck were you doing?" he demanded, eyes scalding.

Hrafn blinked, black eyelashes fluttering. He made it halfway to sitting before rolling onto his side. Siggi breathed through his teeth at the sudden sting of Hrafn's arm and his own vibrant lacerations, and he pulled his hand away so his blood wouldn't drip on Hrafn's face.

"What the fuck." Now Hrafn forced himself upright, shivering and blinking. His voice was frail, even if his resentment wasn't. "Are you hurt? How the fuck did you get hurt fetching water?"

"I didn't…that's not—argh! That's not what happened, you idiot! I had to wake you up!"

"You had to—" Hrafn started.

Siggi slowly held out his hand. Hrafn's eyes went wide, and painful as everything was, Siggi was relieved to see how bright and alive they looked.

"Are you fucking kidding me? Why the fuck did you do that?" Hrafn asked.

216

Honestly, the gall of the vicious little witch Siggi loved. He knew by now that every wound Hrafn inflicted on himself meant very little to him, was as commonplace to him as blinking was to others. Yet whenever Siggi was hurt, he was livid.

Siggi couldn't find the furious words to explain that this stupid, mindless bias hurt much more. As sharp as Hrafn's blade was, it had nothing on his tongue. And maybe Siggi had forgotten, amid their embraces and shared breaths, that Hrafn was a wounded thing, a cat that would scratch as soon as purr, a cat that might not even see the difference.

And even that was wrong to think, because Hrafn was a person, not an animal, no matter how much he maligned himself. How maddening it was that every time he tried to understand Hrafn, or tried to be understood by him, Hrafn's self-loathing rose like a great shattering wave between them, so tangible Siggi could taste the salt of it.

"Holta said you told her to cause you pain if you didn't wake up. So I did."

"I didn't mean—for fuck's sake, that's not what I meant!" Hrafn said. "You could have just hit me or stuck the blade in me. It would have worked."

Siggi shook his head.

"I would have," Holta said, and Siggi frowned. "I was going to try that after we dumped the water on you. But your boy wouldn't let me."

Siggi felt a sudden heat fill his face, not anger. *Your boy*, she called him. Siggi was Hrafn's boy now. Storguð's hands! How could he make Hrafn understand what that meant?

"You're already bleeding," he told Hrafn. "I wasn't going to give you another wound."

"So now we're both bleeding." Hrafn threw up his good hand, but it was trembling like a bloodless thing. "How the fuck is that better?"

"I won't cut you," Siggi said. "So stop arguing with me about it."

Fidelma groaned. "Please, please, stop arguing about it. This is like listening to blackbirds fight over entrails, except the birds at least have more reason. Answer the question, witch. What were you doing?"

"I know where Arnes is," Hrafn said, and Siggi's heart flipped over because he'd refused to hope, but he'd wondered. "Or, to be more accurate, I know where he's going to be in about two days. But he's not close. I don't even know if it's possible to get there in time. Fuck. I'm going to have to ask Ylfa for help."

"You—he's—he's still alive?" Siggi could hear his own breath in his ears, could almost see Arnes in his eyes, could only imagine what Hrafn had seen while doing his magic. "Are you certain?"

Hrafn lowered his eyes and his voice. "He is for now."

The foreboding in Hrafn's words was impossible to mistake, but Siggi couldn't care.

Arnes was alive, and Hrafn had found him.

He threw his arms around Hrafn, heedless of their injuries, a wordless noise escaping him as he pulled Hrafn close. Hrafn's posture was stiff and his clothes were sopping wet, but Siggi didn't let go. Gods, did Hrafn have any idea how fragile he was?

"Thank you," he whispered. "Thank you for finding him again."

"Stop it," Hrafn said. "Don't."

"Yes, please don't," said Holta from somewhere beyond them, as Fidelma snickered.

"Thank you a thousand times, Hrafn."

This time Hrafn pushed him away, hands on Siggi's collarbones. "Stop it, I said."

Siggi frowned at Hrafn's uneasy expression. "But what is it? Was Arnes…? Apart from his finger, was he…? Was he okay?"

Hrafn blinked and turned away. "He's…he's alive." Hrafn cleared his throat, casting his black eyes about the room. "He was with Ketill, of all bastards."

Siggi frowned, thoughts swimming. The burning church in Midfjördur, the mocking man on horseback. "The priest. The frog-mouthed one?"

"Yes." Hrafn frowned, still shaking. "He must be working with

Swift-Eye."

"Who the fuck is Ketill, and why would he be fool enough to work with Haraldar?" Holta asked.

"I *thought* he was nothing more than a piece-of-shit priest. He wanted me to steal"—he looked at Siggi—"a relic from Siggi's village."

"My huldu mother's severed head," Siggi said, and he didn't let his voice tremble, and he didn't look away from Hrafn, willing him to see he wasn't angry, wasn't anything but present.

"If the head belonged to this one's mother," Fidelma mused, gesturing at Siggi, "it must have been a powerful relic indeed."

Holta grimaced, but there was a gleam in her eye. "If he's working with Swift-Eye, his goal must also be a way into the hidden realm."

Siggi looked at Hrafn, who nodded. "I suspect so. He's bringing Siggi's brother to Draugamyr."

"Why, though?" Holta asked. "I understand what a witch like Haraldar wants with huldu magic, but why would a priest risk going to Hulduheimer?"

Hrafn frowned. "I don't know what stake Ketill has in all of this."

"Well," Fidelma hazarded, straightening up. "Isn't it obvious?"

Siggi, Hrafn, and Holta all looked at her and she rolled her eyes. "Oh come on. You say he's a churchman, yes? And if there's one thing I know about *those* particular arse-cocks, the only thing they like more than burning witches is controlling others. If you're the sort who becomes a priest, it's more than likely you don't do it to appease any god, old or new. You do it because you want people to listen to you, and you want power, and what place is more powerful than the long-lost hidden realm, where magic grows wild and free and terrible?"

Siggi gaped at her, and she shrugged. "What? I had the misfortune of being raised by a priest in Akureyvik before I ran away to join the druids. Would-be holy men all want what they shouldn't have, and they all tell others what they refuse to tell themselves."

"Hmm." Holta frowned at her. "Not everyone is that simple."

"Men usually are," Fidelma said sweetly.

"It doesn't matter," Siggi said, pulling himself upright. His hand was still bleeding, and Hrafn still looked unwell, but Siggi had rarely felt so certain. "They have my brother, and we're going to get him back."

"Oh? Still repeating that, are we?" Fidelma looked at him strangely. "You do know that's precisely what this priest wants, don't you? To lure a useful huldu to the Draugamyr? To the Gate of Blood and, ahem, *Bone*?"

"It is most definitely a trap," Holta agreed, and Hrafn pinched his lips shut.

Siggi shrugged, wondering how often he'd have to say it: "So it's a trap. That doesn't matter."

"Doesn't it?" Hrafn asked quietly. "What if this priest brings something back from the hidden realm? What if Fidelma is right, and what he wants is another way to harm people? One that nobody can protect against anymore, because it's been a hundred years since they've had to? Is it worth the risk?"

Siggi opened his mouth, but Hrafn cut him off.

"Don't answer that. I know what you'll say."

"Well, is it a trap if we know about it already? Why not play along and see where it leads?" Holta asked.

"You're Gráinne's child, all right," Fidelma said with a chuckle. "Are we pretending that's all you want? Just to see where it leads?"

Hrafn's eyes narrowed. "What do you mean?"

"Didn't she tell you?" Fidelma said brightly. "This priest isn't the only one who wants a way into the hidden realm. Celestina wants nothing more than to march through one of the gates and take revenge on those who killed her family and banished her."

Silence descended within the close hut. Hrafn looked shocked.

"Fidelma!" Holta shouted.

"What, you never mentioned your lifelong quest for vengeance to them?" Fidelma laughed, then stopped. "Honestly, Celestina. Were you going to keep it a secret until they realized you were trying to open the gate as well?"

"Is it true?" Siggi asked, meeting her eyes. "Did…did the other huldu kill your family?"

"If I say yes, will you pity me?" Holta demanded, eyes gleaming.

"No," Siggi said. "If you say yes, I'll help you."

Holta went quiet, but Fidelma laughed. "Farm boy's got you there, ina. Since when do you care about the power games men play, when all you want is your vengeance? And me? If we get to murder a priest along the way, I won't complain. And we all know this besotted little witch won't let Siggi out of his sight again. Do you have objections?" she asked, looking at Hrafn.

"I…" Hrafn didn't seem to know how to answer. Siggi could not tell what he was thinking. "It's madness. We're more likely to die than succeed. But it's not impossible."

Fidelma held open her arms, and beneath her shawl, Siggi heard a dozen little pouches jangle. "So? Let's walk into the trap. We've all agreed, haven't we?"

Somehow, it seemed they had.

"How are we getting to Draugamyr?"

Holta scowled. "Fidelma, *you're* going the fuck home to Myrkvidor."

"Not a chance, dearest," Fidelma trilled. "I've been so bored of late."

Siggi could see Hrafn and Holta were both about to protest, and so he spoke instead: "Thank you for your help."

Fidelma smiled and Holta muttered something scathing, but Siggi was watching Hrafn. He could feel his thoughts winding and twisting.

"Draugamyr," Siggi echoed, and the word tasted black on his tongue. "Where is it?"

Holta cursed and began to pace. "On the southern side of Grimholl, several days' journey in fair weather. The only path there goes over a high pass between slumbering mountains before descending into the bog and lava field below. The way is treacherous and often fog-choked, and of course, people say Draugamyr itself is little more than an accursed cemetery."

"They also say the swamp moss bleeds after it rains, and the squelching of bootsteps sounds more akin to screaming." Fidelma was grinning as though these rumors were as delicious as they were hideous. Siggi felt like he was listening to Arnes of yesteryear. "It's half marshland and half obsidian, and haunted enough that the wind carries the voices of the dead that melted there."

"Sheepshit and whispers," Hrafn said, "but it's true the place is haunted."

"It's *the most* haunted," Fidelma insisted, pouting. "It's called the Ghost Marsh, for fuck's sake!"

"I know," Hrafn retorted, "because I've *been there*. Are you worried you'll soil yourself at the first angry wail?"

"Enough!" Holta stood up. "Haunted or no, that's where we're going. But how?"

Hrafn pressed his palms into his temples. "That's why I need to contact Ylfa."

Siggi's eyes widened, mind whirring. "Will you ask her to lend us her lyngbakr?"

Fidelma's eyes went wide. "You know someone with a lyngbakr? Holy shit, truly?"

But Holta's shoulders stiffened. "You can't mean Ylfa Sifsdottir."

Siggi wasn't sure, and Hrafn didn't answer.

Holta's gaze darkened. "The selfsame Ylfa Sifsdottir who sealed Gráinne in the Myrkvidor for a decade? Ylfa Sifsdottir, the witch who bound a huldu lover to her will and cursed his offspring? Ylfa Sifsdottir, the vicious witch of Viklaugur, who collects the bones of infants for her spellcraft?"

"Um," Siggi said, looking at Hrafn. "Is Sifsdottir her family name, Hrafn?"

Hrafn let out a dry laugh. "It is, and those stories are rather dramatic, but honestly,who cares if she slept with some huldu in her youth?"

"Just because *you* wanna sleep with a half-huldu," Fidelma muttered, but Holta's mouth was a thin line.

"How do you know Ylfa Sifsdottir, Hrafn?"

Hrafn met her gaze. "Doesn't seem like I have to tell you."

"She's like a guardian to him," Siggi answered, cutting through the tension. "She taught him magic and raised him for a time."

Hrafn's eyes flickered, but for once he kept his mouth shut.

"That may explain *you* somewhat," Holta hissed. "Raised by a thing like that."

Hrafn just looked at her, arms folded.

"Well," Siggi said, watching each of them, shifting his weight from foot to foot. "Hrafn. Are you going to…um, call Ylfa here to help us?"

Hrafn let out a dry laugh. "No one can call Ylfa anywhere. She turns up only when she wants to."

"But she'll want to!" Siggi argued. "She'll *want* to help you, Hrafn!"

"Why should she?" Hrafn asked, as though he genuinely didn't know.

Weeping Stormurkona, Siggi could just smack him, except he never ever would.

"Because she *loves* you, you dolt."

"She doesn't," Hrafn said, scars livid on his flushing cheeks. Siggi felt a spike in Hrafn's pulse, something like genuine shock.

"She definitely does, Hrafn."

"How can you possibly know that?" Hrafn snapped.

"I can just *tell*," Siggi said. "You can't see it because…because *you* just don't know what love looks like."

Hrafn's face twisted.

"Well, we won't know if she'll help until you ask her, will we?" Fidelma said. "If she can bring her lyngbakr, that's a bonus. I've always wanted to see one of those things. Will she let me pet it? Or ride it, even?"

"Clearly *you* haven't met Ylfa," Hrafn said, but Siggi could see he was considering. "I'll call out to her. I've a summoning stave. She may not answer, even if she hears me."

"Please," Siggi said, catching Hrafn's eye.

"Fucking hell," he muttered, using Siggi's shoulder to find his footing. "Siggi. You stay right fucking here. Have Pisslocks bandage your hand."

"No! Last time I left you alone you nearly didn't wake!" Siggi stood. "You're not leaving me again."

"What, never?" Hrafn said coldly, and Siggi felt a shock run through him.

"He won't go alone," Holta said, pulling them apart. "I'll go with him."

Hrafn's gaze was unreadable, but he nodded before turning his back on Siggi. Though the witch-boy tried to hide it, Siggi could feel how exhausted Hrafn was.

Siggi had one more thing to say: "Don't cut yourself more than you have to."

Hrafn didn't answer. Siggi looked to Holta, who nodded. "I'll watch over the little bastard."

Neither she nor Hrafn looked back as they stepped into the fog. The hut's uneven door clattered shut behind them.

"Well," Fidelma said, wiping her hands on her trousers, "let's just hope they don't knife each other."

Fidelma pulled a pot of poultice, a needle, a spool of thread, and a roll of bandage from several of her many belt bags. Now that Siggi was looking at her properly, beneath her oversized shawl the druid girl was completely laden with pouches and pockets and bags, draped in them like an unkempt sheep with overgrown knots of wool. Fidelma was a sturdy, thick-legged girl, steady handed as she moved. Siggi couldn't help but think she'd be a lot of help on the farm.

"Hold your arm up higher or it'll never stop bleeding."

Siggi did as he was asked. She set about wiping his hand and forearm down with a surprisingly spotless rag.

"You have so many pockets."

Fidelma smiled, remaining eye on her work. "Any druid worth

her salt has healing herbs within reach at all times, and several blades in her boot as well."

Siggi's skin pulsated as Fidelma, humming to herself, tied a length of leather around his forearm, a tourniquet to slow the bleeding, but gravity was doing the bulk of the work already. "What else have you got in there?"

"Hold this," she said, pressing a stone into Siggi's other palm. "If the pain's too much, squeeze it tight, and watch you don't bite your tongue. As for what else I've got?" Fidelma stood upright, too short to attend to Siggi's upraised hand otherwise, even though he was kneeling. "You name it, it's likely I've got it. Beads, coins, bread and balms, shells."

"Shells," Siggi said, wincing as she pushed the needle through his palm, pulling the string taut. "Because they're beautiful?"

"Because other people think so, and I've often traded them for more useful things." Again the needle went through, and Siggi flinched. "Which isn't to say I don't have my share of pretty keepsakes. I've a love for obsidian that weighs down my pockets for no good reason. Holta always says keepsakes are pointless, but that's only because *her* favorite keepsake is a place she's never been to."

"The hidden realm," Siggi said, as the needle rose and fell, his hand set alight. He squeezed the cool stone in his other hand, grimacing. "Did she…was she really banished?"

"Well, I don't rightly know, beyond what little she's told me," Fidelma pulled the needle through yet again. "She's been in this realm since she was a child. She doesn't like to talk about what came before that. Or how she alone survived being banished."

"What's the hidden realm like?"

Siggi watched her eye narrow to pinpoint focus. "No one has been for a visit in a century, and those who come out don't say much. You're only the second huldu I've ever met, and no offense, but you know a lot less about it than even she does."

"Were you thrown out of somewhere as a child too?" Siggi asked, before he could think not to.

"I wasn't." The sewing paused, and Fidelma breathed through

her teeth. "But my parents were put to death by the Brotherhood of the Seven Saints when I was six summers old."

Siggi startled, and she tapped his arm to keep him steady. "That's…I'm sorry. But…why?"

Fidelma put the needle down and set about opening her little pot of poultice. She rubbed the yellow, acrid-smelling substance into Siggi's newly puckered hand. First it stung, as though she were rubbing sand into his skin, and then suddenly his hand felt numb.

"They were accused of being witches, if you can believe it. Because Father was not milk skinned and mother was even browner, and he spat a few choice words at the thieving farmer next door, and then that farmer's wife fell ill and gave birth to a dead child, and the church declared that was Father's doing. The priests took me in to reeducate me thereafter, but I never let it go, and ran away to the druids the moment I saw one of them in the harbor. That was Gráinne, and I think it was a bit like love, seeing her with all her knives and beads and skin like mine and red eye simply *not giving a shit* about everyone else."

"What was it like? Being brought up by a priest?"

"Oh." She paused. "Well. You know how churches are."

"I don't." Siggi shook his head. "Father never let me go."

"Aren't you fortunate." She set the poultice pot down and unspooled the bandage around Siggi's stitched palm. "Gods, but this scar is strange, isn't it? It's all hazy in my magic eye, even. So. The church. Well. People in the church say a lot of lofty words and curse a lot of simple joys. It seems everyone is guilty of something, and anything in this world that's enjoyable is frowned upon. And yet priests go on and on about another world, a heavenly realm where things are lovely. But I couldn't help but think that even if we were already in such a place, the priests wouldn't let anyone enjoy any of those happy, lovely things. Happy people don't need church so much, you see. And the church that raised me was a bitter place full of vindictive people who killed my parents and called it goodness. Right. You can put your hand down."

"Thank you." Siggi did so, rubbing the bandage with his other palm, watching Fidelma pocket her objects again. He wondered what Holta and Hrafn were doing, hated that they were doing it out of sight, but he felt no new sting of pain, so at least Hrafn hadn't cut himself. Yet.

"You really love that witch, don't you," Fidelma said, and Siggi realized she was watching him. He didn't know what to say, but she didn't expect a reply. "It's awful, isn't it? Painful even. Loving someone."

Siggi stared at his mismatched hands. "Hrafn…I. We're soul-bonded, but I still don't know what he's thinking, or how to convince him that even if we weren't, I'd still…I'd still want to…"

Fidelma pounded him firmly on the back, almost knocking the wind out of him. "Oh, believe you me, I know how that goes. The thing is, you *never* will know entirely what he's feeling or thinking, soul-bonded or not. I mean, I can't even say I always know what *I'm* feeling, let alone guess at the feelings of the one I love."

"So how can you *convince* anyone you love them?"

"I think you're probably stubborn enough," Fidelma said. "Keep on doing what you're doing. I'd wager it's working."

Siggi lifted his chin, brimming with hope. "It is?"

"Oh come on," Fidelma said with a crooked smile. "That witch-boy's got eyes like obsidian, black as night and thrice as cold. But when he looks at you? They turn to silk."

"Oh." Siggi's heart ached and swelled all at once. He wondered if Hrafn could feel it.

"Hey, tell me something." Fidelma looked at her fingernails, eyelids lowered. "Holta…does she look at me like that?"

"Sorry," Siggi said, after a moment. "I haven't noticed. But I'll try to from now on."

For once, Fidelma looked less than jolly. "Well, thanks anyhow."

A sudden rumbling pulled them to their feet and the walls of the hut rattled. There came a booming roar and a mighty shout from down the hill, and Siggi and Fidelma burst through the door into the open air. The fog hadn't lifted, and even as they ran past the curious warding staves that made his stomach flip, Siggi couldn't see beyond the thick of it.

"Hrafn!" he cried, barreling down the slippery hill with Fidelma at his heels. "Holta!"

Again came a rumbling that nearly bowled them off their feet, followed by another shout that sounded not unlike the braying of a sheep in pain, though it was a hundred times louder.

"What the fuck is that?" Fidelma said as Siggi leaped into the mist and slid down the damp grass.

The mist wasn't mist at all, he realized, as he sucked in deep breaths—it was smoke, and something massive and moving was ablaze at the base of the little hill.

"Ylfa! Ylfa!" That was Hrafn's voice, and suddenly Siggi felt Hrafn's heart racing.

It was Ylfa's lyngbakr. The towering, claw-footed mound of heather trampled the turf to mud as it screamed, mindless in its agony. Siggi spotted Hrafn and Holta, shouting and trying to stop the creature's fitful stampede. The heather burned and cracked, and Siggi couldn't see the creature's face through the flames that licked its hide, razing Ylfa's little turf house to ruins.

"Hrafn!" Siggi cried again, but Hrafn did not seem to hear him. Against all sense, his face bloodless, Hrafn ran toward rather than away from the inferno, calling Ylfa's name until his voice was raw.

The thistles were crumbling to ash as Hrafn neared the creature's furious fore. He tried in vain to climb atop it, but the ladder to Ylfa's door had long since burned away, and the roof of her house atop the lyngbakr's back had caved in. From the lyngbakr's brambles dripped what looked like oil, so much thicker than blood.

Siggi felt Hrafn's hands burning as he fought the flames. Hrafn wouldn't stop unless someone *made* him stop. Siggi leaped forward and grabbed Hrafn around the waist, pulling him back as the creature's feet came down and it crashed to its burning knees, howling in agony.

"Ylfa!" Hrafn fought against Siggi's grip, his arms aflame. "She's inside, Ylfa's inside!"

"Move!" Fidelma said, shoving both of them back into the damp green hill. From another of her pouches she pulled an arrow, long and sharp, and aimed it through her bow at the lyngbakr's burning face.

"No, don't!" Hrafn cried, but the arrow sang through the air, piercing the creature between the obscured eyes, cutting its cries abruptly short.

The lyngbakr crumpled with the cacophony of a forest collapsing, no longer screaming as it met the earth.

Now Holta made her move, leaping in a single bound over Fidelma's kneeling form, boots finding purchase amid the burning brambles of the creature's hide. For the first time, Siggi witnessed the grace of a huldu in action. Holta leaped over the heather ruin and kicked in Ylfa's door. It fell away in a pile of ashes. Holta stepped aside as flames burst from the turf house, then darted inside. Fidelma shouted at her below. Hrafn fought against Siggi's grip, clawing at his skin, but Siggi didn't let go even as Hrafn drew blood.

Finally, Holta reappeared in the sunken doorway, a bundle of cloth in her arms, and Ylfa's orange cat clinging to her neck. Around her head a winged creature flapped: Ylfa's skull-faced utburdur, squalling like a newborn, its cries as piercing as they were futile.

Holta jumped from the ashen heap to the grass below, and finally Siggi let Hrafn go so he could run to her.

Ylfa looked so small in Holta's arms, her body singed and half her clothing burned away. But she was coughing, alive as Holta laid her on the damp grass. The cat slid from her neck and darted away up the hill, but Anna stayed close. Fidelma swatted at the flames on Ylfa's legs and shawls as Hrafn leaned over her, sobbing like a broken thing.

Holta took a step back and met Siggi's eyes, and her gaze told him all he needed to know.

The little utburdur hopped around the grass, mewling piteously.

More than half of Ylfa's body was burned red raw and black, and her breath came in wheezes. Her left side was all but charred to nothing, bone exposed, and one eyeball burned away, half of her mandible visible because her skin was all but absent.

"Hrafn," Ylfa whispered. "You called me just in time. He was going to drag it out, you see. Didn't want me coming to help you."

"I couldn't put the fire out," Hrafn cried, eyes furious. "You taught me how to start them and not to put them out. Fuck's sake, *Ylfa!*"

"You assume *I* ever knew how to put fires out," she rasped. "But no one taught me either. Starting fires, not ending them. That's being a witch."

"Who did this," Hrafn demanded. "Who did this to you."

She coughed, her remaining eye roving, but her wits remained steady. "My old huldu friend was no true friend of mine, it seems. He sent a witchfire sending to do away with me."

"Because of me?" Hrafn said, eyes wide and mad. "Did he—"

"They're all riled up now," she said. "I thought they'd stopped caring, truth be told. Thought they'd stopped caring decades ago."

"But you said this huldu was your friend?" Siggi said, mind reeling, watching Hrafn take that news like another arrow. "How could he do this to you?"

"Oh, stupid farm boy, haven't you learned yet? People can be many contradictory things all at once."

And in that instant, Siggi realized she'd known or suspected Siggi was huldalf all along, and that it no more mattered to her than Hrafn being a witch, that it didn't make either of them less than what they could be.

"Ylfa." Hrafn's words were wet with tears. "Ylfa, I don't know enough healing magic. I don't know anything worthwhile."

"It'd be wasted anyhow. Where's my foolish old cat?"

"He came out with you, Ylfa," Siggi said.

"Course he did," Ylfa murmured. "And may he find the druids more welcoming than I did."

"I'll make sure they spoil him," Fidelma said calmly. "Mice and firesides daily."

"Ylfa…" Hrafn gasped.

"Now stop that crying and listen for a change, child. You've got to reach the gate first. Every fool and his blade will be trying to seize it, now that the idea's in their minds. There's another path to Draugamyr, a quicker one," she said. "Anna will show you the way. Won't you, Anna? She'll help you find it. You and she both, you've walked the borderland between life and death. Trust her."

The utburdur cooed a sorry cry, rubbing its skull against Ylfa's limp hand. Siggi felt a curious buzzing in his ears, and knew that the bones there were broken. Maybe his own magic, wielded by someone wiser, could bind them together, but even that wouldn't change her fate.

"But I hate birds," Hrafn said, voice breaking. "I can't fucking stand them."

"We all tolerate things we can't stand. Anna will take you where you need to go, stubborn boy. There's a tunnel, the old lava tube through Grimholl. If you take that tunnel, perhaps you'll make it in time. The tunnel…it's older than anything human or huldu can recall. Be careful I tell you, though you won't listen."

"Ylfa," Hrafn said, shaking her shoulder, but her skin seemed to peel away at his touch. "Ylfa, please, don't close your eyes!"

"*Eye*, just one," she said with a cackle. "Do you think the druids would like me now?"

Dying though she was, Ylfa remained alert and coy, directing this question to the girls standing behind Hrafn. Fidelma had buried her face in Holta's chest, but Holta nodded at her once. Finally, Ylfa's stare drifted to Siggi.

"Siggi. You look after this idiot, won't you?"

Siggi nodded. "Forever."

"Ha, but he'll hate you for it," she said, and her coughing became a mighty wracking. "Aye, all this trouble. I'd hoped we'd left it in the past."

Ylfa had nothing else to say as her body succumbed to the fiery spasms alongside her fallen lyngbakr. The heather kept burning, a persistent crackling heat, but otherwise the world seemed incredibly quiet at the base of the misty little hill.

Anna tucked her skull beneath a black wing.

For an instant Siggi couldn't tell where he was—was it possible he was still in Midfjördur, watching his father's body burn? Or at the church? Or was he only feeling exactly what Hrafn was feeling, watching a parent turn to ash?

"Hrafn," he said, touching him on the shoulder. He waited for Hrafn to recoil, to scream, to throw him aside. Instead, Hrafn's shoulders sank, and he put his hands in the grass, unable to speak between his wracking, stilted breaths.

"You see what comes of loving me," Hrafn gasped. "If that were ever true."

Siggi pulled Hrafn into his lap and Hrafn wept, tears soaking Siggi's neck.

"That's what comes of loving anyone," Siggi whispered.

Chapter Sixteen
Veins of the World

Once, when Hrafn was living with Ylfa, she woke him in the middle of the night. It was early winter and bitterly cold. The wind howled like a wild animal. Hrafn grumbled and thought about staying tucked beneath the warm blanket no matter how hard Ylfa tried to rouse him, but he didn't know yet how far he could push her before she lost her temper and beat him. It hadn't happened yet, although he had been pushing and pushing, waiting for the snap.

So he rose, dressed in warm clothes, and followed her out of the cozy thicket of heather.

Ylfa didn't explain where they were going. She carried no lantern or torch, followed no trail, only shuffled across the crunching black rocks without even looking to see if he would follow. The lyngbakr had been perched atop a blustery cliff for a few days. Hrafn could hear the ocean, angry and crashing far below. There was no moon, and most of the stars were hidden by high, swift clouds. He didn't ask where they were going. She would tell him, or she wouldn't. What he wanted had very little to do with it.

Perhaps Ylfa had grown tired of him and intended to drop him into the sea.

Two days earlier he had slashed at her with a knife—a kitchen knife, the only one she let him touch—because she had refused to let him try a new spell. He had barely touched her, drawn only the thinnest line of blood, but Hrafn knew she was angry, and he knew her anger would explode eventually. It always did, when somebody was angry with him. And he had never yet met anybody who wasn't always angry with him.

Ylfa stopped abruptly. She tilted her head into the wind and gestured for him to come closer.

"Hear that?" she said.

Hrafn didn't hear anything except the wind. It was so cold his nose was running and his ears ached. He should have stayed in bed, even if it meant Ylfa would beat him bloody in the morning.

"There," she said. The wind grabbed her voice and whipped it away. "Listen."

Finally Hrafn heard it: a cry on that wind, a voice that did not belong to the night air or the seabirds. He tensed and looked around. He couldn't tell where it was coming from.

"It's nothing to be afraid of," Ylfa said, with a hint of laughter in her voice. "Weren't you the one telling me you're more frightening than anything out here?"

The mockery made him bristle, but Ylfa was already turning away.

"This way," she said, and she started walking again.

The ground sloped downward, tufts of grass and clumps of heather giving way to naked rock that crunched and slid beneath his feet. The roar of the ocean waves grew louder.

Then, without warning, the earth dropped away before them. Hrafn stopped and stumbled backward a few steps, his heart racing. They had reached the edge of the cliff.

Ylfa crouched to the ground. There was something dark at her feet. A dead animal, Hrafn thought. A lamb or goat. But the cry rose again, that chilling wail that burrowed into his skin, and the shape moved, revealing itself to be a bundle of cloth with something inside.

"Don't be afraid," Ylfa said. "Come and have a look. You've not seen one of these before, I'd wager."

"What is it?" Hrafn asked.

"Utburdur." Ylfa picked up the bundle to cradle it gently in her arms.

It wailed again, that eerie, piercing cry, and she bounced it softly as she might a child. Hrafn glimpsed black wings and white bone.

"There, there, little one. There's no need for that. You're just a little lost thing, aren't you, looking for what can't be found." Ylfa glanced up from the creature and jerked her chin toward the cliff. "See, there."

The swaddled little creature was not the only thing on that barren cliff top. There was also a pair of simple rope-and-leather shoes, quite small, and a folded garment of undyed wool. Atop the clothing was a handful of shiny pebbles and a necklace made up of a string of wooden beads on rough twine, smudged with oil and clay to give them color. It was something a little girl might have made for herself to wear.

Hrafn swallowed back bile in his throat. The little creature in Ylfa's arms kept crying. She was right; he had never seen an utburdur before, but he had heard of them. They were what became of abandoned and exposed infants. They kept their human skull, but the rest of them took on the form of a raven, giving them flight and voice—more than they'd had in their brief, miserable lives.

It was said they would seek out their mothers, the ones who had abandoned them. It was said that if you followed their cries, you would find the faithless mother.

Hrafn looked again at the shoes, the necklace, the edge of the cliff. He felt sick to his stomach. There was a village down at the seaside, with a new church in its center and a magistrate with a reputation for cruelty. If they went to that village and began asking questions, they might hear of a family with a daughter who had recently gone missing. A girl young enough to wear a string of beads and collect pebbles as she walked, but old enough to know what would become of an unwed mother and unwanted child in such a place.

The utburdur wailed again. It sounded nothing like a child, nor did it sound like a raven. It was caught between and could never be mistaken for either.

Ylfa shook her head. "All right, little one. You probably want some meat, don't you? Nice, fresh meat. We'll get some for you. We'll get some right away."

She rose to her feet and started back to the lyngbakr. Hrafn hesitated to follow. He didn't like leaving the shoes and clothes just sitting there, waiting to be swept away by the wind. It wasn't right, that the last trace of the girl could be erased without anybody ever knowing.

His own mother, whoever she had been, might have chosen the same fate. He knew from the brown of his skin that one or both of his parents had come from far to the east, from the rich and strange lands across oceans and continents, where the sun shone always and kings and emperors battled. But that was all he knew. They had left him nothing else.

He might have become an utburdur himself, if things had gone just a little differently.

He had never realized before why Birtingr had given him the name he had.

With the wind stinging his face and icy knots in his gut, Hrafn hurried after Ylfa. He didn't want to be left on that cliff top alone.

Ylfa was always taking in strays—stray creatures, stray spirits, stray boys—but Anna was the only one she kept. And now Anna was leading them away from her, leaving the burnt husk of the lyngbakr behind.

They had passed the remainder of the night in the druid's hut, although none of them had slept much. Fidelma had wrapped Hrafn's burned hands in a salve and bandages, but not until she had asked him if he couldn't heal it himself. Siggi, of course, had spoken up to say that he had healed Siggi's burns before. Hrafn hadn't denied it, but neither did he try to deal with his own burns. He wanted them to keep hurting. His eyes stung and his throat felt raw, but he was out of tears, scraped empty on the inside. He wished he was still in Siggi's arms.

The morning was grim and cold, with the sun little more than a pale circle behind leaden clouds. Wind buffeted them as they walked. The smell of smoke lingered in Hrafn's hair and clothes. They had not buried Ylfa. The ground outside the Myrkvidor was either rock or marsh, neither suitable for a grave. Fidelma had said the druids would come to see that they had escaped the wood unharmed and bury the witch when they did. Hrafn thought now he should have demanded they bury her. He knew what people might do with the body of a witch as powerful as Ylfa. People who feared her but did not know her. He should have buried her.

Anna led impatiently, flying ahead before circling back, sometimes squawking or wailing to get their attention. They followed the Fossvegur south for a short while, before veering inland on the faintest scar of an old trail, heading toward the slumbering bulk of Grimholl in the distance. They passed no villages and saw evidence of only small and remote farms.

Every once in a while Fidelma would stop abruptly and look around, her beads and braids softly jangling as she whipped her head this way and that, before she muttered something to herself and kept going.

The third or fourth time it happened, Siggi finally asked what was wrong.

Fidelma said, "Not wrong. But not right either. It's taken me awhile to see it, but we're following a corpse road."

"A what?" Siggi asked, alarmed.

Fidelma gestured vaguely at the barren landscape. "A road used by mourners to carry the dead to burial. It leaves an echo that lingers a long time. That's what we're walking along, but it's an old one."

"How old?" Siggi asked.

"Very old," said Fidelma. "Maybe even as old as the first people to come here."

Several paces ahead, Holta let out an unimpressed snort. "What do you know about the first people here? Even the druids have no true understanding of what it is to live a long time."

Fidelma laughed lightly. "Oh, why don't you share with us your wisdom, then, fair hidden one? Tell us what it is to live so long that a corpse road is nothing more than a wisp of a spiderweb to you."

Holta glanced back to glare at Fidelma, but it was not a particularly convincing glare.

"That's not what I meant," she said, her voice grumbling. "The hidden folk were already here when humans arrived. You know that."

"I do," Fidelma agreed. "Just as I know this path is an old one."

"But they weren't alone," Holta went on. "The trylla were here as well. The huldu and the trylla shared this land, but not easily, long before humans showed up with their boats and axes. Although some say there was never any difference between them, or no more than there is between cousins of the same bloodline."

"I've heard of the trylla," Siggi said. He quickened his pace to walk beside Holta, obviously wanting to take advantage of her unexpectedly chatty mood. "But all I've heard is that they live in mountains and eat people."

"That would be the only part humans considered worth remembering," Holta said, with a roll of her eyes. "We killed them off centuries ago and never had any thanks for it."

"Ylfa said the tunnel is older than human or huldu," Siggi said. "Does that mean it might have been made by trylla? Or somebody else? Somebody even the huldu don't remember?"

Holta only shrugged.

Fidelma said, "Maybe. We can't exactly ask them, can we? All I know is it's very old, and the huldu have only been locked behind their gates for a hundred years. It's said the Gate of Blood and Stone is in a tunnel, because in places like that—places between the two worlds but not firmly in either one—it's easier to make the passage."

"Is it this same tunnel?" Siggi asked.

"No," Hrafn said, the first words he had spoken in what felt like hours. "That gate is far to the south, beneath Bryreldfjöll."

"Some would argue that they're all the same, beneath the surface, no matter how far apart they are," Fidelma said. "Distance has a different meaning in the border between realms. How else could it serve as a shortcut to carry us across Grimholl?"

Fidelma turned to cast her gaze on Hrafn for a moment. There was no laughter in her expression, no jest in her eyes. They had all heard Ylfa's words to him: *You've walked the borderland between life and death.*

She walked backward for a few steps before turning again. "Do none of you know this? Never thought I'd be in the company of a huldu, a half-huldu, and a witch, and yet know more than all of them about their own land. It doesn't matter, anyway, whose dead was carried along this road. The echoes are all the same in the end."

She and Holta strode ahead, and Siggi fell back to walk beside Hrafn. He shortened his own steps to match Hrafn's but did not say anything. His silence—no questions, no reassurances, no pointless comments—chafed at Hrafn.

"What?" Hrafn said, after the silence had lasted too long.

"What?" Siggi replied. He had the nerve to sound startled.

Hrafn felt a hot stab of anger. "You obviously want to say something. So fucking say it."

"I don't—" Siggi stopped, took a breath. "I'm just…I'm worried. About you."

He reached out for Hrafn's shoulder, but Hrafn flinched and stepped away. He didn't want Siggi's pity. He didn't need it. He didn't deserve it. Without looking at Siggi, he quickened his pace to take a few steps ahead and said, without even glancing back, "We can't all get over watching somebody burn to death as easily as you can."

He pretended he didn't hear Siggi's quiet gasp, but he couldn't ignore the way Siggi's heart skipped, quick and painful.

Siggi didn't try to talk to him again. He followed behind Hrafn as they climbed up the mountainside, quiet except for the crunch of his boots on stone. Hrafn told himself he couldn't feel the weight of Siggi's gaze with every step.

It began to rain shortly after that, a blustery onslaught that alternated between a spitting mist and brief downpours, and it continued until they reached the northern slope of Grimholl. Anna alighted on Hrafn's shoulder to tuck her skull-face into her wing, rousing again only to squawk and point which way to go. No amount of jostling could dislodge her, so Hrafn let her be. The cold rain dripped through his hair and down his neck. He told himself it was washing the scent of smoke away.

The trail led them into a shallow cirque with a small lake at its lowest point. The water was as gray as the clouds, rippling in the persistent wind. There was nothing alive around it, no moss and lichen clinging to the rocks, no tufts of grass pushing from cracks in the earth.

Anna abandoned Hrafn's shoulder to fly straight across the lake, crying raucously for them to follow. As they rounded the shore, their shoes crunching and clattering on barren rock, she settled on a large jumble of boulders to wait. Only when they were closer did Hrafn realize that it wasn't simply a pile of rocks. It was an archway, but a hidden one, disguised by uncounted centuries of rockfalls and weathering.

Fidelma produced a small lantern and candles from among her many hidden belongings. She lit the lantern first and handed it to Holta. Holta raised her eyebrows.

"You're the most likely to survive if something down there tries to kill us," Fidelma explained as she passed stubby candles to Siggi and Hrafn. "And you've done such a fine job leading us so far."

"Oh. I see. How touching." But Holta accepted the lantern without argument and let Hrafn light it with a quick slice of his fire staves. Anna fluttered down from atop the boulders to perch on her shoulder. "Stay close. If you get lost, you'll probably never find your way out."

The Blade That Binds Us

As Holta slipped between the slabs of black stone, her lantern revealed runes scratched into the stone. She stopped to look at them, then pursed her lips and kept walking. Fidelma followed her, beads and burdens jangling slightly as she turned sideways to fit through the crack.

The runes were old and hard to read, some worn away by time, others scratched or chipped away by tools or weapons. There appeared to be a much newer set carved overtop others so old and strange Hrafn didn't recognize them, nor the language in which they were written. But the meaning of those newer runes was clear enough.

"It's a warning," Hrafn said, even though Siggi could read them just as well. "Go back. Stay out. Certain death beyond. The usual shit."

The underground air flowed past him, teasing at his damp hair and raising bumps on his skin. He clung to the candle and wished he had a dozen more. He reached for his knife, gripped the hilt, and started to draw it again; he could hold more fire in his still-stinging hands than their weak flames could provide.

But Siggi was looking at him, those big blue eyes wide and worried, so Hrafn curled his hand into a fist and pressed his blunt fingernails into the palm of his burned hand instead, relishing the ache that radiated along his arm.

"Let's go," Hrafn said. "The fish-girl will leave us behind."

He slipped through the crack and into the darkness. In any other circumstances, it would have been funny how Siggi had to duck and squeeze to fit, with his height and his ridiculously broad shoulders. But Hrafn had never felt less like laughing. He felt instead like saying, *See, see, even the rocks don't want us in here.*

Holta and Fidelma were waiting a little ways ahead, where the narrow entrance opened into a round cavern five or six ells across. The air had a heavy scent to it, something metallic and warm, altogether unlike the rainy day outside. Two tunnels stretched into darkness like twin throats of a great beast. The entrance to each was framed by a rough-hewn arch, built from the same black stone as the tunnel itself. Neither was marked in any way.

"Well." Holta took a breath. She glanced at Anna on her shoulder. "Any idea which way we should go?"

Anna flapped her wings but did not take flight.

"That's useful," Holta said.

It was strange to see Holta so visibly uneasy, but Hrafn couldn't feel smug about it. There was something *wrong* with this place. His skin felt as though it was crawling all over with spiders and lice, and a dull headache began pounding behind his ears. The sensations were all his own, none of them Siggi's, and Siggi showed no sign of feeling the same discomfort. Hrafn shifted from one foot to the other, but even as he did so he felt something faint and cool brush over his skin. He jerked suddenly to swipe it away—it felt like spiderwebs, although there were none clinging to the rocks—and the others stared at him.

"Are we just going to fucking stand here?" Hrafn's voice didn't echo as it should have. It fell dully between them, like a corpse dropping to the floor.

Holta's only answer was to turn sharply and stomp ahead, following the tunnel to the right.

Anna let out a bloodcurdling screech at the same second Hrafn shouted, "No!"

Siggi gasped, and it was a relief to know he had felt Hrafn's wild stab of fear as soon as Holta had stepped toward the right-hand tunnel.

Fidelma lowered her hands from her ears and looked at Hrafn. "So we don't go that way?"

Hrafn shook his head. "Not that way."

Holta narrowed her eyes. "Maybe you should lead."

"Ylfa did say you and Anna would know the way," Siggi added. He touched Hrafn's shoulder, but Hrafn barely felt it.

There was nothing he wanted less in that moment, but he pushed past Holta and led them into the left tunnel.

The tunnel was straight for a long while, with no branches or turns. Nor were there any more runes. It was both unsettling and boring, but Hrafn regretted thinking as much as soon as they came to the next branch, this one an intersection of three tunnels. He tried one and recoiled immediately. Tried the second and found it felt like nothing. Tried the third just to be sure, and knew it was wrong even before Anna screeched in protest.

Second tunnel, then.

"That feels very odd," Siggi said.

"You can feel what the witch and the bird are feeling?" Holta asked.

"Only because Hrafn feels it," Siggi said. He was speaking very quietly. "It feels…I don't know how to explain it. Unwelcoming."

They continued. The tunnel branched again, and again, and each time Hrafn chose the path based on nothing more than how fearful each direction made him and Anna feel. It was an unsatisfactory way to navigate. It occurred to him that perhaps they were going about it all wrong, perhaps they should be choosing the tunnels that repelled them.

It was too late for that now. The tunnels bore almost no resemblance to lava tubes anymore. They curved and bent, climbed and fell, almost organic in shape, like roots—or veins. That made him think about his own blood in his own veins, and he started to think he could feel how it pulled and pulsed, trying to slip free from his body and join the ancient flow of frozen black stone around them.

There were times he was certain they were doubling back on themselves, even though they never once turned around. Hrafn kept his gaze forward, not daring to look back, lest the tunnels succeed in confusing him. They were trying. He could feel it with every step, a mocking pull, a teasing invitation to get turned around, to tie themselves in knots, to stay, stay, stay.

"Fidelma, can you see anything in here?" Siggi asked after a long while. His voice was low, hesitant in a way that reminded Hrafn too much of Siggi as he had been when they first met.

Fidelma was quiet a moment before answering. "The corpse road is still here, but it follows all of the tunnels, even the ones we don't choose. I don't think—I don't know if there's anything else."

"What do you mean, you don't know?" Hrafn wanted to glare back at her, but not as much as he wanted to keep his eyes fixed on the darkness. "Is that eye of yours useless now?"

"There's nothing wrong with my eye," she said. "We already know this is an unnatural place, born of unnatural magic older than any we know. And these tunnels, they're like…like the hardened veins left behind after their blood of molten stone stops flowing."

Hrafn scowled. He really wished she hadn't thought of veins as well.

Fidelma went on, "They have their own magic. I can tell that what we're seeing is not all that is truly there, but I can't see what else there is."

"What do you mean?" Siggi reached out to touch the wall, brushing his fingertips over the black stone. Hrafn felt the soft, cool pressure in his own fingers. "What else would you expect?"

"This is where the dead were brought to be buried," Fidelma said. "So where are they? Where are the bones, the burial markers, the runestones? They didn't get up and walk away after their mourners left them here, no matter how long ago it was."

"You think somebody took them?" Siggi asked.

"Or took what was offered," Holta said. "If this is—"

Anna screamed.

The sound was like blades driven into the ears. Anna launched herself from Hrafn's shoulder and fluttered wildly back to the others. He hadn't realized how far from the others he had strode ahead. A good ten ells stretched between them, and Anna covered that distance swiftly.

She screamed again, so loud it drowned out what they were saying. Her delicate little jaw opened, drawing breath she didn't need, over and over again. In her panic, she knocked the lantern from Holta's hand. It clattered to the ground and the light winked out, leaving only the candles to illuminate the tunnel.

"Fuck!" Holta shouted. "You stupid bird, what are you doing?"

"That's not helping!" Fidelma replied, even as Anna screamed again. "Calm down!"

"Anna, Anna, it's okay!" That was Siggi, worry lacing his words, because of course he would worry for an undead creature panicking in a corpse-road tunnel beneath a dead ancient mountain, *of course* he would. "Anna! Just come here, girl, just come!"

Hrafn knew he should help. Had he thought he was only ten ells from them? It seemed so much farther now. Their candlelight was so dim, so distant. When Anna screamed the entire mountain shook, a silent response to her unnatural call. With each of her shrieks the black rock rippled, glinted, *changed*. Specks of white appeared, like the crests of choppy waves on a storm-dark sea.

"A quake?" Holta's voice sounded as though it came from very far away.

And a reply from Fidelma, even farther away: "Is Grimholl waking?"

The light from Siggi's candle was so faint now. Hrafn couldn't remember if he had walked away from them, or if they had walked away from him. It was no safe thing, to cling to an undead witch in a place like this, to trust in the strength of his fear to guide them. The candle's tallow dripped on his hand, hot and insistent.

The white glimpses in the black stone took on shapes that were alien for the underside of a mountain, but familiar nonetheless. Pale round globes. Slender curves. Long cylinders. Tiny, delicate specks filling in every crack.

The bones had been around them all along.

Maybe this was what being dead had felt like. Light and noise and companionship pulled away and away, until there was nothing left but the remains of people whose names have been lost for centuries.

Hrafn turned around, and all at once, with the force of a glacier calving, his fear returned.

His heart shuddered in his chest like a wild animal. He felt cold all over, sickly and prickly, and he needed to get back to the others, he needed more light, he needed their voices and their warmth. He needed very much to not be alone, but they were gone. Siggi's candlelight, Anna's scream, Holta's spluttering shouts, they were all gone. If Siggi's heartbeat still echoed his own, he could no longer feel it, buried as it was beneath his fear. The tunnel itself was gone. Without a sound, without any scraping or grinding, the walls of bones had closed around him in every direction.

He stood now in a large chamber. It was constructed entirely of bones, but he knew the bones were themselves enclosed in something larger, something impossibly vast, hinted only in the briefest sensation of space and emptiness, as though the mountain itself had swallowed him whole. The feeling passed, and the chamber was smaller again, closed around him in either reality or illusion. Some of the bones were white, some were yellowed with age, all were draped with green moss that seeped through the seams, damp enough to drip in places, surrounding him with an uneasy patter. The air smelled and tasted like an old bog, like vegetation rotting into soil after spring rains.

Around the chamber there were arches that looked as though they had once been openings. Each one round. The placement needled Hrafn's memory. He knew this shape. He knew the form of this place, because he had examined it before, sliced it out of a corpse and held it in his hand, a mundane task for a witch, a chore entrusted to a useless child.

The huldu heart he had carved out so many years ago had been indistinguishable from human, no matter how hard he had looked for differences. This chamber of bone was shaped like a heart, human or huldu or other, with all but one of the veins and arteries closed.

And in that one stood a towering figure. It formed a long silhouette, with something like an arm extended toward him, but the fingers were too long, like spines or blades. Its head was massive, its shoulders hunched. Teeth gleamed in the candlelight, briefly, before sinking again into the darkness.

Chapter Seventeen
The Burial

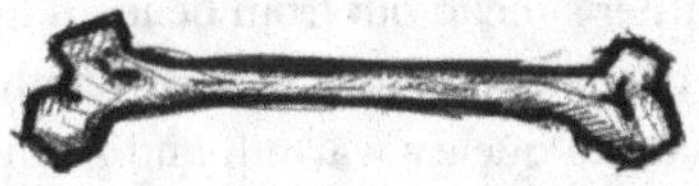

Hrafn was gone.

Siggi's stomach plummeted. "Hrafn?"

Anna screamed again, batlike in the cavernous dark. Fidelma spun around, beads and pouches colliding, aiming her scarlet eye back the way they'd come.

"Where is he?" she said, confused.

Holta ran a few steps ahead, then stopped abruptly. "Witch! Where are you!"

"Hrafn!" Siggi shouted. "Hrafn!"

For some time the tunnels had been as dizzying as they were confined, the darkness overwhelming them like an impenetrable sea. There had been times when Siggi rounded bends and didn't see Hrafn, and he had to run, run until he saw Hrafn's candlelight again, trying to keep up with Hrafn's strange pace. Hrafn's expression was so so hollow that he looked nearly as lifeless as he had when Siggi had first found his corpse on the wagon.

But now there was not even candlelight ahead.

Hrafn was gone

"Trust that idiot to get snatched," Holta said, but concern colored her voice. The light of her lantern, meager though it was, shone bright enough to reveal the gleam of her blade as she drew it from its scabbard.

"Hrafn? Hrafn!" Woozily Siggi stumbled forward until he reached another fork in the tunnel; he still could not see Hrafn's candlelight.

"The walls," Holta hissed suddenly. "Storguð's eyes, look at the fucking walls!"

But Siggi was already looking, mouth agape, blood rushing through him with a sudden intensity that reminded him of the day Arnes had snuck Father's mead out from beneath his pillow and the two brothers had downed half the bottle secretly in the hidden cavern, agreeing that the queasy warmth and giddiness were worth the inevitable beating.

Siggi could only be drunk again, because Hrafn was missing, and the tunnel walls?

The walls were filled with bones. Bones as large as unbroken femurs, bones as small as baby teeth, bones ridged like vertebrae and as smooth as polished crowns: all these cluttered the surfaces of the tunnel in an ornate but haphazard mosaic. And beneath all these, Siggi sensed—could *feel*—other bones still, and more still on and on, filling the very veins of the mountain.

He laughed and it felt like choking. How had it taken him so long to notice?

"I think we found the missing dead," Fidelma said grimly.

Siggi laughed again, a booming outburst that failed to permeate the tunnel's embrace.

Anna squealed and dropped from the air like a hailstone, tucking herself into the tangles of Fidelma's beaded hair.

"What's the matter with you?" Holta demanded.

He couldn't stop laughing. From the instant they'd followed Hrafn down the first branching fork in the darkness, something beneath Siggi's skin had begun to itch, and his bones had begun to feel altogether too loose in his body, dancing in place within his flesh. Now Hrafn had vanished, and bones had taken his place, and the feeling crescendoed, evolving into a heady mania.

Siggi looked to the girls to explain, but in place of faces and scowls

248

and clothes, he saw only their skeletons, and he couldn't stop laughing. If he pinched his fingers together just right, he could break every one of those bones in a heartbeat. That made him laugh, too, to the point of tears.

"Have you gone mad?!" Holta cried.

She smacked Siggi hard across the face. To Siggi she still looked more like a skeleton than a person, although her bones were very different from Fidelma's. Holta's were longer and fewer, iridescent and distinctly inhuman. Was that what Arnes's bones would look like, once they finally found him? Would his skeleton be still and broken like those in the walls, or upright and alive and dancing within his skin?

And if Arnes were dead, couldn't Siggi lift his familiar bones upright and set those two feet on the ground and put him back together? Make him tell Siggi stories, stories enough to make up for his long absence? He could keep his brother in their farmhouse and never let him leave again. As Father had done to Siggi. As Arnes had as well, with the cold clamp of iron around Siggi's wrist.

Siggi began to wheeze.

For all Arnes's kindness, had he really been so different from Father?

He must have fallen over. The bones in the ceiling flickered and rumpled overhead like the aurora in winter. Then Fidelma's skeleton was leaning over him, and he felt her warm skin as she lifted him up and propped him against the cavern wall. The touch of her hand was fire.

"His eyes," Holta hissed.

"He's glutted with magic. Damn near giddy with it. Siggi? Can you hear me?"

"Fidelma," Siggi grinned at her. "There are so many bones down here!"

"Siggi, we need you to breathe. We need to find Hrafn."

"Hrafn," he called to the ceiling, "Come out now, please!"

Though he couldn't *see* Hrafn, Siggi *could* feel him, as though he had tiptoed just out of sight. Siggi felt, too, the instant Hrafn opened one of his staves—the burning one.

Siggi frowned. "Stop that."

"But if *he's* spell-drunk, why aren't you? You're full huldu, and he's only half!" Fidelma said.

"Oh, so I must be just as gormless as a farm boy, though I was raised by druids just as you were?" Holta snapped.

Fidelma faltered. "I didn't mean—"

"Hey!" Siggi said. "Be nice to Fidelma, Holta! She loves you very, very much!"

Fidelma gasped; Holta's tone shifted. "But…I'm saying, does this place look like it's full of fish? This was a corpse road, lined with fucking bones. It's exactly his brand of poison!"

Siggi laughed again. Here they all were, standing inside a tunnel made of bone, talking about bones, these two bickering skeletons.

"Siggi, look into my eye." Fidelma was right in front of him, her bony hands on his shoulders.

Siggi did so, peering at the red stone floating in her eye socket. Gradually and then all at once, Fidelma began to look like a flesh-and-blood person again, her face twisted with worry.

"It's such a pretty eye," he told her. "Holta, Fidelma's eye is pretty. Don't you like it?"

"Goddesses spare us!" Holta too looked like herself again, although Siggi had never seen her cheeks so red, her blush apparent even in the murk.

"Hrafn doesn't like me anymore," Siggi told them, and now his face was soaked with tears, or maybe it had been the whole time. "Because I'm a monster."

"We're all monsters, you tit," Fidelma told him. "And we'll all be dead monsters, too, if you don't snap out of this and find Hrafn!"

Siggi blinked, eyes bleary. "He's gone."

Holta squeezed his hands, gentler than she'd ever been. "Remember when you broke the spine of that sending in the fjord? Or when you cracked the teeth of the darkwolves? Remember that?"

Siggi blinked. "Yes…"

Holta took a deep breath. "Huldu magic is instinctive, and no one's ever taught you how to harness it. Fuck knows I'm not the one to tell you. But I *need* you to think back to how using your magic felt. How did you break all those bones, Siggi?"

"I wanted to." Through the haze of nauseating magic, Siggi recalled the fury he'd felt, watching the sending grab Hrafn, watching the wolves attack *his* witch. "I broke them to save Hrafn."

"And you want to find him now," Holta said. "You can find his skeleton. You *can*."

Siggi lifted his witch-bladed hand, the hand that anchored him to Hrafn. There were thousands of bones in Grimholl, buzzing all around them. And for all the time he'd spent staring at Hrafn, watching his smirking lips and beautiful eyes, what had he seen of his skeleton? Hrafn's smile was rare, but when Hrafn thought hard, one of his incisors peeked over his bottom lip. And Siggi thought Hrafn's shoulder blades spoke a language all their own, a language he longed to understand.

"I can find him," Siggi said. "Hrafn's bones are my favorite bones ever."

"So what are you waiting for, huldalf?" Fidelma said, solitary eye sparkling. "Go on."

Siggi held up his witch-bladed hand and stretched his fingers as wide as he could. He felt as though he was extending great, invisible capillaries into the walls around them, pushing them into the roots of the mountain.

Siggi felt the bones answer, their essence turning toward him like blooms toward sunlight. He squeezed his fist, pinching his fingers into his palm, but not as hard as Hrafn often did, not enough to draw his own blood.

All around him the bones—*his* bones, now—answered his call.

They swarmed him with their stories. This rib belonged to a girl who died at the hand of her lover, this skull was cracked open against a rock, this arm bone had been broken twice before its owner passed. This pelvis had borne several children despite repeated fractures, these teeth had bitten into fruits in a far-off land.

The stories were overwhelming, like trying to count shells on a black beach, like trying to split every blade of grass in a field.

A sharp pain pierced Siggi's hand. But before he surfaced, his heart soared. Because among all the dead he'd found someone living, someone beloved—someone whose bones were as dear to Siggi as life.

Those shoulder blades, that snaggletooth, those long, beautiful fingers. Even as bones, Hrafn was like no one else. Through a tangle of tunnels, through bone-pocked walls of rock older than the wider world, Siggi found Hrafn, alive and bracing for yet another fight.

Siggi stood, swaying like a sail at sea. Anna chirped, alighting on his shoulder at last.

Siggi pointed down the left fork. "This way."

A few stumbling minutes during which Siggi was often caught or held up by the druids. A few forks chosen with the support of Anna's affirmative chirp. Several breaths during which Siggi closed his eyes and listened for the call of Hrafn's bones.

And at last the tunnel gave way to an impossible vision. Siggi, Fidelma, and Holta stood beneath arcing walls of compacted bone, caught inside an archaic chamber made of ribs too large to be human, too large even to be whale or lyngbakr. This chamber was a tunnel in its own right, sixty ells long at least, the floor littered with bone fragments, tattered fabric, and dust.

And near the heart of the chamber was Hrafn, standing before an incongruous figure that towered in the soft glow of bones. Shadows clung to the figure like darkness at the bottom of a deep pool.

Hrafn glared up at the eerie thing, his determined frown illuminated by his telltale lavender flames.

Gods, but he's so fucking beautiful, Siggi thought.

The figure before him was twice as tall as a man but with curiously hunched shoulders, and clad in black, intricate armor. Luminous green lichen coated the armor, tracing each greave, pauldron, and sabbaton in a haze of queasy light, as though the figure were imbued with the aurora. The creature's head and hands alone were exposed, and neither were remotely human. There were far too many fingers, long as branches and many-jointed, and the face was long and featureless, apart from a gaping smile.

Nothing in the world should have so many teeth.

Whatever the teeth were made from, it was not bone. Nor were there organs or flesh within that armor. Through his connection with Hrafn, Siggi knew: the armor was occupied only by gelatinous, molten magic, as sickly as it was old.

The figure slithered closer to Hrafn like moss creeping over stone, its speed accelerated ten thousandfold. Its silhouette expanded as it moved, spreading a cape of decaying lichen behind it. Siggi gagged on the sweet stench of rot as the grinning specter bore down on Hrafn.

Hrafn did not recoil. The flames on Hrafn's palms shone only brighter as the creature's face, four times the size of Hrafn's, leveled with Hrafn's.

"Let us go," Hrafn said.

The walls rumbled, the armor rattled, and the creature grinned wider, snippets of light escaping from between its many teeth.

"The trylla have no place in this world anymore." Hrafn raised his fiery arms, staves dripping. As always, Siggi was taken aback by the terrible, inscrutable loveliness that imbued Hrafn's frame when he performed magic. Hrafn was a star on a cold night, a gleaming bloom at the bottom of a deep, unknowable pool. "Let us *go*."

The fey creature cocked its massive head, turning to face Siggi and the girls. It pointed one long finger toward them and widened its grin, allowing more of that piercing light to escape its maw. The glow pierced Siggi's eyes like another blade, leaving dizzying spots of blindness behind. Beside him Fidelma screamed and stumbled, hands clasped over her face. Holta let go of Siggi to catch her, and Siggi stumbled forward over the detritus of human remains, bones and bones and bones.

"Enough," Hrafn hissed.

Siggi couldn't see it, but he felt it when Hrafn tore the old sheep dagger across his own chest, collarbone to collarbone, a single gouge that split the skin above his rib cage. Siggi almost fell over, the pain was so great. Hrafn remained standing, as inured to agony as ever.

He felt it, too, when Hrafn took in a great breath and exhaled a howling burst of wind, a tempest fierce enough to blow the dried moss from the armored figure, stoking the flames on his palm to roaring heights even as he clutched at his gushing chest with his other hand.

Skulls in the wall grinned in the amethyst glow as Hrafn's inferno expanded, setting fire to the armor's lichen cloak—

But the trylla smiled, and the fire and wind vanished in the vortex of that toothy grin, leaving only smoke and ash trailing through the teeth. The cavern fell into a flameless darkness, lit only by the faintly glowing bones.

Hrafn groaned and fell to his knees, but immediately long fingers wrapped around his torso and lifted him from the ground. From the creature's chest came the rattling imitation of a laugh.

"Hrafn!"

The grinning figure drew Hrafn close and parted its teeth, spreading its jaw wide. Hrafn cried out as the light from its throat struck him.

A cold, deep fury flooded Siggi. "*Enough.*"

He waved a hand and parted the sea of wasted bones as easily as a child blowing seeds from a weed. The skulls on the wall screamed as though alive and the bones nearest the figure rolled together and fused, forming spears of ivory.

One of these spears tore upward in a violent thrust that impaled the age-encrusted armor. The trylla screeched, limbs scraping against ancient metal. From the darkness beside Siggi a lithe form darted forward, loosing a feral scream; Holta leaped nimbly onto the trylla's shoulders and pressed all her formidable strength against its bottom jaw, slamming it shut so sharply that the teeth clashed and broke.

Siggi wiped his bloody nose on his hand. He strode across the cavern. He no longer felt dizzy. A strange calm overtook him. When he reached the trylla where it struggled futilely in Holta's grip, he peeled the creature's long fingers open and pulled Hrafn free.

With Hrafn warm and safe now in his arms, Siggi waved a hand again, and the jerking vines made of bone sprang from the cavern walls and floor to wrap themselves around the monster, piercing its palms and stabbing through its fingers. It tried to cry out, but Holta's hold on its jaw kept any sound but a whimper from escaping. With another twitch of Siggi's hand, the bone shackles began to compress, crunching and snapping, denting the armor and trapping the entity within.

Only when the bones wound tight around the helmet, clamping it shut, did Holta let go.

The armor shuddered, then fell still.

Sickly green still shone through the gaps in its wide grin and the cracks in its armor. The trylla was confined, but not destroyed.

"Release us on the southern side of the mountain," Holta demanded between panting breaths. "At Draugamyr. Do that, or this huldu will use the very bones of your victims to end your long, miserable life, trylla."

For an expansive moment, the smiling figure did not move. Then, fighting against the grip of bones on its chin, it nodded once. With unexpected ease, it freed one of its impaled palms from its bony spear, snapping off several of its own long fingers to do so. It bled only eerie light from the wounds.

With a curling gesture of its mangled hand, the trylla peeled open a wall of the chamber as though it were a curtain. They gazed upon a gaping wide vista of brown, black, red, and white: the lava fields of Draugamyr, desolate beneath an ever-white sky.

"We're already there," Hrafn muttered. "Ancient fucking magic indeed."

Again, the creature's grin widened. Holta hurried to help Fidelma stand, and Siggi hoisted Hrafn up in his arms, gripping him under the armpits, and spun him around like a child.

"Hrafn! I'm so glad you didn't get sacrificed or eaten or

something!"

"What are you doing?" Hrafn rasped as Siggi whirled him about once more and laughed and pulled him close and kissed him as though they weren't bleeding inside a hollowed chamber made of bones, watched by an ancient, grinning man-eater. As if they were instead at home on his farm, or on a farm of their own, scarred but in love and more or less whole.

"I felt so many bones," Siggi said, grinning wide, tasting his own blood. "But I definitely like your bones the best!"

"Your eyes," Hrafn choked, struggling against Siggi's grasp. "Holta, what's happened to him?"

Holta pushed them both forward, Anna squawking indignantly from atop her head.

"Not the time," she muttered, glancing back at the stationary, hulking figure. "Let's get outside first, for fuck's sake!"

Together Holta and Fidelma pulled Hrafn and Siggi through the hole in the chamber wall. Siggi felt the creature's silent gaze trailing him as they hurried through the opening.

They had not defeated it. It was allowing them to leave.

Siggi's head pounded as the first wave of clarity rattled him. He vomited down his front and fell to his knees on the cliffside. Every inch of him felt sapped dry, like a fish left out on the rack for too many months, salted and drawn. Hrafn's hand was warm on his back.

Blearily, Siggi looked back at the mountain.

The smiling figure in the bone chamber dipped its chin one last time, then the edges of the hole began to crumble. The mountain shook, and Holta and Fidelma grabbed hold of the boys, dragging them away from the mountainside as a small rockfall sent cascades of black stones down from above. Before the tunnel closed, Siggi saw the green gleam of that smile in the darkness.

Chapter Eighteen
The Ghosts That Cannot Escape

"Well, that wasn't *so* awful," Fidelma said as the dust settled. She laughed like a madwoman. "That wasn't so awful, now, was it? Taking a shortcut and learning that your lovely huldu kin completely and utterly failed to kill off all the trylla after all? That was *fine*."

She screamed twice into the sky before collapsing on a boulder. She pulled a flask from one of her pockets and downed its contents in one go.

Siggi laughed weakly, and Hrafn felt a sudden riot of pain—not his own, but Siggi's, as his entire skull began to throb as though an ax had fallen through it. Siggi slumped to the ground; Hrafn caught his head to keep it from hitting the rocks. Siggi blinked up at him and smiled sleepily.

"Will you still like me even if I'm bones?" Siggi asked.

"Shut up," Hrafn replied.

Holta crouched beside them as Hrafn pulled Siggi's head onto his lap. "The magic's poisoned him right through. Much more of this and it really could kill him."

"Powerful magic is its own worst enemy," Fidelma said. She scowled and rubbed at her face. For the first time Hrafn realized that her stone eye was broken, cracked right down the middle like an egg. "Too much at once is like breathing smoke until you choke or eating 'til you burst. Poor Siggi's been gorging himself a good while now."

"I can feel it," Hrafn said. He hadn't known what that feeling was before, but it was unmistakable now. "Maybe I can help him."

He took Siggi's knife-bound hand in his own and drew his blade across the palm. He felt the sting, the warm well of blood, although for once he was not the one bleeding. Siggi made a noise of surprise, not quite pain, that turned to a question when Hrafn pressed that palm against a stave on his own cheek. There was no reaction at first, then Hrafn felt the force of Siggi's magic like a kick in the stomach. He let out a gasp, echoed by Siggi, as the magic coursed between them. It was like a flood of glacial water after an ice-dam broke, there was so much of it, and it was so very wild.

"Do you know how I found you, Hrafn?" Siggi mumbled as his blood dripped down Hrafn's face. "I looked through all the bones and I searched for your angry shoulder blades."

"Hush, Siggi."

"Even if your shoulder blades are angry, I still love you."

Hrafn loosened his grip on Siggi's wrist but didn't let go. "Shh. You're out of your head."

"But I mean it! Even when you're mean to me, I love you."

"Tonguð's tongue, if I could stop you talking that might save me," Hrafn said, trembling from the flow of Siggi's magic. No wonder Siggi had gone spell-mad under the mountains. "How you've withstood even a minute of this is beyond me. My magic is nothing compared to yours. It's nothing at all."

"You have really lovely bones," Siggi murmured.

Hrafn pulled Siggi's hand from his cheek and pressed his lips against his fingertips. "Close your eyes. Try not to move. Okay?"

"Mmm," Siggi said. His eyes were back to normal now, the whites once again white, the blue once again the color of a clear summer sky. "You won't leave me?"

"I didn't mean to go off alone. I know better than to do that." He pressed Siggi's fingers against his cheek once more. "We weren't apart very long."

"It was too long," Siggi said.

Siggi fell quiet as the magic funneled through Hrafn's skin and down Hrafn's other arm and into the rocks beside them. There were few bones to cling to outside of Grimholl and the tomb at its heart, so the magic dissipated like steam rising after a storm. Siggi's eyes fluttered closed. Hrafn wondered if he was doing something ridiculous like falling asleep.

But after a moment Siggi inhaled sharply and sat up. He looked at Hrafn, almost sheepishly. "Thanks."

"We're close to Draugamyr," Holta said. She had moved a few paces away; her gaze was fixed on the distant mist of the marsh tucked into the lava field. "We should keep moving."

"In a moment," Hrafn said. "Siggi, give me your hand."

Siggi held out his bloodied palm, but immediately retracted it when he looked at Hrafn. Tears filled his eyes, but there was no lingering vagueness there, no confusion or overwhelming magic. He was, once again, a blue-eyed boy, and he was crying.

"Hrafn," he said, his voice hoarse. "I'm sorry."

Hrafn felt something almost like fear. He didn't know if it was Siggi's or his own. He busied himself grabbing Siggi's hand and fumbling through his bag for a bandage. "For what?"

"About Ylfa."

Hrafn's hands stilled. "I…I know you are. I mean, that's very you, to be sorry about someone you didn't know, and someone unpleasant."

"She wasn't unpleasant."

Hrafn sighed and pinched his eyes shut. "It doesn't change anything, being sorry. So why say it?"

"You're so used to pain." Siggi brushed his fingertips on Hrafn's bleeding chest. "But maybe not this kind. If what happened to Ylfa happened to you, the pain I would feel…that'd be worse than I felt for Father or my mother."

"I shouldn't have said…" Hrafn tied the bandage in a knot and patted it, letting his hand rest on top. He had to say this, but he couldn't meet Siggi's eyes as he did so. "I wasn't being fair to you. I shouldn't have said that. You aren't unfeeling. You aren't cruel."

Siggi squeezed Hrafn's fingers gently. "My father was. You were right about that. And my mother didn't exist, not to me. Even Arnes left me. You're the realest thing I know."

Hrafn looked up at him. His own eyes were hot and stinging now. He leaned forward and kissed the tears away from Siggi's cheek, speaking his next words into Siggi's mouth. "Even if I'm a terrible bastard and a liar and a witch, the truth is…I don't want to be separated from you again. Not even for a moment. Because I'm incredibly selfish, and you're incredibly clumsy, and the only thing worse than seeing you hurt or hurting you myself is not seeing you at all. Understood?"

"Understood," Siggi said. "Although you were the one who vanished, not me."

"I really, really didn't mean to," Hrafn said. "I swear it."

"I know," Siggi said.

Hrafn pulled away and smiled, and Siggi smiled as well, and the feeling that was caught between them was bright and soft, warm enough to chase away a blizzard.

They descended from the slopes of Grimholl as the day waned. To the southwest was the marsh, swathed in heavy fog in spite of the clearness of the sky above. They kept their distance for now. Hrafn was not going to set foot in Draugamyr as night approached, and nobody argued with his decision.

As they skirted the marsh, they climbed a ridge that looked down on a black, lifeless valley.

Siggi shaded his eyes to look toward the west and the sea gleaming in the distance. "I always thought there would be more people once I got out of the Thrandir. What is this place?"

This was how Siggi should be: asking questions, so many questions, stubborn and persistent. Not vague, not strange, not lost in his own magic.

"There were farms here before the battle," Hrafn explained. "It wasn't really a village. It wasn't big enough for that. It was just a few ordinary families who didn't like to involve themselves with witches or huldu."

Siggi frowned. "What happened to them?"

"They were the first to die when the fighting began," Hrafn said.

"Even though they weren't on either side?"

Hrafn laughed humorlessly. "Do you think anybody fighting that day cared? The farmers and shepherds died at the first flare of magic. They were the first ghosts, and they died so fiercely, so angrily, that everybody who followed never had a chance to escape. That's why there are so many ghosts in the Draugamyr."

So many ghosts ensnared in the burnt memories of rich grasses and spring lambs, drowned in the fetid marsh water, smothered in mud and ash. They had been peaceful farmers who wanted no part in any magical fight. Their revenge, in death, was to offer no release to their murderers.

The shallow valley was still barren, even after a hundred years. The ash and charcoal had long since washed away, but not a single sprig of grass grew in what remained of those old farms.

"We'll go around," Hrafn said.

Some steps ahead, Fidelma kept tilting her head and squinting, as though she hoped her cracked eye would heal itself if only she blinked in the right way. "Are you certain? There's nothing here. The ghosts are meant to be down that way." She gestured toward the marsh.

"What do you know about it?" Hrafn asked. "Walk through the valley if you want. We'll hear you screaming from up here."

Siggi squeezed Hrafn's hand slightly. Hrafn didn't know if it was a gentle scold or reassurance, so he took a breath and stamped down on his annoyance. Siggi no longer looked and sounded like he might drift away if Hrafn released him—but Hrafn had no intention of letting go. Siggi had found him. Siggi had saved him from a place that had muddled Hrafn's mind, warped his senses, drawn nightmares from memories, all using power so old the very contemplation of it left him breathless. Hrafn was not letting go unless Siggi told him to.

"He's right," Holta said.

Hrafn was so surprised he looked at her, eyebrows raised.

She only shrugged. "There is anger in this place. We shouldn't linger."

"It's no wonder they're so angry. But aren't most ghosts angry?" Siggi asked. "That's what the stories say."

"That's what witches say too," Hrafn admitted.

"You sound like you don't believe it," Siggi said.

"I'm not sure I do," Hrafn said. "Only the ghosts know, and I don't think anybody's ever asked them in a way they saw fit to answer. I don't think they feel things the same way we do."

When Birtingr had brought Hrafn to Draugamyr years ago, he had been trying to teach Hrafn how to communicate with ghosts. His idea of instruction had been to haul Hrafn to the most ghost-infested place in Lifandfjall, cut a stave into his skin, and throw him into the marsh with no guidance or aid.

Although Hrafn had only been seven or eight at the time, he had picked up the skill rather more quickly than Birtingr expected. He found his way out of the marsh without suffering much injury. For some reason that had infuriated Birtingr. Hrafn had tried to explain that he didn't remember much of what had happened, but what he did remember made him think that perhaps the ghosts had been more frustrated than angry—not at his invasion, but at the fact that somebody had sent a child alone into the Draugamyr. That hadn't lessened Birtingr's anger. He punished Hrafn anyway.

Hrafn stopped walking.

"Oh." The word was little more than a breath, as though it had been squeezed out of him.

"What is it?" Siggi said.

Hrafn's successes, expected or not, always infuriated Birtingr.

Birtingr had never been able to endure the Draugamyr—because he was afraid of the ghosts, Hrafn realized, as many witches were, rightfully so. But Birtingr would never admit to such a fear, so he could not admit that talking to ghosts was a skill he struggled to master.

As a child Hrafn had not feared anything as much as he feared Birtingr. He had thought his teacher knew everything, could do everything, had every power and every secret. Every punishment convinced him that he had done something wrong, because he was always doing something wrong, always making a mistake or messing up in a way that deserved the slaps and the pinches, the bruises left on his skin and hanks of hair ripped from his scalp, the cold nights spent outside a locked door, the chores that left his hands bleeding and raw.

For so long Hrafn had seen Birtingr as the biggest, most powerful man in the world, the one whose shadow fell over everything, the one whose reach was so great that he could never escape it. He owned Hrafn's life so completely, it had taken dying for Hrafn to slip away.

And it had taken Ylfa dying for him to finally understand what she had been trying to tell him all along. What she had seen from the first moment she looked at him. Why she had despaired of trying to help him.

She had believed he deserved better.

But she had been bad at saying it, and Hrafn had been unable to hear it.

He wanted her to know he finally understood. It was too late. He wanted her to know anyway. *She loved you*, Siggi had said, but the words hadn't meant anything to Hrafn, because what did that even mean, when a person was gone and there was nothing left but memories and the scent of smoke?

"Hrafn?" Siggi said softly. "What is it? Are you okay?"

Hrafn blinked. Because he had stopped, Siggi had stopped with him, on that hillside over the dead valley. He felt a little foolish, a little giddy, like he was the one drunk with magic now. Ahead, the girls were looking back with concerned expressions. Well, Holta looked concerned. Fidelma was hitting the side of her own head with the heel of her hand and muttering.

"Yeah, I'm fine," Hrafn said. "It's…"

He thought about saying, *I'm just being stupid.*

He thought about saying, *It's nothing.*

But Siggi wouldn't like it if he called himself stupid or nothing, and that was enough to stop him. It occurred to him that maybe he had never been stupid, and he had never been nothing.

Hrafn lifted himself onto his toes to kiss Siggi's cheek. Siggi looked surprised, and he blushed, and his heart skipped pleasantly. Hrafn liked all of those things so much he did it again.

"I'll tell you later," he said. "We should keep going."

From where they stood they could see the marshes stretched out at the foot of the mountains, hidden by unnatural mist that was never quite still, moving with shadows and shapes that faded from view the moment you looked at them. The warm evening light set the watery pools around the edges aglow in golden hues. The rain that had soaked them relentlessly on the corpse road had stayed on that side of the mountain.

The fourth or fifth time Fidelma cursed loudly as she smacked her own face, Holta grabbed her arms to stop her.

"That's not helping!" Holta said, her voice harsh with frustration.

Fidelma groaned as she pushed Holta away. "I *know* it's not helping, but it's making me crazy. I can see some things normally, but others…like if I look that way, at that great bloody swamp we're marching right into, you want to know what I see when I look over there?"

Holta frowned. "What?"

"Nothing," Fidelma said. "Nothing! I don't see anything! It looks like fog. It looks like a stupid soggy marsh. That's the most haunted place in Lifandfjall, full of ghosts of huldu and witches who all died in a big horrific magical battle, and they left so much wild and wasted magic around that people go mad just from walking nearby and tripping over the wrong log, and it should be blinding me with how much magic there is, it should be overwhelming, but *I can't see a fucking thing.*"

Her shout echoed from the mountainside, and she fell abruptly silent, breathing heavily, her fists clenched at her sides. For a long moment, nobody moved. Siggi released Hrafn's hand to step forward, his expression soft with concern, but Holta was faster. She touched Fidelma's shoulder lightly, a bit awkwardly, as though she didn't quite know what to do.

Fidelma sniffed loudly and rubbed tears from her cheeks. "Ah, I'm being childish. We should—"

"We should stop for a bit," Holta said. She cast a quick glance toward Siggi and Hrafn, daring them to argue. "I can look at your eye. We can't have you tripping over your feet every five steps when we head into the marsh."

"Right." Fidelma took a shaky breath. "Right. Can't have that."

"I think there's a spring up ahead," Holta said, nodding toward the next valley. "We can get washed up. Some of us need it more than others."

Holta turned away quickly as Fidelma looked at her, as though she was afraid to be caught staring. Siggi let out a quiet huff. He was smiling gently. As Holta and Fidelma started walking again, he said, "I guess that answers that question."

"What question?" Hrafn asked.

Siggi shook his head. "Something Fidelma asked me. I'll tell you later."

It didn't seem like something bad, so Hrafn let it go. He liked the sound of that—*later*—reassurance that whatever they faced in the next day or two would have an afterward, and in that afterward they would have time to tell each other things. It felt dangerous to look forward to that, but he let the feeling roll over him anyway.

Holta was right. In the next valley, a spring tumbled down the side of Grimholl, flowing through a series of steaming pools and playful cascades, surrounded by soft moss and summer grass. Holta wasted no time in settling Fidelma beside one of the pools and fussing over her brusquely while Fidelma argued in a way that made it clear she actually quite liked it.

Neither of them paid any attention to Siggi and Hrafn, so Hrafn nudged Siggi's elbow and said, "The fish-girl is right. We need to wash."

There was a perfectly good pool right next to them, but Hrafn turned to climb upstream, away from the girls and their quiet conversation. Siggi followed without a word. All the effects of the magic underground seemed to be gone now, because Siggi was sure-footed and steady again. Every time Hrafn looked back at him his heart skipped.

They climbed up to where the creek spilled from a long, deep pool set in a hollow of soft, green grasses and small summer flowers. Steam softened the edges of everything, but the water was so clear they could see the bottom.

"Ugh," Siggi said, plucking at his shirt and wrinkling his nose. "Suddenly I can smell myself."

Hrafn laughed, delighted by the disgusted look on Siggi's face, but his laughter stopped abruptly when Siggi stripped off his shirt. Siggi knelt to wash his shirt in the outflow from the pond. Hrafn stared at his shoulders and arms for a few seconds before looking away, his cheeks warming. He didn't think Siggi would *mind* his staring—he might even like it—but there was something about this moment that made Hrafn want to preserve their easy companionship for just a little bit longer. At least long enough for them to get clean.

He crouched by the pool, his feet sinking into the grass. The water was hot, but not so hot it scalded. Hrafn removed his own shirt, wincing as he peeled the fabric away from the blood caked across his chest. The wound wasn't deep, certainly no deeper than any other he carried, but it had bled enough that he was fairly sure the shirt was ruined.

After a second he noticed that Siggi had stilled. Hrafn looked up, and Siggi asked, "What's it like? In Draugamyr? You said you've been there before?"

"Oh." The question caught Hrafn off guard. He went back to scrubbing his shirt, wondered if he cared enough about the blood on his trousers to wash them too. They would take too long to dry, he decided. The blood could wait. "It's, um. Hard to explain. I was just a kid, so I didn't understand much of what I saw. And heard."

Siggi frowned, his brow creasing.

Hrafn went on hurriedly, "I don't even know if it will be the same for you. Your magic is—"

Astonishing. Extraordinary. Like the depths of a sulfurous lake, or the explosion of a mountain, or ocean waves powerful enough to gnaw rock into sand. So vast and incomprehensible that it made every spell Hrafn had ever bled to work in his life nothing more than petty wounds carved into feeble flesh. Terrifying.

"Different," Hrafn said. "I was there to learn how to talk to ghosts. I don't even know if that's something huldu can do."

"But what was it like for you?" Siggi asked.

Hrafn thought about it. "You know when you're walking beside a sea cliff, and there are thousands of birds screaming above and below, and it's such a big noise that you can almost feel it? And you know that in that screaming there must be the voices of individual birds, because each of them is screaming alone, but you can't pick out a single one?" He lifted his sodden shirt and squeezed the excess water out. "But at the same time, it was like not being able to hear anything at all, or nothing that was a real sound."

He remembered curling up on the ground and covering his ears, but it hadn't helped. Nothing had helped. The spirit staves Birtingr had carved into his neck had burned as though they had been set aflame.

"We can't hear anything yet," Siggi pointed out.

Hrafn stood to spread his shirt on the grass to dry. "I don't know if you will at all. I have a stave for it."

"Does it help you see them too?" Siggi asked.

"Oh, everybody can see them, if they want to be seen," Hrafn replied. "Day or night. When ghosts haunt a place that long, they become as much a part of the weather as the fog."

Siggi looked thoughtful, but he didn't have any more questions. He was worried about the marsh, Hrafn knew, but it was nothing compared to his worry about his brother.

The wound on Hrafn's chest felt tight, the skin around the cut itchy. He scratched at it idly, grimacing at the feeling of the tacky blood on his fingers, mixed with dirt and who knew what else. It was in his hair too, with the clinging scent of smoke, and something gritty that he suspected was ancient bones ground to dust. He needed to get it all off of him, as soon as possible, so he kicked off his shoes, stripped off his trousers, and plunged into the spring.

Water closed over his head, hot and clean. His feet hit the bottom and his toes curled over rough rock. Eyes closed, breath held, Hrafn scrubbed roughly through his hair and over his face, until he could feel the filth floating away from him. Just as he was going back up for a breath, he heard a muffled splash: Siggi had joined him. Hrafn surfaced and grinned at him, and Siggi smiled before ducking his own head under the water. He had taken his hair out of his usual high knot. When he emerged again, the fair strands were darkened as they fell over his shoulders, but his blue eyes were as bright as gems beneath the summer sky.

His gaze dropped from Hrafn's face, and his smile faltered. Hrafn felt an unpleasant knot in his gut. He knew Siggi was looking at the staves across his neck and shoulders and chest, including the one he had cut open in the bone tunnel, the one that had been a long-faded scar until today. Hrafn turned away to scrub at the cut self-consciously, even though the motion stung enough that Siggi would be feeling that too. He couldn't clean away what lay beneath the blood and grime. He had given up trying years ago. Scars such as his faded, but they never truly vanished. Magic always left a mark.

He kept expecting Siggi to say something, to prod at this sore point between them as he always had before, but Siggi remained silent.

When Hrafn glanced over his shoulder, Siggi wasn't even looking at him. He wasn't hiding disgust behind questions or reassurances. He wasn't looking at much of anything; his gaze was unfocused, his expression thoughtful, as he scooped water over himself.

Hrafn stared for a little while, mesmerized by the motion of those strong hands, the curve of those broad shoulders, the lines of the muscle on his chest. Siggi's skin was pink from the hot water, and the steam curled around him with every motion. Siggi began to absently trace his fingers from one collarbone to the other across his own skin, following the line where Hrafn bore a fresh cut. He didn't seem to know he was doing it, didn't seem to realize that Hrafn could also feel that touch, featherlight beneath the sting of the wound and lap of the spring water. There was no stave on Siggi's chest, of course, but his skin was not unmarred. There were fresh bruises and scrapes. That long stretch of fish-scaled skin on his side. Scars from old wounds, including a couple of very faint lines that curled around his strong shoulder, evidence of a long-ago lashing, no doubt thanks to his useless father.

Siggi started and looked at Hrafn. "What is it? Did I miss a spot of dirt on my face?"

"No," Hrafn said.

Siggi started to smile, a little uncertain.

Hrafn kicked away from the rocks in the pool to push himself over to Siggi, didn't even try to slow himself before bumping right into him. He wrapped his arms around Siggi's neck to pull him even closer. Siggi let out a surprised little laugh, so bright and easy that Hrafn just had to kiss him, to kiss him until that laugh turned into a gasp. Siggi's hands came up first to grip his arms, then to curl around his back, and his palms were big and strong and so very warm pressing into Hrafn's back, his shoulders, the back of his neck. They kissed until they were both breathless, then they parted only to gasp for air, foreheads pressed together, steam from the spring rising between them.

"You said you like my bones," Hrafn said.

"I do like your bones," Siggi replied.

"You said you like them best of all."

"I do."

"That's a really fucking weird thing to say, puffling."

Siggi's grin was wide and easy. "I think you like it when I say really fucking weird things to you."

His hand cupped around the back of Hrafn's head, he drew him in for another kiss. It was so hot in the spring that Hrafn could feel it on every inch of his skin, as he could feel how aroused Siggi was and knew Siggi could feel the same of him. They were as close as they could be, touching everywhere, but Hrafn wanted to press closer still, didn't think he could ever get close enough.

Siggi turned him and pushed him toward the side of the pool. Water sloshed all around them, and Hrafn felt a sharp jag in his backside.

"Ow, fuck, ow!" he gasped.

"What? Did I hurt you?" Siggi's eyes were wide. "Shit, I'm sorry, did I—"

"You didn't do anything except push my ass into a sharp rock," Hrafn said, laughing, before Siggi could worry.

After a second, Siggi laughed too. "Sorry, I guess. Hey, we can—"

Instead of finishing his sentence, he grabbed Hrafn at the waist and lifted him out of the water—just lifted him, as though he weighed no more than a lamb, those ridiculous arms and even more ridiculous shoulders not having to strain even a little bit to set Hrafn on the mossy bank of the pool.

Hrafn had no idea what his face must have looked like, but Siggi crawled out beside him, blinked several times to chase droplets from his eyes, and raised an eyebrow.

"Uh, you liked that?" Siggi asked.

"Shut up," Hrafn said, his face so hot he was sure it was steaming as much as the spring.

"Okay."

Siggi dropped to the ground beside Hrafn and rolled onto his side to pull him close. He kissed him again—Hrafn didn't think he would ever get tired of kissing Siggi—and brushed his thumb over Hrafn's bare shoulder, a light and maddening touch. Only after a moment did Hrafn realize that it wasn't an idle or random touch. Siggi was tracing a stave carved there, an old one that had faded into faint pale lines against Hrafn's brown skin.

270

Hrafn tensed, tried to pull away, but Siggi curled his hand around his shoulder to stop him.

"It's not just your bones that I like," Siggi said, very quietly. "I like this part of you too. Even if you don't."

There were a million things Hrafn could say to that, with Siggi looking at him with such a soft expression, with the warm mist and green moss around them, the evening sky ablaze above. Hrafn surged forward to kiss Siggi again and again, pushing at him until Siggi rolled onto his back and Hrafn could climb atop him.

Then he did stop, suddenly uncertain. "Is this okay? Do you—"

Siggi said, "You idiot. Don't you dare stop."

He was smiling, perfect and playful. Hrafn wanted to make him smile like that forever.

"I won't," he said.

Chapter Nineteen
The Haunted Mire

"You can talk to ghosts," Siggi said, running his fingers through Hrafn's hair.

"I wouldn't call it talking," Hrafn murmured, eyes closed.

"They don't use words?"

"No, but they make their feelings known in other ways."

"Like sheep," Siggi observed. "They don't use words, but they have strong opinions."

Hrafn laughed and pressed closer to Siggi.

The spring water had left Hrafn's black strands silken, downier than lambswool. But what felt even softer than Hrafn's hair was Hrafn's demeanor, the very fact that Hrafn did not recoil no matter how much Siggi touched him, no matter how many times his fingers grazed Hrafn's scalp or traced his staves. He was still Hrafn, still sharp edged and biting and, if their tryst on the moss was anything to go by, absolutely relentless.

But Hrafn was pliant, now, his shoulders relaxed. Hrafn wasn't smirking, but he was smiling, the smallest of lilts gracing his chapped lips. It was as though washing away the grime had washed away some of his pain, at least for a little while.

"Did you ever try to communicate with them?" Siggi asked.

"Them whom?" Hrafn murmured into Siggi's chest. He'd been

272

sprawled there ever since they had finished, his skin all but fused to Siggi's own. Yes, it was cold this white night, and yes their clothes had been forgotten on the rocks, but it was something more than the chill that made them inseparable now.

"The ghosts from the farms," Siggi said. "The ones who died first. Do you think anyone has tried to help them?"

Hrafn groaned and opened his obsidian eyes. Siggi was grateful for the white night, grateful to have seen all Hrafn's expressions throughout their exertions this evening. "Only you would think to."

Siggi stiffened. "Only me. Because I'm—"

"Stop that," Hrafn said, pressing a finger to Siggi's lips. "Before you tell a lie. Only you would think of helping ghosts rather than avoiding them, *not* because you're a magical bone huldu, but because you're *you*, and you were left alone on a farm yourself, and somehow you've grown up too warmhearted for a world so fucking cold."

"Magical bone," Siggi echoed, raising his eyebrows. "Fucking."

Hrafn punched him playfully in the chest, and Siggi laughed and kissed Hrafn's knuckles, counting the scars on them. Hrafn laughed, soft and light, and laid his cheek on Siggi's stomach.

Siggi wrapped his arms tight around Hrafn's shoulders, felt the cutting angles of his shoulder blades. Hrafn was being so honest, so gentle, and their hearts were so closely pressed, Siggi felt they were one soul.

"I think the girls are likely steering well clear of us," Hrafn said.

"I think Fidelma will be glad," Siggi said, feeling rather pleased, "for the time alone with Holta."

"Well, there's not many who'd feel that way."

Siggi frowned. "Holta's a good person."

"I suppose. She's also an intolerable snob."

"You like her," Siggi chided.

"No I don't," Hrafn said. "I only like you, puffling."

Siggi stroked Hrafn's hair, listening to the steady hum of the trickling ponds, and watched the steaming mist rising toward the starless sky. He knew he should be overwhelmed and exhausted, should be sleeping like a corpse, but he felt altogether lighter than he ever had. He thought of all it had taken to arrive in this place, so far from home, but so much closer to who he should be. Those days daydreaming on the Erikson farm, imagining what it might be to have a life of his own while Arnes went to school and Father went to work. All those days alone, had Siggi ever truly believed he might one day belong to the wider world? He'd dreamed but never believed in dreams, and certainly never thought he'd one day do magic or save his brother or love a witch with all his being.

He looked down at Hrafn, those dark brows and scarred skin and those lovely eyelashes, and felt something big and impossible swell in his chest. He yanked Hrafn closer, holding him tight as he could until Hrafn let out a small "Oof!" and pinched Siggi's arm. "Too tight! What's going on with you?"

Siggi smiled, then frowned, loosening his grip. "I'm only thinking."

"Oh, no. Mustn't do that," Hrafn said dryly.

"Hrafn," Siggi said, biting his lip. "Do you know what?"

"*What?*"

"I'm so happy. I just…is it right to be happy? When everything is so wrong?"

Hrafn peered into his eyes. "You're asking the ever-miserable skin-witch."

"I am." He sat up, holding Hrafn's forearms as he slid away, unwilling to part just yet. "Are you happy, too? Is it okay that we found happiness together?"

Hrafn blinked, and a curious expression crossed his face. "I don't know. But…" He seemed to struggle with the words, his whip-smart tongue seemingly tied. "But for once, I don't want to feel bad about feeling good."

Siggi nodded and scooped Hrafn into his arms. He scooted them toward the spring, until he could dangle his legs in the steaming water. He thought Hrafn would do the same, but instead he drew his own legs close and, in the nest of Siggi's thighs, hugged his knees. Siggi wrapped his arms around Hrafn, an embrace around an embrace.

274

"I'll spend forever tracing these staves, if you'll let me," Siggi said, pressing his lips to the ones on Hrafn's back, the ones he hadn't seen properly when Hrafn was atop him. "Once we've got Arnes back, won't you let me?"

"Siggi." When Hrafn spoke again, his voice was hoarse. Siggi pressed his face into Hrafn's hair, listening. "I never thought I could admit it."

"Admit what?"

"Wanting something. Happiness. Love. Kindness. Anything at all."

"Something's changed," Siggi said, nodding once.

"Yes." Warm mist rose from the water as it always had, watched by eyes that had never before seen it. "Something's changed."

Siggi dreamed of the abandoned farm and its ghostly inhabitants. Inside the longhouse, the walls were decorated just as Ylfa's had been, lined with shelves of colored jars. At least a dozen utburdur, perched on a bench beside the fire, watched him. A young boy who looked like Arnes or maybe looked like Hrafn or maybe looked like Siggi or maybe looked like a faceless stranger kicked his feet while he ate at a table laden with a remarkable feast. There was dried fish and mutton and sweet summer jam, all of it dripping down the boy's filthy face. The boy wasn't alone; a woman and a man sat on either side of him, staring at him while he ate, watching his every bite and swallow with hungry eyes.

Siggi stood in the doorway, and when they saw him there, the three of them turned to face him as one.

"What are you doing here?" the ghost-woman demanded, and her voice was tinged in fear or anger.

Her face was sliding away from her, revealing bones underneath. The same decay overtook the boy, but he kept eating all the same, gnawing flesh even as his own melted away.

"I don't know," Siggi said, and then he woke and opened his eyes to find a grinning skull staring down at him.

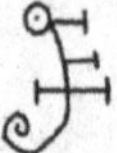

Siggi didn't scream. Instead he froze, breath caught in his chest, sure the pounding of his heart would wake Hrafn, asleep against him—

But it was only Anna, her head cocked to the side, perched on the shore of the pool, peering at the pair of them as though asking a question.

"You frightened me," he whispered, exhaling at last.

Anna lowered her infant skull and began preening her feathers. Siggi stared at her cranium, the small crack down its middle. Inside of Grimholl, when magic made a fool of him, Siggi had felt the presence of every single bone for miles and miles. Not just the bones of the beast and the bones of his traveling companions, but bones far deeper in the earth, bones older than the mountain, bones of creatures that no longer existed. He'd felt it all at once without finding it strange, but now the mere thought of knowing so much scared him.

And yet…the truth was, being overwhelmed by magic had been intoxicating. Not just in a drunken sense, but in a deeply gratifying sense. When the magic flowed through him, Siggi felt as if he were utterly himself, truly strong for the first time in his life. And that memory of wholeness terrified him even as it excited him, because while power was something he'd never thought to want or have, the ease with which magic had come to Siggi in the cave seemed to pose an important question:

If Siggi was only now becoming who he should be, who had he been before?

Arnes might not even recognize him when they reunited on the morrow.

Careful not to wake Hrafn, Siggi ran his fingers over his scaled stomach, the scars that marked his torso.

A dread Siggi couldn't verbalize accompanied every breath he took. As much as Siggi had changed, Arnes must have changed as well.

Because there was something Hrafn wasn't saying, something that flickered across his face whenever Siggi spoke of Arnes.

Hrafn stirred in his sleep, and Siggi pulled him closer. He was so incredibly warm, like a hot coal pulled from the fire, so very alive and furious, yet still carrying the potential of going cold. Siggi remembered the first moment he'd seen Hrafn. Dead and broken in the heap of corpses, a tragedy of stillness.

How unfair it seemed that this boy, gifted with so much talent and power and wit, had never felt loved before.

There was so much Siggi couldn't say, so much he couldn't see inside Hrafn's mind, and on the moss with their feet floating in the warm water, he found himself wondering what would become of them. Should Siggi reunite with Arnes, would they three return together to Midfjördur? And if Hrafn and Siggi severed the bond that knotted their souls together, what then? Would Hrafn leave his side, a witch in the wilderness?

Could they love each other still?

Siggi placed a hand on Hrafn's forehead and let it rest there.

Anna finished her preening and raised her head. She hopped down from the stone, stalked forward, and nestled into the space between Hrafn's scabbing collarbone and skull, the most peculiar of pillows.

"Whatever else, we will keep him safe," he said, and she didn't answer. Though Anna had no eyes to close, Siggi knew she was resting.

But Siggi could not sleep again.

Morning was easy to mistake, given the quiet of the steamy glade. Siggi watched the gray grow lighter so gradually that nothing seemed to change at all. The birds did not sing, the mist clinging to Draugamyr did not lift, the water did not stop pooling. Anna had left them during the night, Hrafn none the wiser. When Hrafn opened his eyes at last, they were shaded by residual nightmares, but when he saw Siggi he smiled.

They rose and dressed and descended to the base of the pools. Holta was nowhere to be seen, but Fidelma was crouched beside a meager fire. She had removed her cloak, revealing all those belt bags and pouches, and she was adjusting their straps and assessing their contents.

"Good morning, Fidelma," Siggi said.

She jumped, dropping a bag that must have been full of glass for the sound it made.

"Sorry," she said, looking up at them. "Not accustomed to being surprised, though I suppose I'll have to get used to it."

Holta had not fixed Fidelma's stone eye. Instead, Fidelma wore a patch of cloth that bore the marks of her needlework, embroidered with a false eye that made her face seem curiously lopsided. All the same, she smiled knowingly as Siggi and Hrafn approached.

"Does it hurt?" Siggi asked her. "Are you okay?"

"It's all right," Fidelma said, though her voice lacked its usual vigor. "A druid's much more than what she sees, you know."

"Haven't you got a spare eye in one of your pouches?" Siggi asked.

"Oh no. A druid gets one seeing stone, and only one. It's made with the menstrual blood of the entire clan, aged by the light of the aurora on the equinox, then fed to a goat until it forms a bezoar that's shaped into a perfect sphere."

"Oh," Siggi said, eyes wide. "I see."

Hrafn chuckled and bumped his elbow against Siggi's. "She's joking."

Fidelma probably winked, but Siggi couldn't be sure.

"Sleep well, then?" Fidelma purred.

"Yes, actually," Hrafn said. Siggi was taken aback by the pride in his voice, the complete lack of sarcasm, when he added, "*Extremely* well."

"Oh ho," Fidelma said with a grin. "Glad to hear it. All right, Siggi?" She tapped her fingers against her neck pointedly, and Siggi clapped his fingers to his own, knowing then that she could clearly see one of the many places Hrafn's lips had rested the night before.

Siggi knew none of them needed a magical eye to see his face burn. Hrafn laughed sweetly and took Siggi's hand—every time he did that, Siggi thought his heart could burst—and pulled him toward the place where their packs lay. He shamelessly rifled through the pockets of Holta's bag and handed Siggi a sheepskin pouch that contained half of a dried fish.

"Where's Holta?" Siggi asked, looking around.

From here, the valley of Draugamyr looked almost unremarkable. Rough fields of rock formed from ancient eruptions were not uncommon in Lifandfjall, and Arnes had once told him even Midfjördur had fallen victim to a lava flow when Father was just a boy. But though lava fields were commonplace, the dark-hued mist clinging to this one and the jaggedness of the rocks seemed too intentional, as if carved by some monstrous hand.

"She's gone off to have a look at the trail ahead. The fog's thick as curdled milk, but she reckons we'll reach that bog in an hour or less."

"You ready or not?" Holta asked, and Siggi and Hrafn both jumped. She had emerged from the thick fog as if from nowhere, Anna on her shoulder once more. "I've found a way down into Draugamyr that isn't so steep, if we follow the stream."

"Oh, there are plenty of ways into Draugamyr," Hrafn said. "It's getting out that's harder."

"Right. So how the hell are we going to find the gate?" Fidelma asked, tapping her eye patch. "I won't be able to see the magic or anything else once we're in the thick of it, surely."

Hrafn stood. "I've been there before. The ghosts might remember me."

"Will that be a help or a hindrance?" Holta asked. "You don't leave the best of impressions."

"Well," Hrafn said, with a smirk that didn't reach his eyes, "neither do they."

They descended in silence. Hrafn led the way, with Siggi at his back, Holta and Fidelma following behind. Soon their bathing the night prior seemed altogether pointless; mist doused them thoroughly as they stepped and slid down the slippery rocks. What Holta had called a path was little more than the narrow, damp space between the trickling stream and the boulders that braced it.

If Siggi had thought there'd be nothing to see, he was badly mistaken. Yes, the ancient lava field was shrouded in that heavy mist, the surrounding mountains and much of the distant field completely obscured. But the myriad pools of dark water in their vicinity remained curiously untouched by the haze. Their surfaces were utterly still, as though the contents were frozen solid despite the sulfurous warmth of the steam rising from the falls beside them

Siggi was so focused on his own feet that he didn't know they'd reached the plateau until Anna let out another of her haunting wails. She went stiff and her talons loosened. She slipped from Holta's shoulder, but the huldu girl caught her in her arms.

"Anna!"

Siggi almost fell over trying to reach Holta's side. "What's happened? Anna! Is she all right?"

Holta cradled Anna, eyes wide. "I don't know. She wasn't breathing to begin with, so how can I know? But she's not moving."

"Then—what's wrong with her?"

"Even without my eye, I can guess," Fidelma said, her tone unusually serious. She pulled her heavy cloak around her and took a step closer to Hrafn. "We're in it now, aren't we?"

Hrafn sighed and nodded. "The ghosts of Draugamyr aren't fond of other monsters. Use your magic to see if she's still with us."

"What? But I…you know I don't know how to do that."

Hrafn looked at him over his shoulder. "I think you do, even if you don't think so. I think you could do almost anything."

There was a hitch in Hrafn's voice, but also a degree of certainty. Siggi placed his palm carefully on Anna's cold little skull. And immediately he felt her fragility, felt that this scarred cranium was the only bone in her strange little body, felt that she had existed for years and though she had no heartbeat, she was still there. He inhaled sharply and pulled his hand away.

"She's just unconscious," he said, and knew it was true. Again, it felt like belonging, knowing the bones of things. Hrafn nodded, facing the bog.

Holta seemed to soften, ever so slightly. "Fidelma?"

"Don't worry, she'll be safer than the rest of us, under my wings," Fidelma said. Carefully she lifted Anna's stiff form from Holta's arms. She tucked the utburdur into one of her many bags, pulling a drawstring shut before letting her cloak fall closed once more. "Don't worry, Tina."

"I'm not worried," Holta said, and then added, "I…thank you."

Siggi tore his eyes away from the pair of them, from the intimate way they were looking at each other. And he saw that Hrafn had gone on ahead of them, just slightly, stepping onto the old path between the pools. Siggi took a step forward, about to say his name, because Hrafn, in his black and bloodied clothes, looked so slight on that horizon, but—

"Siggi," Hrafn warned, without looking back. "Stay put for a moment. There's something I have to do, before we go farther. Okay?"

Even days prior, Siggi would have ignored him, would have asked a dozen questions, but now he bit his tongue. "Okay."

Hrafn drew his knife. He reached over his shoulder, tugged down the collar of his ragged shirt, and pressed the blade into a stave on the back of his neck. Siggi had yet to memorize all the staves on Hrafn's skin, even after they'd spent the night entwined, but he knew he had never seen him use this one. Hrafn let out a soft groan and immediately dropped the knife in order to cover both ears with his palms. Hrafn cursed and staggered—Siggi forced himself to stay put, not to rush to him—but Hrafn did not fall.

After a long moment, Hrafn lowered his hands and drew himself upright, sweat beading his brow. Though his voice was tense, it was also steady. "They're noisier than I remember. A real racket."

"I don't hear anything," Holta said.

"If you want your own ghost-talking stave you'll have to carve it yourself."

Hrafn frowned, ear cocked toward the mist. He winced suddenly, knees buckling, and Siggi couldn't bear it any longer; he rushed to Hrafn's side. The moment he stepped onto the space between the pools, he felt the rocks give way slightly beneath him, and with each step forward the ground seemed to recoil from his feet.

"Hrafn!" he said, catching him as he fell, and he felt a surge of panic when he saw that Hrafn's eyes were leaking tears. "Hrafn? Are you okay?"

"Yeah," Hrafn said hoarsely. "It's just…they *do* remember me."

"Well, you're hard to forget," Siggi said gently, and helped Hrafn to his feet.

"They're going to tell me the way. Stay close to me. Whatever else, don't lose sight of me. It's much easier to be lost here than found."

Holta and Fidelma fell in behind Siggi, and together the four of them gazed into the fog. Though they could see no path, Hrafn seemed to. He took his first steps with intention before pausing.

"And don't look into the pools," Hrafn added.

"Fucking hell, you could have said that before," Fidelma hissed, and Siggi turned to see her staring deep into one of the still pools, her single eye wide in its socket. "This…it's horrible."

"Of course it's horrible!" Hrafn snapped, rounding on them. "And if you think it's bad to look at, imagine existing like that! Thousands died here! It doesn't help to see them suffering! Leave them some degree of dignity!"

Yet Siggi couldn't resist following the line of Fidelma's gaze. The pools revealed the heavy mist for what it really was: an amalgamation of humanoid forms and screaming faces, a slurry of spirits visible only in the mist's reflection. Hrafn had said that everyone could see the ghosts of Draugamyr, he had warned them, but those silent screaming faces…

Hrafn groaned again, and Siggi knew they weren't silent at all.

"What are they saying?" Holta asked. "How far is it to the gate?"

Hrafn listened to voices in the air, brow furrowed. "I don't know."

"Have they seen Arnes? Is Arnes in Draugamyr?" Siggi asked.

"They don't communicate that specifically," Hrafn said, shaking his head. "But no matter where Ketill and Arnes are at this moment, that's where they're going."

"And where we'll be waiting for them," Siggi said solemnly.

"Hey," Fidelma said, and put her hand on Siggi's elbow. She was looking at him with something like apprehension, though Siggi couldn't fathom why. "Are you okay? Not magic-drunk again?"

Siggi frowned. "No, I don't…why?"

"Surely there are thousands of bones buried in this mire, and enough magic to drown in. Will he be all right?" Fidelma said.

Holta looked sharply at Siggi. "Siggi. Do you sense any bones?"

Siggi reached out in his mind with those unseen tendrils. He felt his friends around him, and little Anna tucked away. Beyond that, he felt the dead lying in the mire, but they were spread out, their pull more diffuse than what he had felt beneath Grimholl. They stretched across miles, but every one of them was alone, like wisps of lonely firelight in the dense fog. It was unsettling.

"I feel them," he breathed. "But it's not like the tunnel."

"It wouldn't be," Hrafn said. "Draugamyr is a furious place, but all that fury is in the spirits, not their remains. The ghosts have forgotten they ever had bodies, I think. If you *do* start to feel it again, say something, okay?"

"How do you know so much about the ghosts?" Holta had yet to look into the pools, and seemed fixated on the horizon, on the gate said to lie ahead, the gate that would take her to the hidden realm. "They told you all of this?"

"In their way," Hrafn said tersely, and he turned away from them all. "Not to be obvious but please stay on the path. And…Siggi? If you see the wound beginning to scab on my neck, I need you to…tell me, and I'll cut it open again. Otherwise, we may be lost for good."

Siggi longed as ever to argue, but he knew this was how Hrafn's magic worked, and how he knew to help him. And though he longed for a day when Hrafn wouldn't cut himself to find some degree of control, that day was not today.

"I will."

He leaned down and kissed the whorl at the back of Hrafn's head, and despite all the rest, he felt Hrafn relax ever so slightly.

"And Siggi," he said, more softly now. "Stay close to me."

"I'm not leaving you," Siggi said. "Not ever again. We talked about this."

Hrafn nodded and led them into the whirling fog, and even their footsteps seemed muffled.

Chapter Twenty
The Gate of Blood and Bone

It was difficult to walk on the lumpy, uneven ground, where any misstep might plunge a person into a pool of rancid water. Hrafn chose his steps with care. Siggi was right behind him.

He also listened intently. He wouldn't have thought it possible, that he would recognize the ghosts' voices after nearly ten years, but he did. And he knew, before long, that they remembered him all too well.

Hrafn didn't think anybody had ever sung a lullaby to him when he was a child. Birtingr told him he had been abandoned shortly after he was born, left out in the weather like so much rubbish, and his care had been entrusted to apprentices and fellow witches, people who tended to a squalling baby only because they did not want to anger Birtingr. So when he had first come to Draugamyr, a child alone with a fresh stave on his neck and tears in his eyes, he hadn't recognized the sound when one of the ghosts began to sing.

Perhaps *sing* was the wrong word. It was more like a hum, or the thrum of a stringed instrument that he could feel in his throat, in his teeth, in the bumps rising on his skin. Among the people who had died on Draugamyr a hundred years ago, there had been mothers and fathers along with everybody else, both witch and huldu, people who had left their children behind to fight a battle they would never return from. Somewhere in that maelstrom of rage was at least one spirit who had seen a crying boy wandering alone and decided he needed comfort.

He didn't know if ghosts retained any memory or personality at all. He only knew that the lullaby was his answer, and they were going to show him the way. He had been terrified of them as a child, but he felt no fear now. A ghost existed only in the time after its death, and that was all it knew: the agony of dying, the anger of a life snatched way, and a desperate, hungry yearning for all the pain to go away.

"I think we understand each other a little better now," he whispered. He smiled a little as a set of footsteps hopped from stone to stone ahead of him, parting the mist like a veil.

The fog darkened around them, casting the whole of the mire into a murky gloom, darker than any day should be on the rising crest of summer. There was just light enough to see the shapes gathering around them, defined only by the whirl of mist. Here and there the water rippled, disturbed by presences Hrafn could not see. In other places, the moss compressed and parted in fleeting, light footsteps.

And, everywhere, always, there was the screaming.

The way was slow and treacherous, and Hrafn did not know how much time had passed when he heard Fidelma muttering something to Holta. She was asking if anybody even knew what they were going to *do* when they reached the gate, and Holta grumbled something in answer, something about knowing when they saw it, and he could hear the doubt in her voice—

He could hear her.

He could hear their voices. Their footsteps. Even Siggi's breath, still so close behind him.

"Fuck!" Hrafn stopped abruptly, wobbling on a moss-slick rock. "Fuck, fuck, fuck! I need to—fuck!"

The voices of the spirits were growing softer. Hrafn slapped his hand to the back of his neck. His skin was slick in the heavy fog, but beneath the sheen of water and sweat the wound was scabbing over.

"You were supposed to fucking *tell* me—"

"Sorry!" Siggi was right there. "I'm sorry, I'm sorry, I was looking, but we're all dripping because of this *stupid*—"

"It's fine," Hrafn said sharply. "I just have to open it again."

He raised the knife over his shoulder, but Siggi grabbed his wrist to stop him.

"Let me do it," Siggi said.

For a second Hrafn couldn't answer. He couldn't find the breath.

"You want…to cut me?"

"*No.*" Siggi's voice was low, but so very close to his ear, so close that it drove every other sound away. "No, Hrafn, not like that."

Still holding Hrafn's wrist, he wrapped his other arm around Hrafn from the back to embrace him. He pressed a kiss to the top of Hrafn's head, another right behind his ear.

"Never like that," Siggi said. "I only mean…your hand is shaking, and you can't see the stave. I can help. I can"—a pause as he swallowed—"I can make it a clean cut. It will hurt you less."

"Oh, Siggi." Hrafn closed his eyes and leaned back, letting himself rest against Siggi's broad warmth for one stolen moment of comfort. They didn't have time for more. "Only you. Do it. But hurry."

Siggi took the knife from his hand and stepped back. His fingers were warm on Hrafn's neck as he pushed the fabric of his shirt and strands of damp hair aside. There was a puff of breath right before his lips touched Hrafn's skin, right above the stave.

"You have to spill blood," Hrafn said.

"I know," Siggi said.

Hrafn expected him to hesitate, to wince and worry, but Siggi did no such thing. He felt the press of Siggi's fingers, then the touch of the blade—cool, stinging, steady—and the warm well of blood. Siggi's fingers brushed over his neck again, right above the cut, then dropped away.

The screams of the ghosts returned, but Hrafn was ready for it this time. He took his knife back, gave Siggi a nod, and kept going.

He didn't notice the ground beneath them was changing until he put his foot down and felt the sharp crunch of crumbling rocks rather than the spongy give of overgrown moss. He looked up and blinked water droplets from his eyes.

He stood at the edge of a large black outcropping of stone. It was about fifteen ells across and far too round to be natural, even cracked and weathered as it was; it sloped upward to form a gentle hump above the boggy landscape. The mist shifted and churned, and for a moment the scent of the air changed, with the damp, sulfurous smell of the spring-fed bog giving way to something sickly and sweet, like rotting food in a refuse pile.

Then the rotten smell was gone, and the fog whirled again, and it did not stop whirling, turning and turning in a gentle circle around that outcrop of black rock, spiraling toward the center. Hrafn followed where it led, over stone that was damp and slippery but free of moss, until he could see how the mist twisted and shimmered in the center. Tendrils of fog curved and clung like vines, snaking along the ground before climbing to form an unmistakable shape.

This was what they were looking for.

The Gate of Blood and Bone.

"Oh." Siggi stepped up beside Hrafn. "That's not what I was expecting."

"What were you expecting?" Holta asked. She reached back to help Fidelma step onto the ring of black rock. "Something shiny and golden, like the priests teach?"

"No," Siggi said, "but I was kind of expecting something that was at least, well, *solid*." He looked around for a moment, peering into the heavy fog as though he expected to see something. "Ketill and Arnes aren't here yet."

The wails of the spirits were fading again, but this time Hrafn let them. He walked a slow circle around the gate; it did not change, no matter what angle he looked at it, nor did it react to their presence in any way. Partly obscured by fog and caught between realms, it was visible only as a ghost of itself, transparent and slippery to the eye. There was a glimpse of white bone, a hint of green moss, a quick, faint glimmer of something that might be light.

He reached out tentatively to touch the archway.

"What are you doing?" Holta demanded, while at the same time Fidelma said, "Uh, is that a good idea?"

But Hrafn felt only a prickle of warmth, vaguely sticky, like cooling blood. There was *something* there besides the illusion, but it was not solid under his fingertips. He stepped back and crossed his arms over his chest, scowling. There were no runes, no markings, no signs that indicated how the gate worked or how it had been closed. It was only a ghostly arch, through which all that could be seen was the Draugamyr.

"A magic druid eye would be really fucking useful right about now," Hrafn said.

"Gosh, if only we had thought of that," Fidelma replied. "How silly of us."

"Why don't you try bleeding on it, witch?" Holta said. "That's how you do everything else, isn't it?"

Hrafn made a face at her because he didn't want to admit that he was considering doing exactly that. But there was a problem.

"There's nothing for me to bleed on," Hrafn said. He reached out again to wave his hand through the shadow outline of the gate. "I can't touch it. I can see that it was once made of bone, but what remains isn't enough in this realm for me to do anything to it."

Siggi made a questioning sound in his throat, then said, "Huh, I wonder if…"

He stuck his hand out.

Hrafn grabbed his wrist. "Wait, don't—"

"You stuck your hand in here," Siggi replied, amusement warming his words.

"But that's—"

"Hrafn. Look."

Siggi's hand was curled around the edge of the arch. Where he touched it—because he *was* touching it—the bones were less translucent, more solid, quivering with a strange, undulating motion that made them seem like they were trying to escape his grasp. He wasn't flinching away or wincing in any way; the touch was not causing him pain. But it did make the rest of the gate slightly easier to see. There were a very large number of bones contained within its tall, slender archway.

"Ah, the farm boy is clever as well as handsome," Fidelma said, and Siggi's cheeks pinked. "What does it feel like?"

"It feels weird," Siggi said.

Hrafn poked at the bones just above Siggi's grip. Instead of passing right through, his finger met solid resistance. He tried again, farther from Siggi's hand, and felt only the strange warmth. There was the faintest shadow of a stave marking on the gate, but he couldn't make out the whole of it, nor could he touch it. It looked like part of the stave for locking doors against intrusion, altered and combined with symbols he did not recognize.

Siggi slid his hand over the bones. "It's not like the bones in the mountain, or the ones elsewhere in the marsh."

"It wouldn't be." Holta was standing on Fidelma's other side, her arms crossed, her mouth fixed in a scowl. "Those bones were dead."

"And these aren't?" Fidelma asked.

"No," Siggi breathed. "No. They're definitely not dead."

"How does that even work?" Fidelma asked. She didn't sound like she doubted it, more like she was trying to work it out in her mind. "The huldu gates are ancient. How can the bones still be alive, unless they're—"

"They're huldu bones," Holta said.

Siggi snatched his hand away quickly, and the gate was once again as ephemeral as mist.

"I had always rather assumed the blood and bone referred to…what the huldufolk took from others. From trylla or humans. But you're saying they built it out of their own people?" Fidelma said.

"While they were still alive," Hrafn added. "I don't suppose they asked for volunteers."

Holta was scowling. "Do huldu ever ask before taking what they want?"

One glance at Siggi's face, one moment of feeling the faint ache in his chest, and Hrafn knew what Siggi was thinking. He was thinking about whether he would do something like that, whether there was something in his own blood and his own bones that would make him look at another person and see nothing more than a thing to be broken down into useful tools for magic. Hrafn wanted to reassure him, but he didn't know what to say, so he reached for Siggi's hand. Siggi didn't grasp his in return, so Hrafn settled for loosely looping his fingers around Siggi's wrist, holding him even if, in that moment, he didn't think he deserved to be held.

"I still have no idea how to open it," Hrafn said. "Even if Siggi can touch it."

"Don't you?"

The question came from behind them, rich with laughter and mockery. They all spun to face it, and Hrafn's first thought was *Haraldar, fucking Haraldar*, because what he saw was a figure in the mist draped in stitched-together skins. But that was not Haraldar's voice, and Hrafn's second thought was, *Fuck, I hoped we'd have more time to prepare.*

"Hello, Hrafn," Ketill said. He stepped onto the stone platform and lowered the hood of his skin-cloak. He was smiling. "Good. You're both already here. We have work to do."

Ketill was not alone. Another figure followed him, hands bound by rope, draped in a cloak of skins so long its ragged ends dragged through the moss and mud. Ketill gave a yank on the rope, which was looped through his belt, to tug the other person onto the black stone. That person staggered almost drunkenly but didn't fall; they jerked the rope back and made a displeased noise. One of the bound hands was wrapped in a dirty bandage.

"Behave," Ketill said mildly.

The other person lifted his chin slowly. He was still gagged with a strip of dirty cloth, but the shape of his features and the blue of his eyes staring out from beneath his matted hair were unmistakably familiar.

"*Arnes*." Siggi spoke the name as a gasp. Hrafn felt the thump of Siggi's heart and the sudden tightness in his chest.

Ketill held up a hand. "Ah. Not so fast."

Siggi ignored him; he tugged his hand from Hrafn's grasp to run forward. Ketill twitched the rope again, tugging Arnes a few steps out of Siggi's reach. Arnes made a sound of protest, low and angry in his throat, and Siggi stopped uncertainly.

"I said not so fast, Sigbert," Ketill said.

"Arnes," Siggi said. "I'm—I've been looking for you. It'll be okay now. I found you."

Arnes looked at Siggi, looked at Ketill, then looked past both of them. When his gaze settled on Hrafn, his eyes narrowed.

Siggi didn't seem to notice. "He doesn't need to be gagged. Can't I just—"

Ketill gestured carelessly. "Fine. The gag only. I'm sure we're all eager to hear this heartwarming reunion. Leave his hands bound."

Siggi touched Arnes's shoulder lightly, so very lightly, before reaching around his head to untie the strip of cloth. Now that they were out of the fog, Hrafn could see the staves painted on both of the skin-cloaks—for sneaking, for warding off spirits. That was how they had remained hidden in the marsh.

"What have you done to him?" Siggi asked, with tears in his eyes. "And why is this knotted so *tight*? I need—"

"No blades. I'm not that careless, boy," Ketill said. "To answer your question, I didn't do anything to him. Nothing that will last, anyway. I've simply given him a little concoction to slow those impressive huldalf reflexes. All of his little bumps and bruises are courtesy of Swift-Eye. Disgusting man." He looked around mildly, eyebrows raised. "I rather thought he might be here already."

"The wolves of Myrkvidor caught him," Holta said.

Ketill laughed. "He was stupid enough to go into the forest? He won't be mourned."

"Why were you working with him, if he was so stupid?" Fidelma asked.

"I said he was stupid, not that he was useless," Ketill replied. "He was, in fact, very useful—or so I thought. If I had known our little raven-haired beauty would be so willing to help, I would have gone about it the easy way. Shall we get started?"

"So you are here to open the gate," Holta said, her eyes narrow.

"Isn't that why we're all here?"

"Why do you want it open?" Fidelma asked. "You know that it's mad, don't you? Whatever it is you want from that realm, they won't make it easy for you. They'll make you into a pet when they catch you."

Ketill raised his eyebrows. "Don't the old women of the forest teach their daughters about the value of pursuing difficult goals?"

"There," Siggi said suddenly, and the cloth finally fell from Arnes's mouth.

Arnes grabbed Siggi with his bound hands and stepped in front of him. "Stay away from them, Siggi," he said, his voice low. He glared at Hrafn. Hrafn glared right back. "That's a witch."

"That's—what? I know," Siggi said. "Arnes, I know. It's okay. He's okay."

"Step away now, boys." Ketill pulled Arnes to his side with a solid jerk of the rope.

With a quick, smooth motion, he drew a knife from his belt. He kicked at Arnes's knees, not hard, but there must have been an injury there already, because Arnes let out a shout of pain and fell to the ground. Ketill extended his arm to place the knife almost lazily against the side of Arnes's throat.

"Yes, stupid boy, that is a witch," Ketill said to Arnes. "My favorite witch, in fact. I need him for this to work. He and your brother are going to do everything I say, because if they don't you'll be dead before you hit the ground. You might think your huldu half is enough to keep you alive, but your human half is so very, very weak, and both are dulled right now. I have no idea how much blood you can afford to lose."

Arnes looked up at him through his long, dirty hair. His bound hands were clenching and unclenching, his jaw rigid with anger. He spat at Ketill's feet, but he didn't rise, and he didn't try to fight.

"Good boy. Now. Siggi. Back over there." Ketill waved with the knife. "Let's open this gate."

"But we don't know *how*," Siggi said.

Ketill wasn't looking at him. He was looking at Hrafn with a small smile that made his skin crawl.

"Don't we?" Ketill said. "Don't we all know the story of how the gates came to be closed? Witches know. The druids know—they were there, after all, watching without raising a finger to help either side. The huldu know. I suppose dullard farm boys from the Thrandir might not know. Tell him, Hrafn. Tell him why you're both here."

"A witch and a huldu closed the gates," Siggi said. "They worked together, combined witchcraft and huldu magic."

Arnes let out a low growl: "*Witch.*"

"Is that the pretty tale the witches tell? The truth is the human witch killed his huldu lover," Ketill said flatly. "They had promised to live together in peace after the gates were closed. He cut her throat and mingled her blood with his own. When the others finally broke through the fighting, his arms were red to the elbow, and she was so drained she had aged a hundred years. The witch didn't even pause to kiss his lover as she died. He was too greedy for her blood."

Holta began, "That's not—"

Hrafn interrupted her with a snort. "Oh, for fuck's sake, that's the stupidest thing I've ever heard. It takes more than that to kill a huldu, and the witch would only need that much blood if he was really *incredibly* shit at magic. Besides, if all it took was draining a huldu of blood, you wouldn't need their cooperation, would you? So you know there's more to it than that. Siggi, come here."

"Keep your distance," Arnes snapped. "Stay away from it. You don't know what it can do."

Siggi's lips parted, and Hrafn could see that he was trying to figure out what to say, but in the end he only said, "I do know. It's okay. I'll be okay. I just need to do this." He looked at Ketill before joining Hrafn at the gate. His heartbeat was calmer now; it felt like a steady echo to Hrafn's own. "You'll let him go if we do this for you."

"I don't want him," Ketill said, with a quick smile. "I've never wanted him. He wouldn't even be here still if he had cooperated before, but, well, he was stubborn."

"So you'll let him go."

"He'll be all yours. You can take him home and patch him up and raise sheep, or whatever it is farm boys dream about doing. You'll never see me again." Ketill looked down at Arnes, then twirled his knife in his fingers. "But only if you succeed."

Hrafn didn't know if Ketill was lying, because Ketill wore the same amused mask whether he lied or spoke the truth. But they had only two choices: believe him or attack him. Arnes was drugged, Siggi wouldn't do anything to risk Arnes, and Hrafn didn't know if even Holta could move fast enough to keep Arnes safe. Her huldu strength and speed meant nothing if the knife could sink into Arnes's neck in less than a heartbeat. He might survive that, but he might not.

Ketill smiled at Hrafn, and he winked.

"Siggi," Hrafn said, turning away quickly.

Siggi rejoined Hrafn at the gate. "You know what to do?"

"I need to see the markings on the gate, to figure out which ones to break," Hrafn said. "And I think to do that we need, um."

Siggi pushed up his sleeve and extended his left hand. "Go ahead."

"You can just touch it first, so we can look at it. You don't have to—"

"But this will work better, won't it? This is what we have to do anyway," Siggi said. "Go ahead."

Hrafn drew his knife—the knife Siggi had given to him after Hrafn had crawled out of his own funeral pyre, after he had murdered Siggi's father. Siggi had shown no hesitation, no fear about placing a blade into the hands of an abomination and a killer, and there was no fear on his face now. Only streaks of tears, and a look of determination. Through their bond, forged with the blade Siggi had plucked from Hrafn's dead body, Siggi's heartbeat was still so very steady. It was staggeringly unfair that he could look so strong and kind and beautiful even when he was crying. Hrafn reached up to brush the tears away.

"Don't you fucking touch him," Arnes said. He started to lunge forward, then hissed as Ketill's blade pressed into his skin. "Keep your filthy hands to yourself, witch."

Hrafn dropped his hand and grabbed Siggi's wrist instead, held it perhaps tighter than he needed to, and pressed the tip of the blade to Siggi's forearm.

"Start with tracing any staves you see," he said. "I need to see them clearly."

"Right. Okay."

Siggi didn't wince as the blade cut into his skin and blood flowed from the wound. Hrafn felt the sting of the cut himself, like a thousand cuts he had felt before, but softer. Siggi touched the gateway in a few places, stirring the bones to react to his presence, then swiped his fingers through the blood to trace the first of the staves.

There was one stave to the east, where the sun would rise on the equinox. Another to the west, where it would set. There was a stave carved across a threshold of femurs laid flat on the ground, and another at the highest point of the arch, which Siggi could only reach by asking Holta for a boost in height. Siggi traced all of them with his blood, painting them with a red that remained unnaturally bright, even as the white of the bones seemed to glow from within. When he was finished, he stepped back and absently closed his bloody hand over the wound on his arm.

Within the arch was a gate, also made of bones, set in a starburst of curving ribs held together with a knot of sinew in the center. Nothing was visible beyond, except more fog.

Hrafn reached for the gate. He could touch it now, both the gate itself and the arch around it. They were solid and oddly warm, even a bit slick, and the bones trembled with the faintest hum beneath his fingertips.

Siggi walked around the arch to look it over again. "That's it. There are only those four."

"Do you recognize them?" Holta asked.

Hrafn didn't answer right away. While they had elements that were as familiar to him as the oldest of his own scars, that mad witch from a century ago had combined and altered them in ways he didn't fully understand. He had woven his own magic with huldu magic to ensure that the spell could not be undone, because even if there were another pair willing to work together, any huldu with the right kind of magic was likely to be sealed away beyond reach. It would take days or weeks of study—and probably quite a bit of trial and error—for him to be able to deconstruct them thoroughly, to see every thread of magic well enough to unwind it. He didn't know how to do that.

But that was fine. Hrafn wasn't here to be careful. He'd never been very good at that anyway.

He lifted the knife and drew the blade across the fire stave on his right wrist, swiftly opening three cuts. He switched the blade to the other hand, his palm slick with fresh blood, and did the same with his left palm. Then he tucked the knife away and pressed his hands together.

When he brought them apart, he was holding fire in each palm.

He slammed one hand first into the western stave on the gate, hard enough to make the structure tremble. The fire crackled and burned, instantly scorching the bones. Black lines spread to follow Siggi's blood, and the stave beneath cracked open with a loud tearing sound. The entire gate shuddered; a groan came from everywhere and nowhere at once. Hrafn stepped quickly to the eastern stave and did the same there. The fire was hot, much hotter than he would normally make it. He could feel his own skin stinging, but he ignored it. He burned the stave until Siggi's blood was charred and the stave broken open by the heat.

Then he stepped back and looked at the stave at the top of the arch.

"So, I think I need a, uh, I need a big strong farm boy to help me reach that one? If you could—"

"Like this?" Siggi's hands were already at his waist, lifting him easily.

"Perfect."

Hrafn used both hands to burn the topmost stave, holding the fire there until every last line was burnt as black as ink. Siggi lowered him to the ground.

"Now for the huldu's work," Ketill said.

"I don't know what to do," Siggi said. "Hrafn? What do I do?"

"Wait." Fidelma stepped forward, her beads clinking softly. "Have you thought about what will happen if you do this? What will *really* happen? Because what you faced in the fjord—that was what the huldu can do when they *aren't* in this realm."

"We talked about this," Holta said shortly. "I told you—"

"I know, I know," Fidelma said. "But the gates weren't closed for a lark. The pair that did it, they did it to stop a war. They did it because people were dying."

"I always forget how tiresome druid morality is," Ketill said. He grabbed Arnes by the hair and tilted his head back. There was a trickle of blood on Arnes's throat where the blade had sliced his skin. "All the trouble your brother went through to find your mother's family, and you're going to fail him at the last step? You're going to let him die?"

Siggi turned away from Ketill. "Hrafn, what do I have to do?"

Hrafn knelt at the threshold. This last stave was a strange and complicated thing, almost organic in its shape, completely unlike any he had seen before. In it there were hints of familiar lines—for entrapment, for security—but all of it was twisted and whirled around a sinuous knot that was very clearly huldu in origin, or even older. It even reminded him a bit of the veined labyrinth beneath Grimholl.

"Come here," he said to Siggi. He placed his hand over the stave. "Put your hand over mine. The one—"

"I know," Siggi said. He knelt as well and closed his left hand, the one marked by Hrafn's witch-blade, over Hrafn's smaller hand. "You've hurt yourself again."

"Sorry, puffling," Hrafn said softly. "This is probably going to hurt both of us now. We have to break this seal. I can break the stave on the surface, but you need to break it within the bone."

"I don't know what to do."

"You do," Hrafn said. He looked at Siggi until Siggi met his eyes. "That's the difference between your magic and mine. Yours is part of you, a natural part. It's not something you have to learn. It's part of your will—your instincts. That's why this works. Ketill's version of the story is horseshit. They had to work together. There's no other way. A witch can't break the huldu part of the magic alone, and a huldu can't break the witch part. The pair who sealed the gates were counting on the fact that witches and huldu would never get along well enough to undo it."

"I won't let them hurt you," Siggi said quietly. "I know Fidelma is right that this is dangerous. But I don't care if they're my family. I won't let them. I promise."

Hrafn had no answer for that. He wanted to believe Siggi's promise so much it terrified him.

"Ready?" he said. "Follow the blood and fire into the cracks to break the bones apart."

Siggi took a breath, squeezed Hrafn's hand, and said, "Ready."

Hrafn drew forth the fire again. It licked between his fingers and danced over the threshold stave, filling the gaps between the bones with smoke and char. Pain crept up his arms, burning and strong. He felt it for both of them, passed back and forth between their bond.

He felt it, as well, when Siggi began working his magic.

It was like nothing he had ever felt before. It wasn't pain, wasn't anything like that, but he felt Siggi's attention and focus in every single one of his bones, from the tips of his fingers to a sudden ringing in his ears, from a squeeze in his chest to a hum in his head. His bones were no longer his own; he could not move them even if he wanted to. Siggi was too powerful, too encompassing, and it would be so easy to let him take everything, to give in to that overwhelming strength, that magic so unlike his own.

The snap of the threshold brought Hrafn back to himself.

The femurs set into the base of the arch shattered into long splinters, their edges charred and brittle, as magic and fire flowed through them. The breakage spread outward in both directions from their hands, cracking bones into jagged pieces inch by inch. The bones blackened as they broke, and the air filled with sooty black dust that stung Hrafn's eyes. The fires burning deep within the old bones spread across the gate itself, along the slender ribs that obscured the realm beyond. Shards of bone broke from the sides of the archway and pattered around them like rain, and Hrafn felt something deep within the structure shift.

He looked up to see the gateway turning black and mottled, like wood charring in a fire, up both sides until it reached the top. The bones that formed the top of the archway cracked once more, loudly, but did not fall.

Hrafn let the fire go out. The air was thick with smoke and ash. For a moment there was no sound except the settling of the burnt bones.

Then a new sound: soft, crisp. So out of place in the center of the Draugamyr that it took Hrafn a moment to recognize it.

It was the sound of footsteps through fallen leaves.

"Shit," he whispered, his heart thumping with fear. "*Fuck.*"

There wasn't supposed to be somebody on the other side. Not already, not close enough to hear. Open the gate, let Ketill and Holta sneak in, do it without being seen. The huldu had lost interest in the human realm, absorbed in their own concerns—that's what Ylfa had said.

But Ylfa's huldu friend had lied to her.

The smell in the air changed, and something heavy and sweet swept over them, carried on a warm breeze that stirred from nowhere. The sweet scent turned ripe, even rotten, as it grew stronger and stronger. Siggi released Hrafn's hand to grab his elbow and pull him backward. They had stumbled only a few steps away when the center of the gate burst outward with a gust of fetid air.

The ribs shattered, and shards of bone sliced across Hrafn's face. Siggi rolled to protect him without a second's hesitation.

When the onslaught of bone splinters ceased, Hrafn shoved at

Siggi's shoulder to sit up. There was a slice across Siggi's cheek, a line of blood where a shard of bone had struck him. Hrafn touched it gently, marveling at the way Siggi's hair looked even fairer in the light—the light that was coming from behind him.

From the gateway.

Hrafn pushed Siggi aside and scrambled to his feet.

The gate was gone. The net of rib bones was completely broken, shattered to pieces apart from a few last bits dangling from sinews on the sides. Also gone was the fog on the other side of the gate. It had been replaced by sunlight. Bright, golden, midday sunlight, illuminating the humid, hazy air. The glow had a green tinge to it, like the morning mist of a verdant pond, and that smell, too much like rotting food or low tide, was pervasive. Something moved in the golden light beyond the gate: a swirl of motion that resolved into an indistinct shape, before revealing itself to be a person. A woman stepped through the gate. She was tall and fair, with hair so pale it was nearly white, and eyes of a sharp, bright green. Her dress was the same color, the green of new spring grass and the freshest unfurling leaves on blossoming trees.

She looked around, taking in each of them with a cool, unblinking stare, before her gaze finally settled on Hrafn.

"Finally," she said. Her voice was deep and sonorous, the voice of someone who knew she would be heard when she spoke. "I was growing so very *bored*. Are you the witch who killed my sister?"

Chapter Twenty-One
The Hidden Realm

In his mind, he thinks it must have been a dream.

In his heart, he knows better.

Here is Siggi, so much smaller, crouching in the struggling grass near the snaggletoothed sow and the goat that gives milk no longer. Here is Siggi, dragging a stone across muddied peat in the afternoon breeze, left alone on the homestead while Father and Arnes are away. Father has tied a rope from his ankle to the fence post, so that Siggi will stay where he is put.

Siggi doesn't mean to dig, but with little else to do, dig he does, gouging the sulfurous muck with a jagged stone until the turf peels away. He digs a hole hoping to find the treasure of the seafaring men Arnes so often speaks of.

Siggi digs, and he sees the glimmer of something beautiful.

His heart catches, but as he drops the stone and pushes his pudgy fingers into the mud, he realizes it is not gold, but a bone. No, it is several bones, small and delicate, the remains of a lamb that did not survive its first moments.

Siggi feels a sharp sting in his chest, an ache of empathy he is far too young to understand. When he puts his hand on the bones, his eyes are already running. When the bones respond to his touch, twitching and jostling, Siggi isn't afraid.

When he wraps his arms around the lamb skeleton, it kicks against him like any other infant. It is not soft and warm and bleating, but hard and cold and silent. The goat and the sow are pressing themselves as far from the little grave as the fence will allow, terror in their wide eyes. Siggi doesn't care.

He sets the bones in the grass and slowly the creature finds its footing. It is missing pieces here and there. A fox has claimed one of its legs, and ravens may have notched those divots in its skull. All the same, the lamb stands with uncanny grace, and Siggi stares into its dark eye sockets and sees in them something like kinship. It takes a few wobbling steps. He reaches forward to touch the jagged remnants of its snout—

"What are you doing?"

Siggi falls back. "F-father."

Father's face is veined with red. He grips an iron mallet tight in his hand.

Just behind him, Arnes stares with fearful eyes.

Siggi says, stumbling over the words, "It's just a little l-lamb…"

But Arnes isn't looking at the lamb. His terror is reserved for Siggi.

Father steps over the fence, and within three strides he has Siggi by the nape. He throws him backward and then swings the mallet down upon the skeletal lamb. There is no bleat of pain as Father shatters it, but Siggi feels a cry in his heart. He's sobbing as Father unties the knot from his ankle and drags him, heels scraping stone, into their little house.

"Father," Siggi cries, but Father says nothing as he pulls the switch from its place above the door.

"Foul as your mother," Father utters, after the first blow lands. "A beast in the making."

Head swimming, Siggi looks toward the open doorway. Arnes is silhouetted against the green grass and the dark mountains.

"Arnes," Siggi pleads, but Arnes takes a step away. Face wan and hands shaking, he pulls the door closed, leaving Siggi in the darkness with Father.

This was never a dream, but it was a nightmare all the same.

Reeling from the stench of another world that roiled through the gate in the wake of the fey, fearsome huldu woman, Siggi could only think, *Is this who Arnes was seeking?*

Her voice was mild, but it felt like a thunderclap in Siggi's chest when she asked, "Are you the witch who killed my sister?"

For once, Hrafn seemed at a loss for words. His hands were blistered red, his dark irises mirroring the green light of the hidden realm. If Hrafn noticed the devastation he'd done to himself, he did not show it. His familiar stoicism made Siggi want to cry. This was all wrong. There wasn't supposed to be somebody waiting at the gate.

The huldu drew nearer, carrying that blinding chartreuse haze with her. Her features were muddled, as though they were seeing her through an ell of misty water. She stood taller than Siggi by several heads, neck long and willowy like a sapling. Her face was angular, her ears pointed, her hair as thin and pale as morning light. Her dress was embroidered with vines and studded with jewels. Her stature was reminiscent of the trylla in the mountain, but she stood perfectly upright, with straight shoulders, and bore the features of a real person. Her teeth, however sharp, did not number in the hundreds. Her every motion carried with it that strange, rotting stench, as if she were an open jar of fermented fish, forgotten in the sun.

A thick layer of dust coated her skin, as though she had been stationary for an era.

"Yfirnáttúrulegt! Oh, ethereal being!" Ketill cried suddenly, falling to his knees on the black stone.

Arnes yelped in surprise as his leash was pulled. White anger sparked in Siggi's temples, but Hrafn restrained him, one ruined hand on Siggi's sleeve.

The huldu shifted her stare from Hrafn to Ketill.

Ketill lifted his head. For the first time, emotion colored his features, emotion so strong it bordered on manic. "Oh how I have longed for this day! I have sought it with all my being, ever since I was cast out from the brotherhood of blasphemers who could not see the truth. I joined the Brotherhood of the Seven Saints seeking heavenly grace and the wisdom of the Godhead. But though my brothers studied the very same scriptures as I, they *would not see the truth!*"

"The truth," the huldu said. "What truth?"

"They seek heaven after death, but I know that heaven is here, beyond this very gate. I know that gods once walked among us! You and your kind are holy, Yfirnáttúrulegt, celestial souls that the foolish, mortal settlers failed to worship. I knew you would be beautiful," he added as a tear slipped down his freckled cheek. "Yet you are more exquisite than I ever imagined. Heed my prayers, Yfirnáttúrulegt!"

She raised a narrow eyebrow. "How very dull. I did not stand guard over this wretched gate for one hundred years to bandy words with a feckless panderer."

The huldu kicked Ketill with the toe of her pointed slipper. Delicate though she appeared, Ketill crumpled and yelped, clutching his stomach. He dropped the rope that bound. Although he was in obvious pain, he crawled forward toward the huldu, staring up at her with wide, beseeching eyes.

"You don't understand!" he cried. "I've come here for you! I did this all for you!"

"Do you think," said the woman, "that I have need of gifts from a mortal maggot? You insult me."

As she stepped farther from the gate, the otherworldly haze abandoned her skin and the gray light of Draugamyr revealed the truth.

Her garment wasn't embroidered after all, but overgrown with a branching, minute gray fungus that clung to her like lichen. The would-be jewels at her collar and hem were writhing insects that had burrowed dozens of holes into her flesh, as though she were made of rotting bark; their iridescent shells glittered as they squirmed. Her hair was so thin her papery scalp was exposed. She was altogether too pale, every artery visible through her translucent, dust-caked skin.

With each step the huldu took, the ground behind her churned. A hundred tiny seedlings sprouted in her footsteps, grew and bloomed, and then withered and died and rotted in quick succession, the cycle of life amplified and destroyed by her presence.

"You have something of her in your face, helmingbarn," she said, meeting Siggi's eyes, before looking to Arnes as well. "The both of you do. Though your humanity has most assuredly dampened her charms. You share her proclivity for sordid company, it seems." Her eyes fixed on Siggi's witch-bladed hand. "Tell me, are the human swine so bland that you've bound yourself to a murderous witch?"

Hrafn freed himself from Siggi's grasp. When at last he spoke, his voice had lost none of its defiance. "I'm sorry, are you talking about me?"

The woman shifted her gaze to Hrafn. "Are you not the witch who killed my sister?"

"I may have, or I may not have," Hrafn said dryly. "What did she look like?"

"Do not taunt me, witch. You have burned her skull and bedded her offspring, I'd wager." Arnes made an outraged sound, but she ignored it to return her gaze to Siggi. Though her eyes were green, not blue, there was something of Arnes in her cheekbones, something of Siggi in her chin. "Nephew, we all have our whims, but this witch is an especially insignificant creature."

"Thank you," Hrafn said sweetly.

"He isn't," Siggi said.

"Rich coming from a decaying hag!" Fidelma blurted.

The huldu yawned, revealing several rows of incisors. "My sister chose to bed a mortal, and he cut her head from her shoulders. Your own dalliance is hardly a surprise."

Siggi reeled, and the earth seemed to fall away beneath his feet. "But…Father…*Father* killed our mother?"

"No," Arnes breathed.

Hrafn's face registered grim resignation. How long had he suspected this?

Siggi felt blood pounding through his ears.

Ketill began to laugh, a ragged, broken sound. Clutching his stomach, he drew himself upright. Blood dribbled down his chin, but his eyes shone brightly. "Oh, he surely *tried* to kill her. According to Brother Hamon, your heathen father only learned what she was after she gave birth to her second monstrous son. He panicked, believing he had sinned, and pulled her from her children and lopped her head away. Imagine his disappointment when she continued to scream. He tried to kill a holy thing, a goddess! The damned fool!"

"*No.*" Arnes shook his head, his filthy hair whipping about his face. The cloak of warded skin still clung to his shoulders. "Father would not have!"

"Well," the huldu said. "Certainly it was a task easier said than done. No clumsy beheading would have killed my sister."

Siggi felt turmoil roiling within him, an amorphous mass of tangled emotions that numbed him from the inside out.

"But he tried," Ketill said. "Oh, he tried. When decapitation did not end her sobbing cries, your father brought her remains to the church. Brother Hamon is a fool, but the pettiest priests know power when they see it. In exchange for sparing your father's life and keeping his secrets, they claimed her vessel and distributed it as church relics."

"Relics," Hrafn said, eyes wide. "More than one."

"Oh, yes. She was divided eight times over, for that is their sacred number." Ketill held up a hand to tick off fingers as he went on. "Her torso, her head, her two legs, her two arms, and her eyes. Each in a sanctified burial place, blessing the land and warding away evil."

"No," Arnes said again.

Siggi fought back the gorge in his throat. His mother's head in Midfjördur was the least of it. Other churches held the rest of her, wrapped in bone and buried, objects instead of the pieces of a person.

"Alas, it is the truth. Had I known of her suffering, I would have never done her such a disservice." Ketill's voice turned earnest, almost pleading. "I would have served her. I would have protected her. I would have worshiped her living form, as your wretched father should have done."

"Father didn't kill Mother!" Arnes shouted.

"Arnes…" Siggi whispered.

"No," Arnes said, eyes roving. "You never loved him, and he never loved you. You know just as I know that *you're* the true reason Mother's dead."

Siggi flinched, grounded only by Hrafn's warmth against his shoulder. "Arnes…"

"You're no brother of mine," Arnes snarled.

Bile rose in Siggi's throat, and a true chill pierced his heart, but for once he could not cry.

"Well, I'm afraid you can't ask the old blacksmith yourself, pet," Ketill chided, with a little laugh. His strength seemed to be returning, along with his mocking tone. "As this little witch killed him in turn."

Arnes let out a feral howl and lunged for Hrafn, clawing at his face as Ketill laughed and Siggi tried to wedge himself between them and Fidelma tried to pull Arnes away.

"Enough!" Hrafn shouted, and despite his mangled hands, despite their profound difference in stature, he gripped Arnes by his filthy tunic and shoved him away. "It's true. I killed your mother, and your father! Your mother I regret, but your father? Your piece-of-shit father?" Hrafn laughed, his expression suddenly vicious. "Your father tried to *burn your brother alive*, and I'd kill that bastard a dozen times over if he tried it again! I don't regret it. I regret only that *you* didn't do it when you had the chance to spare Siggi years of suffering!" Siggi had never seen Hrafn so livid, his scars so luminous. "You say he's no brother of yours? Well, you were no kind of brother to him!"

"Hrafn!" Siggi cried, forcing the two of them apart. Hrafn stumbled backward. "Stop it!"

Arnes staggered backward, shoulders shaking with the sobs he held back. Siggi reached for him—he would *always* reach for him—

but Arnes smacked his hand away.

When Siggi turned to face Hrafn, the witch's eyes were wounded but resolute.

"I'm not wrong, Siggi."

"Hrafn…"

The huldu clapped her crusted palms together. "I must say," she purred, "as I brooded and stood watch on the gate, in the midst of my annoyance I forgot how entertaining mortals can be."

"Mortals have forgotten your kind entirely," Hrafn said, "and they're better off for it."

"Oh?" The huldu frowned, seemingly nonplussed. "But why should it matter, whether swine recall their keepers? They taste the same once they're slaughtered, regardless of what they know. And though we may forget the pointless squabbles of humanity, we haven't forgotten the indignity of this gray realm being stolen from us. A century is nothing but an inconvenience, and yet…we do not like to be inconvenienced."

Siggi's head was spinning as she spoke. They had known the huldu were angry with Hrafn, but the woman's words said more than that. She did not speak of a single family stirred to action. It sounded instead as though she was speaking of an entire people, locked away behind closed gates, whose grudge had been festering for a hundred years.

Ylfa had tried to warn them. He understood now, and he knew from a glance that Hrafn did as well. She had tried to warn them, but she had died too quickly, and they had not understood.

"My lady," Ketill pleaded, "I beseech you, let me serve you. I have no magic of my own. But I will serve you well."

"You're a sickly thing," she observed, with a wicked grin. "Reproachable, certainly."

"I am. And still I ask: grant me access to your holy realm."

"Holy, you say," she mused. "You think I'm a goddess, but that is simply untrue. We are but people, and you are but vermin."

"Heed me, fair one." Ketill drew himself up, confidence blossoming. "I long conspired to reopen the passage between our worlds. And I—I am *owed* your blessing, Yfirnáttúrulegt!"

"Owed," she echoed, grin vanishing.

Siggi did not see her move, yet suddenly the huldu was bent double, clutching Ketill's face in one enormous, hole-pocked hand. From the earth around her feet vines grew, weaving their way up Ketill's legs and constricting, pulling him to the ground. Fungal threads sprouted from the holes in her hands and spread to Ketill's cheeks, burrowing into his skin and taking root beneath it, sliding their way up his nostrils. It must have been agony, but his expression remained euphoric.

"Owed, you say, but you have given me nothing. Are vermin owed anything other than disgust and death?"

"I have…brought you…your nephews," Ketill gasped.

"One nephew brought himself, and the other you have trussed like livestock." She squeezed his face tighter, her fingers leaving gouges in his cheeks. They bled, and from the open wounds sprang tiny yellow seedlings.

"I opened the g-gate!"

"You did *not*. My blood and his witch lover did. No, I can't see what you are *owed* at all, worthless human that you are."

"Please," Ketill begged, as figwort bloomed and died on his cheek.

"Begging, are we? How droll."

She shoved her hand right through Ketill's torso as easily as slicing lard, and when she withdrew with a sigh, every open wound and orifice on Ketill's body sprouted with greenery. From his nostrils grew vines of ivy, seedlings sprang from his tear ducts, and from the pores of his skin, moss and mold slithered and spread. He screamed in agony, writhing where he fell, until his throat was filled entirely with lilies and he could scream no more. Roots sprouted from the hole in his stomach and bent toward the ground. They unfurled and stretched, before curling over the edge of the black stone and burrowing deep into the marshy ground. He could do no more than wheeze and whine as the roots dragged him away from the gate and into the watery mulch of the ghost marsh. His boots sank into the mud with a wet sucking sound, and he let out one last, pained cough before falling silent.

Within moments, Ketill was gone, and in his place stood a barrow covered in flowers, incongruous in the sopping mire. Only those looking closely would see the screaming mouth and open eyes tucked between the leaves and blooms.

Arnes whimpered, and Fidelma shushed him with a finger, her own face pale as the moon. Siggi felt Hrafn tremble, but neither of them wavered, neither looked away.

It was so easy for her to end him, like crushing a slug. Ketill, the monster who had so long tormented Arnes, was nothing but a pest to her. How would any human in Lifandfjall fare any better against the huldu?

"Another mess, tidied." The huldu used the largest leaves of the barrow to wipe the blood from her sharp-nailed hand. "And soon we'll tidy your foolish mother's as well, before cleansing this land of its mortal infestation."

Of all the awful things this woman had said, these unnerved Siggi most.

"But…she was your sister, wasn't she?" Siggi asked.

She sighed. "She was, though it pains me to admit it."

"Don't you…aren't you…" Siggi floundered. He stared at Hrafn, who would no longer meet his eyes. He stared at Fidelma, at the mound where Ketill was trapped, and finally at Arnes's shaking form. "Didn't you love her?"

"Oh?" She tilted her head. "Need I have loved her?"

"You aren't angry about her fate…?"

"Angry?" The huldu mulled over the word. "It's been some decades since I felt proper anger. Though your mother disdained her bloodline and abandoned her duties to pursue mortal dalliances, anger seems like rather a lot of bother." She considered her own words. "Ah! But perhaps I was *embarrassed*. But then, Alva was always an embarrassment to us all."

"Salka," Siggi said, and the word felt whole on his tongue. "Her name was Salka."

"Salka? No, that's not right. She was Alva, Daughter of Frode. She Who Bent the Earth," she scoffed. "A mighty title for one so utterly unfit to rule."

"To rule," Hrafn echoed.

"Our family has long since ruled the courts of Hulduheim. Even half-blood children will be admired by many of our kind, especially the grovelers. And given you have opened the gate?" She showed her teeth to Siggi. "Oh! That will be seen as most impressive. Perhaps you'll be gifted a fjord of your own, once we've swept the human remains away. Would you like that, dear nephew?"

"I opened it with Hrafn's help," Siggi said, feeling ill. "Only with the help of the witch."

"I shall not lie, that *is* distasteful. If humans are vermin, witches are wolves, and we'll be sure to slaughter them first. Oh, but I've an idea! Kill this one now, and you'll be redeemed."

Siggi gaped at her. "What?"

"Come now. The witches have been very naughty, closing our gate, and this one has a foul mouth on him as well. So here's what we shall do, nephew: end this loathsome little witch, and then you and your brother will accompany me to your true home, where you will reclaim your dignity and princely thrones."

Siggi gawped at her, blood boiling. "Never."

She frowned. "Oh? Then I will kill him in your stead, and I will be less than gentle about it. I have patience enough to prolong his punishment, now that the gate is open."

She closed her eyes. A great wheezing sound like a mighty breath pulled at the air around them. Siggi thought she must be inhaling, but her lips remained shut and her nostrils did not flare. Instead, the air was being siphoned through the holes in her skin, tickling the tattered edges of them, dislodging the beetles that clung to her limbs.

And then, the exhale: her eyes shot open, and from each of those pits shot fetid air, foul and stinking enough that Siggi braced himself against it; Fidelma coughed and Hrafn ducked his head. Siggi could see yellow spores spit from inside her, like clouds of pollen in the spring. Blown from their dens, worms and midges clung to her,

312

fighting the tempest, coating her broken flesh in their shells and wings, stretching their antennae toward the poisoned air.

Everywhere her spores fell, the bog began to churn. The water and mud bubbled at first, like it was boiling, then those eruptions began to spew whiplike saplings that twisted and shuddered, every one of them crooked, pus-colored, marked with blight sores, rising from the pools of the marsh like hair from a scalp. As they watched in horror, the saplings began to grow, hardening into woody trunks and branches, still twisted, still diseased, but armored now with a sickly green-gray bark that seeped yellow sap from tortured cracks. The air filled with the sound of stretching, creaking wood as a monstrous forest filled the landscape that had been bleak marshland only moments ago.

With that noise came another, one that struck Hrafn before it reached Siggi's ears. He saw Hrafn flinch, saw him clap his hands over his ears, but there was no escaping it when the newly born forest began to scream. The rot-softened trunks of the trees shuddered with every wail, and in the shadowed gaps Siggi saw glimpses of bones: white, gray, and bog-rusted brown. The dead things who had rested, semipreserved in those pools ever since the great battle, were now caught in the trees, their skeletons growing skin and eyes and faces just long enough for each of them to scream and die and rot again, trapped in the bark, or dangling from the branches, or reaching with futile panic from beneath the spreading roots.

"For one hundred years I waited," the huldu rasped over the cacophony of crying undead. "It was no time at all, really. But it was time enough for humanity to forget whose land this was before they stumbled from their leaking boats. It will take significantly less time to do away with them, but we will relish every moment."

Chapter Twenty-Two
The Return

Hrafn's mind was a white storm of panic and rage. The world was filled with horrific sounds—the creaking of wood, the boiling of mud, the screams of the ghosts as the huldu magic trapped them back in their long-dead bodies—but in his mind it became a single howl, a furious cry, because they had forgotten.

Not just he and Siggi and the girls, not just in this moment, but every human, every witch in Lifandfjall, every idiot fisherman or shepherd or child telling tales of the hidden folk to amuse themselves, they had all forgotten what it meant for a cruel and fickle people to wield magic strong enough to remake the world.

The huldu had not forgotten.

Their patience infinite, their pride hurt, their greed ravenous, they had been waiting, and Hrafn had shattered the gate that kept them away.

A sudden yelp punctured his thoughts. Fidelma, several steps away, slashed at a web of growing vines with her knife, stumbling as they unfurled in long, slithering tendrils to wind around her ankles.

The huldu woman gestured with one long hand, moths fluttering around her fingers, and more vines erupted from the black stone in front of Hrafn and Siggi.

Siggi grabbed Hrafn by the shoulders and hauled him backward. There was still fresh blood on Hrafn's hands, enough for him to bring forth a vivid purple flame. He flung it at the nearest vines and was pleased when they crumbled to ash.

"If you think stealing this realm will be easy," he snarled, cupping palms of flame again, "you've forgotten your own miserable history!"

The woman smiled. "Humans do indeed know how to be pests, but they have never been more than that. We are patient, and our magic is pure."

"Pure?" Fidelma spluttered incredulously. "You call this *pure*? You've got worms crawling out of your ears!"

The woman twisted her hand ever so slightly, and the unnatural forest around them shuddered. A copse of the nearest trees convulsed as mossy skeleton hands peeled their barks open from the inside. There was a flash of yellow hair and a sickening crunch as Holta kicked apart two of the undead before they could crawl through the mud toward Fidelma.

The huldu spoke with amusement in her voice, light and mocking. "The humans who work their crude magic might have been powerful once, when we were caught unawares, but they have withered to insignificance so quickly. Come now." She tilted her head and met Hrafn's eyes. "We will outlast you and your filthy curses."

Siggi took two angry steps forward, but on the third he staggered as one of the vines wrapped around his leg. That was enough to finally snap useless Arnes from his shock. He had Ketill's knife in hand; he threw himself at Siggi and began hacking at the vines.

"What will you do to the people?" Siggi demanded. "The ones who aren't witches? The ones who never fought you?"

"You are huldu, more or less," the woman said, cocking her head. "Why do you care?"

"Clearly you've no idea what kind of person your nephew is," Fidelma said, with a laugh.

"I'm not like you," Siggi said. "*We're* not like you. And neither was our mother."

Hrafn had never heard so much scorn in his voice; he was almost proud, even though it hurt to hear Siggi so angry.

And Siggi wasn't finished. "We're not going to let you—"

"Your pleas bore me, nephew," she said. Her gaze passed over Fidelma and Holta, over the hummock that had once been Ketill, and over Hrafn too, taking in the ring of singed plants that encircled him. His fire was such feeble protection against her wild magic. "Mortals serve no purpose. This land will be more pleasing without them. They won't be missed."

Languidly she extended her hands. She twitched one to shake a clinging beetle from her fingers, and then she twisted both hands at the wrists, a gesture so graceful it might have been part of some infernal dance. A new vine burst from the stone at her feet. It was so black in color it seemed to draw light into itself as it grew. Tight spirals unfurled into tendrils along its length, whipping and reaching toward the huldu's outstretched hands.

A bud formed at its end, as large as a fist, angular as a chunk of basalt. With another twitch of the woman's hands, the bud blossomed into a pitch-black flower. It was as long as her forearm, slender for most of its length but spreading out at the end.

"No!" Holta shouted. Hrafn had never heard her like that before, her voice high and full of panic. "No! Stop her! Don't let her—"

With a choking cry, Holta jerked backward and fell.

"Burn it, witch!" she shouted. "The fucking flower, burn it! Burn it before she can call them!"

Hrafn charged forward, past Siggi and Arnes, reaching for that dire black flower with flames in both hands. As he sprinted, Holta scrambled to her feet and wrenched herself free of the vines. She flung herself at the woman with dizzying speed. The woman swept one arm out to stop her, but Holta dodged her hand and slammed into the woman's side.

He was only a few steps from the flower when he felt something grasp his ankle—another of those fucking vines. He lurched forward and fell to his knees, but the hold on his foot loosened almost immediately. Siggi was right behind him, slashing at the vines, and Hrafn stood again and threw himself at the black flower. It hurt to look at it, it was so empty of color and light, so hollow it seemed to be an absence of a thing rather than a thing itself.

There was an shout as the woman flung Holta away with a furious blow. She landed with a crack; Fidelma was at her side in an instant.

Hrafn closed both hands around the stalk of the flower. He ignored the radiating pain in his palms, already so scorched and tender from breaking the gate. He ignored Siggi's gasp. Ignored Fidelma calling Holta's name, the vines snaking around his legs, the screams of the spirits trapped now in the huldu's monstrous forest. He focused only on the fire and that wretched flower, and felt a spark of satisfaction when the flames licked along its stalk, caught, and spread up and up, devouring the black flower from its base.

"You are very foolish," said the huldu woman. "And your efforts are pointless."

She stood over him, so close that the ragged filth of her gown brushed his fingers. Licks of flame caught on her dress but quickly died. She was smiling.

She plucked the black flower from the stalk even as his flames reached the end. The stalk crumbled to ash, but the flower was untouched. She raised it to her lips. Hrafn thought at first she meant to eat it when her lips parted.

"*No!*" Holta screamed again. "Stop her! Hrafn, stop her!"

He tried. He surged to his feet and jumped, flinging flames even as he grasped for the flower, but the woman pushed him away easily, as though he were nothing more than one of the insects that tumbled from her parted lips. He felt the blow in his chest, the sensation of falling, then he was on the ground several steps away, dazed and breathless.

Siggi was at his side, helping him to sit up. "Hrafn, are you—"

A deep, powerful sound drowned out the rest of his question.

The huldu had tilted her chin upward, her long neck elegant in spite of the grotesqueness that enveloped her. Pressing her lips to the stem, she breathed into the base of the flower's bell. The sound it emitted was steady and strange and overpowering, like the deep, dangerous howl of some impossible animal.

The flower was a horn.

It was not loud enough to cover the screams of the spirits, but it was low, strong, and resonant enough to make every bone in Hrafn's body shake.

The sound faded as the flower withered in her hands. She dropped the remains to the ground and said, "There. Come along, nephews. We have no need to concern ourselves with this anymore."

"We won't go anywhere with you," Siggi said.

The huldu laughed. "Do you have a choice? My vines have caught you. The others will soon arrive to deal with"—she cast a disdainful eye around her—"this."

Hrafn felt the moment when Siggi understood, felt it as a jolt of renewed fear. They both understood now why Holta had been so frantic to stop her. The flower was a war horn: a summons.

Siggi stood, pulling Hrafn up beside him. "We can't let them come through."

Hrafn felt Siggi's focus sharpen as he reached outward. Wherever there were bones, Siggi had power, and there were so very many bones all around them. Hrafn leaned against him, lending Siggi his strength through their bond. Their magic twisted and braided together like it could not bear to be parted. The gate began to shake, casting dust across the doorway. The screams of the dead heightened.

"Stop that," the huldu snapped. "You are being ridiculous."

The huldu cast a rope of vines out like a whip. It struck Siggi across the face; he flinched but did not fall, only gritted his teeth and braced himself. The woman flung her whip again, and this time it hit Hrafn, not Siggi. It coiled around his wrist and yanked him so hard he felt it wrench his shoulder as he fell away from Siggi's side.

"Only you?" the woman said, with bland disappointment. That made no sense, not until Hrafn looked up to see that she was not speaking to him but looking back through the gate. She gestured impatiently. "Well, come on, then. Make yourselves useful."

From beneath the shaking archway emerged three more huldu. They were a trio of burgundy-haired youths clad in polished black

318

volcanic armor not dissimilar to that of the trylla in Grimholl. They were triplets, with identical fine-boned features, all three of them shorter and younger than the woman, and devoid of decay. Their eyes were bloodshot, their grins malicious. All that distinguished them were their weapons and the color of their eyes: the yellow-eyed one carried a spear; the red-eyed one a bow; the blue-eyed one a spiked mace.

"You, bind this one! You, the other!" The woman pointed at Siggi and Arnes. "They are my nephews and worth more than your lives, so do no damage that cannot be fixed." She gestured to the third triplet. "You? *Kill the witch.*"

Even as the words left her lips, the yellow-eyed huldu ran Siggi through the stomach with his spear. Hrafn felt the pain across their bond, setting his torso ablaze, as Siggi screamed and fell. Through the waves of pain and sudden tears, Hrafn saw Arnes fling himself at the yellow-eyed youth with an outraged cry, but before he could reach him the red-eyed triplet notched an arrow in his bow and loosed it with inhuman speed. The arrow struck Arnes right above the collarbone. Another arrow followed, this one landing in his shoulder, and Arnes dropped to his knees, coughing and spitting blood.

The huldu raised another arrow, but before he could fire, Holta was upon him. She grabbed his crimson hair and wrenched his head back with one hand, snatching the bow with the other. There was a sickening *crack*, a startled gasp, and Holta shoved the boy aside and spun around.

Siggi was crying out, struggling to tear himself free, but the spear was not made of bone, the vines were not made of bone, and the pain he felt as he tried and tried and *tried* was so overwhelming, so terrible, it overwhelmed all Hrafn's thoughts, shattered his concentration. All he could hear was Siggi's cries. All he could feel was the agony as the vines wrapped around the spear and drove it deeper into Siggi's abdomen.

"Hrafn! Look out!" Fidelma's shout broke through their shared agony.

Hrafn snapped back to himself to see the blue-eyed youth leaping toward him with his spiny mace upraised. He flung both hands up to catch it—the head was metal but the handle was wooden, the handle could *burn*—but when he grabbed it and fire burst from his palms, the force of the blow was so strong he felt a searing burst of pain unlike any he had felt from his flames before. He could not keep hold of the weapon. His hands were too weak, no longer obeying his commands. The huldu boy raised the mace again, grinning wildly, and swung it down.

Siggi shouted, but it was Fidelma who blocked the blow. She threw herself between Hrafn and the huldu boy. She took hold of the mace's handle with both hands and shoved, but the huldu boy was stronger. He sneered at her efforts and spat, and with both hands on his weapon, his face contorted with disdain, he pressed his weight against Fidelma and kicked her in the navel. She gasped and let go, tumbling backward. The boy raised the mace again.

From under Fidelma's heavy cloak came a screech of fury. Anna burst forth and flew directly toward the huldu boy, gouging at his face with her talons, sending the gore of his eyes down his pale cheeks. The huldu boy howled and fell back. Fidelma pulled Hrafn away from the furious, blind swings of his mace.

The wayward mace landed a crunching blow on Anna's skull. The utburdur shattered and fell like a stone, and Siggi roared. It was a roar Hrafn felt in his heart, in his bones, more powerful even than their shared pain. Siggi's magic burst from him in a furious torrent.

It was the eruption Hrafn had been expecting since he had first met Siggi. It was more terrible than he had imagined—and more incredible.

The blinded triplet screamed as both of his arms snapped backward, forearms broken in two, golden huldu bones jutting from white skin like spires. He screamed and screamed, twisting and writhing, unable to escape. The yellow-eyed huldu let go of his spear abruptly and ran to his brother's side.

The red-eyed huldu was dragging a dazed and bloodied Arnes toward the gate, but he stopped at the sound of his brother's screams.

He dropped Arnes roughly to pull another arrow from his quiver—he had no bow anymore, not since Holta had tossed it aside, but he flung the arrow at Siggi with unerring aim and reached for another. Even as he drew again, Fidelma barreled toward him, bowling him over, slamming his head against the base of the gate. It was enough to stun him but not knock him out entirely. As soon as Fidelma moved away, he rose shakily to his feet.

It wasn't enough. Siggi's anger, Fidelma's stubbornness, Holta's strength and speed, it wasn't enough. The huldu would keep fighting. The horn had summoned them, and it would summon more. They were not strong enough to fight them alone.

But they weren't alone.

Hrafn didn't let himself hesitate. His hands were clumsy and useless now, but he didn't need a blade for this. He twisted his head and bit himself hard on the shoulder, opening a stave he had never used before. Ylfa had been horrified when he carved it; Birtingr had been furious. They had both told him, in their own ways, that using that stave was more dangerous than any problem he might seek to solve with it.

Maybe they were right. But they weren't here now. Hrafn didn't have another choice.

"Enough!" cried the huldu woman. She had remained near the gateway, watching the struggle without engaging in it, but now her voice was heavy with malice. "You have made me remember anger after all."

Vines surged around Fidelma, grasping her hands and wrapping around her forearms and neck, and constricting like sailors' knots. She let out a strangled wheeze, and her face turned red as she fought to free herself. The vine around her neck tightened and her eyes rolled back. Holta leaped over to her to help, but even she could not dislodge them.

"Let her go! Stop this!" Siggi cried.

The huldu woman was not going to stop. There were vines tightening around Hrafn's legs again, and soon they would be reaching for his neck. While he still could, he licked at the blood from his shoulder stave, then bit down hard on his own tongue.

Then he opened his mouth again, and he screamed.

His scream carried through the Draugamyr, through the mists and the misshapen trees, through the mossy humps and fetid pools. The fog itself shuddered with the sound, and every one of the huldu's foul saplings trembled. Wood cracked and split, branches swayed, and skeletal limbs jerked and lurched. The wail of the spirits, omnipresent until now, began to slacken, then ceased, until Hrafn's was the one voice that remained.

Then Siggi was there in front of him. Bleeding from the wound in his gut. Eyes wild and blue. Reaching for Hrafn.

"What are you doing?" Siggi asked. "Hrafn? What are you doing?"

The huldu woman was shouting something, but Hrafn didn't hear it, didn't care, because he could feel the force of Siggi's concentration, even through all the pain. He finally stopped to take a breath. Siggi's hands were warm on his arms.

"We have to close the gate," he said. "While the spirits distract her. We have to close it."

Silence surrounded them for a moment, the hush of a gathered breath.

And the ghosts attacked.

Chapter Twenty-Three
The Orchard

From the very grain of the bewitched bark, from the pools beneath the water, from the depths of the bog they came, rising like steam: the dead of Draugamyr, heeding Hrafn's call. They were hardly corporeal, thinner than fog, but their humanity was undeniable. Their faces might have belonged to anyone in Lifandfjall, were it not for the staves many of them bore. Freed now from the prison of huldu magic and damp graves, they circled Hrafn and Siggi, running spectral fingers across Hrafn's face, cooing softly to him. Lavender hued they were, an echo of Hrafn's flames.

Or perhaps Hrafn's magic was always lavender, soft even in its violence. Gently, he ducked out of Siggi's grasp and allowed the ghosts to ensconce him like a glacial cloak. "They won't hurt us."

Siggi nodded and took a step away, allowing the specters to encase Hrafn, to caress his limbs and cheeks and whisper softly over his many wounds.

Hrafn raised one singed, ruined hand and pointed.

"Her," he said simply.

And the ghosts of Draugamyr's fallen witches, in their spectral aged clothing, with their stave-marked skin, convened with a roaring hiss of fury and moved as one force. Like a wave trapped ashore they crashed down upon the huldu woman. Liberated from bone, bark, and bog, the witches remembered their true enemy.

"How dare you!" she cried, swatting at them, her smirk at last dismantled. "Back to your graves!"

They heeded her no more than an ocean heeds a ship.

They were something to behold, but Siggi was hardly looking. Instead, he looked at Hrafn, captivated by the tranquil smile on his exhausted face. For once, he looked his age: a boy on the cusp of manhood, a boy with a future before him.

Hrafn so often spoke as though he were a sordid, lonely creature, but here were dozens of souls that mirrored his own in a way that even Siggi's did not. These specters, the witches of Draugamyr, shared his power and his pain even one hundred years after their demise. And like Hrafn, they sought to do good, not evil.

Hrafn had been wrong all along, Siggi thought, tears burning his eyes. His magic was so much bigger than Siggi's, so much brighter, and Siggi only hoped Hrafn could feel the joy and pride Siggi felt at the thought, despite it all.

The huldu woman became more frantic, slashing at the spirits with her clawlike hands and lashing vines. But her blows could not pierce them, for there was nothing of them to pierce. The ghosts obscured her view and eased into the holes in her skin, so that she shuddered and screamed in discomfort, trying to pluck them out, but her fingers made no more mark on them than it might on the air.

Siggi tore his gaze from the unholy sight, and Hrafn was gone. Not far, but stumbling toward the gate again, his bloody palms upraised, ready again to ignite them.

Siggi snarled, past words, and rushed up behind him, wrapping arms around his waist. "No more fire! Enough!"

Siggi's shoulder still throbbed with the indentations of Hrafn's teeth, and he knew Hrafn was in no state to bleed again. All those times Siggi had asked Hrafn not to hurt himself, had he ever said it firmly enough? Or had Siggi been too lenient because Hrafn's pain so often benefited him, because he could so easily make excuses to justify the way Hrafn so easily maimed himself?

"We have to close the gate," Hrafn said. "And that means more blood, more fire. But I can't bring it down by myself. I don't think that's how it works."

"Hrafn," Siggi cried, sobbing. "Your hands."

"Admittedly, I may have overdone it," Hrafn said weakly.

"Enough, I said!" cried the huldu, and after another profound inhale, she expunged all the sordid air from her body again, spitting the ghosts away with the paltry remains of the decimated insects within her.

The witches' wails were all too human as she scattered them to the breeze, as their wayward souls were sent away from the clearing as though carried by a storm, lost in the torrent of her exhalation.

Hrafn made a choking sound and clutched at his heart, watching them vanish in the mists.

"Listen, now, nephew!" Her hair a nest of insect carapaces, her wounds sprouting new plants, the fungus covering all of her now as she struggled to recover, the huldu limped toward the gate. "Do as you're told and come home. Your pitiful brother's on the other side already. Or didn't you notice?"

All the air left Siggi's lungs.

A trail of blood led from where Arnes had lain through the emerald glow of the gate.

They had not seen the huldu boy drag Arnes past his unconscious brothers and into another world. But the woman wasn't lying. While two of the triplets lay inert on the ground, one broken and limp, the other bleeding from his skull, the third was nowhere to be seen.

Siggi willed the woman's bones to break. But he could not feel them. There were so many bones all around, living and dead, but she was only a void in his awareness. She laughed as he grimaced, her spine unbent despite his exertions.

"Oh, I know what you're trying to do. But I've long since replaced my old bones with wooden ones," she said sweetly. "You can't break the roots of me."

"Arnes!" Siggi cried. "Give him back!"

"You've nothing left to barter." She shook her head. "Come along now. Soon this will be a battlefield once again."

She smiled wickedly, blood between her teeth, and stepped backward out of Lifandfjall.

Siggi could shout no longer. Behind him, the groans of their friends were indistinguishable from the groans of the huldu boys. Before him, Hrafn slid down the black bone gate with a heavy sigh.

"Siggi." Siggi turned as Hrafn spoke. Merely leaning against the archway seemed to cost his remaining strength. Blood slipped down his chin. "That's it. You have to go after him."

"But you're hurt…and you can't let them get you, it's too dangerous for you to cross—"

"Without me. I told you. We have to close the gate."

"Hrafn." Ignoring the wound in his stomach, the agony in his chest, Siggi knelt beside him. "I won't leave you again! Look at what's been done to you!"

"When we met I was a corpse. A pair of mangled hands is hardly a comparison. Besides, I did it to myself," Hrafn argued, voice garbled. "And I'd do it again."

"I know," Siggi choked, pressing his lips into Hrafn's blood-soaked hair. "I know you would, but gods how I wish you wouldn't. Hrafn, how can I leave you, knowing that?"

"The choice here is obvious," Hrafn said. "Your brother or the murderous witch."

"My brother or the one I love," Siggi said, tears slipping down his nose.

"Siggi. Listen…" Hrafn's black eyes flickered to the gate looming above them. "It's not about me. It's not about Arnes. The story of the lovers who closed the gates. What do you really think happened to the huldu in that story?"

"If they loved each other," Siggi said, tears sliding down his cheeks, "the witch would never have killed her."

"But she vanished thereafter, never again to be seen," Hrafn said. "So where do you think she went?"

Siggi frowned. "Hrafn…"

"There are two sides to this gate," Hrafn insisted. "And both need sealing."

326

Siggi saw then what Hrafn was suggesting, what it would take to separate the worlds once more. "You can't know that for certain."

"Of course I can't, but what choice do we have?" Hrafn said, with a weak laugh. "She's sounded her horn. Those three won't be the only ones who answer. Fidelma was right. They closed the gates to stop a war. We can't be the reason it starts again. Siggi. Siggi. *Go.* Holta's already gone through. You and Arnes won't be alone there. Isn't this an easy choice?"

Siggi looked around frantically and realized Hrafn was right. Holta had slipped through the gate at some point during the fight, exactly as she had wanted all along.

"That's her choice. This is mine. How can you say that it's easy?" Siggi demanded, taking him by the shoulders.

"Reunite with your brother and spare Lifandfjall from all of—all of *this*." Hrafn jerked his chin toward the forest around them. "Or stay here and cry over the wasted body of a stubborn, foul-mouthed witch?" Hrafn's smirk, so familiar, had rarely seemed so sad. "Come now, puffling. We both know you're too good to choose wrongly here."

"You're not supposed to be like this," Siggi pleaded. "You're supposed to be selfish."

"I am selfish. I want us both to live."

"Ask me to stay! Do that, Hrafn, and I will! We'll find another way to close the gate. We'll fight them when they come. Fuck all the rest, I will stay."

"You might," Hrafn said, turning his chin away, "but you'd regret it. Don't think I don't know your heart when it's half mine."

"More than half," Siggi said, burying his face in Hrafn's neck. "It's yours entirely."

"Then you know I'm not changing my mind."

Siggi felt himself bristling. "You think you're past saving. Is that it?"

Hrafn squeezed his eyes shut. "Gods, I wish that was it. Siggi, I wish I felt as small and worthless as I did when I met you. But you never let me feel that way. I don't think I'll ever have another self-deprecating thought for as long as I live without hearing your voice in my head. If I'm past saving, it's only because you've already saved me, for fuck's sake."

"Hrafn, I *know* you," Siggi said. "If I leave you alone, you'll set yourself on fire again."

"It'll be okay. I can heal myself."

"You never heal yourself."

"Maybe I will this time." Hrafn grinned, blood in his teeth. "But if you stay I'll set us both on fire to stop those huldu coming through."

"Liar," Siggi said, wiping his eyes on his filthy sleeve.

"Of course I'm a liar. I'm a witch."

"My witch," Siggi whispered.

He cupped Hrafn's face with his hands and kissed him deeply. Hrafn tilted his face to meet Siggi's lips and the little noise he made struck Siggi right in the heart. He didn't want to let go. He couldn't let go, not until he heard another sound, low and ominous. Another horn, sounding through the gate. Distant but drawing closer.

Siggi let go of Hrafn and turned away from those lovely, horrible eyes. He couldn't bear to say goodbye, so he said nothing at all as he walked toward the gate.

"I love you, Siggi Arnesson," Hrafn called.

Siggi almost stumbled then, because he had never heard Hrafn sound so frail. But if he dared look back, he knew he would let the world burn just to hold him again. His other half. His heart.

Siggi couldn't fathom Hrafn's pain, couldn't distinguish it from his own. He knew only it was immeasurable.

Siggi passed through the gate with his hand on his chest, stepping into the fetid green light, leaving the churning ghosts of the Draugamyr and his broken heart behind.

Siggi wasn't simple. Siggi had spent no short amount of time beside Hrafn, and cunningness had a tendency to spread.

Siggi found himself standing in a putrid, overgrown orchard, caught between trees whose overripe fruit lay gathering worms in soggy heaps on the sodden earth. There was no advancing army to be seen, and the only waiting huldu was the woman, who stood with Arnes bleeding at her feet, and the yellow-eyed youth beside her.

But he heard the horn again. He didn't know how much time they had.

Siggi noted the rotten softness of the soil, the sour yellow of the sky, and the victorious grin on the woman's face. Arnes was panting, his chest rising and falling like a choppy sea. He was hurt but alive.

"Come to your senses, nephew mine?" the woman said.

Siggi didn't answer. He was thinking about Hrafn, and how wrong he was.

Saving Lifandfjall was not an easy decision, not at all. Because how could the entire span of Lifandfjall be worth even half as much as Hrafn's affections? The bristling witch who softened only around Siggi, the powerful young man who hurt himself to spare others? Who never saw how very wondrous he was, but remained wondrous all the same? All that Hrafn was, weighed against a cruel land that had never once embraced Siggi for who or what he was?

Siggi wept openly, standing in the decrepit orchard. He glanced once more at Arnes's supine form in the grass before gritting his teeth and exerting every thought toward a single intention.

In his chest, he felt a sudden strain in Hrafn's heartbeat, mirroring his own.

Because he wasn't doing this alone. It was a spell for two minds, two hearts joined in a single desire. There was no other way. On the other side of the gate, Hrafn bled and worked his magic against the stone, completing the circle between them, sealing the gate's demise.

Siggi's magic reached beyond his body like another mist, encompassing the Gate of Blood and Bone, wrapping around it like a woolen blanket. And then he clenched his witch-bladed fist, willing the magic to compound, willing himself not to cry.

At first there was no change. Siggi stood in a wasted glade of putridity and sordid overgrowth that felt as warm and choking as

Father's forge, and thought he'd never breathe again.

And then the gate groaned. Tiny cracks appeared all across its ivory surface and a shrieking sound pierced the air. The cracks widened as fragments of bone chipped and fell away, and where the cracks grew, the surrounding bones shifted and began to fall.

The Gate of Blood and Bone was collapsing.

"No!" the huldu woman screamed. She took Siggi by the shoulders and shook him violently; his knees gave out as the spear in his stomach shifted and the wound began to leak. "What are you doing? Stop this poor behavior! Stop it now!"

But it was already in motion. As the ancient structure crumbled, the hidden realm's famished magical plants grew to overtake the wreckage, ensconcing the ruins in foliage that rotted even as it spread. The yellow-eyed triplet leaped away from Arnes's side, running toward the collapse even as the path between worlds closed in an avalanche of cascading bones and dust.

The gate was gone, and the huldu woman let Siggi fall from her hands so that she could pull her hair and scream.

The sole triplet sobbed and clawed at the rubble, calling for his brothers in a strangled voice. Dazed though he was, Siggi could not look away. Perhaps because the huldu boy was younger, or perhaps because not all huldu were unfeeling monsters, the yellow-eyed triplet's grief seemed genuine as he vied against gravity and space. But the verdant earth continued pushing vines and mosses over the debris, aging the bone fragments and burying them anew. Within minutes, a grassy barrow obscured all but a few spiny ribs. The way out of the hidden realm was gone, as if it had never existed.

"*This* won't win you any friends here," the huldu hissed, adjusting her hair, hands trembling with fury. "They are going to be so disappointed in you! They are always reminiscing about disemboweling humans…"

Siggi didn't reply. He was spent in every sense of the word, and he could not dislodge Hrafn's broken voice from his ears any more than he could dislodge the splintered spear from his stomach. He stumbled toward the place where Arnes lay in the overlong, dewy grass. Someone—the yellow-eyed triplet?—had pulled the arrows from his chest and plugged his wounds with grass to staunch the bleeding.

"Arnes." Siggi pulled his brother's head onto his sodden lap and brushed the hair from his forehead.

Arnes's eyes were closed, and he was so very thin, but his skin was warm and his hands, despite the missing finger, were as familiar to Siggi as his own.

"Arnes is alive," he whispered, and at long last the words were undeniable.

Many times Arnes had been by Siggi's side when he was sad or beaten. So many times Arnes had dressed the wounds Father left and soothed Siggi's restless mind with stories.

"You were right, Arnes. The world is so vast," he whispered. "And I've so many tales to tell you."

Siggi listened to the screeches of thousands of otherworldly insects, watched the ascent of rotting magpies with white eyes who abandoned the fruit in the grass, sated already several times over, and not truly living anyhow. The green sunlight cut through Siggi's drooping eyelids and he wondered if there were any lambs in these fields, any true ravens, anything that wasn't half dead already.

Anyone might succumb to sorrow in such a place.

But there, beneath his scattered heartbeat, he could still feel Hrafn's pulse, the searing pain in his beloved's bleeding hands. Worlds away from one another, perhaps divided forever, still they were bound. Siggi focused what remained of his consciousness on the witch-blade scar on his palm. He could almost feel Hrafn there, holding his hand.

Acknowledgements

We want to thank our editor, Joshua Dean Perry, who believed in this book and made a place for it at Tiny Ghost. It was both a joy and a relief to work with an editor who loved this dark, bloody little story, with all its monsters and scars, and only ever wanted it to be the best version of itself. We also want to thank everybody else at Tiny Ghost Press involved in making the book a reality, including Reuben Davies-Hoare, Thomas Shah, Carla Jones, and Lewis Hughes.

And we want to give a special shout out to copyeditor Dana Keller, who is so good at her job that she made a couple of veteran authors fangirl over her attention to detail. We're afraid she's set a standard that's going to be hard for other copyeditors to match.

We also want to thank Corey Brickely for their beautiful cover illustration and [illustrator] for the wonderful map.

Any fantasy book that borrows from history and folklore draws on countless sources of inspiration. One that we truly appreciate is artist Arngrimur Sigurðsson and his book *Museum of Hidden Beings*. The weirdness and beauty he captures in his paintings of creatures from Icelandic folklore was always in the back of our minds. Similarly, a visit to the Museum of Sorcery and Witchcraft, a tiny museum in a very remote part of the Strandir in Iceland, planted the fundamental seeds for this book. In short, this book was partly brought to you by necropants. Iceland, as a whole, is a country that bleeds inspiration.

On a personal note, writing this book during a pandemic was far from easy. Leah would like to thank her sister, Erin Thomas, for all her compassion and care, and for being the best person in the world to see an erupting volcano with. Both authors would like to thank their numerous cats for providing comfort with a side of sharp claws, which certainly helped inspire Hrafn's characterization.

And strange as it may seem, the authors would also like to thank each other. We were roomies for almost 8 years before circumstances separated us and we ended up on opposite sides of the planet, but it was only once we lived separately that we managed to cowrite a book together. We can't wait to write more.

About the Authors

Leah Thomas writes stories mostly about queer kids and monsters (sometimes human-shaped). Her debut novel, *Because You'll Never Meet Me*, was a Morris Award Finalist. An educator by day, by night she writes about anime and admires her cat. She currently lives in Tottori Prefecture, Japan.

Kali Wallace studied geology and earned a PhD in geophysics before she realized she enjoyed inventing imaginary worlds more than she liked researching the real one. She is the author of science fiction, fantasy, and horror novels for adults, teens, and children, as well as a number of short stories and essays. She lives in the Pacific Northwest.